HORN

By D. Keith Mano

Bishop's Progress
Horn

HORN

D. KEITH MANO

HOUGHTON MIFFLIN COMPANY
BOSTON

To my wife, Jo—

Whose patience, wit, good humor, economy, diligent typing,
careful supervision in matters practical, and
superb cooking have made not merely
this book — but my very existence
as a writer — possible.

PART ONE

Getting Out

HORN IT SAID. Someone had scrawled it in black marker on the back of my seat. Tentatively, I ran my fingers over the word, searching perhaps for some significant texture. Caret-shaped figures, abstract horns I supposed, were scattered at random over the seat's back — their apexes directed at that single word HORN. The bus, I knew, had passed through Harlem; in passing, even its unfeeling bulk had been scarred. And now I was passing through. Nervous and excited as I was, fearful as I am even to this day, I was sensitive to all supposed prophetic meaning.

Now he is dead: George Horn Smith, my friend of a single day. In the two years since his assassination, ten books and more than three hundred articles have been written about him. They have conspired to make him what, in death, he is today — a Negro folk legend. It is all very difficult for me. I want, it is my love's instinct, to compound this splendid misconception. But I cannot. Each of those books, each article without exception, is fundamentally untrue — as much a fraud as my friend, himself, was a fraud. I knew him. No one knew him better than I.

I remember that day. A timid, foolish white clergyman making his very first journey into Harlem. To remain a year and

more. Harlem, in the early seventies, was Smith. As I sat in the
bus, staring at the seat back, I thought of him. At that time I
knew no more than the legends would allow. Essentially that
he was a freak — a magnificent freak with an eleven inch horn
jutting up, out of his forehead. It was, in fact, a skin disease:
Cornu cutaneum, which shows a preference for the forehead and
scalp. Very much like an animal horn, though attached only
to the skin and containing no bone. Had he been like you or me,
an ordinary man, George Horn Smith would probably have remained just that: a sport, a victim of some queer dermatological
condition.

But he was so very much more than that. Middleweight
champion of the world. A compelling orator. An illiterate
who had, single-handedly, brought a measure of economic sta-
bility and hope to the despairing ghetto of Harlem. A professed
enemy of the white man. Founder of the Horn Power Movement which had violently repudiated all white, liberal connec-
tions three years before. An unscrupulous man with an oddly
consistent reputation for honesty among his own people. A
striking and a paradoxical figure.

The horn was real. He was a boxer of great ability. He did
more for the American Negro than any man of his time. But,
beyond that, George Horn Smith was, as I have already suggested, an absolute and unmitigated fraud. Remembering now
how I felt on that first day — fresh from having read Smith's
autobiography — I can imagine how incredible that statement
seems. I will have to proceed very slowly, therefore; I will have
to begin at the beginning. I will try to make the slow process
of my enlightenment the process of your enlightenment as
well. Then, perhaps, you will understand what I mean. And
about his murderers — I must tell you especially about them.

The beginning then. I had intended, the first of many intentions, to walk a good part of the way north from the Port Authority Building — to acclimatize my obstinate ruralness. But, after just a few blocks, my shins began to ache from the sharp, unaccustomed slap of sole against hard pavement. I began to pant. Excitement interfered with the easy flow of breath into my lungs. In fact, I didn't walk much beyond the Forty-second Street Library. The dingy lions, hunched in their postures of unremitting comfort, seemed to counsel moderation. I sat on the library steps, lifting my thighs now and again as the cool stone enforced a sensation of incontinence about my loins. I considered. After a few moments I acquiesced. I made my first compromise: I took a Number 3 bus at 43rd Street and Fifth Avenue — up, as again there is two-way traffic on the avenues.

It was a pleasant morning, the Wednesday after Labor Day. Summer had barely begun its capitulation. The dawn hours had been chilly in Greensprings. Now, though the air held sufficient promise of warmth, the paraphernalia of autumn was already implicit. Even in the city, even without the litmus test of the leaves, there was anticipation of the equinoctial change. A stressing of shadows primarily; shadows that have been perfunctorily cast and ignored during the long summer days. Objects assert themselves in chiaroscuro as hard, three dimensional things. Sounds and aromas begin to lose their insistence. I like the autumn. I am not a man of warmth and light.

I had been to New York only four times in my life. From my seat behind the rear exit door, I peered out with a naïve and excited curiosity. Central Park was approaching on my left. Surreptitiously, so as not to betray my provincial insecureness, I patted each laden pocket in its turn: my wallet; my tobacco pouch; notebook; spare eyeglasses; vitamin pills — both bottles. All there. All taken from the bureau top where Eleanor had placed them, in careful order, the night before.

This, you must understand, was a great moment in a life not previously distinguished by great moments. My sister Eleanor had stressed its significance often enough — to my mute discomfort. Eleanor knows me very well. She sensed at once what I was trying to do: trying to minimize the event, to fit it into familiar perspectives. And so, during that last week, she had worked against my complacency. "You're getting out," she would say, digging her fingertips into my ribs as I shaved, nose to the mirror. "You're getting out," as I filled a cup, upsetting my tenuous coordination, causing me to spill tea on the transparent petals of a Steuben lily. Shouted in my ear as I lay somnolent on Saturday morning. Written on the icing of a cake. "You're getting out."

I was. For the first time in just over forty years I was leaving the only milieu I had ever known. Getting out, involving myself, becoming committed to serious and unfamiliar responsibilities. My friends had been quite uniformly appalled. Tall and yet fat; clumsy and very shortsighted; dedicated to my books, my butterflies, my comfortable routines. Not precisely the missionary type. "Are you sure, Pratt?" But Eleanor had glared at them until each had broken off nervously and was silent. No. Not precisely. Not at all sure. "Getting out," I said under my breath. "Out. Really out."

To my left I could see the fantastic rooftops of the Children's Zoo. There were only five other passengers, all white persons. A red-haired woman with freckles — a middle-aged Catholic, certainly — sat at right angles to my seat. She held a knitted bag in her lap; her right hand was buried in the bag's throat. I could see her fingers moving inside, fondling something. Her eyes were set straight ahead, as though unwilling to countenance the movements of her hand.

Two high school boys sprawled on the back seat. They whispered in low, excited tones, and, every now and then, the larger would punch the smaller's biceps. An old man with impressive, white muttonchops slept in the seat just ahead of them, his chin supported on his upper ribs. And last, directly across from me, sat a nattily dressed, graying, crew-cut man. An executive. He was thumbing through a *Wall Street Journal*. At intervals, he would extract a cleverly folded handkerchief from his vest pocket. Then he would unfold the handkerchief once, place it near his mouth and "hmmmmm" delicately — an altogether paltry motivation, I thought, for so elaborate a gesture. While doing this, he would stare with discerning apathy at the priest across the aisle.

I peered self-consciously at my own legs. A white, hairless calf peered back, whiter yet between black cuff and black sock. I uncrossed my legs. The executive crackled his paper, expressing mild approval. In rebuttal, I pulled out my expensive Sasieni pipe and jammed it between bared teeth. The paper applauded again. I sat up stiffly, hoping to compensate somewhat for my ugly, bulging pockets. The red-haired Catholic woman, supposing me to be one of her own, pursed her lips and then smiled. A clergyman is always the focus of speculation, and I was most patently a clergyman. I had deliberately come in uniform on that special day — lest I be shot as a spy.

I leaned forward in sudden agitation. An elderly Negro man, his pockets stuffed with brown paper bags, was proceeding uncertainly down the aisle. When he was almost even with the exit door, I stood suddenly — quite irrationally — to give him my seat in the near-empty bus. An outward and visible manifestation of the terrific tensions to which, for weeks, I had been subjected. The old man squeezed past me, his bags rustling; he sat in the last seat but one. The executive interrogated his handkerchief. I sat down in confusion. The old man with the muttonchops rose and walked slowly toward the exit door.

I stared, without subterfuge, at the new passenger. "Make a

wish, C.B.," I thought, ridiculously enough. I had seen Negroes
before, of course; even unsophisticated Greensprings had had
its share. And still I stared, quite unable to will my glance
elsewhere. As a man on shipboard might survey some inscruta-
ble expanse of green jungle just on the horizon; a jungle at
whose heart he fully expected to pass a lifetime. I saw the complex of wrinkles in which the man's features were embedded. I
watched as, with preoccupation, he took a brown paper bag
from his left trouser pocket and poured its undisclosed contents
into a bag from his right jacket pocket. And each movement
held, for me, the particular significance of ritual.

The red-haired woman left us at 79th Street. She smiled as
she stepped into the stairwell. Smiled at my collar — an unspoken admission of shared faith, shared experience. The larger
boy knocked the smaller boy's books to the floor. A pretty Negro woman boarded the bus. She selected a seat just opposite
the exit door. The executive leaned circumspectly backward in
order to study her excellent profile. Two Negroes, four whites
— the bus driver uncommitted behind his curtain. We proceeded through the Eighties. Now I had perhaps thirty blocks
left. I examined my two Negroes hastily: first one, then the
other, then back again. I was looking, I know now, for inti-
mations of hostility. But the jungle's surface was homogeneous
and mute.

We passed the Guggenheim, a massive symbol in search of
massive meaning. I squirmed around to look. Below, a pair of
Negro boys, their books borne like footballs, were racing to
catch the bus. The driver started, hesitated, then slowed to pick
them up. The two boys sat on either side of the aisle, several
rows from the front. They chattered noisily. One of the boys
leaned across the aisle and punched the other in the biceps. I felt
a sharp twinge in my lower abdomen. The signal buzzer
sounded. The high school boys from the rear seat were getting

off. I pressed my hands together between my thighs. Then I smiled at the executive — an unspoken admission of shared faith, shared experience. The executive raised his eyebrows. He raised his *Wall Street Journal*.

I watched the boys as they descended. The smaller, after a moment's calculation, punched the larger boy's books out from under his arm. Then he ran, laughing, down 92nd Street, past the quiet brownstones, out between two bright, rich Cadillacs parked at the curb. I put my hand on the window's metal rim and squeezed until my thumb ached. The bus crossed 96th Street. Already the side streets seemed dark and cluttered. House walls were stained, rights of way obstructed; children knelt on all fours in gutters. Beneath their Fifth Avenue canopies, doormen suggested sentries on outpost duty. I ran a hand across my forehead. "You're getting out," I said. And I almost did.

The bus made a left at 110th Street. The signal buzzer sounded once again. I turned quickly from the window, my palm held upward in an instinctive plea. The executive had stood. He tucked the *Wall Street Journal* in the crook of his armpit, and, ignoring my call to fellowship, began walking up the aisle. I closed my palm and pressed the knuckles of my fist against my kneecap. A young Negro man boarded. He stood aside as the executive passed. He was dressed in a fashionable, dark green suit; a handkerchief, intricately folded, appeared over his vest pocket lip. As he walked down the aisle, I saw that there was a newspaper — a *Daily News,* but a newspaper — tucked in the crook of his armpit. He sat opposite me, his buttocks warmed in a residue of the executive's body heat. "A sea change," I thought, "into something rich and strange." But I felt, instead, that I had been the dupe of some cheap and vaguely ominous magical trick.

And outside . . . I brought my head slowly around. The

people — yes, there was no doubt about it — now the people were different. Sewers at the curb wore garlands of current-sucked refuse. Sounds were strident and sudden. A smell of burning fat. Of fish. Of urine. Of beer splashings and vomit. Store fronts, the plate glass broken and filthy. Garbage cans, battered and greasy, themselves no better than garbage. A torn shirt, a brown, shiny shoulder blade protruding. Children playing, pummeling each other, terrifically violent. Half a shoe. Rags, gray and wet, lying in the shape of drowned animals.

The bus hesitated, dwelling on the gray, broken shell of a building. I looked up. The windows were gone. Strange, long strands of material hung like seaweed from the broken roof. Two derelicts, back to back, discarded bookends, drowsed in the doorway. A pool of something wet spilled over from the junction of their bodies. Desolate — even in the bright morning sunlight. And yet, at each level of the crumbling façade, I saw a small bas-relief tableau. Here a Medusa, mouth wide, hair insane; there a brace of naked cherubs or a fig-leaved warrior, his sword upraised in futile rearguard action against time and corruption. The ineluctable remnants of our classical tradition. Eclectic, meretricious and yet hopeful. Suggesting some colonial Roman ruin swallowed up by a pernicious and vital undergrowth.

The bus began to fill. Something hard and metallic thudded against the exit door. I drew my head in. As though blindered, I stared up at an advertisement — woman's hosiery on brown legs. My heart was beating a violent tempo. I felt it along the circumference of my collar. My hands, imprudently white, began to moisten. "I have come in peace," I said. "I have come in peace. Don't hurt me."

St. Bartholomew's was situated on a side street; it was somewhat nearer to Lenox Avenue than to Seventh. A huge, vulgar tin cross was attached at right angles to the façade, intended, no doubt, to attract a religious clientele from the busier avenues. Yellow or yellowed lettering spelled out ST. BARTHOLOMEW'S on the twelve foot vertical; CHURCH on the shorter horizontal — a method of advertising then much in vogue. From where I was standing, I could see similar crosses: TRANSIENT'S/HOTEL, PRETTY JOE'S/BAR, DOUBLE Q/BILLIARDS. But my cross was incontestably the largest. The morning breezes were barely noticeable, even so the sign wavered, creaking on its rusted supports. I touched the top of my head involuntarily. Then I stepped out from under the cross.

An empty lot, two brownstones in width, lay opposite St. Bart's. I crossed over to it, meaning to place the entire front of my church in perspective. The empty lot distracted me. I hooked my fingertips into the diamond mesh of a wire fence and peered in. There was a pervasive odor of wet dog's fur. Three shredded mattresses lay side to side to side near a burly, rusted fifty-five-gallon drum. The island's primitive topography had been preserved in the lot. Here and there the naked, tough granite of Manhattan poked through an epidermal layer of weeds and refuse. Not more than ten or fifteen yards from the sidewalk, the land fell away, forming a shallow gully. A stream bed once, I supposed. There were several of those pseudo-tropical, fern-branched trees that flourish in undeveloped portions of the city. Their stunted offspring, as yet nothing more than weeds, lay scattered beneath their branches. I heard, partly saw, a rustling in the gully. A fat, gray animal — a rat, certainly, but with an oddly thick tail — squeezed between two boulders and then scurried into the undergrowth. Still a wilderness of one or another sort. As inimical now as when the first Europeans had arrived three centuries before.

I turned to look at my church. Strictly speaking, of course,

St. Bart's could no longer be called a church. It was listed now as an Episcopal Mission and soon, in a matter of eighteen months, it would cease to be even that. It was quite a large building, constructed at the height of the nineteenth-century Gothic revival; there were seats for nearly five hundred parishioners. Lately, from what Father Pierre and Bishop Hawkes had intimated, I gathered that there had been many fewer than that in attendance. Once, when Harlem had represented quite different nationalities, St. Bart's Parish had been a thriving member of the New York Diocese. There was an altar guild then and a Sunday school; a choir and an organ that worked. Now, ninety years after its dedication, St. Bart's persisted as an outsized, gray symbol of ethnographic change.

There was a single tall portal. The statues of the apostles lining its arch were mostly faceless, their drapery as imprecise as the shafts of melted candles. A low, wide flight of four steps led up to the entrance. But the door, I knew, was locked, for the instruments of worship were no longer sacrosanct. Above, leaded in a spider-web pattern, there was a pretentious rose window containing less than half its original glass. The walls were blotched by efflorescence. A stubby, steepleless tower poked without much assurance toward God's heaven. The metal cross, seen in profile, cheapened what little was left of architectural merit in the Gothic façade. It was an altogether depressing prospect.

Three Negro boys approached from the direction of Seventh Avenue. I turned and saw them — saw them when they joined arms and began walking toward me, shoulder to shoulder to shoulder — then I turned away in dread of giving provocation. They were no older than twelve or thirteen and scarcely half my six feet two inches. I heard a high-pitched giggle. I hesitated. I longed to cross the street, but that seemed a shabby concession to my fears. The three boys penetrated the periphery of my vision. They were set on a collision course, ignoring me with their eyes, grimacing in conspiracy. Closer now — fifteen feet. The boy on the right had an immense cigar, unlit, between naked teeth. Ten feet. I began to hum, to smile. Still arm to arm, as in a game of Red Rover. Five feet. Three. One. At the last moment, they broke arms and flowed around me, running. A brown hand challenged my grip on the traveling bag. It tugged just once; having failed, it prudently ceased to dispute my hold. I watched as the three of them ran down the block, their pocked sneaker soles flying up from the pavement. At the corner, the three turned as one and spat. They made allusion to my skin and to the tenor of my sexual life. I smiled. Waved. They disappeared around the corner.

I let the traveling bag slip from my hand. Eyes . . . They had watched my encounter with the boys; now they were watching me. I took the old-fashioned rectory key from my pocket, and the movement was carried out self-consciously, performed. A scalloped bureau edge peered out from beyond the frame of a third story window. I smiled up at the dark profile, engaging its supposed single eye, until its thingness became apparent. Then I laughed. The sidewalks were deserted. I crossed the street.

St. Bart's rectory was attached at its left wing to the apsidial end of the church. Ninety years before there had been lawns on either side of St. Bart's, a lawn in front as well, gently sloping toward the gully in the empty lot. Now faded, pastel brownstones shouldered St. Bart's on either flank. To the right an alley, barely six feet wide, ran along the nave to the rectory at the rear, separating the church from a salmon-pink brownstone. But for a small portion of the left wing, glimpsed at the alley's end, the rectory was entirely hidden from the street.

Four lidless garbage cans obstructed the alley's mouth. I shoved one aside with my heel. Strange items of trash — thick, green strands very much like vines; bulbous fruits, exotic in their rottenness — dropped to the pavement with each a moist, pliant sound. I kicked them aside. Then I scraped my soles dry on the rough cement. The word HORNETS in green lettering had been sprayed on the salmon-pink wall. I noticed that the basement windows of St. Bart's had been mortared over; those of the nave were protected by heavy gratings and a venerable crust of pigeon dung. The alley was in twilight even then — at just after eleven in the morning. I inhaled. I started walking toward my rectory.

I looked up and to my right. An old man with empty, active jaws leaned, ruminating, from his second story window. The man spat down apathetically. I heard a sharp snap as his wad of saliva met the pavement ten steps in front of me. I seemed to cause a somewhat Pavlovian reaction wherever I went in Harlem. I smiled as though I considered spitting a salutation; nonetheless, my scalp prickled as I passed beneath the window. A tabby cat galloped across the alley some distance ahead of me. It disappeared into the rectory foundations.

I stepped out into a fairly spacious, paved court. This court was bounded on its north and west sides by the front of my rectory and the apsidial end of St. Bart's respectively. The southern line of the rectangle ran across the alley's mouth and along the rear of the salmon-pink brownstone. On the east were the backs of three buildings that fronted on Lenox Avenue. Even at that early hour there were lights at each window of these three. I could see the heads and shoulders of several Negro men. A telephone rang. And another. There was laughter, then scattered applause. I stood on tiptoe in the middle of the court and peered to the east. A window was slammed. I turned away, fearing that my curiosity had been impertinent.

The rectory was two stories tall. The upper story was orna-

mented with elaborate gabling; a cone-topped turret — a sorcerer's hat — surmounted the front part of the right wing. A
weather vane had stood at the cone's apex, but now only the E,
W, N, indicators remained, tilted at quite inappropriate angles.
The upper story had been sealed off just before the Second World War; most of its windows were shuttered, though
some, especially those in the turret, had been boarded over.
The shingles were maroon. Where the gutters were rusted
through, rain had discolored the wooden siding in icicle-
shaped, brown stains. My rectory was, essentially, a modest
country mansion; it seemed abashed by its unfamiliar, urban
surroundings.

The entrance was three steps up from the pavement, set in under a Corinthian-columned portico. I walked toward it with
sudden reluctance. Father Pierre had made the situation quite
explicit during my first visit two weeks before. I knew there
was no hot water. I knew that only four rooms in the entire
building were habitable. I had seen the roaches: Father Pierre
had pointed them out with great relish. I set my traveling bag
down beside the door. I sighed and straightened up, slowly
accumulating my resolve.

The stoop was covered with large duck-foot-shaped leaves. I
thought that odd: there were no trees in the immediate area.
Brown discolorations — like the erratic wrigglings of snakes —
crossed backward and forward over the landing. I scraped at
them with the tip of my toe. Someone said, "Damn it. That
does it! That does it!" in a very loud voice. I peered toward
the three buildings, tilting my glasses in order to achieve maxi-
mum magnification. But the outburst had no audible sequel.
I shrugged and slid my key into the lock. I hesitated, listening.
Then I quickly turned the key and pushed the door inward. I
had heard a dreadful noise.

Every light was on. Indeed, every electrical device in the place had been left running. Somewhere to my right I could hear the terribly determined rush of pouring water. I slammed the front door shut and hurried down the hall. It was the tub: someone had left the faucets on. The bathroom and a good part of the hall were already flooded. I kicked my shoes off and waded forward. Every few seconds a miniature wave would slurp over the edge of the brimful tub. I stared into the water. Six or seven of those strange duck-foot leaves — God only knew how they had gotten there — were blocking the drain. I leaned over the ancient, high tub, straining at the middle to avoid breakers cresting on its rim; I turned the cold tap all the way to the right. There was no improvement. The water numbed my toes. All the way to the left . . . The flow did not diminish. I gnawed at my lower lip. Cold water was filling my cuffs: sopping trouser legs adhered to my shins. I grabbed at the hot water tap. It turned with difficulty, but the stream of water appeared to abate somewhat. I applied the full leverage of my arm and upper body — the handle came off and slipped silently under the ripples. I toppled forward, catching hold of the soap dish at the ultimate moment. I hung there, bowed, for several seconds, while water seeped into my trousers at the belt-line.

I shoved my body away from the wall and stood, motionless, eyes closed until my composure returned. Then I took off my jacket and splashed with determination to the bathroom door. I hung my jacket on a hook. There was a pipping sound: hook and jacket fell into an inch of water. I blasphemed without the slightest compunction. The pipes gibbered. I draped my jacket over the toilet seat. Then I rolled up my right sleeve. After a moment's unpleasant groping, I managed to salvage the HOT handle. Water, displaced by my arm, ran in an eddying current around my ankles. I fitted the handle onto its hexagonal shaft. I turned once, very carefully. The lights went out.

It took me until noon to find and replace the fuse. At three o'clock the floors were reasonably dry. And all that while I thought of Rufus Clagger. He was the part-time sexton, referred to simply as "that damned devil" by Father Pierre. Father Pierre had left on Tuesday for his second ulcer operation; during my short stay he had intimated that, in large part, his internal trouble was the fault of Rufus Clagger. Father Pierre hadn't looked well. His eyes were haloed with blue-black rings, and he walked with the stoop of an elderly person, though he was only two years older than I. Father Pierre didn't think I was fit to assume his post. I saw that at once. He, himself, had not done too well in it. The advice he gave me was of the most perfunctory sort. I don't think he wanted me to succeed in Harlem.

I made a cup of tea and carried it into my office, the rectory's one pleasant room. My belongings had been sent on ahead. One trunk and three cartons of books stood near the desk. I unlocked the trunk and began removing my more intimate possessions. My pipes and their rack. My pen set. A pound tin of Peterson's Mixture, unopened. A photograph of Eleanor. My Bible. My Book of Common Prayer. A copy of George Horn Smith's autobiography. A family photograph — my mother, Eleanor and my two older sisters grouped around an adolescent me. The worry bird with the clerical collar given me by Eleanor just after my ordination. I arranged these things on my new desk much as they had been arranged on my desk in Greensprings.

My office was slightly longer than it was wide. The bedroom was immediately to its right. The two rooms were at the far end of the hall and, together, comprised the tip of the rectory's left wing. The kitchen was down the hall and to the left; it was separated from the bedroom by a staircase that led to the abandoned second story. The door at the foot of the stairs had been locked for some time. The kitchen was wide and spacious, with a double door, having been intended for very large pastoral families. An equally large, disused, dining room stood opposite the kitchen. The right wing, which contained a long meeting room, another office and a recreation room of some sort, was in a state of perfect neglect, the furniture sheeted, and the sheets, in turn, covered with dust. Except for the bathroom. . . . This stood at the far right end of the corridor — as far from my convenience as was architecturally possible.

Two doors entered my office. One, as mentioned, led in from the hall near my bedroom door. The other, in the far wall of the wing, led out into the chancel of St. Bart's. A peephole with a sliding panel afforded a fragmentary view of the nave. Bookshelves lined the two doorless walls. A plain wood cross, the knots quite visible, hung above my desk; it had hung there since the rectory's dedicaton in 1881. A reproduction of Brueghel's wintery "Adoration of the Magi" hung near the internal door. The furnishings were old and spare: a desk, its cork mat etched with doodles; a comfortable swivel chair; a table on which stood a globe of the world, so rusted that it could present only an African face to the room; an armchair, the arms splayed, the slipcovers blotched with monstrous peonies; a threadbare green carpet bearing an illustrative pattern now quite indecipherable. Best of all, a small electric heater. I turned the heater on.

I took off my wet socks and draped them across the heater. Gingerly, I tilted backward in the swivel chair until I could safely place my fat, reddish heels on the desk top. I lit a pipe. It was nearly four o'clock. The single window looked out onto the court through a substantial grating. Shadows from the alley's mouth were rising up the rear wall of the salmon-pink brownstone, repulsing sunlight in the diurnal give and take. It was already dark in my office. I switched on my desk lamp.

I had been most unceremoniously installed — partly rebaptized in the process as well. But now — for the first time — I was rector of a church. Though my tenure, thus far, resembled merely some death vigil beside the bed of an aged stranger, I could not help feeling both pride and exhilaration. A priest should be this, no matter the circumstances, at least once in his life. I knew that. Yet, even so, I did not enter St. Bart's that first day. I had seen enough on my last visit to know the old church would only dishearten me. Instead, I knelt in thanksgiving before the knotted, wooden cross.

After a while, I took Horn Smith's book down from the desk top and held it, open at random, in my lap. There was a striking watercolor on the jacket, just the man's head with the great horn curving upward at the hairline — half of a rainbow's arc. I don't know who painted the cover. But, whoever the artist was, I owe to him all — the good and the bad — of my Harlem experience. Months before, that watercolor had caught my eye in Polk's, the Greensprings bookstore. I had no interest in contemporary writing and yet, compelled by that astonishing profile, I bought *My Head Lies Heavy*. I read it in a single afternoon. I was deeply moved by it; I have never found anyone who was not. It was Horn Smith's book, in fact, that had brought me there— to the swivel chair in my little office as evening descended on Harlem.

And yet the book was a fraud. Certainly the most elaborate of all Horn Smith's hoaxes. I cannot write about the past without foreknowledge of the present. I had come, as a pilgrim, to find the man of the autobiography. If not the man himself, then the world which he so completely dominated. But neither the world nor the man were what I, in my gross naïveté, had expected them to be. On that day almost three years ago I had still a great deal to learn. I learned it with difficulty. But the

intense, painful experience of those six months in Harlem gave
me a greater respect for human courage and ingenuity than has
anything I have seen or read, before or since. And now, to the
best of a very limited ability, I will teach you as I was taught.

Excerpt from the Autobiography of George Horn Smith

Some men, when they are babies, they walk at one year. And
some other men, they say whole words. At one year I, George Horn
Smith, first tried to lift my head.

They say now that the earth shook when I was born. The earth
shook and a great wave came to drown the fishermen at Old Shark
Cay. That is what they say — but I do not believe them. My people,
you will forgive them, they are superstitious. Birth frightens them.
And death — death is so terrible a man will not think of it. Now
my people call me a god. Thirty years ago they thought me the
most evil of jumbie-things. I love my people, but they have much
to learn.

My horn was not so big then — when it came slicing from my
lovely mother's body. But it was big enough. My poor, lovely
mother . . . She was alone, with only her sister, Reseda, to help
in the birthing. The rain tapped, then it knocked, then it hammered at the walls of our metal and wood shack — as big only as
eight coffins stacked together. The flame of one candle flickered in
the wind. The walls shook and the cross with Jesus on it fell to its
face on the floor. The rain came in through the holes we called windows. Red ants and mahogany bugs ran up the legs of our broken
table. They, too, did not like the rain. They huddled on bits of
mango and tanya, on the rim of our iron wee-wee bowl. And they
crawled between my mother's naked thighs as she shrieked with me.

It came from my mother like an iguana's ugly snout. Brown and
wet, glittering with blood. My mother quivered as if a great,
wooden stake had been driven through her body. Aunt Reseda
screamed and then she struck her fist against her forehead. It moved
again. It squirmed like a snake shedding its skin. It was me. Aunt
Reseda threw herself backward on her heels. "Mary mother! Joom-

bie! Oh, Mary mother!" she screamed. Then she ran out of our shack and into the rain. And there, on the edge of the hill, she prayed, pushing the shark's-tooth charm hard into the soft places of her palm.

My aunt said the Lord's Prayer — and when that was not long enough — she said a spell the obeah doctor had told her. Then she felt guilt, she tells me that, guilt and the cold rain that was falling so hard. My aunt climbed back up the hill. By then my mother's blood was running down the hillside with the rain water. And I was born — born, almost drowned in the water. My aunt cut my body free. She did not look at my head. She pushed her shark's-tooth charm between my empty gums. Then she wrapped me in an old burlap rag and ran out again into the rain. I could not cry, for I was almost dead. In the morning, the old Cha-Cha doctor came from Mafolie on the hill, and he made my lovely mother well.

My aunt hid me for three days. She told my mother that I was dead, and my mother believed her, for she had lost five children before me. In all that time I lay like one of many logs, wrapped in the burlap rag, in the woodpile near my uncle's little house. The big roaches, they left their dung on my body. The tiny lizards crawled into my armpits and took warmth from my groin. The mosquitoes sucked me, as I should have sucked my own mother. I lay, more animal than man, not feeling it when my aunt touched my chest to see if I was dead.

But then the Cha-Cha doctor, when my aunt wouldn't speak to him, went and told the police. The two mulatto policemen were very brave when they entered my uncle's house. They were very brave when they searched all the rooms, when they poked under the beds and in the closets, when they beat my uncle's shins with their sticks. But, when they looked behind the woodpile, then they were no longer brave. Then the two policemen forgot how to speak, and, before they could remember, they were down the hill, far from my uncle's house. But the old Cha-Cha doctor was white and more knowing than men of my race. He took me in his arms and carried me down to the city. I was important to him for my horn. The doctor brought me to his little hospital below the Catholic Chapel. He put me in a womb machine. And many white men came to marvel at my horn and be disgusted.

And so I was born. An animal. A freak. Unknown to my lovely mother. Feared by my aunt. Hated by my people, who are, themselves, a hated race. I had no father — for my mother, may God bless her, is a woman who loves easily and does not remember. I lay asleep in the machine — unaware of the fear and the hatred and the loneliness.

Unaware, too, of the greatness that was to come . . .

It began to rain late that first night. Father Pierre had left the bedroom window open nearly four inches at the top; the opening was directly above my head. I awoke just before six, having dreamed, at intervals, of a great and malicious baptismal font. My pillow was damp; the hairs of the right arm were hung with tiny globules of water, very like dewdrops. I stood — one foot on the mattress, one foot on the sill — and pawed ineffectually at the window frame. I succeeded only in opening it another two inches. In exasperation, I pounded at the window with the heel of my palm. The panes, however, rattled so violently in their casings that I was afraid to persist. I climbed down and stood, barefooted, in the center of my bedroom floor. Finally I brought some waxed paper from the kitchen and, using adhesive tape, managed temporarily to seal the gap.

By that time, of course, I was wide awake. I went into the kitchen. Father Pierre had bequeathed me a fully stocked refrigerator and a note stating, in Latin, that condemned men should *semper* eat a hearty meal. I made myself a cup of coffee. There was a box of instant oatmeal and a miniature cornflakes package in the cupboard. I took down the latter and emptied its contents into a small bowl. Instead of cornflakes, however, a handful of white letters poured out — letters for the announcement board. I poured the letters onto the table and began playing anagrams. I tried spelling "Reverend C. Beecher Pratt" but there weren't enough "e's" and the one "v" was needed for "services." I unreverenced myself and tried again.

C.B. PRATT

SERV. 10 AM

Rather terse, but I needed the letters for something more significant.

BCK DOR

ALWYS OPEN

COME IN FOR

COFEE & TALK

I liked that. It sounded amiable, inviting. The sentiment was expressed with simplicity; the spelling was particularly unpretentious. When I had finished, however, there were very few letters remaining. That could mean only one thing: Father Pierre had already tried the COFEE & TALK gambit. The response, I suspected, had been disheartening.

The rain let up just before ten. I put on my rubbers and walked out of the rectory, down the alley, to the front of St. Bart's. It would have been more convenient, certainly drier, had I walked through the church itself — but I wasn't ready for that as yet. I had Eleanor's tiny, flowered umbrella over my head; she had lent it to me the week before, and I, in my preoccupation, had forgotten to return it. The sidewalks were nearly deserted. Few people passed as I hunched in front of the announcement board, inserting the letters of my telegram. During the night — at least I assumed it was during the night, for I could not remember having seen it the afternoon before — someone had hung a long banner between the windows of a beige brownstone. The banner said, THE HORN'S POWER IS YOUR POWER. A menacing, brown horn had been painted on a yellow background. The horn seemed to be goring an abstract human stomach. Lines of force, representing impact, radiated out in all directions.

I glanced once again at my handiwork on the wall to the left of the church door and started walking back toward the alley's mouth. After just a few steps, however, I hesitated: my attention was drawn to an extraordinary black turd. Such things are not my usual study, but this turd was so enormous that its presence on the steps of St. Bart's quite confounded me. It was all of ten inches across and more or less exactly rounded. I wondered just what Brobdingnagian species of dog had dropped it there. I frowned. The turd dwarfed even cow pats I had seen in the fields around Greensprings.

While I pondered this, slightly embarrassed by my own fascination, I detected a hymn tune — Hymn 530, I think — being whistled to inappropriate jazz rhythms. I peered toward Lenox Avenue. A short, wiry man was approaching, his lips puckered. He wore a Horn Smith hat: I recognized it from pictures I had seen in *Time* magazine. The Horn hat was, essentially, an immense hack's cap — the peak grotesquely exaggerated. Smith himself had worn just such a cap, as a child, to conceal his deformity. They were quite the rage then, even outside Negro communities. Each was sold with a telescoping metal rod that prevented the huge peak from sagging down over the eyes. In April, a Paris designer had brought out a chic variation for women. These latter had silvered plastic horns that were attached to the forehead with a kind of spirit gum.

The wiry man continued to walk toward me. As he came, I stared at his costume. From throat to knee he was dressed in a tabard-like garment. The whole was orange and as phosphorescent in hue as an automobile reflector. It had puffed sleeves. There was a wide belt at the waist. Below the tabard, he wore green tights over a pair of bandy legs. Pert orange bootlets covered his feet and ankles. When he was but twenty feet away, I descried an emblem in the tabard's center: a silver unicorn prancing on a blue field. Underneath, in silver lettering, there were the numerals 174-66-0. The unicorn, forehooves upraised, seemed somehow familiar — though, at the time, I couldn't imagine why.

The man hesitated as he came even with St. Bart's. He paused, nodding his head in time to the rhythm of his whistling. Then he climbed the steps and halted only when he was standing directly in front of me. I sensed some menace in him. Instinctively, I took a step backward, afraid, perhaps, that my unabashed curiosity had been offensive. But he was still whistling and did not speak until, at leisure, he had brought the stanza to an end.

"You Pratt?" He pointed at my solar plexus — as though that were named quite differently from the rest of me.

"Yes," I said. "Pratt. Yes, I am." The little man cleared his throat. He put his hands on his hips. The slight drizzle made glossy the paper-thin skin over his cheekbones. It reminded me of fine, Greek pastry. He was much shorter than I and probably less than half my weight; nonetheless, I decided to take yet another cautious step backward, skirting the mysterious turd as I moved.

"Well," he said. "I'm the janitor. Father Pierre tell you about me?"

"Yes," I said enthusiastically. "The sexton. You must be Clagger. Rufus, I think." I put out my hand. My palm was the larger of the two and yet, when we applied the pressure of greeting, I felt a sharp ache along the line of my knuckles.

"No," he said. He shook his head. "Two no's. I'm the janitor and my name's Nicholas Breakspeare."

"Breakspeare?" I inclined my ear toward him, certain that I had misheard.

"Nich-o-las," he repeated, separating the syllables. "Break

as in break. Speare as in spear. And don't hand me that sexton stuff. A janitor's a janitor. Even if he's in a church."

"But . . ."

"Rufus Clagger's dead, friend. He died to the Horn. Break-speare's my Horn name. Father Pierre, he don't care for the Horn. He kept on callin' me Rufus. I told him an' I told him, but he's a stubborn man."

"I — I don't think I understand."

"Okay. I'll 'splain to you sometime. Meanwhile you got a pretty umbrella and me, I don't got nothin'. What say we step inside? I don't dig the wet."

"Oh," I said. "No. Of course not. Sorry."

I looked up at my pretty umbrella and then beyond it to the overcast sky. Clagger-Breakspeare had already begun walking toward the alley, kicking imaginary objects out of his way as he went. There were slit pockets high on the sides of his tabard; he had hooked his thumbs negligently into these. I smiled as I watched him walk. As many short persons will, he affected the wide, sweeping gait of a six-foot athlete. The Horn cap made his head seem quite the largest part of his body. Nicholas Break-speare . . . It was an extraordinary name. And, like the prancing unicorn, it seemed somehow familiar.

My nose wrinkled involuntarily. I jammed Eleanor's um-brella rather roughly into the hall stand. Nicholas Break-speare hadn't closed the bathroom door. He was using my toilet with a noisy familiarity. The high-pitched sound of the stream reminded me of another, louder splash heard the afternoon be-fore. As I walked toward my office, I phrased certain sentences of firm but temperate reprimand. Responsibility. Economy. Neatness. Cooperation. Respect for property. I suppose the hat and the orange tabard made me think of children on Hal-loween. The tone I meant to take was certainly condescending, a bit scout-masterish. I reconsidered, however, as soon as Nicholas Breakspeare sauntered into my office. Reprimands of any sort, I realized, would be very poorly received.

He stood in the doorway for several moments, standing contraposto, wiping his fingers with seeming intense preoccupation along the inside of his betighted left knee. He was pacing himself, studying me as I, in my turn, studied him. Having dried his hand, Nicholas Breakspeare sniffed between the fingers and seemed satisfied. He was of indeterminate age. His ears protruded on either side of his head. The light brown skin of his cheek and forehead wrinkled extensively under the urging of even the slightest facial expression. And Nicholas Breakspeare's face was very expressive. He had, especially, a habit of drawing his upper lip back over his teeth in a neutral grimace. He resembled — I censured the comparison even as I made it — he resembled one of those small, agile monkeys.

"Okay," he said. "Let's us get down t' business."

"Would you like some coffee first?"

"Coffee? No. No coffee. I want t'get things straightened out."

"All right," I said. "Let's do that." I sat in my swivel chair and smiled blandly up at him. There was a tempered hostility in his voice. He had planned what he was going to say, planned even the tones of it. And so, in self-defense, I sought to foul his careful timing.

"What Father Pierre say 'bout me?" Anticipating, he struck a pose of angry intransigence. Hands on hips. One leg before the other.

"Say? He didn't say much. Why don't you sit down? The chair doesn't look like much, but — "

"Never mind sittin'. What he say 'bout me?"

"Uh. He mentioned your name. Said you were the sexton,

that's all." I pretended to think for a moment. Then I nodded.
"No. Nothing else."

"Yeah?" He deliberated, his lips pouting. "Have it your
way. I don't care what he said. All I want's a fair deal."
He cleared his throat again. Despite his assumed anger, I knew
he was worried. I felt sorry for him.

"A fair deal. Fine," I said. Nicholas Breakspeare took two
steps forward, leaning over me as I sat. He was coming to the
crux of his argument and he wanted a physical advantage. I
reached behind me and took my aluminum and nylon butterfly net from where it stood against the wall. Then I began making wide, aimless sweeps in front of me. This effectually
negated his advantage; moreover, it distracted him from his
prime intention.

"What's that for, fish?"

"No. Butterflies. I catch them."

"Yeah? There ain't no butterflies around here."

"No?" I nodded thoughtfully. "Suppose not. Never can tell,
though. But you were saying — about a fair deal . . ."

"Yeah. Right. Uh — " He became confused. I think he had
forgotten his purpose in speaking to me. He stared uneasily
at the moving net until he had collected his thoughts. "Salary
and working times," he said. "That's it. I get forty-five a week.
Right? Just like before."

"Yes." I made an over-the-head-flip snatch with my net. Very
difficult to execute.

"Okay. I work nine to one."

"Fine."

"I work Monday, Tuesday, Wednesday, Friday, Saturday."
He counted off the days on the five fingers of his left hand. I
waited for him to extend his right thumb as well. He didn't.

"And Sunday," I said.

"No Sunday." He crossed his arms over his narrow chest.

"No Sunday?" My net hung motionless in the air. "That's when I need you. What d'you think I am — a Seventh Day Adventist?"

"Man — I know what you are — don't you worry about that. No Sunday. Father Pierre went along with that."

"I don't believe it." I got my net moving again, but now the sweeps were sharper, agitated.

"Believe it or not. I don't care. I gotta go to church Sunday. I gotta have my freedom of religion. It's the law."

"The law?" I ran my hand over my lips and lower jaw. "Am I to take it then — you're not an Episcopalian?"

"That's just it — that's just the way you take it. I'm a Baptist and proud of it. Tabernacle of the Burnin' Lamb. Around the corner on Lenox."

"Look," I said reasonably. "Let's not get ourselves upset. You want to go to church, that's fine with me. Some of my best friends are Baptists. All I ask is that you give me an hour or so on Sunday morning. There's no altar guild here. I'll have a thousand things to do. If it snows — "

"God makes the snow. I don't. Remind me, I'll show you where the shovel is." I paused. I leaned my net against the wall. Then I began filling my pipe. Nicholas Breakspeare cleared his throat again. "I know what you're thinkin'," he said. "You're thinkin' you're gonna fire me. Well don't try it. Father Pierre fired me for a month first day he got here. But he didn't get nobody else. I saw to that."

"No," I said. "I wasn't thinking of that. Didn't even cross my mind." Nicholas Breakspeare tapped his foot on the carpet. His body was terrifically tense. He had expected an argument. His left eye began to twitch. He brushed irritably at it with the back of his hand.

"Well?" he said.

"Well . . . What's there to say? You win. You've got me over a barrel." I stuck my hand out. The gesture was so unexpected that he backed away at first. When finally he shook my hand, he did so without trying to maim me. I sighed. Father Pierre, I thought, would have enjoyed my defeat.

"Glad of that," said Nicholas Breakspeare, his little body relaxing visibly. He pressed his palms together as the tension ebbed out of him. "Glad you see it my way. I don't want no trouble. Just my rights. Come on in the church. There's some things I gotta show you."

We left my office through the rear door and emerged in the chancel of St. Bart's, just below the choir stalls. It was perceptibly cooler, almost cold. The dampness was pervasive; it had become embedded in the wood of the pews, the threads of the tattered carpeting. Nicholas Breakspeare turned on the lights and waited patiently while I reverenced the cross. An unpleasant draft circulated near the floor. I felt it on my knees and ankles as I knelt before the altar. St. Bart's was not the most pleasant place to worship God. If I, a priest, felt that — how, I wondered, did the few remaining parishioners feel?

Nicholas Breakspeare showed me around. I knew he was enjoying my discomfort. He pointed out the light switches — the ones that worked and the ones that didn't. The rear of the nave had been without lights for several years. Nicholas Breakspeare had rigged a droplight. The ugly, black cord ran from the chancel, up the center aisle, to the vestibule. There a naked light bulb hung in a cage from a bar in the coat stand. I held my hand flat over my eyebrows to subdue the glare. There were no hangers in the coat stand. That seemed ominous, but I refrained from making the obvious inference.

"Place's rotten. Rotten. Rotten. Just plain rotten." Nicholas Breakspeare made complacent clucking sounds with his

tongue and lips. "Roof leaks. That there's the worst spot —
leaks there even when it ain't rainin' out." We were in the
right-hand aisle. Nicholas Breakspeare indicated a point at the
corner of a small pseudo-Gothic vault. In a mesh of fan tracery, near where the groining met the wall of the church, I saw
the greenish glint of water. I followed the glint with my eye;
it descended the wall, ending in a wetness just under my feet.
The vault was at least eight feet above my head. The main
vaults were twice that height. I shivered involuntarily. Nicholas Breakspeare giggled.

"Yeah," he said. "Even bums don't come in here. January,
February — cold as a polar bear's behind." He drew his upper
lip back over his teeth. "See your breath in April — "
He breathed out heartily, but we couldn't see anything in the
gloom.

"The boiler — I don't suppose . . . There's nothing we
can do about it?"

"Metal's like paper. You can push your finger through." He
pushed his forefinger through a slight and imaginary obstruc-
tion in the air.

"Is there anything below this? I saw some windows out in
the alley."

"No," he said and he shook his head vigorously. "I mean —
yeah, there's rooms. But, man, you don't wanna go down there.
Place's a holy mess. Dirt, dust. Broken furniture. Used to be a
'musement place for kids. Old, flat basketballs. Ping-pong pad-
dles. Stuff like that. Staircase down's ready to collapse. You
better steer clear. Take my advice."

"I will," I said. He led me between two rows of pews, into
the center aisle. We walked slowly toward the apse. Nicholas
Breakspeare continued his discourse on corruption. I listened
without looking at him.

"Pews're pretty shaky. Full of splinters, too. I hadda take the

pads off — they got real mildewed, stunk to high heaven.
Watch it." I had tripped over a loose corner of the carpeting.
There were treacherous rents in every square yard of the fabric.
"We got books only for the first four, five rows. That's plenty,
believe me. Guys backed a truck up t'the door. Took the
whole kit an' kaboodle. The Bible off the lectern. Candlesticks. Left the cross, though. Funny. Probably it's bad luck
t'steal a cross." He halted under the chancel arch. "And whatever you do, man — don't go up in that pulpit-thing. It shakes
like. You come down like the walls of Jericho. Mark my
words."

Nicholas Breakspeare sat on the steps of the chancel, leaning
back on his elbows. His orange tabard with the prancing unicorn seemed welcome, cheerful. I nudged the pulpit experi-
mentally. It creaked.

"Excuse me?" He had spoken, but I, in my preoccupation,
had not quite heard him.

"Why'd you come here? Huh?" I stammered, confused by
the frankness of his question. Then I shook my head. Nicholas
Breakspeare went on. "Father Pierre — I could figure him. He
wanted t'do something — wanted t'be a big cat here. Like
John Meeker. But now it's too late. The man is dead. They
gonna tear him down. So, like I say, why'd you come here?" He
stared at me for a long while without blinking. I looked at my
feet.

"I don't know really," I said. "I wanted to do my part,
whatever that means."

"You know what?"

"What?"

"I think you're a tourist." He shoved a thumb in my direction. I laughed.

"That's just what I am. Want to be my guide?"

"Me?" Nicholas Breakspeare waved a bony hand in front of his face. "Not me. I'm not crazy. Man — you want my advice — you do your sightseeing right here. Me? I don't mind white people. Race, color and creed. I'm not prejudiced. But things're changin', brother. Out there, out there the wind's blowin' black. Lotta guys in the movement — cut out a white man's heart soon's look at him." He slammed his fist against the wooden arch. The vaults echoed dully. Nicholas Breakspeare watched me to see what effect his grisly pronouncement would have. I ran my fingers along the ridge of my left cheekbone. Then I changed the subject.

"Why d'you wear that?"

"This thing? You like it? This is my Horn suit." He stood up and turned around, pirouetting. "Got it three years ago. First color's orange, then green, then blue. Someday I be a blue." He looked toward the cross and his eyes deepened.

"What do you do?"

"One thing I don't do — I don't answer silly questions." He smiled. "But for you — I give you a hint — I'm a runner for the Horn."

"George Horn Smith?"

"No. Lena Horne. Trader Horn. Little boy blue and his horn."

"George Horn Smith — I've read his book."

"Yeah? Me, I don't read much."

"What — what's a runner do?"

"There you go again." He shook his head. But he was too proud to be perfectly reticent. "A runner's someone who does — who gets things done. Does."

"Does what?"

"Does." He shrugged, as though the word in itself had sufficient meaning. "You know — when you go into the rectory?"

I nodded. "On your right hand — take a look some time — that's the back of Horn's Place."

"Those three buildings? Where the lights are on?"

"That's the place. Reason I tell you: it's not smart for you — for any white cat — t'go walkin' by that place. Up on Lenox. Y'get what I mean?"

"Yes." I was thinking. Father Pierre hadn't told me about Horn's Place. I felt a tightening in my abdomen. Nicholas Breakspeare stretched, yawning.

"So. You got the word. Can't say nobody warned you."

"Why do you call yourself that — Nicholas Breakspeare?"

"I dunno. Smith knows." He started walking toward the door to my office. The conversation had ceased to interest him. "Oh," he said, as an afterthought. "I saw your sign on the board. Come in and talk, that stuff. You're gonna get yourself robbed." I shrugged. "Yeah. That's the way Father Pierre was. All the same — it got on his nerves. Robbed him six or seven times. Think he was insulted more'n anything else. No coffee and no doughnuts and no talk. Nobody wanted to say nothin'." He paused. "My advice — don't do no resistin'. Give 'em what they want and don't talk too much. Nobody likes a talkin' white man."

He saluted. Then he turned and walked out past the choir stalls.

I wandered aimlessly back up the center aisle. A fat drop of water struck my temple, spattering into a thousand bits. I stared up at the high Gothic vault, but, of course, I could see nothing. Nicholas Breakspeare had begun whistling again. He was happy; he had made a fool of me. Disconsolate, I walked to the far right-hand side of a pew, near the back. There I sat, drying my glasses, my head balanced against a pillar. From where I was, the four-foot cross above the altar seemed infinitely far away. I knew the acoustics were execrable; beyond twenty rows, my thin voice would not be heard. The lighting in the apse was haphazard; the altar and altar screen were actually in shadow, while the walls to the left and right were subjected to an arid glare. The pew seat felt cold and moist under my buttocks. The kneeler had come loose from its hinges. I hunched down. I was embarrassed, I think, to be found in such a shabby derelict.

Daylight filtered down and through a stained glass window on my right. I stared at it. For a long moment, I had difficulty identifying the window's theme, so much of the original glass had been destroyed. At the bottom, a yard-square piece of plywood covered an irreparable break; in places the leading was bent jaggedly inward. There was a figure on the left somewhat more elevated than the others. This window, I decided finally, had once portrayed Our Lord's glorious Ascension.

There was an Ascension window in our church at Greensprings. As a work of art, it was hardly more valid, I suppose, than this had been in the time of its wholeness. But I had loved that window in St. Mark's Chapel. A great weeping willow stood just outside, between the window and the morning sun. Shadows cast by the slender branches were projected onto the glass; they rose and fell gently — animating the nimbus above the risen Christ's head. In a slight breeze the motion was hypnotic. If you concentrated diligently on the shadows, the figure would seem to come free from the vitreous, white clouds and, at last, from the window itself. I always led my family there. In time it became known as Pratt's Pew.

A stream called Little Jordan meandered around St. Mark's forming a gentle moat on three sides. Little Jordan's course

had once been tampered with, for it ran only in straight lines
and at right angles. It paralleled St. Mark's on the right, then
crossed in front and turned again to run parallel along the left
hand side of the nave. A little, arched cedar plank bridge led
up to the entrance. Pots of flowers hung suspended from the
railings. In the years before the bridge was built, parishioners
had to cross Little Jordan barefoot — pants rolled, skirts held
high — at the time of the spring thaws.

Sequestered. Enclosed. That was our way in Greensprings.
Every building had its fence or its wall or its moat. Every field
had a hedge or a brake of some sort encircling it. My own home
was surrounded by a thick, stone wall. The mortar joints were
green with moss; pompous toads lived in the innumerable
chinks and crannies. The house itself had been constructed
in a natural hollow. The wall followed the rim of this hollow
and, as a result, only the roof and the windows of my attic room
looked out over it to the road beyond.

We are an old family, complacent and self-regarding. My
mother was a great grandniece of that most illustrious of Beech-
ers. My father was a gentleman lawyer — that is to say, he prac-
ticed only as a favor to friends or when some particular legal
matter seemed of interest to him. There were, and still are,
several large family landholdings in western Massachusetts.
The income from these allowed my father — and, to a lesser
extent, his four children — considerable economic freedom.
In his leisure, George Danforth Pratt wrote three very well-re-
spected books on New England wild flowers. Two of my older
sisters, Harriet and Charlotte, have told me of long hikes
through Vermont and New Hampshire, of twinleaf and ad-
der's-tongue, of Solomon's seal and Dutchman's breeches, and of
a rare species of lupine called, even now, Pratt's lupine.

My father died before my second birthday. I was a late child,

born almost twenty years after Harriet, the first child. My
mother wanted a manchild, but her experience had been only
of daughters, and she was perhaps uncertain how to treat me. I
was reared, I imagine, as some superior sort of female: I have
seen photographs of my infant clothing and of my playroom
decorations. The death of my father intensified this bias both
for my mother and for my sisters. Eleanor, I fear, still considers
me some special kind of doll. And so I grew to manhood behind thick walls, sedulously coddled and adored by women.

My attic room was made ready on the day before my thirteenth birthday. Except for my time in Harlem and my years
in college, I have known no other room. Later — after my
mother had died and Harriet and Charlotte had moved away
— Eleanor and her husband inherited our house. I rented my
attic room from them. Everything but the terms of my tenancy
was the same. The bed that I slept in at forty was the bed that
I slept in at thirteen. The high school pennant still hangs
over my headboard. My adolescent toys are the bric-a-brac of
my mature years. Few people have ever visited my room, so
I have been spared the trouble of redecorating in honor of my
middle age. You will, I trust, forgive me these revelations. I
write of them not because I am proud of my narrowness, but so
that you may understand my inadequacy in the face of what was
to come.

I had no close friends until my junior year in college. I cannot remember a time when I was not the tallest and most awkward of my contemporaries. We Pratts are big people who
move slowly. Our bones are large, especially the jointing
bones — ankles, knees, wrists — and our extremities seem
grafted from some more substantial species. Once my playmates had ascertained that no great strength or coordination
attended my tallness, they delighted in playing Jack the Giant

Toppler. I fell a great deal in those early years. Perhaps the slight stammer, which returns to me even in my middle age, was the result of a long uncertain state of equilibrium. I still feel, though I know better, that "prat-fall" has a personal significance.

I bore the topplings with a good grace. It was, after all, the only thing I had to offer: they the topplers, I the toppled. It was an intense, intimate relationship. I was happy to be the source of their enjoyment. But, in time, my collapses became too predictable; the excitement waned. My contemporaries abandoned me to topple other, less certain, things — football players, careers and, increasingly, young ladies.

The seminary was midway on the road from Greensprings to Sturgis Forge. Sometimes, when I bicycled along that road, crossing and recrossing Little Jordan, I would stop at the foot of the path that led up, between the stone gate posts, to the seminary itself. I liked to walk in the little flowerless garden with its self-consciously pagan fountain. I liked to sit on cool benches hewn out of native granite. I read there; it was a good place to read. I saw many men in the garden who wore glasses, some as thick as mine. I spoke to them. I found their company pleasant. And now I, too, am a priest.

It was not quite that simple. It never is. But there was no sudden and dreadful revelation, no visionary gleam. Some of my fellows have had that. I see it in their eyes: victims of an unwilling rape that will not be forgotten. I do not envy them. For me, it was an intrinsic thing; an elaboration, more or less inevitable, of things that already were. I believed in God and in His church. I accepted the commitment with a sense, often, of presumption, but never of doubt. The road led that way; it led out through my middle name, beside Little Jordan, in the direction of Sturgis Forge. And, afterward, it seemed fitting that I stay on at the seminary, that I continue bicycling along that road. I became, in time, a passable New Testament scholar. The life was pleasant, and there was God to sanction my complacency. I had my books; my butterfly net clipped conveniently to the handlebars of my bicycle. I might never have left. But God, with His fine sense of irony, had made quite other plans for me.

Cleveland Palmer was one of my students during that final term. He and Laurence Ashbrook, who was T. C. Coughlin lecturer that year, exerted an inordinate influence on everyone from Dean Polk to Hubert the janitor. Ashbrook's lectures were cynical and very amusing: he called them "Secular Fantasies." Palmer edited our monthly newspaper and was a boy of immense physical presence. Both were excited by the God Is Dead controversy then prevalent. They quoted bits of Robinson and Belknap and Bonhoeffer. They were phenomenologists; that is, they judged things by what they meant to men, not by traditional norms of the real or the unreal. A democratic naturalism: if the majority of men had ceased to believe in God, then God, by human fiat, no longer existed. Palmer and Ashbrook considered themselves Christians. Of course they weren't — not in any meaningful sense. They wanted to rid Christianity of its archaic trappings and its medieval world view. They wanted to pull God down from heaven and then reinstall him somewhere in among the human viscera. They were good men and I respected them, but they certainly caused us a good deal of trouble.

Dean Polk collaborated unwittingly. He was an undogmatic man, rather less assertive than any administrator can afford to be. He assumed, having seen his own gray hair and sagging jowls, that he was an old man, irretrievably behind the times. He felt an ambiguous guilt, as do most victims of the Progress

God. Dean Polk never presumed to reprimand Palmer; Ashbrook, whom he had invited to lecture, became gradually the
leader of our faculty. In time liberal-radical factions in the
student body began to challenge our curriculum. They pick-
eted my class and that of my friend Hans Bowlder, who taught
liturgics. There was confusion, as you can well imagine. Sec-
ularize, they said. Theology is obsolete. Get out and do. Make
our church a powerful arm of the welfare state. "Action and
love. Action and love," said Laurence Ashbrook. And Cleveland Palmer, who liked to put things his own way, said "Love
and action. Love and action." For a while, the road from
Greensprings to Sturgis Forge was traveled by reporters and
network sound trucks. We had quite a time.

I found myself shamefully unmoved by it all. My familiar
routines persisted throughout, and they proved a mighty bul-
wark against the prevailing chaos. Hans Bowdler and a few
others tried to organize a counter-reformation. I gave them
token support, but I never became very much involved. My
apathy infuriated Hans, but I was right — life in the seminary
soon returned to normal. Ashbrook and Palmer left to find
more prominent rostra. Students came back to their classes.
Dean Polk's complexion cleared up. And then something happened. Of all people, it happened to the most complacent, the
most unmoved member of the community. It happened to me.

There is a water fountain just outside my classroom. I remember it was late afternoon, near the end of our spring term.
I was standing there, wiping my spattered glasses. The corridor
turns left ten feet past my fountain. As I stood there, I could
hear two students conversing just beyond the turn. What they
said was, for the most part, unintelligible. Then one voice
raised itself in an impassioned monologue.

"Teach?" the voice asked in rhetorical indignation. "Teach?

And end up like fat Pratt the Pharisee? He's never had a parish. He's a graven image. A pot-bellied hypocrite. A Christian? Him? Satan was a saint compared to Pratt. At least Satan
got out and met people. At least he was real and alive — "

I turned away then. I didn't want my presence to confound
and embarrass them. Half blind, glasses in hand, I opened the
first door my fingers encountered and walked through. I had
time to meditate after that: the door was a fire exit and didn't
open from the outside. I sat for two hours on the little balcony,
experiencing guilt while simultaneously plotting acts of revenge. Every ten minutes I'd puzzle with the escape ladder
mechanism or bang irresolutely on the door. Pharisee, I muttered. Pharisee, indeed. Graven image. But my time had
come: Hubert the janitor led a radically changed man in off
that balcony. Like St. Paul, I had heard a voice, and, though
the voice had not struck me blind — only momentarily more
shortsighted — the effect was quite as traumatic.

I found George Horn Smith's book a week later. Two
months after that Bishop Hawkes happened to mention Father
Johann Pierre and his ulcer condition. Bishop Hawkes blew
into his pipe when I volunteered to take over at St. Bart's. Pipe
ash settled on his white, wild hair. But he finally agreed; he
wasn't, after all, very likely to get many other applications for
the job. Much pipe ash flew around Greensprings that week.
Hans Bowdler said I was mad. He cursed Palmer and Ashbrook. At dinner he begged Eleanor to reason with me. When
Eleanor said she was all for it, Hans dug a dull spoon into his
tomato half and spattered his vest with little, pink seeds.

It was God's hand. Let us make no mistake about that. The
hand of a God who exists, even though His meaning among
men may be in eclipse. It was God working in and through the
unlikely instrument of my anger and my pride. And it was

God working, as He so often does, to just the opposite end that
I, in my human presumption, had intended. For, you see, nothing has changed. I am here once again. In Greensprings. At
the seminary. At my desk, writing these words in the room of
my adolescence.

Excerpt from the Autobiography of George Horn Smith

. . . The muscles in my neck grew thick and strong. I stood
straight, my shoulders pulled back, my spine stiffened, to balance
that strange weight in my head. As I grew, it grew. As my muscles
hardened, it hardened. I knew it was there — I could reach up and
touch it with my hands — but I could never see it. There is little
water on our island — no pools to see your own face in. Only,
sometimes, a tip of its darkness when I looked up, or my head and
its pointed shadow cast by the sun on a wall. When I was crying
and afraid, I could never dry my eyes against my lovely mother's
body — it stood out so from my head. Then, in those lonely days,
I wore my horn like a crown and I was not ashamed.

Our little shack stood high on the hill that watches over the big,
busy city and the sea. No people came there — only my aunt and
sometimes the old Cha-cha doctor to tap my body and to measure
the thing on my head. Until I was seven years old, no one else saw
me and I saw no one else. I was busy. I ran and threw things.
I made long jumps and climbed the trees behind our shack. I
learned to walk on the palms of my hands. There was an old
burlap sack — it was filled with wood chips and it sat on a big
rock beside our house. I made believe the sack was an evil man.
I hit it again and again with my fists. The chips bruised my
knuckles. Then my knuckles, too, grew hard. In a very little time
my hands had torn big holes in the sack. And there, beside our
house, the middleweight champion of the world first learned to
strike and kill . . .

One day — a day I remember like this day — my mother took
me down to the big city by the sea. My mother, she did not want

to do this. But, on that dreadful day, there was no other way for us. A great hurricane was coming. My mother and me, we were playing in the field, throwing an old beanbag back and forth. We were playing when we heard the boom-boom-boom of the warning cannon in old Fort Louis. My mother, she put her hands to her ears and she screamed.

We ran then, we stumbled, down the rocky goat path that leads to Cliff Street and to the City. I remember feeling the wind's rough hands, slapping at the sides of my head like a mother slaps her child. It was all so new to me — the City and the people — as new as the wind and the big, black clouds that broke in a thousand pieces in the sky. I was not afraid. A child is not frightened by the things that frighten men. Those things are too big to know the fear of. A child is frightened only by harmless things — darkness and old uncles and small animals. I did not want to run from the wind. I wanted to stand for long minutes and see all that strange, new world.

We come to a street on the City's high edge — Victoria Street where the rich white men lived. I have never seen so many people. And white people — I did not know there were such wonderful things. The old Cha-cha doctor was white, yes — but he was old, and I, with my child's thinking, thought that a man's hair and his skin together became white with the years.

Everyone is running. The black men run clumsily with fear. The white people run easily, for they know where they are running. A white man's house can be closed up tight and where the wind can't get in, it cannot tear the roof away. A white man, in those days, was always safe. But soon his time of fear will come.

The cannon booms again. My mother screams. It is a long way to Fort Louis where the poor can hide from the storm. The trees shake their heads in terror. Their branches snap against the walls with the sound of a hundred whips. The wind strikes me a blow in the face. Then it digs its knuckles into the middle of my back, and I fall to my knees. We come to a corner, and I can see, down the long hillside, to the bay. Little ships are huddling near the reef. A sail rips loose. I see it fly into the air, a terrible bird. But I am a child, and I don't know that men are dying. I laugh with joy.

The rain begins to fall. Big drops, cold and hard like ice. We cannot see now where our steps will take us. The wind pulls our eyelids open and then our eyes are filled with rain. My mother presses her thin body against the wall. Shutters bang with the sound of bullets. Rain pours off my horn, down my face. I begin to shiver. I want to hug close to the wet dress of my mother, but she is pulling me along — along to a place where the wind will not snatch me away.

There is a great rushing sound. Suddenly my eardrums are being sucked out of their holes. We have come to a square. There the wind plays in circles, like a giant dragon chasing its tail. Across, on the other side of the square, there is a big, old warehouse. The double doors are open. My mother points and the wind throws her pointing hand high in the air. We try to cross the square, but we cannot. The wind is too terrible. It pulls us around the square like paper in a flushing toilet. We stumble forward. We fall. Then we are standing on a man's body. The man is dead and his stomach was once big and fat. We walk on his stomach, like poor mules on a treadmill. We walk on him until the skin of his belly is raw and torn. Then the wind blows us ahead.

A roof comes off like the top of my tiny toy jack-in-the-box. The insides of a house vomit up into the sky. Chairs and tables. A bathtub. A spotted dog. Then they are all gone and there is only the sky — orange purple like an old bruise. Two great roof rafters come walking at us like a man on stilts. They stumble. They fall just ten feet from our bodies. The top of a palm tree explodes and is gone. My mother and I crawl toward the warehouse on our hands and knees. A dozen coconuts come rolling across the square. They bowl into us like we are tenpins. The side of my head hits against the cobblestones and it is night inside my mind.

We are in the warehouse. I try to stand. The side of my right thigh is torn away where my mother has dragged my body over the cobblestones. Sharp pieces of glass break loose from the high, shattered windows of the warehouse. There is a terrible tinkling, like the buzzing of deadly bees. The lightning flashes — once, twice. In its light I can see men and women, little children, a burro, all huddling at the far end of the warehouse. Then it happens. A gust of wind blows the dress up, over my mother's face. The lightning flashes again and now there are screams. I hear the word "Joombie! Joombie!" They have seen us.

A woman is pointing. Her mouth is frozen wide with fear and the sound that comes from her throat seems to have no end. We were a sight from hell — I know that now. Monsters of the storm, standing there hand-in-hand. My mother, headless, her body naked from the navel down. And me, bloody — bloody with a great horn sticking out of my head. I do not wonder now at their fear. I do not wonder now that they tried to kill us.

My mother pulls her dress down. Then she walks toward them. The children scream. One man picks up a brick. Another man picks up a bar of iron. My mother does not understand. She understands only that her child will be safe in here. And then the wind thrusts its big shoulder high against the wall of the warehouse. It tears loose a big window frame and the frame comes crashing to the floor. Brick chips and bits of glass, they lash at our faces. My mother panics. She runs at them — to be safe among their bodies. The children shriek. The man with the bar stands away and then he brings it down across my lovely mother's neck. She falls and does not move. "Get him," cries the man. "Get the devil and his horn." Men and women — even the little children — they pick up bricks and stones. They rush toward me. I turn from them and run out into the storm.

And I have been there ever since — out there — in the heart of the storm . . .

There were sounds on all six sides of me. Traffic noises came from both north and south, and, occasionally, from Lenox Avenue as well. From the west came sounds of a Spanish family in endless and complicated discord. From the east, from Horn's Place, sounds of typewriters and telephones, angry men, laughing men, insistent men with strident, unreasonable voices. Above, helicopters puttered and planes gnashed their teeth. Then, from the streets, came frightening, unexplained sounds — thuds, metallic crashes, running feet. Once, in the night, I heard a sound very much like three gunshots in rapid succession. Even the floor denied relief: I heard, or imagined I heard, unaccountable bangs, footsteps, whole bars of music, emanating from just beneath me. Strange, chthonic noises. The old building's slow settling, I thought. Echoes. Trolls, perhaps. I didn't investigate. This besetting hubbub disquieted me — accustomed only, as I had been in Greensprings, to the intermittent cry of birds or the crunch of a single pair of feet on a gravel path.

I, alone in all of Harlem, had not been assimilated; a vacuum, unabhorred by nature. In more than one hundred hours, from Tuesday afternoon to Friday night, I neither spoke to nor saw anyone. Anyone, that is, but Nicholas Breakspeare, and he ignored me when he was not testing the strength of my Christian forbearance. I found his petty harassments more a relief than a nuisance. Nicholas Breakspeare left the lights on, the water running, the windows open and his equipment wherever I would most likely run foul of it. On Friday he did not appear at all. On Saturday he placed a wet, filthy rag in the middle of my desk. I smiled, and received the same smile in response. Then Nicholas Breakspeare would mention a certain unfortunate white man who had been killed or maimed or despoiled of his property, "Right near here. Last night. Honest. You could spit t'where it happened." And I would smile again.

I didn't leave my rectory once during those first five days. I ate almost nothing; I smoked until I was quite dizzy. For hours on end I sat beside my electric heater, sketching an inaugural sermon, thumbing through a book of butterfly reproductions. My own church appalled me. The rear parts of the nave were already, in September, as cold as an ice cave. Dirty stalactites hung from the ceiling wherever water dripped down from between limestone slabs. Given the circumstances, my reluctance was understandable. I justified it: I needed a little time to settle down, to get my sea legs. That was all. A little time and, perhaps, a little courage as well. I was terribly afraid. Frightened enough by the sounds of Harlem to dread their fierce embodiments.

On Friday, in defiance, I opened the doors of St. Bart's. But no one entered — either to worship or to pilfer there. Later that same afternoon I saw the first and only acknowledgment of my presence. The glass front on my announcement board had been expertly removed. There were no glass fragments, no evidence of forcing. My pathetic, misspelled plea for friendship had been rearranged to form an equally misspelled exhortation to strange and difficult auto-erotic practices. I pulled out the letters, leaving only SERV. 10 AM. Then I threw them high into the air. They tinkled weakly on a car hood.

The cat appeared early that same day. It sat in the middle of my front yard, miaowing to no apparent purpose. I stepped out onto my little stoop. The cat's back was turned to me — a back eyed and striated rather like the wing of a large, dirty Polyphemus moth. Every few seconds the cat would throw its head back and scream toward the roof of the salmon-pink brownstone. "Puss. Puss," I said tentatively. The cat looked back over its shoulder, fixed me with squinting eyes, then returned to its original posture and business. A human being possesses certain conditioned responses. A miaow: a bowl of milk. The cat is hungry, I thought.

"Wait, puss," I said, with that complacent faith that we all have in human language. "Don't go 'way." I went inside and filled a soup bowl with milk. When I returned, the cat had moved nearer the rectory foundation. It was sniffing at a crack in the pavement. I held the brimful plate out at arm's length to demonstrate my charitable intentions. I took one step forward. The cat leaped away, protesting as it went. I followed awkwardly. The milk splashed over my thumbs. "Nice milk. Yum. Yum." I said. The cat, sensing my resolution, shrieked once and then disappeared through a gap in the boarded basement window.

"Darn," I said. I made my way to the gap and placed the bowl near it on the pavement. I peered in. A concerted high mewing answered my curiosity. Kittens. Spontaneous benevolence welled up within me. I reached between the boards to pet. There was a sudden roaring, as of a small engine in ignition. "Purr?" I said stupidly. And then a steam valve exploded and countless hard needles forced themselves into my hand. I was pulled inexorably into the gap, so terrific was that initial onslaught. My head struck the wall. I yelped. The cat was now methodically scarring my hand and wrist. Some of her claws became caught in my cuff and, for long moments, neither of us was able to fight free. I yelped again, yanking hard against the little, impaling hooks. My hand came out. Someone laughed hoarsely in Horn's Place.

From watchband to fingertips, my left hand was a garish, unmitigated red. In places, my blood actually bubbled in its rush to the surface. "Bad cat," I said. "Bad damn cat." A sharp hiss came from the basement window. I jumped back awkwardly, stumbled and put my left knee in the milk bowl. Another hoarse laugh from Horn's Place. I stood uncertainly, dripping white and red. The sight of blood momentarily caused my vision to become unfocused. I ran up the steps and into my rectory.

There were five deep gashes in my hand and dozens of minor cuts. The rectory's medicine chest was almost bare, but I finally found a squat, ancient iodine bottle on the top shelf near the back. I jammed my hand under the cold water tap. Hurriedly then, I doused it with iodine. After five seconds, I thought the worst infection highly preferable. My fingers went into convulsions from the sting. I waited for the pain to reach its apex, but, as cut after cut absorbed the iodine, my discomfort increased. I began to dance on one foot from the sink to the toilet and back again. It was a one-step, done to the rhythm of damn cat, damn-cat, damncat, damnctdamctdmct. After about ten minutes I was calm enough to sit on the toilet seat and begin swathing my hand in yards of ancient, brittle gauze.

I staggered to the kitchen. I took my milk container and carried it out to the yard. Warily, I refilled the plate, pushing it near the window with my foot. As I did so, I heard the sound of music — triumphant music. I walked quickly toward St. Bart's and peered down the alley to the street. I was in time to catch only the last marchers. They were dressed in tabards, green for the most part. Two held trumpets to their lips; two others held saxophones solar plexus high. The music was march-jazz and it was very thrilling. A small group of people stood at the curb, watching the procession with respectful interest. I wanted to rush down the alley, to peer out and see. But I was afraid. I contented myself by shyly, nervously tapping my foot to the rhythm.

I had a caller on Saturday afternoon: John Meeker, the rector of St. Catharine's Church. St. Catharine's was just twenty blocks to the north. From what I had heard, it was an attractive church, smaller and more economical to maintain than St. Bart's. It was more conveniently located — just half a block from the Eighth Avenue Subway — and, thanks to Meeker, it already possessed a large, enthusiastic congregation. The diocese had decided to concentrate all its efforts on St. Cat's, hoping, in a year or so, to combine the two parishes into one. Bishop Hawkes had mentioned John Meeker several times. So had Nicholas Breakspeare. I was eager to meet him.

Meeker burst through the front door when I opened it. He was halfway to my office before he acknowledged, or cared to acknowledge, my presence. When we shook hands, he peered at me strangely, as a personnel man might examine some laborer. He looked at my shoulders and at my legs; his hand clasp was, in itself, a difficult test. He said, "Hmmm. Hmmm" several times, oblivious to any affront he might be giving. Then he led me into my own office — as though I were the visitor, and he were short of time.

Meeker was nearly as tall as I, but very much thinner. He wore a sports jacket and a very stylish plaid shirt. The shirt, however, was covered with grease spots. In fact, nothing Meeker wore seemed quite clean. His jacket and shirt were frayed at the cuff; his pants had a hole where the crotch is seamed. He wore a pair of high-backed, soft shoes — desert boots, I think they are called — and these were covered with splotches of red and yellow paint. When I passed close to him, I noticed a strong, unpleasant body odor. I offered him coffee, but he only closed his eyes and then made a short, impatient gesture with his hand.

"Welcome," he said. "Welcome to Harlem. Can't stay now — just dropped in to welcome you." I stammered my thanks. "From upstate, huh?" I nodded. "From the seminary?" I nodded again. "Different isn't it? God-damned different. Be a long time before you know these people. A long time." He nodded in self-affirmation. Then he began, methodically, to examine my belongings — picking up things from my desk, weighing them, grunting "Hmmm. Hmmm," thoughtfully. He quite ignored my presence.

John Meeker was a handsome man. His voice was deep and pliant. His eyes were vivid. "A saint's eyes," I thought. I noticed that his left sideburn had been shaved off close, while his right extended almost to his earlobe. Meeker had picked up my worry bird and was holding it near his eyes. He began to address the bird in monitory tones.

"Tough here," he said. "Damn tough. They tell me you haven't had much experience — not in this line." This still to the bird. "Taught mostly. That right?"

"Yes. New Testament theology." He puckered his lips and nodded.

"Idiots. That's what they are. Sending a babe like you down here." He flicked his finger at the bird's head. "I don't suppose they told you? Hawkes, I mean. Told you what you'd be getting into."

"I asked to come," I said. "I knew what it'd be like — pretty much."

"Yeah?" He came toward me with an odd aggressiveness. "Theology won't help you here. This is what you need." He made a fist and brought it close to my throat. My head shied away instinctively. "Think you could handle yourself? In a fight? Can you use these?"

"No," I said. Meeker shook his head.

"See." He made a disparaging gesture. "That's the game right there. I mean, they can smell it like a dog. They know when you're afraid."

"I didn't say I was afraid."

"But you are. You are, aren't you?"

"Yes," I admitted. "I am a bit."

"Well . . ." He spread his hands flat in an umpire's "safe" sign. "Q.E.D. Got a butt?"

"No. I only smoke a pipe." He laughed.

"A pipe. Oh, brother — who has time for pipes? You're not a man of leisure, Pratt — not any more. A pipe." He laughed again. Then he walked over to the bookshelf and began glancing cursorily at my titles.

"I've heard a lot about you," I said, wishing to placate him. "Have you been here long?"

"Four years and some. Four years and still alive. If a white man can use his fists — if he can shoot a good basketball, dribble around them, foul them going up — if he can say Goddamn and worse — then he has a chance. Then they might treat him like one of their own. God, they're beautiful athletes."

"So I've been told," I said. I smiled, but he ignored my mild irreverence.

"Don't get me wrong, Pratt. I know how you must feel. I know, and I don't want to act like a wet blanket. But this isn't going to be a picnic — you'd better get that straight right now. And you won't get much help from the big boy upstairs." I started when he said that. Meeker smiled. "From Bishop Hawkes, I mean. He doesn't like to drive up here — not since the neighborhood went to hell. He's always at St. James' or St. Thomas' or up at the Cathedral. A real Sutton Place Bishop, he is. But get him to come up here . . . I wonder, Pratt. D'you think Bishop Hawkes is afraid?"

"I'm sure — ah, I'm sure I wouldn't know. I've only met him once or twice." Meeker stared at me, smiling. His single-mindedness was distressing. "Sure you won't have some coffee? I can make it in a minute." Meeker came away from the bookshelves. He stood in front of me for a long moment.

"Why'd you come here, Pratt?"

"Everyone asks me that." I tried to laugh, but only swallowed, gagging slightly.

"Well . . . ?"

"I'm not sure. Thought I'd try it, that's all. Maybe fill a place no one else wanted. Something like that."

"No," said Meeker. "No. That's not the reason. I know why you came here." He grinned. It was not a pleasant grin. "Want me to tell you?"

"Yes. Please do."

"Are you sure? I don't beat around the bush. You might be offended."

"Let me be offended then."

"All right." He folded his arms across his chest. At either elbow crook, his thumb and forefinger were rubbing, working at each other. "All right. It's because you don't like them — black men. It's because you're a good Christian filled up to the Adam's apple with guilt. Don't shake your head, Pratt — admit it. I'm not condemning you. God knows, it's natural enough."

"Yes. Perhaps. But, all the same, it's just not true. Not for me. I'm sure of that. You see, I'm — well . . . I'm not a very passionate man. I don't go out of my way to hate — or to love — unless someone gives me some very good reason. It's not a virtue, unless laxness is a virtue. It's just my unfortunate make-up." Meeker had begun staring at the ceiling. His tongue danced in his cheek. "But you're right — in one sense. I have felt guilty. About being a teacher for so long, about not doing my share of the work. The hard work. The good work. The work you're doing."

"Well. Could be I'm wrong. Exception proves the rule and all that." He stared at my feet. "Got a butt? No. You only smoke pipes. Been around much? Been outside?"

"No. Not yet."

"They won't accept you. Won't be like tea at the local dowager's — you realize that."

"Yes. I haven't had much luck — so far. You're the first person I've seen. I appreciate your coming." But Meeker ignored my gratitude. His eyes had become strangely dull, as though he were reading something at a far distance.

"Try to forgive them," he said. He put his hand on my arm. It was a strangely compassionate gesture. He squeezed my biceps. Then he patted it. And all the while he stared at the wall above and to the right of my head. "Forgive them. It's not their fault. We've done it. D'you know how they came here?"

"How they came?"

"Yes. They . . . We — we packed them into those ships. Three foot decks, one fitted against the other — like spoons. Each man with his head in the groin of the man above. If one had to shit — " I looked up shocked by the word. "Yes, shit. That's what I said. That's the right word. Because it sounds like the thing and the thing is dirty. Would you prefer defecate? Evacuate? Some other euphemism? All right, the man made pooh-pooh on the other's head. Just like that. The stench, Pratt. For months and months and months. The puke. The whips. The chains. The degradation. You and me, what do we know? Pratt and Meeker. Old names. Names of men who, way back then, held shares in those stinking ships. You wonder they don't welcome you with outstretched arms?"

"I — I suppose not."

"Let me make a suggestion," he said after a few seconds. "It might help. D'you mind, Pratt?" I shook my head emphatically. "I've been around. I know the score. A word to the wise can't hurt. All that stuff — " he pointed at my bookshelves, "even that — " he indicated the Bible on my desk. "Even that. It's not what they want. They want love. Want — in the old sense — need. Need love. And love for them, it's got to show itself in things. In doing. In spontaneous, unselfish action. They're magnificent. Raw and strong. They understand what they can see and feel. Not theology. Not prophecy and promises. Real things. When they come to trust you — if they do — then, my friend, then you'll be king. And you won't need revelation to tell you what's right and what's wrong."

"I guess — yes, you're right," I said. "Yes. Of course."

"You don't really believe me. I can tell. But the proof of the pudding, Pratt — it's easy enough to see. Ask anyone. I've got two hundred families in my parish. My services are crowded — strictly standing room only. They like me, Pratt. I know it. I know it. They've forgotten I'm white. I — I forget sometimes." He walked slowly over to my globe of the world. He gave it a flick with his hand; he meant to make it spin. But it was rusted and wouldn't turn at all. He pushed again, harder. The mechanism protested, but gave a few degrees in longitude. Meeker took the globe between both hands and, using terrific force, turned it a full half revolution. The ball came loose at its upper socket. Meeker, with deep preoccupation, fitted the axis back into its hole. "Damn cheap thing," he said. "Old and useless."

"I've — I've just read this," I said, hoping to please him.

"Oh . . . Smith's book." Meeker came over to my desk. He picked up the book and tapped at its cover with his finger. "A great man. Can you imagine the life he led — with that horn in his head and black to boot? Now look at him. Smith runs this place, don't kid yourself. He's got it covered from one end to the other. A man doesn't belch in Harlem without apologizing to Smith — before and after. If things're changing here, it's because of him. If things're tougher on the Jew storekeeper, it's because of him. He's performing miracles and his people know it. Horn Power — brother, some day it's gonna set us big, white daddies right back on our big, white asses. If you'll excuse my French."

"Really? Do you think so?"

"Do I think so? Don't be dense, Pratt. I know it — everyone with a brain in his head knows it. It's the death knell of white supremacy."

"I'm sorry. I really am out of my depths. I need a little time."

"No." Meeker shook his head. "It's my fault. I forget your background. Look, I was brought up on the South Side of Chicago. I've had some experience — nasty experience. I was a pretty tough kid — had to be. You should have seen John Meeker ten years ago. I was in reform school — cooled it twice. Three months the first time. Second time — almost a year. Did you know?"

"No."

"Of course not. But it helps. I'm white, but I've had a bad time or two. It makes it easier — the empathy, on both sides." He looked to the door. Then at his wrist. But he had no watch. "What time d'you have?"

"Nearly one."

"I've got to go. Look, why don't you come up to St. Cat's — say week from tomorrow? Catch my three o'clock service. I'll introduce you around."

"I'd like that," I said. Meeker had already started walking toward the office door. I followed him quickly.

"Place's falling to bits. Hawkes tell you that?" He stared at the cracked ceiling as we walked down the hall and then turned right to the front door. "Poor Joe Pierre. He couldn't take it. Poor old Joe." I opened the door for him. Meeker stood on my front stoop for a moment.

"Thanks for coming," I said.

"Don't mention it. I was in the neighborhood anyway. Doing a little poaching. Couple of my people live a block from here."

"I'll speak to the game warden." I said it in an attempt at levity, but Meeker's face had become serious, distant.

"Pratt," he said. "Did you know I was on the Okaloosa march?"

"No," I said. "No. Were you?"

"I was there — not further than I am from you now — I was there when Don Herring and Doug Banner were shot in the back by Otis Kulp. This scar here under my eye — flying glass from a state trooper's side mirror. Doug Banner died in my arms."

"Oh my God," I said. "A terrible thing."

"Yes," said Meeker. "Terrible. You don't know how terrible. But they remember me for it. When I speak to them, they remember." He raised his hand in a salute. "Good luck, Pratt. Welcome to Harlem."

I was busy that night. I spread my vestments on the kitchen table. Then I pressed them with Eleanor's tiny traveling iron. It was Saturday night, the first such in my Harlem experience; from ten o'clock onward the street clatter became, hourly, more and more intimidating. Just before midnight the rhythmic chant of a large mob rose up, over Horn's Place from somewhere on or near Lenox Avenue. The sense of their words was lost, but I knew they were savage, short syllables uttered in anger. I turned my radio up. There was a decrepit carpet sweeper in the hall closet. I carried it into the chancel and began making nervous, wild strokes across the tattered rug. The mechanism squeaked, and the sweeper had a tendency to deposit neat dust droppings in its wake, but I, in my agitated state, was grateful for the mere exertion.

I was apprehensive of my first Sunday service. A congregation of ten or of a hundred — I hardly knew what to expect.

My inaugural sermon had been written and rewritten several times. The text was taken from St. Peter's vision in chapter ten of Acts. In its final form, it had become an apology for my whiteness and very little else. The language, I suppose, was rather condescending. I spent two hours Saturday night hand-printing fifty 5 x 8 cards. These requested "Name," "Address" and "Telephone No." of the parishioners. I slipped them between the pages of my Books of Common Prayer, and, when I had done this, there were more than a dozen cards remaining. I placed them on a table in the vestibule.

It was nearly two o'clock before I had finished my preparations. The mob's chanting had subsided. I stepped outside and stood for a few minutes in my little courtyard. The night was cool and very clear. Even at that hour there were bright lights on at each window in Horn's Place. Someone threw a lit cigarette butt from a second story window; it fell with a momentary flicker like a midsummer shooting star. I prayed as I stood there; I asked God to make me a more valid, more eloquent witness to His Word. The cat ran across the courtyard and disappeared into its nest. I looked up. In the square of the yard — superimposed and magnified a billion times against the sky — I saw Andromeda and Perseus in the Big Dipper's handle. They seemed as serene, as beautiful, as much a symbol of God's magnificent universe, as they had always seemed in Greensprings. But, truthfully, I was little comforted by their great aloofness.

I was up that next morning at six. By seven I had prepared the altar. It was a dismal sight, rather like a cheerless shop-window. The lighting was ineffectual, and, when I snapped the switch, one of the four bulbs in the chancel blew out with a flash. New shadows appeared to the left of the cross. I washed some filthy artificial flowers that I discovered in the dining room. They were meant to be chrysanthemums, flowers that, even in their natural state, are rather tasteless. I placed them in niches at either end of the altar screen. Then I lit the candles. It was not yet nine o'clock, but I could no longer abide the funereal gloom.

I opened the front doors at a quarter past nine. The morning was gray and unappealing. There was a mist in the air that, when but slightly prevailed on, became an annoying drizzle. My SERV. 10 AM notice had not been tampered with. A smell drifted toward me from across the street; it seemed to emanate from the empty lot. The smell was unfamiliar, but I knew it was the odor of something no longer whole. Men and women passed quickly along the street. I saw two ladies dressed like massive, varicolored hassocks. Men walked gingerly inside precisely pressed suits — those odd hats with high crowns and vestigial brims perched on their heads. Going to church, I thought. Not to my church. The great tin cross protested mildly on its supports.

I felt something tug at my shirt. I looked down. It was my own right hand. The fingers were flexing spontaneously, kneading the material of my shirt. I restrained them. Then I took several deep breaths, but my lungs had lost their capacity. "It is good to see you here today," I said aloud. "It is — " I cleared my throat, seeking an inflection of easy friendliness. I looked at my watch; it was only twenty past nine. I walked inside. For several moments I knelt in prayer before the cross, but it was a futile exercise. My distraught mind kept intoning, "Dear God, it is good to see you here today." I hurried into my office to review the Epistle and Gospel for the day. I am not a facile reader. My eyes jump from one line to another, and strange sounds of hesitation intrude between the words. I read my little sermon once again. Then I vested.

I sat in my swivel chair. Methodically, I began tearing pages of the Anglican Digest into tiny, thin strips. At just before ten I rose and walked over to the peephole. I slid the panel aside. The first ten rows seemed quite empty. I clapped my hands together in agitation. Then I started pacing my office, from peephole to window and back again, playing a disoriented game of hopscotch on the faded rug pattern. At five minutes past, I peered through the peephole once again. This time I managed to squeeze my entire head through the square aperture. No one in the first fifteen rows. I retracted my head with difficulty. Then I returned to my chair. At seven minutes past ten my impatience became intolerable. I rose and hurried through the door, out into the chancel of my church. Without looking toward the nave, I rushed over to the ombre and began making meaningless adjustments. Church-goers are shy. Few people will sit in the front pews of a church. I turned from the ombre and glanced hastily out into the nave. Then I looked more carefully. Then I stared. But for myself, St. Bartholomew's was empty.

My arms fell limp at my sides. "It is good — good to see you here today." I said it in a very loud voice, and a very loud echo repeated my sarcasm. I was, simultaneously, disappointed and amused and relieved. The damp emptiness of St. Bart's seemed to be touching a like hollowness in my own body. I walked down the aisle. When I reached the front door, I glanced cursorily outside. I looked at my watch; I checked the announcement board. Then I went in. I closed the doors behind me that neither I nor my church would be embarrassed in our loneliness.

I spent some time with my God. It is forbidden for a priest, alone, to eat of the flesh and the blood. But I could still prepare myself for Holy Eucharists yet to come. And, of course, I was not alone. My reedy voice rose unhopefully into the vaults

— but it returned to me an affirmation. Let there be no misunderstanding. I was granted neither encouragement nor any abiding assurance. God does not traffic with us in so blunt a manner. But I felt a certain expectation of those things. And it was good.

When I had finished, when, with unsure hands, I had doused the candles, I made my way irresolutely back up the center aisle. As I did so, I noticed strips of green paper sticking, like insolent tongues, from my Books of Common Prayer. I stopped. Then I leaned into the pew and removed one of the sheets. It was a thin, badly mimeographed leaflet bearing the words "Reform Tabernacle of the Burning Lamb." A crude ink drawing of a lamb in flames dominated the cover. The lamb was being worshipped or incinerated, it was hard to say which, by three men and two women — all Negroes. In the corner, in bold letters, was written "Approved by the Horn." There was a green leaflet in every prayer book. Each of my painstakingly hand-printed cards had been replaced. I folded the sheet into a paper airplane and tossed it toward the vestibule. Perversely, it curved back over my head. "Pratt," I said. "Pratt, you are a victim of subversion."

Excerpt from the Autobiography of George Horn Smith

. . . I remain in the islands until I am ten years of age. The great Hurricane has taught me many, many things. Now my lovely mother cannot keep me with her. I wander in the streets of the city — sometimes I do not come home for days. The children, they spit and they call me "joombie." They throw stones. But the children never come near — they have already felt the joombie's hard fists, and his horn, they know, can give a bloody nose. In all those years I do not have one friend. Alone, I swim at Gnats Point. Alone, I play pirates by Redbeard's Castle on Old Spanish Hill. When the tourist boats come, it is the joombie that dives deepest for coins. And when joombie's head breaks water, the tourist women, they cry "ooooh" in their surprise. All the coins, I bring them home to my lovely mother.

My people are very superstitious and very silly. It is a game to play with their fear. A joombie, you know, is a spirit that causes only evil to men. Many times the obeah doctors say, a joombie will come in the body of a goat. I have heard this. So, in the mornings, I go to a little farm down the hill from where we live. There the people keep many goats. I rub my hands between a billy goat's legs, I rub the smell on my horn and over my naked ribs. Then I go to the market square. The women, they stop in their haggling. They stop and then they sniff at the air. Joombie! Before they can stop me, I bend my head and touch their fish or their melons with the tip of my horn. No island woman buys food that a joombie has touched. So the women in the square, they are very nice to me. They give me fruit and beads. Sometimes they give me little coins and say, "Go, take your ugly horn. Go touch Mother Marfa's melons. She makes too much money today." No one dares make the little joombie angry. I had no friends, but, even in those days, I had much power . . .

. . . It is a sunny day in October, that day when the joombie makes his vow. Siesta is just over. Men are sitting, leaning against the white walls that line Mulhaney's Way. One by one they stretch, and their arms rise high above their heads. Then their bodies slump. They talk in low voices, and the spit falls between their feet. The sun is very hot. The light cuts the eyes like a razor blade. There is no breeze. The branches of the Tyre palm droop, like a fat man trying to touch his toes. Even the mosquitoes are asleep. Children come down Mulhaney's Way. They chase each other near the legs of their sleepy fathers. The men slap out at them with their voices. A dog pisses against the wall. Then it rolls on its back in the dust. From where I am standing, in the mouth of an alley, I watch these useless men and their useless children. I am filled with bitter hate.

Suddenly then the talking stops. The children stand still, their hands behind their backs. The men struggle to their feet. One by one they take their hats from their heads. I look to the left — yes, a funeral is coming slowly down Mulhaney's Way. A funeral, you must understand, is the most important thing in the life of an island man. He will be judged by his funeral. If it is a miserable thing, if few people come — then they will say he was a nothing, a little snap of the fingers and no more. I hear bells ring. A child speaks and his father, without looking, slaps his head. I stand back in the alley. A joombie should not come to funerals.

Old Mister Moki, the priest, he is first to come along the Way. He carries a big, black book in his hand, and his old feet shuffle when he walks. Already I know this is a poor man's funeral, for Mister Moki, he is the poor man's priest. Now I see the hearse. A box on wheels, no more, but the sides are made of glass. The glass is scratched and dusty. The coffin is made of unpainted wood, and it jumps when the wheels of the old hearse hit against the cobblestones. The old tired horse; he looks like a skeleton, his skin is like paper on his ribs — that old horse has dragged many, many men down Mullhaney's Way to the earth.

The men wear black. The women wear white. In their hands they carry chairs to lay the coffin on. The poor man's family comes last. It is a small family — an old woman, an old man and a little girl. The family carries flowers, but the flowers are already dead in the hot sun. The old man looks stupidly from right to left. His mouth gapes. The fly on his pants is open. He has no socks. There is quiet — only the bells, the snorting of the horse and the squeal of the hearse on its wheels. Already the body is rotting. The sun is not kind to lifeless flesh.

And then they have passed. The men slouch against the wall. The children shriek in spite against the silence. But the joombie does not move, he does not speak. Slowly his strong hand breaks bits of clay from the wall. And, inside his head, the joombie is shouting, "No!" He is shouting, "No. Not me. No — I will not die like that. My body will not lie in that glass box. No. When I die, the whole world will shriek with weeping. The train of my funeral will fill all of the winding, wide Way. The flowers will be like a jungle, and they will not wilt. No." I shake my fist at the clanging belfry. My horn points to heaven.

No. Not like that. I swear it . . .

My second week in Harlem evolved slowly and with an un-deviating sameness. The weather was clear and bright; it

made me yearn for autumn in Greensprings. Bright sunlight
mitigated the dulling effect of dark corners and cluttered, noi-
some alleys — at least during the day's unchallenged supremacy. I stood for long moments at my rectory door, staring into
the limpid blue-whiteness of the sky. Odd green birds, no bigger than sparrows, settled to feed on bread that I had scattered.
Parakeets, I thought, escaped from their cages. I liked to watch
them basking in the rich residue of the dying year. But my
complacency was forced. I knew, by Tuesday afternoon, that it
was time I started getting around.

I went out at noon that day. As I locked my front door, I
tucked my glasses deep into an inside jacket pocket — hoping,
I think, to palliate the sordidness, the hostility in the soft, in-
definite blurs of my shortsightedness. I emptied my wallet and
tucked a dollar bill into the toe of each shoe. That made walking rather uncomfortable, as the bills tended to bunch near my
little toes, but I was morbidly afraid of a mugging. I wore
my collar, of course. I carried a prayer book in my hand as well
— a prayer book with a very large cross on the cover — so that
there should be no misunderstanding. My knees were trembling as I walked down the alley. I had no idea where I was
going or what I would do. I was urged forward by the sharp
goading of my guilt.

I headed toward Seventh Avenue — clearly away from
Horn's Place. Then I started walking north on the Avenue. I
trusted, with vain hopefulness, that some spontaneous encounter would bestow belonging on me — painlessly and without
any instigating effort on my part. It was not laziness, nor was it
pride. I am shy, incorrigibly so, and the most perfunctory com-
munications are difficult for me. I walked for two hours. But
the eyes I passed did not see me. The voices I heard did not
address me. A profound vacuum accompanied me north on
Seventh Avenue.

As I walked, the slow recognition of one fact became my mind's entire business: there are no white people in Harlem. I would have laughed, had someone told me that two weeks before. No white people? Of course not, Harlem is a Negro community. But we — we of the presumptuous white race — we assume that here and there, standing on a corner, leaning out a window, we will find at least one brotherly countenance. I walked on Tuesday, I walked on Wednesday, Thursday and Friday — and in all that time I saw not one white person. I saw faces that mocked whiteness, and faces that bore the trace of a white heredity. But there were no faces that mitigated my loneliness. It was a harsh lesson. I learned what, so often, the isolated Negro must suffer in this great, white land of ours. I was a blemish. A sport. A freak. And, with concerted embarrassment, the entire community ignored me. By the third day, despite the urging of my best intentions, all my wandering was directed toward a single purpose. I walked not to find communication. Not to assist. Not to learn. I walked to find another white man.

In the end, I abandoned my futile searches. I discovered a park just three blocks south of St. Bart's; it nested at the heart of a large, lower income housing development. A bench stood in the farthest corner. I sat there for several hours on Wednesday and Thursday. The park was a cheerful, compact place. The children played upon devices abstracted from some cubist fantasy — tunnels and great dice and hollow, perforated spheres. There I was conspicuous, but ignored. The children seldom troubled to harass me. Once a little boy spat near my shoes. I smiled when he stared at me; I smiled when, bored, he turned away. It was a studied, not a malicious affront — the result, perhaps, of some parental hatred overheard but not clearly understood. Horn Smith had begun enforcing his anti-white doctrine in Harlem. There had already been several in-

cidents. But, during those first days, I went unmolested. The
bills remained in my shoes. No firm decision had been made
regarding my person: I was neither black, nor sufficiently
white. I simply did not exist.

By Thursday I had become quite irrationally resentful.
Frustration had unbalanced the objectivity that, as a priest, I
had sought to maintain. With these symptoms of human frailty
came a certain obstinate courage. I reacted as would any lonely
and intimidated man. Friday morning, in sheer spite, I turned
to my left as I stepped out of the alley. I walked slowly toward
Lenox Avenue. Threat or no threat, I would look at Horn's
Place.

I bought a few necessities in a Spanish grocery around the
corner on Lenox. I speak Latin fluently and Greek just slightly
less well — but I do not speak Spanish at all. Brown faces
laughed at me. In my ignorance, I was a child again. No one
would offer assistance — though, doubtless, everyone knew at
least sufficient English. I had to pantomine scrubbing for soap,
brushing for toothpaste and, as a final willing degradation, wiping for toilet paper. The toilet paper bit went over especially
well. There was laughter, and, notwithstanding the hectic
spots high on my cheeks, I was glad I had done it. "Come to
my church," I said as I left. "St. Bart's Church. Down the
block. Come. *Venite.*" But it was not yet time for that.

I crossed Lenox Avenue without once looking toward my left.
The grocery bag was propped high on my chest, and most of
my face was hidden behind its paper fringes. The unwhole-
some color of my hands was camouflaged by a pair of plaid
gloves. As I reached the other side of Lenox, I increased my
pace considerably. Thus far my strategy had worked reasonably well. I continued to walk quickly, my head poking up
now and then above the fringes of my grocery bag. But, in the

middle of the block, I stopped with a studied hesitation. I walked over to a pick-up truck parked near the curb. I put my bag on the fender. I shook my head. Then I fumbled in the bag, as though I had forgotten some essential item. While performing this charade, I took my first furtive look at Horn's Place.

The entrance was long and low — three store fronts vaguely joined. The words, "Horn's Place," had been painted in badly syllablized segments on the three glass fronts: HOR-N'SP-LACE. I squinted as I stared across the Avenue, my hands still fumbling unconsciously in the paper bag. Men dressed in green tabards lounged at the entrance. Now and then a short man with steel-rimmed glasses would appear at the center door. On these occasions he would hand an envelope to one or another of the Horn Greens. These were to be delivered on one of the half-dozen green motorcycles parked near the curb, each with a two-foot golden horn attached just below the handlebars. Suddenly one of the lounging men became alert. He touched a fellow near the crook of his elbow. Then he pointed across the Avenue. "Oh God," I said beneath my breath. I began fumbling in my paper bag again. It was time I started moving.

But, in turning to leave, I first clearly perceived the fence. The stores that, together, composed Horn's Place were set two steps down from the street level. A heavy metal fence ran along the edges of this slight depression; it was broken in front of each store entrance. The fence itself didn't disturb me — it was the thing's ornamentation. Crowning each vertical support there was a sphere: each of these balls was larger than those commonly used for bowling. There were twelve balls, all different. Some, though generally round, had pointed shafts driven through them; another had been sliced flat at the top; yet another had an ugly protrusion at the temple. I let my

breath out sharply. My arms pressed the paper bag against my
ribs until both arms and ribs began to ache. Heads, I thought.
Decapitated heads. Dreadfully mutilated. A bitter taste of fear
was exuded by the roots of my tongue. I tried to swallow, but
found that I couldn't. The framework of the fence was rusted
in several places, but the balls were new. Grisly trophies of
some anticipated massacre. I stared in horrid fascination and,
for the first time, I truly feared Horn Smith.

I drew my eyes away, up the façade of Horn's Place. Above,
I could see the forlorn, truncated steeple of St. Bart's. A large
bird took off from a niche in the crenellation. It flew toward
the west. Horn Smith, I knew, despised all forms of religion.
He had said, in his famous Randall's Island speech, that Christ
was the first segregationist. But he tolerated certain churches
— those that lent themselves passively to his movement. Nicholas Breakspeare's Church of the Burning Lamb stood in the
shadow of those twelve balls. Its door was wide open. I
peered toward it. And then a hand touched my shoulder.

I was so startled that I drew the bag into my stomach and
swung clumsily around. The tormented paper gave way, a milk
container dropped through the bottom. I bent my knees and
caught the container in my hastily improvised lap. "God. God.
God," I thought, as my mind fumbled for some familiar prayer.
Two men in green tabards stood on either side of me. They
were burly men with broad shoulders, each had a wide, thick
mustache. In my panic I could distinguish no difference between them. Together they seemed some single phantom of
malevolence.

"You better get," said the man on my right. And the man
on my left said, "Get."

"Yes," I said. "Sorry. I didn't know." In my willingness to
show good faith, I moved too quickly. My tomatoes dropped

through the hole. I moaned. Two tomatoes rolled under the pick-up truck. I looked to the man on my right. I looked to the man on my left. "My tomatoes have dropped," I said.

"Oliver. Get the man's tomatoes." The Negro on my left bent down. He put the two tomatoes, bruised and split, in the top of my bag.

"Well," I said. "Thanks. Thanks a lot." I nodded several more times. The two equal faces remained impassive. "I'll be going now. I was just resting a moment. Bad heart, you know. Overweight. Too much cholesterol." I nodded toward my chest, but my lie was made no more plausible by this gesture.

"Where do you come from?" said the man on my right. "Come from?" said his image in the mirror.

"The church," I said. I nodded back over my shoulder. "St. Bart's." Then I nodded several more times, but this excess of affirmation went unnoticed.

"Okay," said the man on my right. "That's where you belong. Don't come round here again." And the man on my left lifted a thick forefinger, paused, and then said, "Don't come here again."

"No," I said. "No. Of course not. A mistake, that's all. No harm done. No harm." I started to walk sideways along the pavement. The two Horn Greens moved slowly behind me, their pace synchronized. A small crowd had gathered to enjoy the white man's humiliation. My knees quivered. I began to intone a prayer that turned, instead, into a soft drink jingle. There was tittering. I turned my eyes toward the Avenue. Someone said, "White son-of-a-bitch," in a very resonant voice. There was more tittering. Half a rotted grapefruit rind sailed high in the air and dropped, with an unpleasant sound, three feet in front of me. Despite my better judgment I began trotting clumsily.

I don't know if they followed any further. By that time panic had quite unmanned me. I wanted only to reach sanctuary. I crossed Lenox at the corner, running blindered. I saw vaguely the blur of an oncoming bus. I halted, expecting annihilation, my body tensed to meet the impact. What remained of my bag disintegrated in the death grip of my arms. The milk dropped. The tomatoes rolled crazily. A can of mushroom soup, less fortunate than I, geysered with a swoosh beneath the bus's wheel. The driver began screaming. His obscenities were senseless and wild. I dropped the shredded paper remnants. I stood erect and stepped carefully over my fallen groceries. Then I began walking, with a hopeless sort of dignity, toward the dismal tower of my church.

I shared my service that next Sunday with a very large, moribund fly. Just the two of us in the whole of that great stone place. The fly was, I recall, quite the biggest I'd ever seen. It had the wing-spread of a considerable moth, its buzz was the sound of a frayed electric wire grating, sputtering against wet branches. Winter was approaching and the fly was tired after its one strenuous summer of life — tired, but not beyond contesting this mortal summons felt in the autumn air. It threw itself again and again at the Annunciation window above the altar. And each time it would fall, sizzling, on its wings. At first I found the noise irritating, coming, as it did, after my second consecutive Sabbath disappointment. In time, however, I welcomed it. A small fissure in the serene, changeless ice-wall of my solitude.

On Saturday afternoon I found a magazine on the floor of my hall closet. It was a popular, high-circulation magazine, and it featured a series on "The Negro In America Today." On the cover, in large red letters, were the words "OKALOOSA!

An Eye-witness Account by Rev. John Meeker." The article was dramatic, written with blunt emotion; to it was appended an italicized prayer for love. There were photographs of Doug Banner's body, and of Otis Kulp, the killer, looking stupid and cowed. A photograph, too, of John Meeker — his eyes wild, his face and neck spattered with blood. The blood, I thought, seemed strangely congruous.

Meeker's article had been annotated — by Father Pierre, I supposed. The remarks were written in a crabbed, ink scrawl, and they were quite uncompromisingly rude. "Pompous ass." "What do you know about love?" "What about poor Helen?" Father Pierre, too, had been disconcerted by Meeker's oppressive, holy genius, the crude, blind fury of the young Saul. I understood Father Pierre's bitterness, though I could not then condone his coarse marginalia. I looked forward, with a nervous anticipation, to my next day's appointment at St. Catharine's.

There was an article, too, on Horn Smith — "A Horn Of Plenty," it was called. The article began with a description of his then recent fight with Henry McMillan at the new Madison Square Garden. Horn Smith had already killed one white man; another he had left to languish in an eight-month coma. And yet, the writer indicated, Smith had knocked out only fifteen of thirty-eight Negro opponents in his ten-year professional career. By contrast, his record against white men was perfect: eighteen fought, eighteen knocked out. Smith's interracial contests were object lessons in black superiority. They possessed the certainty, the ceremony of a matador's conquest of his bull. Pitted against white men, Smith was a killer, and his people loved him for it.

Smith had been middleweight champ for three years when he fought poor McMillan. That night eighty percent of the

Garden attendance was Negro — Smith himself had purchased
six thousand tickets, and he had given them away at an outlet
on 125th Street. A billboard above had stated, "Free. See The
White Man Fall. See Him Crawl. Free." It was a deliberate
move on Smith's part. It marked the beginning of his ascend-
ancy in Harlem. Two night later, at a press conference, Smith
had first used the words Horn Power.

McMillan was a blood sacrifice. He had a mediocre record,
the outcome was preordained. A brutal cheer greeted Smith's
entrance. His horn arched upward, magnificent despite the
foam rubber taped around it. The matador and the bull, the
master and the animal, the white man and the slave — now,
after ten thousand years of dominance and submission, their
roles savagely reversed. He bowed, and the murderous shouts
of the crowd were his anointment. Smith carried McMillan
for six rounds. By then the victim was bleeding from the nose
and from two deep cuts just above either eyebrow. As the two
men came out for the seventh, Smith gestured with his gloved
right hand, his thumb directed downward in the ancient, im-
perial signal of death. McMillan was unconscious thirty seconds
later; in his blood Smith's coronation was sanctified. The crowd
carried their champion up Eighth Avenue, from Penn Station to
125th Street — carried him still half naked, his fists encased in
white tape. It was an awesome moment.

And now Horn's Place was the capital of Black America. No
white man knew what happened inside those three store
fronts. There were evidences, however; dramatic evidences of
change. The illegitimacy rate in Harlem had fallen an incredible eighty percent since the sixties — due, it was surmised, to a
large medical staff specializing in the sciences of contraception
and abortion. The crime rate had been cut in half, and a tabarded Negro police force had taken over all but the nominal

control of Harlem. Welfare benefits had risen by a third; un-employment had been reduced by a third; the number of Ne-gro-owned businesses had tripled in two years. The mayor visited Smith at a certain hotel near 125th Street on the first of every second month. Cubert Mody, Smith's man, had defeated the long-incumbent Harlem congressman. A staff of lawyers, white and black, had appeared to defend Negroes charged with even petty offenses. The cornerstone of Harlem College had been laid six months before. No one knew where the money came from — Smith had repudiated all the various Federal Poverty War hand-outs — and no one but the most naïve sup-posed that his sources were strictly legal. But the Manhattan district attorney did not propose an investigation. And Smith, the man who created this vast and beneficial empire — Smith could neither read nor sign his name.

At half-past two on Sunday I walked down Seventh Avenue and attempted, in vain, to hail a cab. No one stopped for me — though some drivers slowed, stared and then accelerated. I learned later that Horn Smith had ordered all Negro cab driv-ers to bypass whites: a reciprocal action intended to counter dis-crimination by white cab drivers. I wondered, as I hurried north on Seventh Avenue, whether cabs stopped for John Meeker, veteran of Okaloosa. I had only ten minutes in which to walk more than eighteen blocks. I began to pant after five. My shins ached and the dollar bills stubbed at my toes. Per-spiration formed on my body; my scalp began to itch as the beads of sweat raced through my thinning hair. Despite my exertion, I arrived a full half-hour late.

St. Catharine's was a charming colonial-style church. It was constructed of red brick and had a single, square bell tower. I hurried up a small flight of stairs to the vestibule. A Negro

usher handed me a program and held the door until I had
passed through. The church was filled to its capacity. Several
men were standing. I found a place behind the rear left pew.
Meeker turned to the congregation as I knelt. "Let us pray,"
he said, "for the whole state of Christ's Church." I was indeed
late. I had missed Meeker's sermon.

I peered about St. Catharine's with an avid curiosity, while
the familiar phrases of the communion passed, uncompre-
hended, through my mind. Meeker seemed tall and very white
among his young Negro servers. The altar had been moved
forward. He stood behind it, facing the congregation. I could
see no white parishioners. Here and there I marked the phosphorescent glow of tabards — orange, green and blue. I stared
at the rough-hewn rafters of the chancel arch. Then I noticed
the altar window. There the stained glass presented a grotesque scene. A Christ. At His feet, evidently, were the twelve
apostles — each listening face a black face. Behind the Christ
figure, arms outstretched in exhortation, was not the arid land
of Galilee — instead I saw the unmistakable skyline of New
York. I glanced quickly at the other windows. Each was the
same. A mélange of styles and periods. First-century robes and
the steel skeletons of nascent skyscrapers. Negro faces predom-
inated, in fact, only Christ and the Virgin Mary had not yet
undergone metamorphosis. A black St. Peter, a black St. Anne,
a black Mary Magdalene. Little black cherubim with very
white grins. Hebrew-Negro tribes fasting in the deserts of
Central Park. Not the best intentions, I thought, could render
those windows tasteful. Boldly they proclaimed a new world,
and yet, with characteristic insipidity, they clung to the paraphernalia of the old. Then, for the first time, I heard John
Meeker's words.

"And grant that all those who respect the Negro race may

agree in the truth of Thy holy word and live in unity and godly love. We beseech thee also, so to direct and dispose the hearts of all Christian rulers — and especially the governors of our southern states, the tyrants of South Africa and Southern Rhodesia — that they may truly and impartially administer justice, to the punishment of discrimination and segregation and to the maintenance of Thy true religion — which is equality among the races, love and brotherhood."

I was indignant. I almost stood up amidst all those kneeling forms. The words of the Holy Eucharist are not sacrosanct. They are the words of a man, more or less inspired in his writing. And yet those words should not lightly be tampered with, for the Eucharist is, itself, the most sacred temporal act that men can aspire to — the sharing of the body and blood of God. The preparation for that sharing is a holy business. There are places, in the sermon, in the prayers, for mundane concerns, but the sacrifice itself surpasses political, social, special considerations. It surpasses life; to be meaningful it must surpass life. It presumes transcendence in its affirmation of the transcending event of the Resurrection. And Meeker went on, ". . . comfort and succor all those who, in this transitory life, suffer on civil rights marches . . ." And the congregation of its own accord, said, "Amen" where there was no amen to be said. Meeker spread his arms, as, above him, the uniquely white Christ spread his arms. His black congregation knew he was speaking not to all men, but only to them, to their hopes and needs. And, some, to their hatreds.

My indignation did not long endure. After the general confession, Meeker's congregation stood to sing. This was not the proper place for a hymn. My program indicated that nine hymns had been scheduled — twice as many as are commonly thought sufficient. I stood, singing the words that I knew,

humming those I didn't. The massed voices overspread the
Church. There was enthusiasm, a fervor, in their singing that
I did not dare gainsay. Meeker despite — because of — his
crudeness had obviously succeeded in a difficult mission. My
precious conservatism seemed an empty thing, as empty as my
own church had been that morning. It was a painful judgment,
and one that I did not comfortably make. With a new willingness I listened to this strange communion.

Beside me at the rail, brown hands accepted the holy wafer.
I thought the extreme contrast a symbolic thing — light boring
through a round hole. Then, momentarily it lay at my own
palm's heart. In my hands, sickly and white, it had no such explicit meaning. Meeker's hands were white, too — but they
were sinewy and covered with thin, brown hairs that lay in
whorls. They hesitated above my opened palms, barely reluc-
tant. I fed, nonetheless. As I walked back, I noticed that the
congregation was not entirely Negro. A white woman with
two blond-haired girls sat in the second row. The woman was
kneeling. Her head moved oddly, rhythmically and, for just a
moment, I thought that she was crying. One of the girls, the
smaller, touched her mother's shoulder with a tentative finger.
The older girl, herself no more than six, gently took the other's
hand away. Then she pressed two fingers against her own lips.
I walked back to my place at the rear of the nave. I had prayers of my own to make.

I waited in the vestibule while Meeker greeted his parishioners with an elaborate cordiality. He knew every name,
every recent event in a family's life. He shook the men's hands
with tournament firmness. He complimented the women on
their loveliness, their hats, their well-behaved children. A little boy, aged nine or ten, drove a playful, testing fist into his
solar plexus. Meeker squared off comically, his agile fists barely

missing the boy's ears. Everybody laughed. Sweat was shining on Meeker's forehead when, at last, he walked over to where I had been standing.

"How did you like it? My sermon. Hot stuff, no?"

"Fine," I said, not wishing to confess my tardiness. "Very exciting."

"Got the idea from Smith. Something he said in Shea Stadium about the richness of dark things. God-damn, if I didn't know he was an illiterate — the man talks like a poet." He pointed covertly toward two blue-tabarded Negroes.

"They're Blues. Right-hand men. Someday — someday soon — he'll come. I know it. He'll come. That's all I need now."

"But," I said, "doesn't Horn Smith — I mean, he doesn't seem religious. Frankly, I thought he hated religion." Meeker made a strangely feminine, flicking gesture with his hand.

"Sure. Religion. Don't you hate it? This isn't religion — here at St. Cat's we worship love. And we worship by doing. Half of those people that took communion — I doubt they're even baptized, let alone confirmed. Anyway, I don't ask stupid questions."

"Not confirmed, but — "

"Don't get your bowels in an uproar. What does it matter? So an old bigot like Hawkes doesn't lay his hands on their heads. Hell, he don't like to touch them anyway. Wake up, Pratt. All we're doing here — we're sharing a significant meal. And that's plenty. Plenty."

"Yes," I said, hoping to appease him. "You've done a great job. Forgive me. I catch on slowly. All I need is time — and a good teacher."

"Sure. Sure, Pratt. I understand. Hey, come meet the family. Helen." His wife came over, the woman I had seen in the second row. Her eyes seemed red, and I was suddenly sure that she'd been crying.

"How do you do?" I said.

"Helen. This is — ah . . . What's your first name, Pratt? I didn't catch it."

"Calvin." I shook hands with Mrs. Meeker. She saw my eyes as they quickly examined her eyes. Her free hand made an involuntary move toward her brow.

"Glad to meet you," she said. She smiled shyly, a pleasant smile. "Excuse my looks I — I have an allergy. Irritates my eyes."

"Poor Helen," said Meeker. "She's allergic to me." He smiled slowly, the smile directed at his wife. She returned his smile. I smiled, too, for I felt a tension between them.

"Have you seen a doctor? They're very good with allergies today. It's a shame to suffer."

"Helen's been, Cal. She goes to doctors all the time. Helen, why don't we invite Cal over to dinner some time? Give us a ring. We can spend a few hours at God's work — overthrowing the church."

Meeker laughed. I nodded and half cleared my throat, half joined uneasily in his laughter. A tall Negro approached us. He wore a large diamond ring on his left pinky finger. Meeker turned toward him eagerly. Helen Meeker touched my arm.

"The children," she said. "I have to go. Hope we'll see you soon." She left.

"Samuel," said Meeker. "Say, did I see Cubert Mody here?"

"Yes sir, Reverend."

"Cubert Mody, Pratt. Harlem congressman. Smith's best friend. Isn't that right, Samuel?"

"Yes sir. What I wanted to ask. There's a rally tonight. Want the boys to pick you up?"

"Sure. Sure I do. Eight o'clock — same place?"

"And this gentleman? Will we see him?" Samuel turned to me, his eyebrows raised.

"Well . . ." I said.

"No," said Meeker with emphasis. "Oh no. No. He's just visiting. Has to go soon."

"Oh," said Samuel. "I'm sorry." I wanted to protest, but Meeker's glance was savage in its intensity. I nodded to Samuel, seconding the fabrication.

"That's right," I said.

"Okay. See you then, Reverend." When Samuel left us, Meeker began to laugh. He wiped his forehead as though it were very hot. Then he slapped me rather soundly across the shoulders.

"That was close," he said. "Just saved you. Those rallies are rough, man. You've gotta know how to handle yourself." He made a fist. "It's not for you. Not yet. You wouldn't want to go there."

The Meekers didn't invite me to dinner after all. I called a week later, but Helen Meeker said her husband was too busy just then, would be too busy for some time. I asked if, perhaps, he needed any help. He didn't; Mrs. Meeker seemed to find my suggestion somewhat amusing, even outlandish. I had hoped Meeker would invite me to officiate at St. Catharine's. But a man's parish is inviolable, and I was too shy to assert myself. Meeker's preoccupation frustrated my hopes. I knew no one else in Harlem; in time I gave up my futile walks. By early October I had sufficient justification for being remiss. On the first of the month seven white persons — men and women — were brutally killed by a mob near 125th Street. Investigation showed them to be innocent Swedish tourists. While the October nights remained warm, a continual state of

riot sputtered and flared. Buildings were set on fire and the
responding firemen stoned. Police cars were overturned. An
army surplus mortar was leveled at Park Avenue from somewhere on 96th Street. The two shells that dropped were both
duds. My own experience, of course, was entirely limited to
radio reports. Smith, it was said, had tried everything to re-
store order. I doubted that. And John Meeker . . . My
radio was mute, but I knew he was out there — his saint's eyes
glowing — recommending calm or fomenting violence. In either case, being heard.

October passed very slowly. By the first of November a cold
snap had made my church quite uninhabitable. Snow fell a
week later. It fell regularly throughout December — chiefly
whenever Nicholas Breakspeare was absent. It seemed as
though I spent every afternoon with my shovel, pushing backward and forward, as the street lamps blinked on in the early
gloom. The cold had its benevolent aspects. Street violence
was no longer practicable. The people of Harlem gathered only
for their mutual warmth.

As for myself — nothing changed. My loneliness and isola-
tion had become habitual, and, with custom, I found that a certain pleasure could be derived from them. I had accepted my
fate: now I was content simply to await the final, physical
demise of my church. Guilt perturbed me only when, twice
weekly, I received a letter from Eleanor. She persisted in her
faith. She asked continually for "impressions," in fact, dreams
of love and Christian sacrifice. Totally abject, I neglected to
write until she suggested a Thanksgiving visit. Then I pleaded
business. My failure was so palpable, so without mitigation,
that I could not relate it — even to the one person who understood and loved me perfectly.

Bishop Hawkes dropped in just after Thanksgiving. I was

apologetic. I explained, with a stammering embarrassment, just what had occurred during my short tenure. But there was no episcopal reprimand. Bishop Hawkes didn't seem to mind or to care very much at all. He talked of Bach and drank a great deal of coffee in the hour he spent with me. I walked him to his car. Bishop Hawkes cursed heroically when he discovered the antenna of his white Lincoln Continental had been ripped off. I didn't think I would see him again — not for some time — and I wondered if John Meeker had been right after all.

I developed a case of nervous colitis soon thereafter. It remained throughout my stay in Harlem and resulted in a salutary fifteen pound weight loss. Christmas came and went: I had a private service and a branch of evergreen hung with Reynolds Wrap balls. Every morning, as a Christian martyr should, I placed milk and cat food by the basement window. I sat, during those long winter afternoons, feet up beside my warm electric fire; some nights, unwilling to confront the chill in my bedroom, I slept in the same position. I read. I wrote a monograph on the Council of Trent. I listened to the scratching and scraping of the busy ghosts beneath me. Despite Nicholas Breakspeare's admonitions, I never once was robbed. As I dozed, my net in my lap, I often wondered, as did old Chuang Tzu, whether I was a man dreaming of butterflies or a butterfly dreaming of men.

I had come to be involved, and I was less involved than I had ever been. I had come to do, and I had done nothing. I had come to evidence Christian love, and no one seemed to care. Guilt alternated with complacency, fear with boredom, irritation with relief. Of human beings, I was surely the most useless.

But God is wonderful. God is subtle. Nothing occurs without His premeditation. My moment was approaching and its approach was irresistible. Now, as I remember my ignorance, I am both awed and amused at God's facility in using the poor instruments at hand. I might have guessed — as I sat, hour after hour, in that little office — I might have guessed there was a reason for it all. And there was. Oh my, yes — there certainly was . . .

PART TWO

Dummies in Red Cloth

Excerpt from the Autobiography of George Horn Smith

. . . A boy of ten, I come to this great giant of a country. The city of New York makes my lovely mother's eyes go wide with fear. My own poor legs ache with the need to run. So many people. So many colored skins. Men with skin like milk. Men with skin like old paper. White men who were almost black men. And men, too, the deep, rich color that I am. These men, they spoke English but their speech was ugly. Thick and clumsy, the words all together. I cannot understand what they say, and I fear what I cannot understand. My mother, too, was afraid, but she has money between her breasts, and Dr. Oddie — he can talk birds down from the sky.

Dr. Oddie, short and fat, with tiny feet and a big mustache. He comes to our house like the hurricane. I think the thin walls will crumble with his shouting, "Think of it, Mother Cerela, think of it. The chance of a lifetime. Your son — your own son — a famous man. I can see the headlines, the posters. The Boy With The Horn. Crowned heads of the world will come to marvel at him. A shower of money, the coins as thick as raindrops. Think of it. Little Georgie, why he'll be the toast of New York City. New York — the metropolis of the world. Not this miserable, filthy, mosquito-infested backwater. And you, Cerela Smith, the proud mother. Your heart filled with love and joy. Photographers. Reporters. Thank your lucky stars. Get down on your knees and praise God. Rich. Famous. The chance of a lifetime. I promise you."

My mother, she puts her fingers in her ears, but still she can hear.
Only deaf men could not hear Dr. Oddie. My mother was afraid.
She wants him to go away. But then Dr. Oddie takes dollar bills
from his wallet — more dollar bills than my mother has ever seen
— and he drops them in her lap. In her life, in our life, there had
been much need for money. My mother touches the bills with her
fingers, then she picks them up. Then she rubs them on the sides
of her cheeks. And so Dr. Oddie leads us with his trumpet voice
down from the hills, to a great boat and to the city of New York.
Swinging his cane with its head like a man's. His own head almost
bald, looking from left to right like a proud cock rooster. In New
York I was to learn much. I was to learn that it is better, in America,
to be a freak than to be a Negro. But to be both . . . That is to be
like a dog's dung, scraped from the sole of some man's shoe.

Dr. Oddie, he owned a place for freaks in Coney Island, which is
not an island. An old building, that groans and rattles when the
big, black snakes of the subway train shake the ground. The little
freak — he wants to see the crowned heads, the coins that will
shower down like drops of rain. But they do not come. There
were posters, oh yes — and on them pictures that did not look like
me. Pictures that give me a doll's body, without my strong muscles,
and lips like big, pink shrimps. And my horn — a great arm reach-
ing high into the sky. There were words on the posters. I could
not read them, but once Dr. Oddie told me what they said. "THE
HORNED BOY. Captured In Far Off Borneo Where He Was Moth-
ered By A Great She-Boar. AMAZING. GROTESQUE. DISGUSTING. The
Sensation of Coney Island. See Him for Only FIFTEEN Cents."

Dr. Oddie puts me in a little stall. The floor is covered with
rough straw and hard, old bits of dung. Dr. Oddie's old, two-headed
lamb lived there, but the long, cold winter has killed it. For fifteen
cents people could see the four-legged chicken and the skeleton of a
child with two bodies and one head. For fifteen cents they could
see Judy the cow, who had a leg like jelly growing from her back.
But I was the big-time freak. "Georgie, my boy," says Dr. Oddie.
"You're bringing them in. The hit of Coney Island." But I saw no
men with crowns on their heads. No photographers. No reporters.
Just a dirty, old building, and the heat of New York which lays
on your back like a great hand.

They came and they stared. Screaming children not older than

me. Old men who smelled from their mouths and their armpits.
Young girls with their dolls and their cotton candy, hugging the
warm hips of their men. The young girls would make little, squeal-
ing sounds, and the men would say, "Don't be scared. It's not real.
It's a fake made out of paper." And a woman with flowers on her
hat, she pokes at the man who is her husband. "If I had a child
like that," she says, "I would strangle him with my own two hands."
But to them I was no woman's child. An animal only — too disgusting for pity. Of all who come, only one man understands me.
A young man, and he comes four times to Dr. Oddie's. He comes
alone on crutches, for one of his legs is gone. He stands by my stall
and stares a long time at my horn. And I, with the curiosity of a
child, I stare at the place where his leg has been. Once he nods.
Once he smiles a little smile. We understand each other.

I was four years at Dr. Oddie's. In all those many years I speak
words only to my mother. Dr. Oddie, he smile and shake his head.
"No brain," he says. "Horn ate his brain away." Dr. Oddie was
not a cruel man — I will speak the truth of him. He feeds me well,
as well as he feeds Judy and the chicken with four legs. At night
my mother and me, we sleep in a little box of a room in the back
of Dr. Oddie's place. There is a yard behind, a yard with a high
fence around it. In the mornings Dr. Oddie let me play there. But
only in the mornings. For the rest of the day, for twelve hours, for
fourteen hours, I sit in my little stall. "Sorry, Georgie," Dr. Oddie
say, and I believe he was sorry. "Like to take you to the beach.
Like to. But it wouldn't be right. The attractions can't go see the
people, Georgie — then the people, they wouldn't pay fifteen cents
to see that nasty horn of yours." He puts the head of his cane in
his mouth and sucks it like a baby sucks a tit. I don't mind Dr.
Oddie. I don't mind the stall and the stupid faces. I know I am
earning green dollar bills for my lovely mother.

Winter is the best time. After the Labor Day weekend, when no
one wants to see freaks any more, Dr. Oddie, he would rent a trailer
and take us all away. Sometimes we went to country fairs, sometimes to other cities. But, when it gets cold, Dr. Oddie takes us to
his farm near the city of Albany. There he lets me run free — if I
promise not to go past the thin barbed wire fences. "Don't do that,
boy. Scare the neighbors. They don't care t'have me around as it is.

Don't like freaks. Matter of fact, don't like niggers either." It was
very nice on Dr. Oddie's farm. Even Judy forgets the jelly leg in
her back. She moos at the trees and watches me when I jump or
walk on my hands or hit a sack full of corn cobs with my two hard
fists. Her wet, cold nose feels good on the back of my neck. We
were friends — friends who know what it is like to have no friends.

I am very sick at the Christmas of that first winter. The cold . . .
In the islands a man's mind cannot imagine such a thing. My
breath comes like steam, and, when I see it, I run screaming. My
body shakes and my fingers will not bend. I see snow for the first
time when I am deep in a great, burning fever. I think it is a big,
white monster of my nightmares. Even today, when the snow falls
in Harlem — gray before it touches the ground — I feel my child's
fear. In time, yes, snow becomes my friend. I throw it and I run
my sled in it. I shape its flatness with my strong, brown fingers.
But, like all white things, I do not, did not — no, I will never trust
it . . .

Washington's Birthday eve: thick sleet fell, bullied about by
a spiraling wind. Half frozen puddles, some ankle-bone deep,
became treacherous pitfalls on the pavement. I spent the early
evening chipping, scraping at the slush on St. Bart's steps. Again
and again my shovel caught on the uneven pavement. The
hard shocks struck at my solar plexus, winding me. Patches of
wet snow accumulated on my scalp; when they grew top heavy,
they cascaded down the nape of my neck. Once, at about seven
o'clock, a lone snowball struck me just under the ear. I turned
and peered through my sleet-spotted glasses. But the attack
was without sequel, and its perpetrator did not reveal himself.

I constructed myself a warm bath that night. "Construct"
was the proper word; more appropriate than mere "make."
The water had first to be heated on the stove and then carried a
good twenty-five paces to the bathroom. I had two cauldrons,
each barely a gallon in capacity: six cauldrons were a minimal
bath; eight covered my thighs when I lay perfectly flat; sixteen

were delightful as far as sheer immersion was concerned, but,
by the time I had added the second eight cauldrons, the first
eight had cooled perceptibly. It was a necessary effort, however. There are two sorts of people in God's creation — bath
people and shower people. I will not presume to judge the latter but I, myself, am a bath person. On Washington's Birthday
eve I settled for ten cauldrons. I was shivering as I let my body
down into the tepid water.

I toweled hastily and hurried along the chilly hall to my office. For several moments I hopped up and down in front of
the electric fire. Then I slipped on my underwear and the
warm bathrobe Eleanor had given me. I was very tired, too
tired just then to make exhausting preparations for sleep in my
cold, somber bedroom. When I was reasonably warmed, I went
over to my bookcase. I took down my copy of Thucydides'
Peloponnesian Wars. I sat in my swivel chair and read, at random, of Alcibiades and his disgrace. I dozed in time — the
swivel chair balancing and unbalancing beneath me — half
asleep in Harlem, barely awake in the Peloponnese.

In a period of just less than six months, from early September to late February, I had come to relish my odd, sterile existence in the rectory of St. Bartholomew's. Expectation and
its uncertainty no longer unsettled me. I had no duties to fulfill. As safe routine established itself, even the annoying in-
conveniences gradually became amicable, reassuring. I read. I
wrote. In truth, I did just those things that I had always done
in Greensprings. My newly assumed radicalism was now bland
and merely academic. I had tried — albeit not very sedulously
— to communicate and to serve. For my inconsiderable pains,
I had been ignored, threatened. Now the responsibility was no
longer mine. Despite infrequent, ephemeral moments of guilt,
I felt profoundly relieved.

I yawned. I stared with interest at my hands, as though their presence in my lap were mysterious and unprecedented. The sleet tapped insistently at my window pane. I yawned again. I looked at my watch without comprehension. Then I rubbed my palms slowly over my cheeks. Tap. Tap. Tap-tap. I righted my chair, my bare feet rigid as they touched the worn carpet. Tap-tap-tap-tap. "Hail?" I wondered. Each tap was too sharp, too clearly defined to be mere sleet. I drew my glasses down from my temples. I stood and walked over to the window. The sleet had stopped. And then I realized what was happening. My door. Someone was knocking at my door.

"Hold on!" I shouted. "Hold on, I'm coming!" But all composure deserted me on making that one, vocal gesture. I ran to my chair and sat, trying futilely to locate my shoes beneath the desk. Only one was in evidence. I squeezed it on and leaped to my feet, sending the swivel chair backward in a conclusive demonstration of Newton's Third Law. That was my last constructive act. I stood in the middle of my office, muttering curses, my hands sawing at the air. The bridegroom had come and I was unprepared, out of oil, out of uniform — very nearly naked. The tapping was now less determined. I picked up my collar and limped quickly out of my office, down the hall. "Coming! Coming! Coming!" I screamed.

As my hand touched the cold door handle, I realized, quite suddenly, that I had reason to be afraid. What if it were the wrong parable — the thief, not the bridegroom? "Good grief," I said. "They've come. They've finally come to rob you." I backed away from the door, but, at that moment, the knocking ceased abruptly.

"Who? Who's there?" I asked.

"Hee—meee . . ." said something hardly discernible as a human voice.

"Who?" I said. I began fumbling with the bolt.

"Heeee . . ." repeated the high, thin sound. It reminded me of operatic tremolos, barely audible on some ancient Mapleson cylinder. "Good God protect me," I said. "Here goes nothing." I opened the door. No one was there. The wind blew cold sleet refuse against my eyes. I blinked. I stepped out onto the stoop. And then I saw it — a brown sack slumped against the door jamb. I approached cautiously. The sack moved, and I jumped backward, my clad and unclad heels clicking painfully together. "What? Who?" I stammered.

"Heee . . . Come in fess." The top of the brown sack wavered. Then a small portion at the side disengaged itself: the brown, balding head of an old, Negro woman, her chin driven by age against her concave chest. She was no higher than the belt of my bathrobe. The hump formed by her shoulders crested several inches above her scalp, and her hands, busy rodent hands, were buried in her stomach cavity. The old woman stepped toward me, peering from the tops of her eyes.

"Hi," I said in a loud, uncertain voice. "Hi. Come on in."

"Mo-keee. Mister. Make him pray to God." The old woman tottered through the doorway with surprising speed, leaving me alone at my own threshold. I hurried after her. When she began pawing ineffectually at the door of my linen closet, I took her gently by the shoulders and led her toward my office.

"This way," I said. "It's warmer in here. Much nicer."

"Granpa say . . ." She stopped, as though to deliberate. Her neck and head were set at a forty-five-degree angle to her collarbone. They bobbed and jiggled rather like the heads of those inane, plastic automobile dolls. "Granpa say . . . Say . . ." I put my ear close to her mouth.

"What — what did he say?"

"Pig. Old pig smell."

"Yes," I said. "I imagine he was right. Old pigs do. Young pigs, too — some of them." Under cover of this nonsense, I tried to lead her to my armchair, but she surprised me again with her agility — turning suddenly to the right, stamping on my bare toe in the process. She rushed to my swivel chair and knelt before it as though my chair were some strange deity in need of worship.

"Aaah . . ." she mumbled. "Aaaah . . . Mother God."

"Well," I said, clapping my hands together soundlessly. "Well now . . . sure you'll be comfortable there? Wouldn't this nice chair be better?" But she continued to mutter, fingers working just under her rib cage. "I'll tell you what — why don't we have some nice tea?" I began to speak more loudly: old people are hard of hearing and they always drink tea. They also get toast crumbs in the corners of their mouths, where little hairs grow. "I had some cookies, but nobody wanted them. So I ate the whole box myself." This insane confession had no effect on her thinking. "Never mind," I said. "I'll make the tea."

I hurried out to the kitchen. When I returned, she was still on her knees, her forehead balanced against the arm of my chair. I went over to her. She wore a shapeless, brown dress and a tattered pair of tennis sneakers. Her hair was white and pathetically thin; her brown scalp shone through at the pate. I knelt beside her. "Are you all right?" I asked. There was an answering sound, but it was not intelligible. Her mouth twitched; she seemed agitated. I looked down at her waist — she held a rosary in her thin, knuckly hands.

"Tea'll be right in." I put my head very close to hers. "It's nice to have you here. I don't get much company. Won't you tell me your name?"

"Cheeses! Cheeses!" she said with loud and perplexing emphasis. I walked backward, knee after knee, as though I'd been bitten by some small innocent-seeming animal. "Mary mother . . . Give me . . . Give . . ."

I stood up and walked over to my armchair. For some time I sat, scraping at my cuticles with my right canine tooth. She was confessing, there could be no doubt of that. Confessing to an empty swivel chair. Another mistake. Another irony. I now possessed a congregation of one — one senile, deranged Catholic.

"Blessed . . ." Incoherence. "One, two, three . . . Devil not for meeee . . ." Agitated incoherence. "Mother God . . . It ain't my child. Save meee — heeeee . . ." Incoherence. The old woman began to cough. The cough convulsed her upper torso, and yet, despite her difficulty, she persisted in speaking. Something had seriously upset her. Her hands fisted; she dropped the rosary and then fumbled for it on the floor. She'll have a fit, I thought. Tea. I jumped up and sprinted to the kitchen. I poured a cup of hot, weak tea; then I carried it back, moaning as the splashings scalded my thumbs. The old woman had stopped coughing. She was standing now. Her fingers, still entwined in the rosary, were pressed over her open, toothless mouth. She was staring at the doorway, and her eyes were filled with an exquisite terror.

"What's the matter?" I asked, almost shouting. "What's wrong?"

"She's okay, Mr. Priest," said a deep, disembodied voice.

I fell backward, away from the voice. The cup leaped into the air. I saw them — cup and saucer suspended intact — at the level of my eyes. I screamed, and my hands at my own throat aborted the sound as I made it. A man was standing beside my office door. A Negro man. A man with a jagged bone jutting up, out of his forehead. "God in heaven — protect me," I squealed. It seemed that only then, after this long moment of recognition, did the cup of tea strike home with a dull shattering. My legs refused to respond; I slumped to one knee. Ankles, insteps, toes burned where the hot tea had splattered them. My heart pounded in my stomach. I drove my fingernails into the skin of my throat, seeking the cross that hung there.

"She's a bother," said the man. "I take her home now." His face was without expression. He seemed not to have noticed my confusion or the physical dismay his appearance had caused me. I tried to stand, but it was too soon for that. I sat, leaned, on the arm of the chair.

"I'm a dead man. A hollow shell." I clutched my chest, my stomach, my abdomen. "Vital organs — they've all gone haywire. You scared me half to death."

"So," he said. "I am sorry for that. I only want to find my mother." He bent then to pick up my cup, his horn pointed like a huge, indicating forefinger at a spot on the carpet. It was a complex thing, not the simple, monolithic outthrust that I had expected. Three long, cylindrical barrels, welded together, converging at a single point. It rose up from his forehead like the span of an arched bridge from the shore. The thing's texture was rough, it was as brown as his skin. I recalled lacquered mammoth bones when first I looked at it. Smith grinned when he saw that I was staring. He tapped lightly at the horn's base with the tip of his right-hand middle finger.

"I guess," I said, fumbling at my open bathrobe. "I guess you're George Horn Smith."

"I am all those things. And this is my poor mother. We have troubled you and we are sorry. Are we not, Mother Smith?" The tiny woman chirped like an excited sparrow. She peered from left to right, but she made no attempt to join her son. "She says she is sorry, but your church, it casts a spell on her. My mother is old — silly with her age — she still likes churches. But we will go now."

"No need. No need. Really. Stay a minute. I'll make more tea, or coffee if you prefer."

"No. I do not drink such things, and time I do not have." He smiled. It was a smile of great charm. He spoke with that lovely, hypnotic Caribbean lilt, the voice rising, falling irrespective of emphasis or meaning. He was shorter than I by several inches. Dressed very much as I was — in the famous bathrobe, for it is said that he had only a bathrobe to wear at Dr. Oddie's Freak House. But this bathrobe was of rich material, collared in fur. It seemed rather the dress of some prosperous, medieval burgher. And the horn — now vicious, now beguiling, as might be the horn of some great, mythical bovine. An instrument. Used, I knew even then, in many different ways and for many different purposes. A horn for all seasons.

"Moki," said Cerela Smith. "Moki. Moki. Moki." Horn Smith nodded. His mother backed away, fingering the edges of my desk.

"Mother. Come. We must leave this man." He turned to me, winking. "She has told you some things, has she not? Poor mother. She is a Catholic and a Catholic must confess. But now, in her old age, she forgets the things she has done. You must understand — just now she thinks I am not her child. She tells everyone that."

"I understand. Actually, most of what she said was, well . . . incoherent."

"Ah . . ." He frowned. "There was another man here — his name I do not remember."

"Father Pierre you mean?"

"Yes. He left?"

"Ill—ulcers."

"I see. And the big, old church — They will tear it down?"

"In a year or so," I said. "I'm standing the death watch as best I can. You're the first — " But Horn Smith was not listening. He had started walking toward his mother. The latter, her humped shoulders pressed against my desk, began to whimper in a sickening manner. Bending, Smith placed his arm gently around her shoulder. The old woman trembled at his touch; her head jiggled excitedly. "Joombie!" she hissed. I started at the word, at her vehemence, and Smith glanced quickly toward me.

"She is very odd tonight. She don't take her pills. The juices in her old body — they dry up. Make her say crazy things. And this church business — it's no good for her."

"Of course," I said. Smith edged his mother toward the door. He seemed to trip as he passed my desk, but managed to regain his balance.

"A lot of books here, Mr. Pratt. You read them all?"

"Yes. Most of them. At one time or another." He stopped in the middle of my office. Then he bent and wiped his mother's saliva-moist mouth with the corner of his robe.

"What is it like, I wonder — to read a book? You know, Mr. Pratt, I cannot read." His mother belched. She began beating her son's hand ineffectually with the end of her rosary chain.

"Do you need any help?"

"No, Mr. Pratt. Only a favor — if you would be so kind. My mother is old, but she is still clever like a fox. I have two ladies, nurses, to look after her. But this church of yours, she has seen it. She is all mixed up inside. She may escape again — and I would be worried." He removed a little card from the vest pocket of his robe. "On this you will find the numbers for my private telephone. If my mother comes — please, if you will, call me. And please, Mr. Pratt — keep these numbers to yourself. Only six people in all this island know of it. Will you do that for me?"

"Yes. Certainly."

"We will go now." Horn Smith began leading his mother down the corridor. I hurried ahead, but the front door would not open when I tried it. The bolt had been shot home.

"It's locked," I said. "How can that be?"

"Yes. When I came in, Mr. Pratt — I turned the lock. You should be careful. This Harlem is a dangerous place to live. Murderers. Rapists. Robbers. And Negroes. Many, many Negroes."

"But I locked it myself — when your mother came in. I'm sure of it."

"No, Mr. Pratt. You must be mistaken."

I opened the door for Horn Smith and his mother. It had begun sleeting again. When he had stepped over my threshold, Horn Smith bent and took the old lady up in his arms. I watched, as he crossed my courtyard, striding toward the rear of Horn's Place. Together they made a strangely grotesque and striking single form — the man with the horn and the tiny, shriveled infant in his arms. I thought, as I closed my front door, that I had heard Horn Smith singing in a high, pleasant voice.

I clapped my hands together. Then I began hopping down the corridor on my right bare foot. Nervous energy danced in my muscles. I returned to my office and tried to appease my body by scrubbing at the new stains in my threadbare carpet. Then I decided to leave them: a monument to the evening's experience. I had met Horn Smith. I had stood within inches of him. He had given me his private number. I hurried to my desk and put the card in my left top drawer. I sat in my chair. Absently, then, I reached out for my Thucydides. It wasn't there.

I looked on the desk top, under the desk, on my chair. I searched through my bookcase. My copy of the *Peloponnesian Wars* had disappeared. Gone. And in the original Greek.

Heavy dripping awakened me that next morning. Outside, tepid sunlight had begun to melt the night's accumulation of sleet. Ponderous drops spattered down from the eaves: a thin spray bore witness to their impact on my windowsill. I lay for several minutes, reassessing my encounter with George Horn Smith. Then I arose. It was after nine o'clock. Despite the previous evening's excitement, I had slept surprisingly well. A phantomless sleep. I slipped into my bathrobe; then I proceeded down the hall. At the kitchen door I nearly fell over the prone body of Nicholas Breakspeare. He was lying on his back, head and naked torso inserted between my stove and the kitchen wall.

"Good grief," I said. "I just walked across your stomach."

"Y'can use the burners, Cap."

"Um . . ." I muttered. I went to the sink and filled a saucepan with water. Metallic clashes came from behind the stove. Nicholas Breakspeare, dressed only in green tights, bootlets and suspenders, began to snort with his exertions. Several rags and a pail of greasy, black water cluttered the floor. I stepped gingerly between them and set my saucepan on the stove. Even with only half-conscious awareness, I sensed that something very suspicious was afoot.

"Nicholas?"

"Yo?"

"Want some coffee?"

"No. No. Nothing for me." I put two teaspoons of coffee and four of sugar in my cup. Then I sat at the kitchen table. I watched his headless, shoulderless body patiently for a moment. I cleared my throat.

"Nicholas?"

"Yo?"

"Just what're you up to?"

"Nothin' much. Smelled some gas when I come in. Y'had a little leak in back here so I tightened her up and slapped on some joint compound. Nothin' to worry about — "

"Nicholas — "

"Yo, Cap?"

"Nicholas, that's not what I meant. Not at all. There's something wrong. I want you to tell me the truth." Nicholas extracted his head. Then he ran several fingers through his kinky hair.

"Tight back there. Push that pot over, huh?" I got up and shoved it toward him with the side of my foot. Then I poured boiling water into my cup, turned off the burner and sat again.

"Nicholas?"

"Yo?"

"Know what day it is?"

"Sure, Cap. Washington's Birthday." I stared at the ceiling. Then I nodded.

"Figures. He doesn't work on ordinary days. Just on holidays." Nicholas Breakspeare sat up. There was a black smudge on his left nipple. Sweat glistened in the hollow of his breastbone.

"No, Cap. I stay home — my wife drag me to a big shoppin' sale. Or maybe I gotta fix the washin' machine."

"I see — you prefer fixing my stove instead. I see." Nicholas grinned. He plucked at his suspender straps. They made light, slapping sounds against his skin. "No. It doesn't wash. Something is very rotten in the state of Denmark."

"Hey — you sure talk funny. Come to think of it, Father Pierre talk funny too. You priest guys — "

"You can't blame me," I said, ignoring his gambit. "Up until this very moment — the truth will out, Nicholas — up 'til now you haven't exactly been famous for your industry. In fact — if someone were to come by on a trolley car and ask me — well, I'd have to say you were pretty much of a goldbrick." Nicholas Breakspeare giggled. "Not that I mind. Not that I should complain. There isn't much worth doing here. But, still, when Washington's Birthday rolls around, and I find you under my stove at nine in the morning . . ." I trailed off, meditating as I sipped my coffee.

"Well, reverend . . ." Nicholas Breakspeare began collecting his rags. "Let me ask you a question."

"Go ahead. Go on — confuse me."

"Am I co — rect? Seems I heard Mr. George Washington kept slaves. Black men. Yes or no?"

"Yes. I suppose." Nicholas made a tocking sound with his thumb and middle finger.

"See. He ain't no father t'me. He's a segregationist."

"De mortius nil nisi bonum."

"Kneebones?"

"Okay. Okay. You're too deep for me." I yawned. "Oh, say, in your wanderings, did you happen to see my Thucydides?"

"What's that?"

"A green book. Thick. Oldish. Written in Greek — little squiggly letters. It disappeared last night."

"Don't look at me, Cap. Them books make me an honest man. I can't find no place t'sell 'em."

"You remain refreshingly frank. Well . . . Keep an eye peeled."

I went back to my bedroom and dressed quickly. The day seemed inviting. I thought I'd chance a little walk. Outside, I found the courtyard, the long alley, the front sidewalks cleared of snow and ice. To accomplish all that Nicholas Breakspeare would have had to start working before seven o'clock. I shook my head. The sun shone brightly, a spring sun. An airplane, reflecting its light, flashed momentarily like a nova against the blue sky. I strolled down my alley to the street. When I turned right, I saw an elderly Negro clergyman standing before the portal of St. Bart's. He had just knocked. Then he stepped backward and stared up, craning his neck — as though some-one were concealed in the steeple.

"Hello there," I said.

"Hello. Hello," he replied. He cupped his hand and shouted at the sky: evidently my greeting had confirmed his suspicions about the steeple. I ran up the steps and tapped him lightly on the shoulder. He turned to the left, then swiveled slowly back before he found me.

"I'm Father Pratt. Rector here. Can I help you?" He bowed ceremoniously, removing his hat in a neat, simultaneous gesture.

"De doo, brother. I'm Uriah Pogue." He held his hat up-side down. He ran his finger nervously around the band. "I come from the Tab'nacle — around the corner. Come t'say hello, brother Christian."

"Dog-gone," I said. "Come around back." I led Father Pogue toward the alley. He was a very old man: had he been white, I would have said seventy, perhaps eighty, years old. But different races age differently, and it was hard to judge with any sureness. His hand, when I took it, seemed slack and without bones. He walked with quick, short steps — unwilling to commit himself totally to any one direction. The comparative darkness of the rectory seemed to blind him. He stood, staring at his feet, until I offered to guide him forward.

"Coffee?" I asked.

"Just water. If you please, sir." I led him to my armchair.

Then I went to the kitchen and poured a cold glass of water from the bottle I kept in the refrigerator. When I returned, Nicholas Breakspeare was standing near the chancel door. Father Pogue had been addressing him. The old man's forefinger waved in erratic emphasis.

"Brother Breakspeare," he was saying. "You didn't do me a favor — you should have told me Father Pratt was here. What must he think of us?"

"Didn't I say?" Nicholas Breakspeare pressed his tongue against the wall of his cheek. "Maybe I didn't." He turned to me. "Think I fix that stuck window in your bedroom."

"Fine," I said. "Fine. Get it good and shut in time for the hot weather." Nicholas Breakspeare shrugged, undisturbed by my sarcasm. Then he tipped an imaginary hat to Father Pogue. "Well," I said, as Nicholas left, "I can't tell you how much this means to me. Really. I've been here five long months. Believe it or not — with ah . . . one or two exceptions — you're the first one who's cared to visit me."

"These are hard times for friendliness. I'm sorry, brother." Father Pogue drank his water noisily. The skin of his face was heavy, it hung in thick ridges at his cheekbones, at his chin, below his ears, just under his eyes. He spoke with little variation and no emphasis. When he had finished his water, he smiled, the curtain of his lips parting very slowly. He had white teeth and gold-capped teeth, alternately spaced. "Ah. Adam's ale. Always the best. Very nice and cold." He paused as he placed the glass near his feet. "This must make you very sad."

"Well . . . It's been disappointing to say the least. Probably my own fault as much as anything." Father Pogue shook his head. "But your kindness makes up for a good deal. Tell me things — tell me how I should proceed in this terrifying place."

"What can I say?" Father Pogue began bending the brim of his hat. His collar was yellow, and one end had come undone. He moved his buttocks uneasily as though the chair seat was wet. He sighed. "Mr. Pratt. I will tell you the truth, sir. I am as frightened as you are. Harlem has changed. Thirty years ago when I came here, yes, sometimes I was afraid of the white man. Fear is not a good thing. But there was respect, too. God help me, should my sons or my friends' sons hear me now. The white man knew many things that my people have yet to learn. You used your centuries well. Why? I don't know. I would not say you were — what is the word — that you were superior. But you have learned, worked harder I think." He paused, licking his wide, cracked lower lip. "But now we, too, have learned a few things. Children who are growing up. We don't want to fear our fathers any more. But we are afraid even so. That is human nature. Being afraid, we want to destroy the things we fear. We want to kill our fathers. Angry children. Children who are almost men."

"Kill. Surely you don't mean that. Surely it's only talk."

"Pardon me, Mr. Pratt — but you don't know." His eyes opened wide and he brought his hands together over his hat in an oddly compelling gesture. "It's the young men and their leaders. They take us by the throat and they say, 'Do you want segregation, old man? Old Uncle Tom. You want the white man to spit on you?' And we say, 'No — no we don't want that.' These young men they are so wild in the eyes, so full of strength. I tell you. My own children are stranger to me than the white man is."

"What about Horn Smith?" Father Pogue sat up. He seemed excited.

"Smith? I will say something about him. Perhaps you will understand. Perhaps you will think I am old and crazy." He hesitated. He put his fingers to his lips. "Horn Smith — I think Horn Smith is a white man."

"A white man? Whatever do you mean?"

"Strange, is it not? And how to explain?" His eyes closed; I thought, for a moment, that he had fallen asleep. "There was a white man once in Alabama. An important white man, he owned many, many miles of land. One day my brother Ezra — may he rest in peace — I remember we were playing one day in the road. The white man, he comes along in his big yellow open car. My brother and I, we were too slow. We did not see who it was. We stood in the road too long. I remember, this white man, he stood up in his car and he made us get out of his way. Made us. But not with shouting, you understand. With his eyes and with his hands. Like — " He made a vague gesture. "I cannot do it. How could I? But we moved — oh, my friend, we ran. He knew, you see, he knew of his great power."

"Yes."

"And Horn Smith is like that. He knows. He moves his hands. He speaks in a little voice and he is shouting. He is angry and there is no anger in his face. He is strong without moving his great muscles. Perhaps it is that devil thing of a horn. I don't know. But he commands my people, as if his mother and father, his grandmother and grandfather had commanded men for many hundreds of years. And it is not so. His people were like the rest of us."

"That's intriguing. Very interesting."

"Is it? Maybe so?" He shrugged in self-deprecation. "But it doesn't help you, Mr. Pratt. I feel for a white man here — in these times."

"Don't worry about me. I have the sensitivity of an old wart hog. You've given me food for thought. I'll have to ask John Meeker what he thinks — when and if I see him again."

"John Meeker. You know him?"

"Yes. Do you?"

"Of course. He is a famous man here. Many of my own people worship at St. Catharine's Church."

"He's done wonders. I know. I wish I knew his secret."

"There is no secret." Father Pogue smiled sadly.

"No?"

"He tells my young men what they want to hear. He is young. They are young. He is angry. They are angry. There is no magic in that, my friend."

"I guess you're right." I filled my pipe. Then I lit it. "Even so, I couldn't do it. Even if I tried. They'd laugh at me."

"I'm afraid that's because you're a white man, Mr. Pratt. You aren't angry. You aren't afraid. You don't want to kill." I leaned forward, puzzled.

"But Reverend Meeker is a white man — surely you know that. Or — " My pipe went out. I tamped it with my middle finger. A figurative dawn had broken in my mind. Father Pogue rested his head on the antimacassar. His eyes were closed; his fingers moved as though in an unconscious spasm. "Are you — " I hesitated. "Are you suggesting what I think you're suggesting?"

"Please. I suggest nothing, Brother Pratt."

"Yes you do." I stood up. "You're a wise man, Father Pogue. You've given me a big lump to chew on. Black and white — the color doesn't matter. It's the color of — of the emotion. That's what you mean, isn't it?" I began pacing the floor. "No, not the emotions. The Apollonian and the Dionysiac. That's what it is. Have you read Nietzsche?"

"I read the Bible, Brother Pratt — and not that since my eyes have gone bad."

"Meeker is— " I plucked at my lower lip.

"Brother Pratt, excuse me. You are a scholar — I see that.

But talk like this . . . Talk doesn't help Christians in their
work."

"Perhaps not." I walked over to where he was sitting. "Father
Pogue, I think I know what would help me."

"And what is that?"

"Let me preach a sermon in your church." Father Pogue
seemed stricken. He smiled, smiled several times in quick succession. Then he grabbed for his hat with such a sudden
movement that it leaped from his knees. I bent to pick
it up. Father Pogue stood.

"I must go now. You frighten me, Mr. Pratt."

"No. Please don't go. Would that be such a terrible thing?
Just a short sermon, nothing more."

"I see. You've made a mistake and it's my fault. You think
I run my own church. No — no one runs anything here. Only
Horn Smith. Your coming, that would be the end of me. When
you said that, my whole body began to sweat and it is quite cold
in here. See?" He showed me his hand. Indeed, it glistened
with perspiration.

"I'm sorry," I said. Father Pogue acknowledged my apology
with a slight inclination of his head; nonetheless, he commenced
walking with determination toward the door. "Your hat," I
said. He took it without reducing his pace. "Couldn't you stay
a little longer?"

"No. I must go." He walked so resolutely that he quite
missed the turning and was some way into the disused wing of
the rectory before I could halt him.

"Promise me you'll come again."

"I will. I will."

"No," I said. "I don't think you will." We had come to the
front door. As I stopped to release the bolt, Father Pogue placed
his hand on my shoulder.

"Forgive me. I'm not a fearless man like you, Mr. Pratt. And this is not a time for fearless love. It would only make them angry, those we want to love."

"You misjudge me. I'm scared half to death — every minute of the day." I opened the door.

"Please — don't think bad things of me." He put on his hat, adjusting the brim with painstaking care. "Spring is coming, Mr. Pratt."

"Yes. I'm a country boy myself. I'll miss the crocuses."

"They're here. Sometimes you see them. Flowers grow in the cracks of the pavement. On the dust of the roof tops. Last night . . . Last night I thought I saw rabbit tracks in the snow. Like when I was a boy and we would go hunting. But a rat, I guess. Only a rat." He sighed. "Good-bye, Mr. Pratt. I wish you well in your work."

"Good-bye. And thanks for coming . . ." He started down the steps. "Oh — I meant to ask. What made you come today? I mean, how did you know I was here?" Father Pogue reached the bottom step. Then he turned slowly toward me.

"Horn Smith told me," he said.

Excerpt from the Autobiography of George Horn Smith

. . . I stay with Dr. Oddie for four summers and three long winters. In the August month of that last summer, I will have my fourteenth birthday. Now Dr. Oddie, he must look up when he speaks to me. The muscles in my arms are thick and hard; I can jump over sticks that hang five feet or more from the ground. Once, in play, I put my back under Judy's warm belly, and I lift her from the ground. I am very strong, yes — but still I do not speak. No one has taught me to read or to make the marks that mean my name. I am the body of a young man, and the mind of a tiny child.

Even then — even when the fireworks explode on the Fourth of

July — even then my time at Dr. Oddie's will almost come to an end. Midge is there, you see. Midge is Dr. Oddie's new attraction. She calls herself the bearded lady, but even my face has more beard than her face has. Midge is a white woman, very white. The white of a sick man's eyes. She is short like Dr. Oddie, and her body is fatter even than his. Her hair is black, but, near her scalp, each hair is white already. I do not like Midge, even from the first minute I see her. She drinks whisky from a flat bottle that she keeps behind her chair, and her breath stinks from it. Every day she puts on a black beard with some stuff like glue that makes my eyes water. That beard, it would fool no one — but Dr. Oddie, he puts the lights down very low near Midge's corner.

Midge makes poor Dr. Oddie love her. I know that. And, from the first minute, Midge is trouble for all of us. She tells Dr. Oddie that he must move my mother and me to a little, hot place in the attic. There are no windows in this place, and, at night, the heat sucks at us like an ugly, hot mouth. There are holes between the boards in the floor. Gray, crinkly stuff — like sharp cotton — sticks up through the holes. It hurts our feet. Dr. Oddie buys two old army cots, but we cannot sleep. In the night, sweat fills the hollow part of my chest, it fills the holes where my eyes are, it bubbles at my nose. I would go to the yard and sleep there in the dust, but I must keep my poor mother company. We talk much, my mother and me. Talk about our nice life in the islands. We talk, too, so that we cannot hear the noises.

Strange noises, terrible noises. And all night long we hear them. Snap, snap, snap — like sticks that are broken across a man's knees. And then the groans come. My mother, she would begin to talk, to laugh and sing — so that I will not hear. But I hear and I know — I know these are Dr. Oddie's groans. In the morning Dr. Oddie, he looks like a very old man. His eyes are heavy and he stumbles when he tries to walk. His cane with the head of a man — he does not carry it any more. He mumbles. Sometimes he bites his lips until there are little spots of blood on them. I feel very sorry for him.

It happened in July, late at night. Dr. Oddie has gone away. My mother, too, she is not there — she is asleep upstairs with a pain in her head. There is only Midge and me, and Midge, she is very drunk this night. She belches. Her black beard hangs loose from

one side of her face. Dr. Oddie, I think, has made her angry. Together we pull down the big, iron door. Then I go to feed the
chickens, which is my job for every night. I hear Midge curse. She
is on her hands and knees in front of Judy's stall. The key, she has
dropped it in the straw.

I go to help her. I must not make Midge more angry, not when
Dr. Oddie is away. I know that. The key is there by her foot, but
Midge's eyes are crazy with drinking and she does not see. Midge
stands up, then she falls against Judy's stall. Poor Judy, she is
surprised and she makes a moo very loud. Midge jumps. "Dirty
freak," she says. Then she stretches her arm over the stall and
punches Judy very hard in her big, soft nose. I have never once
hurt an animal, not in all my life. I am, myself, too much an animal.
And so I am angry — I do what I never dare do before, I kick
Midge, a white woman, in the shin bone below the knee. She
screams and the beard falls off her chin. She raises her fist. Then
she comes at me.

I am strong, stronger than Midge. But, like all my people, I am
frightened by a white man's anger. Midge snarls like a dog. Her
teeth are black and ugly. Her eyes are pink with the whisky she has
had. "Stinkin' nigger freak," she shouts. I back away from her,
ducking my head so that her fist will not hit me. But, instead, she
catches my ear between the sharp, red nails of her thumb and forefinger. She twists and I swing my fist at her, but the pain in my ear,
it makes me miss. "Kick Midge, will you?" she hisses. "Kick Midge,
you dirty savage! I'll teach you to kick." She twists again. And now
she drags me by the ear to Dr. Oddie's room.

The room smells sour from whisky and the odor of human bodies
and something that is like curdled milk. Bed sheets are on the
floor. A woman's things hang from the back of the chair. I see
empty whisky bottles under the bed. Midge pulls my face up to
her face. She laughs and I am afraid. Her hair is like wire and
it is full of black pins. Her nose is bloodied by lipstick. There are
tiny deep holes in her skin. Long hairs from her beard stick out
of her face. She pulls my head down to her belly. Then she smacks
me — one, two, three — on the side of my face. "Bad black boy.
Bad black boy. Bad black boy," she says.

Now Midge pulls me to the bed. She sits on the edge, and I can
hear the springs crack with her weight. Midge laughs. She pulls

me down over her lap, still holding with her devil's grip to my ear.
I feel her hand on my legs. Then my bathrobe is lifted up, over my
shoulders. I struggle. "No! No! No!" I scream. But she is strong
and now — I feel it — she is full of an evil desire. Midge pulls down
my underpants, pulls them down to my knees. I feel her soft fingers
on my naked behind. She pinches me there. I jump, kicking, but
her other hand still holds my ear and there is blood where her nails
meet through my skin. I hear Midge breathing like a man who has
run many miles.

"Bad black boy. Bad black boy. Yes — oh, yes. I've got something for a bad black boy." Midge puts her hand under the bed.
Now she is holding this thing in front of my eyes — it is Dr. Oddie's
cane. I bite at her thigh, but there is no hope for me. A pain like
fire whips across my legs. And another. And another. I hear the
snap, snap, snap and I know now why Dr. Oddie groans. The pain
is so bad that I cannot hold my body still. I jump and I dance.
In all my life of violence, in all the rounds I have fought, never
have felt such pain. I scream out loud for my mother. I weep like a
child.

And then I am lying on the bed. My fists are at my eyes and I
cannot breathe for the sobbing in my chest. Midge is on the bed —
I feel her weight as it shakes the mattress. Then I feel her hands
on my face. Soft like worms. Her hands move up and down on
my horn. Up and down. Squeezing it. Touching the tip with her
thumb. Midge is singing a song for babies. Her hands play with
my chest where the bathrobe opens. Her tongue licks at my nipples.
I hear her. The breath in her throat gurgles like a man's before he
vomits. I sit up. I shake the tears from my eyes.

Midge is naked, kneeling. Her breasts hang down to her thighs.
Her nipples are orange and big as beer coasters. Saliva falls from
her mouth in a stream — she sucks it up. "Nice boy," she says.
"Momma kiss it better." She bends her head down over my waist.
And I — disgust overcomes even my fear of her — I bring my knee
up then with all the strength that is in my young body. My knee
hits Midge in the chin, and her tongue, out to lick, is cut across by
her sharp, black teeth. I roll off the bed, kicking. Midge grabs at
me, but she is blind still with the pain. My fingers reach out for
the back door knob. "Come here you slimy, rotten freak!" Midge

shouts. "Come back here you ugly, ungrateful animal! Come back you nigger!" But by then I have run, still sobbing, out through the yard, out into the hot night. Alone . . .

During the rest of that week, and on into the first days of March, Nicholas Breakspeare was hard at his work long before I arose. Instead of quitting at one, as had been his custom, he stayed late — often until four or five. On two occasions, a special project wasn't completed until well after dark. I became increasingly suspicious, the more so because Nicholas Breakspeare did not suggest a raise in his pay. Whatever his reason, things began to change radically. The lights in the nave were expeditiously repaired; leaks dried up as though they had never been; loose corners of the carpet became secure; dust vanished from window sills and from behind large, immovable objects. When, on Sunday, I officiated at my regular solitary service, I began to regret, for the first time in months, that St. Bart's had no congregation.

Sunday night I heard a radio debate on which the Reverend John Meeker appeared. There were two other guests; Hamilton Harper, a relatively conservative NAACP officer and one Aylbrous Purston, a Horn Blue, whose reputation for extremism, evidently, was quite notorious. Purston was the more controversial figure and, accordingly, received the moderator's particular attentions. He treated all questions, all statements, all commercial breaks as an affront to his race. He used the conversational interplay as an opportunity for bitter, shouted monologues. Purston inveighed against white oppression, comparing it with easy carelessness to Hitler's persecution of the Jews, the *auto-da-fé*, and, incredibly, to vivisection. He advocated extreme civil disobedience. He spoke of fighting fire with fire, of extracting two eyes for one eye, two teeth for one tooth. I found his threats at least as foolish and hyperbolic as they were disconcerting.

I, however, was considerably more interested in what my colleague, John Meeker, would say. Significantly, I thought, he made no attempt to mitigate the tone of Purston's radicalism, and Purston seemed to appreciate this. He never interrupted Meeker or chided him as he did Harper and the painfully neutral moderator. Meeker spoke with a calm obdurateness; his arguments were couched in a seeming rationality, that contrasted with Purston's rhetoric in intensity but not in content. When Hamilton Harper suggested restraint, Meeker simply refused to extend the dialogue. He would say, "I live in Harlem," as though that remark were sufficient and irrefutable. And Purston would second these non sequiturs with a resounding "You'd better believe it, Uncle Tom." Hamilton Harper had the temerity to live elsewhere, to be a wealthy lawyer. His opinions were effectually negated by his own unfortunate prosperity. The debate taught me to envy Meeker's tactics and perseverance. His influential position in Harlem appeared secure.

Tuesday was a warm and lovely day, at least during the hours of high sunlight. Spring teased the city like some coy girl child only half sure of her charms. I took a kitchen chair into my courtyard and read the *Times* for an hour or so. The windows were open in Horn's Place; sounds of laughter and earnest dialogue seemed very near. The *Times* carried the story of an alleged attempt on Horn Smith's life. It was relegated to a half-column on the last page but one; the assassins, if such they really had been, appeared to have operated rather ineffectually. Later that afternoon I walked to the little park and spent a few moments on my bench for the first time since October. When I returned, I found that all my kitchen cupboards had been painted a bright blue. The rectory had begun to seem almost cheerful.

That evening Cerela Smith paid her second visit to my rectory. I was considerably more prepared than I had been on the eve of Washington's Birthday — yet, even so, that tiny, befuddled apparition dismayed my small reserve of self-possession. She trotted to the office without my direction, chattering as she went. By the time I found Horn Smith's private number, she had comfortably juxtaposed herself near my swivel chair. She twittered, whistled as I dialed. I heard disconnected references to her son's deformity, to devils and to joombies, to God's unfailing retribution. Smith answered on the second ring. He appeared, just five minutes later at my rectory door.

"She's inside," I said, whispering as though in some sleeping child's presence. He nodded. When we reached my office, Cerela Smith stood up with an astonishing swiftness — though, ostensibly, she had not seen us enter. She hid the rosary in her hands. Smith smiled and shook a reproachful forefinger at her. With a child's imitativeness, she reproduced the gesture. Then she scurried to the far corner of the room and pressed her body to the wall near my sliding peephole. It was a pathetic sight: the little varicose-veined calves; the balding head; the toothless, active mouth; the gestures like an excited bird. Smith seemed to appreciate my embarrassment. He sighed.

"What shall I do? She will not eat her medicine. I crush the pills in little bits, you know. I put the bits in a spoon. Then I cover this spoon with nice applesauce — and she spits it out at me. It's not good, Mr. Pratt. Not good for a man to see his mother so."

"I know," I said. "My mother died of a brain tumor. A long time ago, but sometimes I dream of it. She was a proud, intelligent woman — as I'm sure your mother is." Smith turned to stare at me. Then a laugh burst from his chest with such harsh quickness that it left no evidence of mirth on his face.

"Proud? No — I think not. Not as Mrs. Pratt must have been. The rich, Mr. Pratt, they have time to be proud. Time to be, as you say, intelligent." He stared across the room. His mother had begun to pluck at her elbow as though some small insect were eluding the probe of her fingertips. "My mother — until now when it is too late — until now she has had strength only just to live. No more than that."

"Proud is proud," I said. "To each their own kind of pride. I know about your mother. I know about her courage. I — I've read your book." Smith displayed no interest; he stared at his mother, musing. "I was deeply moved. If you'll pardon me — it may seem fawning — but your book . . . yes, it's the reason I'm here in Harlem today."

"Is that so?" he said in a neutral tone. "It is a very good book — so they say. Many people have paid money to read it. The man who wrote it down for me, he promised he would make it say only what I told him. But I don't know . . . Someday, perhaps, I will read it."

"Why don't you learn to read? It'd be easy for you — I'm sure of that."

"No. Too late, Mr. Pratt. The king must not let others teach him."

"I'd be glad to help. No one would have to know." Smith turned to me. His eyes engaged mine in an implacable, searing gaze.

"Thank you so much. The church, always quick to teach the poor, black savage. But you mistake me, Mr. Pratt — bookman. I am not poor. I have many men who will do my reading for me. I don't need the white man's knowledge or the white man's bribes."

"I'm sorry. That was tactless of me. I didn't mean to sound

condescending." He laughed. He found me, I think, too poor an adversary.

"I don't know what the word is, Mr. Pratt. But I'm sure you didn't mean it." He walked toward his mother, but hesitated as he passed my bookshelves. "You read all the time. It is your life, Mr. Pratt — am I right? You are an educated man." He said those three words slowly, separating the syllables, as though they were words in a foreign tongue. Then he took out a green silk handkerchief and began wiping his mother's nose. She stamped her feet in annoyance, pulling her nose away, hiding it. He whispered in her ear. The old lady slapped the side of her own face, stunned by his disclosure.

"Yes," I said. "I ought to be. I've spent all my life in school — either teaching or being taught."

"These books, are they all in English?" He began guiding his mother towards me.

"No," I said. "Many are in Greek and Latin, languages of men who died long ago. Some Hebrew, some Sanskrit."

"And you can read them all?"

"Yes. Oh, I'm not so hot when it comes to Hebrew. Or Sanskrit, for that matter. I just scrape along." He grimaced. "It's my business, Mr. Smith. You box. I'm a biblical scholar. I make a living that way."

"Are you a poor man or a rich man?"

"I'm — uh . . . Comfortable."

"That must be nice — to be comfortable."

"Money doesn't buy everything, Mr. Smith. I — I envy you many, many things."

"Yes," he said. "I'm sure. You see this?" He pointed at his horn and I was surprised to see it there. After the initial seeing, I disregarded it as I would have another man's eyebrow or chin or nose. It suited his arrogance so perfectly, jutting there, overreaching. An appurtenance of his power.

"Yes," I said.

"Mr. Pratt, would you agree — there have never been two people so different as you and me. Would you say that?"

"I suppose. Superficially at least. I don't know you very well. I — " And then I watched, incredulous, as Horn Smith proceeded to seat himself in my armchair. He lifted his tiny mother up, onto his lap.

"This interests me — for now. Have a seat, Mr. Pratt. Make some coffee for yourself. We will talk just a moment."

"Yes. Yes, indeed. Certainly. Won't you join me?"

"No, Mr. Pratt. But my mother, she would like a cup of milk. If you please."

I nodded several times. Then I hurried to the kitchen. The reaction set in as I poured his mother's milk. My fingers shook; my knees flexed and unflexed of their own spontaneous accord. For a few seconds I clung to the table's edge, inhaling deeply. Smith's interest in me was more ominous than his strong indifference. I murmured a prayer while, with uncertain hands, I set the water on to boil. Horn Smith was crooning to his mother, rocking her, as I reentered the room. I hesitated; once again, I apperceived his extraordinary and emblematic profile.

"Thank you," he said as I handed him the glass. "Please sit down." I did so, backing to the chair, observing him warily throughout this short retreat. "So, you have read my book, you know my life. But I know nothing of you."

"There's little to tell. I come from a town upstate. I've lived there all my life. I'm a priest and a teacher. I — " I shrugged. "There's nothing else."

"Your family was rich. You were born with a silver spoon in your mouth, and I — I did not even have my mother's tit to suck. Is that not so?"

"You persist in seeing me as a capitalist. I assure you, Mr.

Smith . . . It isn't so. We own a little land, that's all." Cerela
Smith held the glass near her mouth, fondling the rim with
her lower lip. Then, meditatively, she began dunking her
rosary. Smith took it away from her; he wiped it dry with his
green silk handkerchief.

"But when you were a boy, the other children did not spit
at you, did not throw rocks at you. You had many friends."

"Sorry. Sorry to disillusion you. I had few friends — even
today I have few friends. And my fondest childhood mem-
ories are of beatings. Beatings administered by my playmates."

"Hmmm . . ." muttered Smith. "But, Mr. Pratt, you would
not say this life you led was bad. You were fortunate, no? A
few cloudy days. Just a few."

"Yes," I said. "God has been gracious."

"And now you are a respected man. A scholar of the Bible."

"Yes." He nodded thoughtfully.

"Yes. And I — I am a king. Does a scholar, does he have
men who would die for him?"

"No."

"Does he make people happy? Do good for them? Put
money in their pockets?"

"Not the way you do. No . . ."

"I see. Mr. Pratt, may I ask — may a man ask who cannot
read — what use then is a biblical scholar?"

"None, I guess." He smiled, pleased by my admission. "But
that's why I came here, Mr. Smith. To do something. I
wanted to help."

"And have you?"

"No. Not at all." Cerela Smith shrieked. Her son extracted
the empty milk glass from between her fingers.

"Who is then the better person, Mr. Pratt? The Negro. The
freak. Or the rich white man?"

"I don't — you. You are, I guess."

"You guess?" He laughed. I felt a hot flush rise along my throat and cheeks.

"Well. I mean — you said the better person, Mr. Smith. In God's sight we all have a special, a unique reason for living."

"Oh, yes . . . God. This rich man's toy. I have heard that even He likes men who do good deeds. Am I right?"

"Yes."

"Then even the Christian God — He thinks I am a better man."

"Well. I won't argue it. We all know what you've done for your people."

"Mr. Pratt. Why are you afraid of me?" Instinctively, I wanted to protest this judgment, but it was a senseless reflex. Cerela Smith began smacking her lips. Horn Smith patted his mother gently on her balding pate. She reached up to touch his horn.

"I'm a timid man, Mr. Smith. You have a reputation — excuse me — for violence. You hate white men or so you say. Think: I'm here alone in a country you made. I feel I've been set down on Mars. I don't know if I dare breathe the air. It's all very frightening."

"Have you ever fought with your hands — fought for something you wanted?"

"No. I hope I never have to."

"Have you ever had a woman?"

"I — Mr. Smith, I don't think that's any of your business. Excuse me. I don't."

"No. You have had no woman. You are a priest — I forget that. And how is the religion business here, Mr. Pratt?"

"Here? No one comes here."

"So," he nodded, "not even a good priest."

"I haven't had much of a chance."

"No, Mr. Pratt. But I have had no chances either. I make my chances." He stared at the ceiling. "You know what, Mr. Pratt?"

"What?" He leaned forward, his horn and forefinger pointing an intended menace.

"If I ruled this country — ruled it as it should be ruled, Mr. Pratt, I would have you killed. One day the men would come for you. They would take you to some farmer's field, before the plowing. One bullet, perhaps a strangling cord. Then, at least, your rotting body, it would make the corn fields grow." Cerela Smith shrieked her approval. I swallowed and the sound of my working throat filled my ears.

"You don't mean that. I know it." He stood up, setting his mother carefully on her tiny feet.

"No, Mr. Pratt. Maybe I don't. Not now. But sometimes, sometimes when the restaurant man says, 'Nigger, you can't eat here.' Then I mean it. You, Mr. Biblical Scholar, you can eat where you please. And you — you are a useless thing." He began walking toward the door. "I must go. We are taking up your time."

"Thank you for coming."

"Oh yes, Mr. Pratt. Indeed. You are welcome. Hurry along little mother, Mr. Pratt is a very busy man." He laughed. "Tell me — all these long days — what do you do here, Mr. Pratt?"

"I read. Write things. Study butterflies. I catch them at home — in the country."

"Butterflies? Oh, yes . . . They need catching, Mr. Pratt. There are so many of them. They bite the children in the night."

"You enjoy mocking me. You're very good at it."

"Forgive me, Mr. Pratt. Will you not? I'm a black savage, a jungle ape. I know no better." He opened the front door. "We are very grateful to you, my mother and I." In response his mother snapped at my knee like a small dog. "But you will be happy, we go to Washington on Thursday. For a while we will not bother you." He sniffed at the air. "Something is burning."

"Oh, my God. The coffee water."

"Good-bye, Mr. Pratt."

I hurried down the hall to my kitchen. The water had boiled away, and the bottom of the pot was blackening. An acrid mist drifted in the air. Little embers glowed where the painted wood handle had begun to burn. I carried the pot to my sink and poured cold water over it. Steam, hot and nauseating, enveloped my head. I backed away, hands over my smarting eyes. "Oh my God," I said. "God. God. God." I might have cried — it is not easy for a man to learn, with such brutal frankness that his life has been futile and ridiculous in that futility. I might have cried but I did not. I looked up, suddenly pensive. Then I walked quickly into my office. I stared at my bookcase for several minutes. Yes. There they were — the gaps. My *Aeneid* and my Augustine. Both in Latin and both gone. For all his scorn, I thought, Horn Smith was stealing my books.

Late Saturday night I was made wretchedly sick by a bad swordfish steak. I had purchased a pound or so on Friday morning, and even then, as I recall, it had looked somewhat suspicious — a scaly green around the edges. I did inquire about it; at least I tried to. But the quality "freshness" does not readily lend itself to pantomime. I am, moreover, especially fond of swordfish steak; perhaps I was less critical of its appearance than I would have been in the case of some other fish. It tasted quite nice, but I was foolish enough to fry a leftover bit on Saturday evening. By then the greenness had clearly crept beyond the edges; the taste strongly savored of cod liver oil. I ate it, my suspicions notwithstanding.

Heavy, sweet puddings began to appear in my dreams at about two o'clock Sunday morning. I ate them as they appeared and, by three o'clock, the eating was made compulsory by some undivulged but dreadful authority. I rolled from side to side. I pulled my knees up to my stomach and squeezed them there. I sucked at my pillow; I sucked at my fingers; I sucked at my own tongue. The nausea intensified. My throat became unpleasantly dry. Sweat dripped into my eyes. I awoke finally from this sweet surfeit of my unconscious to the reality of an irrepressible retching. I ran, stumbling, to the bathroom.

I was awake the remainder of that morning. After I had thrown up the first time, an equal and opposite urge convulsed my system. Perhaps the Friday night meal — dynamite with a longer fuse — had reached my lower bowel just as the more recent swordfish had begun to torment my stomach. Whatever the reason, my colitis, my impish companion of long winter afternoons, had been transformed into an irresistible and malevolent dysentery. My internal equipment was harshly wrenched in two directions. I doubled over. I sat. I doubled over. Each quick movement and its converse required a nice precision. In a very short while I was confused, exhausted and very afraid.

To be continually alone is distressing in itself. But a loneliness shared with disease is profound and absolute. I found myself remembering childhood illnesses and the compulsory delights that accompanied them. The apple-sweet crook of my mother's arm. Her fingers as they massaged my neck and shoulders. The smell and the coolness of rubbing alcohol. Toast and tea in bed. Clean sheets. Afternoon radio serials. The special attentions of my three sisters. As I lay on the bathroom floor, reamed out and weak, I yearned in stolid middle age for all those vanished things.

I stood up. I bent to flush the toilet — and then it happened. I heard another toilet, an echo of my own, rushing in the thick morning silence. I stepped back, startled. My own toilet coughed and then swallowed with considerable difficulty. I listened, but a dense noiselessness had returned to the rectory. It had been an eerie sound, heard partly in my ears, partly in my fingers as they touched the flush handle. In my Greensprings home, I recalled, all the toilets were diminished in their force when flushed simultaneously with other toilets. But here there were no other toilets. I touched my scalp tentatively. Or were there?

I walked over to the sink. I poured cold water over my face, down over the nape of my neck. The shock soothed me at first. Then it caused a moment's vertigo. I bent forward; my hands gripped the hot and cold taps. Leaning there, I felt a muffled rumbling in the hot faucet — the one I had not turned on. It lasted only three or four seconds. "What the ding-dong hell?" I asked aloud. My mirror image peered back over its own shoulder in comic trepidation. "Spooks?" I turned off the water and waited, hands on faucets, like some patient medium before his Ouija board. Again. This time it was almost ten seconds before the distant vibrations had ceased. I swallowed. Someone had tapped my plumbing.

"Oh boy," I said. "Oh boy. Oh boy." I walked cautiously down the long darkened corridor to my kitchen, muttering encouragements as I went. I hesitated halfway. My hand touched the door, hitherto unopened and unsuspect, that led to the disused second story. It was locked. I crouched and put my ear against the keyhole. A slight draft tickled my lobe but there were no revealing noises. "Get a good hold on yourself, Pratt.

Don't let go." I continued into the kitchen, and there I poured a glass of cold water. The water gurgled audibly down through my dehydrated insides. Then with an uncustomary resolution, I hurried into my office and opened the upper right-hand drawer of my desk.

I took out a ring of large, odd keys — some of them three inches in length — that Father Pierre had left behind. Then I went into the linen closet and removed a tall altar candle. I carried the candle and some kitchen matches out into the hall, placing them carefully in front of the upstairs door. To my chagrin, the very first key on Father Pierre's ring proved to be the correct one; the door stuck but finally opened outward with moaning reluctance. I peered in. Darkness was impenetrable beyond the fifth or sixth stair. "Wait," I said. "Wait until it's light." But my anticipation was more intolerable than reality. I bent down and lit the candle.

I had determined to proceed stealthily, to surprise the mysterious flusher, and, to that end, I had left my slippers on the lowest step. But my tactics proved futile: the ancient staircase answered my weight with a fierce audibility. Before I had climbed five steps, my exhausted body had begun to shudder with cold and dread. My heart thumped fearfully in my chest and the candle — held at full arm's length — dipped and rose with its pulsations. A smell of old canvas and mildew drooped apathetically in the air. Large flakes of dust showered down from the bannister. I stared upward, but the candle-light was pathetically limited in its radius. A bedtime prayer of my childhood began to form and reform itself on my lips: "If I should die before I wake, I pray the Lord my soul to take. If I should die — " I stopped. I listened. The silence was unalleviated.

There were eighteen steps in the flight. It took me almost

ten minutes, beset by fearful hesitation and weariness, to complete the short ascent. At the head of the stairs a murky corridor stretched an undetermined distance in either direction. I stepped toward the right, my hand probing at the wall, my candle darting here and there. A closed door . . . I listened for a moment. Then I inhaled, held my breath and turned the knob. Nothing: a square, unfurnished room. I proceeded ten steps further along the corridor. Another room, exactly similar but for an overturned table, its ornate legs kicking at the air. I backed out: I leaned my shoulders momentarily against the wall. Then, suddenly, I heard a very faint crackling sound. My free hand fisted. I peered into the darkness. Light — the light was increasing. I looked to my right, to my left. I leaped forward. My candle had set fire to a large, loose piece of wallpaper. I dropped the candle and beat at the flames with my fists. Total darkness returned to the corridor.

My candle had rolled several yards back toward the staircase. As I searched for it on hands and knees, my painful, exacting caution turned to irritation. I cursed aloud, heedless now of secret trespassers. My knees thumped against the flooring. I found the candle, relit it, stood and stomped angrily down the long hall. I discovered what I had been seeking almost at once: the bathroom was at the far east end, located directly over my own bathroom. The toilet bowl was shattered. The sink lay on its side in the shower stall. No one had used the plumbing — not in twenty long years. "Ghosts," I said. "Damn, stupid ghost's ablutions."

Through a crevice in the boarded bathroom window I saw that dawn had already begun to break. Jagged waves of exhaustion wriggled up, through my thighs, along my spine — settling in a pit at the rear of my skull. I walked with scant coordination back down the dismal corridor. There was no hope of sleep; my senses were yet too aware, too strongly agitated. I closed the door behind me, relocked it and staggered into the kitchen. Sunday . . . The dawn light sparkled on newly clean windows: the embryo, it seemed, of a pleasant day. I drank five cups of coffee, enjoying the hot, wet steam that rose into my face as much as the liquid itself. My stomach shrieked like moist rubber sheets squeezed together. Just then I hardly felt capable of officiating, even for myself, in that somber, empty church. But routine, I knew, was the most efficient antidote for my nervousness. I dressed at nine o'clock.

Fatigue quite unmanned me as I prepared the altar table. Holy things slipped from my fingers, were misplaced; I giggled at my helplessness before the cross. The long taper refused, for several moments, to make contact with one candle's wick. My tormented stomach muscles ached and, to accommodate them, I began walking with a pronounced stoop. At nine thirty I returned to my office. I vested. Then I sat, for an intended short moment's rest, in my swivel chair. The chair tilted slowly backward; I was asleep before it came completely to rest.

I awakened with a quick, harsh gasp, aware suddenly of something that threatened me. My watch dial was blurred before my eyes; I held it steady against my chest. The hands and their significance baffled me momentarily — ten . . . It was five after ten. And then I heard it. I reached instinctively for my radio, for the sound was a rustling whistle very like that between station frequencies. My radio was not on. I spun my chair around. Then I slapped my face soundly below each ear. It wasn't possible. I stood. I walked, foot placed deliberately before foot, to the peephole. I slid it open. I peered through.

St. Bartholomew's was packed. From the front row to the fifteenth — as far as my peephole allowed vision — there was not an empty place. Negroes. All Negroes and hundreds of them. They were waiting patiently, some in prayer, some talking softly to their neighbors, as though they had come to worship there every Sunday of their lives. Someone sneezed: that homely sound convinced me that this, at least, was no dream, no colossal wish fulfillment. They were waiting for their priest, and I was late. I rubbed my eyes. Then I walked quickly, with a shocked steadiness, out into the chancel.

The sound of their concerted rising drove a thrill through my body. They were standing, I realized, to acknowledge the presence of God in His minister on earth. Only the experience of many Eucharists bore me through those first distressing moments. I read the Epistle, the Gospel, as though the whole concept and practice of reading were unknown to me. When we came to the Creed, and I heard those several hundred "I believes" muttered strongly in the gloom behind me, the hair roots at the back of my neck seemed to harden with the excitement. I was first aware then of my existence, of their existence in a specific time and place. Specific: it was time to welcome them.

Perhaps it was a death wish. Perhaps I hoped only to postpone that first, dreadful confrontation. Whatever my motive, I forgot Nicholas Breakspeare's admonition — I began to climb up, into the pulpit. The treads sagged under my weight. Groans were emitted, crackles, sputtering pops; at one moment the entire structure seemed to settle a full three inches. The floor of the platform was littered with rags and cans, a painter's disused paraphernalia. I cleared a passage to the lectern with my foot. Then I stepped forward. I leaned my arms casually on either edge of the lectern, as though my silence were some planned trick of rhetoric. Interrogatory noises escaped from my throat. In row after row, anticipating faces

stared upward, shoulders pressed against pew backs. Silence.
I tried to capture the thumb of my left hand in the fingers of my
right. Silence. And then someone sneezed.

"Gesundheit," I said.

"Thank you," said the sneezer.

There was an embarrassed tittering, then genuine laughter.
People craned to see the sneezer, who was, evidently, a popular
fellow. He saluted with his handkerchief and a fresh spattering
of laughter ensued.

"And Gesundheit to you all," I said. "Gesundheit means
'to your health' in German. So Gesundheit and God bless you
for coming here today." I cleared my throat. Momentarily confounded, I looked down over the pulpit edge. My acrophobia
returned. The pulpit wall seemed to bend and I imagined
the floor's upward rush to impact. My head darted back.

"Let me tell you," I said, my voice thin with tension. "I
don't believe this — not for one moment — I don't believe
you're all down there. My name isn't Thomas, but I'm doubt-
ing." I paused. "Don't get me wrong. I'm very, very glad to
see you. You don't know how glad. I've been here in this great,
old church for almost half a year now. Yes, and every Sunday
I stood right down there, alone, blessing myself and the mice.
Six months. That's at least two dozen Sundays. I was feeling
very sorry for myself. You know how people are. And now, like
a lot of very nice, very substantial ghosts, a whole great congregation has come to worship with me. God is good. You've
made me a very happy man.

"Well . . . I hope you won't be too disappointed. There's
a church but not much else. The roof leaks when a bird passes
over. The organ broke down a long, long time ago. That's
okay, too, because there can't be more than thirty hymn books
altogether. The pews are damp and, if you sit quick, you may

get splinters. The kneelers, I've tried them, they're harder than the floor. Tell the truth, the way it sounds, I wouldn't be surprised if this pulpit came tumbling down like the walls of Jericho. So nobody, please, blow a trumpet. Worst of all, I'm a terrible speaker. My voice is weak and there's no sound system. But if you've come here to worship God; to give thanks for His Hope in Christ; to ask forgiveness; to pray for God's blessing and his salvation . . . Well, if you've come for those things and I know you have — then maybe you won't mind so much. Forgive me. Forgive my poor, old church. We welcome you.

"My name is C. Beecher Pratt. C. B. is fine. Maybe I shouldn't mention this. Maybe I should pretend it isn't so. But the light's not that bad in here — you can see it. I'm not a Negro. Perhaps then you know just how lonely I've been these long six months. I came here to help, if I could . . . Maybe no help is needed. But I'll be here, God willing, as long as this building remains a place of worship. Come and share your problems with me — forgive me for having, without proper introduction, shared my problems with you. I hope to meet you all very soon. There must be many, many things we can talk about. Help we can give each other. That's why I'm here. I thank you all again."

I stepped down from the pulpit. Two young Negro boys had appeared at either end of the altar. They aided me very expertly in preparing the Eucharist. It was a long service. There were so many mouths to feed; I could never have managed it alone. When all was done and the table had been cleared, I walked very slowly toward the chancel arch. I remember thinking, "It's warm here." And it was: the conjoined heat of bodies pierced through the chilly nave. I raised my hand in blessing and, as I made the sign of the cross, my fingers, I thought, stiffened in the outflowing of grace. I prayed even as I ended the benediction. Prayed that I might be proved more deserving of this sudden, great opportunity.

I exited through the door to my office. While the boys were dousing the altar candles, I rushed out, down the alley, to the front of St. Bart's. Everyone seemed delighted. I was complimented on my impromptu sermon; favorite passages were recapitulated. Each person wrote their "Name. Address. Telephone No." on my little cards, or on scraps taken from their wallets and inside pockets. One lady mentioned a baptism; another, a double wedding. And yet, throughout, a dreadful temptation darkened my rejoicing. I wanted to ask them why they had come, where they had come from. But I didn't dare. And they, in cheerful opacity, conspired to ignore their massive and simultaneous migration.

When the last family had departed, a very dynamic-seeming middle-aged woman approached me. She crooked her finger, then led me back up the center aisle of my church with a confidential expression on her face. She wore a hat like an upended flower pot, the flower, a huge daffodil, growing from the pot's bottom. The daffodil bobbed above her eyes like an auxiliary head.

"My name is Puppet Prather. You just call me Puppet, Father. The ladies asked me t'speak to you — about the altar guild an'all."

"Altar guild. My. That's wonderful." Puppet Prather nodded; the daffodil nodded.

"Well, Father. We got a pretty fine org'nization already — if I do say so myself. I'm treasurer 'cause I'm real tight with money. Mrs. Stevens, she's the president, she's got a bad cold otherwise she'd be here herself. Now we'd all like to meet with you. Thursday — that's our regular night. We'd like t'come Thursday. Eight o'clock okay?"

"Fine. In the rectory. I'll have coffee waiting."

"You gotta show us around — so's we know what's here t'work with. Mrs. Mott, she'll lend us her spinet. We could set it up over there. Most folks have a hymn book. I got a few extras."

"Good. I'll try to dig some up myself."

"Now, Father — excuse me askin'." The daffodil touched my eyebrow as Puppet Prather leaned close, her strong forefinger pecking at my breastbone. "Excuse my askin' — but who does the cleanin' up around here?"

"Uh — I have a man. Nicholas Breakspeare. Perhaps you know him?" Puppet Prather's nose wrinkled on either side of its bridge.

"That's a funny name — he a Horn, huh?"

"Yes. An orange."

"Well, see — them Horns don't got much time for nothin' — nothin' but Horn business that is." She raised her hand flat and brought it very quickly up to her face. "Not that I got nothin' against Horns. Don't be thinkin' that. I just don't have time for politics. I'm a very busy woman, that's all."

"I understand."

"Now I hate to say it — but there's plenty gotta be done around here. This place — it's like an old barn. A dirty old barn."

"You're right, Mrs. Prather. That's just what it's like."

"Okay . . . Glad you see it my way. What we'll do I figure — we'll have a little Saturday volunteer clean up. By spring time proper, you ain't gonna recognize this place, Father."

"I bet I won't — and I won't miss the old place either."

"Let's see. What else I got down . . . Oh yes. Is there a large meeting room here someplace?"

"Yes. Downstairs, I believe. It's been boarded up a while. Why?"

"Well, Mr. Pratt. What this place needs is a little Bingo game. I happen to know — Monday nights there ain't no competition. Anyhow, there ain't from here on in. Make a little money. Make some friends. Get this church on the map, so to speak."

"Mrs. Prather — I take my hat off to you. You're an entrepreneur." She couldn't repress a smile of satisfaction, and the daffodil, though it lacked proper equipment, seemed to smile as well.

"Call me Puppet, Father. I let you go back t'work now." We walked slowly back, up the aisle. "I liked your sermon," she said in a subdued voice. "It was honest and good. Not — not the kinda stuff we're used to hearing."

"You're very kind, I — was taken by surprise. Didn't have time to be anything but honest." Puppet Prather muttered something. Then she pointed toward the vestibule.

"I'd better go. Seems there's somebody got business with you." She walked with pointed swiftness, up the aisle, out the door, past a young man in a blue tabard who was standing there. The young man appraised her ankles. Then he grinned at her apparent distaste. He came toward me.

"Yes?" I said. "Can I help you?" The young man cleared his throat. Then he smiled. He was tall and boyishly handsome. He held his Horn cap upside down between his hands.

"My name's G'wain, Father." He bowed politely.

"Pleased to meet you, G'wain. Were you at the service?"

"No. No — I ain't a churchman, Father. I been sent here to speak to you, that's all." The tiredness and the fear of the night before reinvested my legs. I stepped backward.

"Nothing wrong, I hope."

"No sir — not that I know of. I'm a Horn Blue, head of transportation in Harlem Section Two." He paused.

"Yes?" I said.

"We're havin' a rally tonight, up at the Rabazz Ballroom. Thought maybe you'd like to join us."

"Could I? I'd be honored."

"Don't have t'do nothin' — just be up on the platform when Mr. Purston speaks. Show the friendship between races, you know. There'll be other white men, so you don't have t'worry."

"That's Aylbrous Purston?"

"Yes sir. Mr. Horn Smith's best friend."

"Fine. Fine. How do I get there?"

"Don't worry — that's where I come in. We pick you up about seven o'clock, okay?"

"Okay. I'll be waiting."

We shook hands. G'wain strolled with athletic grace down the entrance steps. At the pavement he donned his cap, carefully adjusting the metal horn. I turned to go in, excitement and satisfaction eddying within me. The collection plate in the vestibule was filled far beyond its small capacity. Bills overspread the table. Some caught by a light breeze, had drifted to the floor. I scooped them up. Then I carried the plate down the aisle to the altar. There I knelt.

"Lord God our Father." I prayed, "I thank You. If You don't mind, I won't ask any questions just now. Mine is not to reason why. Thou art gracious and merciful and Thy ways, indeed, are beyond our understanding. Thank You. Thank You." I bowed my head and there, on my knees, I fell asleep.

Excerpt from the Autobiography of George Horn Smith

. . . I follow the big, iron legs of the subway until it runs to hide in the ground. And from that place I follow the square holes where, deep in the earth, it breathes and growls. When the hot sun rises,

I do not know where I am walking. I am very thirsty, very tired, very afraid. There are no coins in my bathrobe's pocket — only the big, floppy hat that will almost cover my horn. People are waking up. Trucks hurry very fast through the empty streets. Alarm bells ring. White faces, sleepy faces look out from windows. I must find a place to hide, for soon, in the light, people will know my horn.

Then I see it. A big, green arrow pointing. A magic arrow. An arrow that will change my life, though then I cannot know it. The street is quiet. All the buildings, they are the same — sleepy boxes, three stories tall, all dirty red, with big, high staircases walking up to their doors. The magic arrow, it points at one of those doors. There are words under the arrow. The green paint on them is old and peeling. I stop. Far down the street, a policeman comes around the corner. His stick spins on its leather chain. Before he can see me, I run up the stairs, through where the arrow is pointing. Inside there is another high staircase, and, under it, there is a little, square hole. An old baby's carriage, an old tricycle and, yes, an old mattress that smells of a man's pee. I squeeze my body into the hole. Then I pull the carriage and the tricycle up close to hide me. I lay down with my face toward the door. Like a smart, old cat, I will not sleep until my back has been made safe from enemies.

My body is tired, but my mind is like a hooked worm that wriggles and will not die. I dream as I sleep, and the dreams, they are things a young boy should never know. Midge is there, on four legs and as big as Judy the cow. Her breasts drag on the ground. Midge sees me. I run and she comes running after me. I turn and suddenly the green arrow is in front of me, burning like a fire. I pull the arrow down by the tips of my fingers. Now it is a sharp spear in my hands. I stab the point deep between Midge's jiggling breasts. The spear sticks like a knife in a soft watermelon. I pull it out and the blood pours, bubbles down. Thick. Dark red. Streaming over my head, choking me when I reach up to stab. Midge screams. She holds the places where her blood is coming out. I begin to shout. Shout with joy. The blood runs like a river over my knees. And now Midge is many people. She shatters like a china bowl. Every piece is a white man and I am killing them. Killing them. And the joy I feel in that dream is the joy I feel now when a woman lies beneath my body.

The dream has stopped. Someone's hand is on my neck. I wake and my fingers make fists to cover my face. A man is standing over me. The man is tall and white — he has thick, gray curls. His lip goes up and he snarls like a dog. I see the man has no teeth in his mouth. He shakes me very hard by the shoulders. I pull away from his big hand, and my hat falls off.

"Jeee-sus God!" he says. His voice is high like a woman's. He falls back, his hand waves in the air — as if my horn is the clicking of a sharp switch blade. The tricycle crashes over. Before the man can move, I lower my head and my horn hits him hard on the bone just above where his groin hair grows. He shrieks and falls on his knees. I run, crazy with my fear, up the high flight of stairs.

There are doors at the top of the stairs — double doors with round glass windows in them. I push my shoulders through. Behind me, the man is now on the stairs, gasping, falling but still coming after me. I stop, frightened, inside the double doors. A big room full of men — white men, black men, men in shorts, men in their Sunday suits. Their backs are to me. I press my body against the wall. Then I run, my knees bent, my head low, along the wall. No one sees me. I crawl under a big, square platform. Feet thump above my head. I look out — yes, the man with no teeth comes slamming through the doors. He is holding his hands near his groin.

"Hey!" he screams. "Hey, you guys!" The men turn to look at him. "Nigger kid come in here? Kid with a big god-damned horn — here in his head? A horn. He busted me in the chops with it. A horn. Honest to God, big as my arm."

"Curly's drunk again." The men laugh. Curly comes forward, his hands are waving in the air. Saliva drips from his mouth.

"No. I swear. He must be in here somewhere. I swear, you guys. A horn — it scared the piss outa me. I thought it's the devil, a nigger devil."

The thumping stops. Men look around, still laughing, not seeing. But a little, old man in a suit walks near to where I am hiding. I crawl back, into the dark shadows but there is nothing to hide me. The man kneels down — he has a cigar and a gold watch chain. His head is bald. He makes me think of Dr. Oddie.

"There he is," says the man. His voice is quiet, surprised — and the other men, too, they go down on their knees.

"There."

"Yeah."

"Hey — I see it. A horn. Curly's right, he has a horn."

"A god-damn horn."

"He hit me in the chops with it. Man, I saw stars."

"Can't be — it's a halloween trick. A mask."

"No, sir — that's real. Hard like a bone. I bet I'm bleeding."

"Look. See, when he turns his head."

"Hey, kid, come on out — let's see that thing."

"A monster. What they call those animals?"

"Unicorns."

"Yeah. A unicorn, that's what."

"Come on, kid — come on out here."

"Hey — somebody pull him out."

There is a noise. Behind me, a man has dropped down from the ring. He starts crawling toward me. He smiles. There are gloves on his hands, and big muscles in his arms that bulge when he moves. I crawl fast, away from him, out the side. I climb to my feet, but men are standing in my way, ten, twelve of them. I turn around. The man with the gloves crawls out from under the ring. I am trapped.

"I got him," says the man with the gloves. "Chase him this way."

The men walk toward me, arm in arm. They laugh. The man with the gloves jumps forward, his gloves are out to hold my horn away. He is bent at the waist. Grinning — sure of himself, of his great strength and my weakness. But this white man — like all white men — he has something to learn. I run at him, my head down. He gets ready to catch my horn, still grinning. But I stop before I reach him. I take one step to my left. I set my leg and then I throw a left hook, with all the strength of my body, hard and just behind his glove. A sack full of corn cobs. I hit him high on the cheek. My fist stings. The big man blinks, his eyes jump around in his head, and then he falls with a thud on his behind. I try to run over his body, but someone grabs my bathrobe. I pull away — too late. I am caught.

Three men are holding me on the floor. I struggle, kicking, butting with my horn. A strong arm squeezes under my throat, lifts my chin until the bones in my neck begin to crack. I choke.

I hear someone say, "Ohhhh . . . That little black bastard." It is
the man with gloves. He sits on the floor and someone is holding a
small, round thing under his nose. Every time he smells, the man's
head jerks backward. A hand touches my horn, and the hand is
gentle. It is the little, bald-headed man.

"Not so tight, Harry. You'll choke him." The little man steps
back. He puts his hands on his hips. Around him the men are
standing, talking about me.

"Left hook it was."

"Yeah. Lookit the mean little bugger. Wants to kill us all."

"Ssssh," says the little man. They stop talking. "Kid. Kid." He
bends over. I try to bite at him. "Cut it out, kid. Don't be crazy.
We ain't gonna hurt you." The little man has many wrinkles on his
face. His nose is pushed in so far I cannot see the nostrils. His left
eye is dead — white like an egg with no yolk.

"He ain't gonna talk, Barney. Maybe he can't."

"Shut up, all of you. The kid's scared — can't you see that?" The
little man bends over. "My name is Barney Koch. What's yours?"
I try to spit at him, but my throat is held too tight. "You can speak
English — I see you watchin' what we say. Come on now, tell us
your name."

I shake my head.

"Kid. You know, that's a heavyweight boxer you just knocked
out? A pretty good one. How old are you?"

"He ain't more'n fifteen, sixteen."

"Shut up, Charlie. Kid. Where'd you learn t'do that? Who
taught you? Nobody learns t'hit like that by himself." Mr. Koch,
he is smart. My great pride makes me speak. "Nobody teach me,"
I say very fast. "I teach myself, and I am only fourteen years this
month." Mr. Koch smiles.

"I'll be damned. Let's see those fists." I put my hands out. Mr.
Koch whistles. "Big. Big fists — and lookit those knuckles. Cal-
louses. How'd you get those?"

"I hit a bag with wood in it, all the day long."

"With wood — why'd you do that?" Mr. Koch cocks his head, and
his big, white eye looks at me but does not see. "You want to be a
boxer?"

I shrug my shoulders. "Don't know," I say.

"Well, I know. I think you should try. And, believe me, kid —
Barney Koch's been around this business for a long, long time. You
gonna tell me your name now?"

"George."

"How much do you weigh, George?" I shrug my shoulders. "Well
— it don't matter. We'll find out easy enough."

"Hey, Barney. You crazy or something? He can't fight — not with
that thing in his head. One butt, he'd split a guy's skull."

"Yeah."

"Pop an eye out."

"Get out of here, all of you." Mr. Koch is angry. He stamps his
foot. The men step back. "Let him up, you guys. Let him up and
clear out. Me an' George gotta talk." Mr. Koch comes close. "Kid,
you wanna be rich? I'll make you rich."

"Like Dr. Oddie make me rich?"

"Who's this Dr. Oddie guy?"

"A man — he talk like you, but he don't make me rich."

"No? Well, I will. We will. You're a natural, kid. That horn —
well, so maybe there's some problems, but we'll figure 'em out.
Seems to me, seems that horn might make you famous. Plenty
famous. Work hard and I'll see you're champ. Coupla years you'll
be — let's see — one-fifty, maybe one-fifty-five. Middleweight champion. How's that sound, George?"

"Mr. Koch. If I work hard — you bring my mother here?"

"Sure. Sure, kid. Just tell me where she is. I'll take care of everything. Come on in my office. Trust me, George. Trust me."

And so I go to Mr. Koch's office. Oh yes, he was right. I am
middleweight champion. I am a rich man. But no, I never trust
Mr. Koch . . .

I was praying when G'wain knocked, and the sharp raps
drove me forward onto my palms. With the approach of night,
some two hours before, a sorry trepidation had possessed me. I
recognized my cowardice for what it was; I named it before
God; in self-rebuke I called chastisement down on my own
wretched head. I now constantly remembered Meeker's words

and their threatening emphasis — pretty rough those rallies. Rallies? Rallies for what? Against what? In my hurry to be involved, I had failed to ascertain just what I had become involved in. Something reprehensible, perhaps even illegal. A black mass; a love-in; an opium orgy. Something that might require bravery or, worse yet, physical conditioning. As the evening progressed, I began to examine my fists doubtfully. Now and then I struck a cautious blow at soft, unresisting things — pillows, chair arms, my own shadow. I was still determined to attend, but my final prayer had been for a colorless and unchallenged anonymity.

G'wain was wearing regulation issue earmuffs — a matching phosphorescent blue. A cluster of special ribbons was pinned just under the heart of his tabard. He grinned when he saw me: he had anticipated my present fear and the expression on my face, I thought, had not disappointed him; G'wain looked forward with interest to my discomfiture. I wanted to question him, but I had already encountered the reticence of those in the Horn Movement. G'wain bowed with convincing deference.

"Ready, Father?"

"Just have t'lock the door."

"Take your coat. 'S chilly out."

I pulled on my overcoat and untangled a dark scarf from the rack. I buttoned all but the very top button so that my collar, my badge of an impartial harmlessness, was clearly visible. G'wain whistled as we walked down the alley. Isometrics, I wondered, was it too late for them? I slapped a gloved fist into a gloved palm. My glasses danced on the bridge of my nose, and I was hard pressed to save them from falling off. Too late . . .

When we reached the street, I looked to left and right fearfully, but no golden-horned motorcycles were in evidence.

G'wain pointed. A battered, red laundry truck was double-parked near the alley's mouth. My guide took me by the elbow and led me around to the truck's rear. He unlatched the double doors. Then he gave me a helpful boost up. I entered with some hesitation.

"Why this?" I asked, as G'wain prepared to close the doors behind me.

"No offense, Father. Where we goin', some cats don't care for white men."

"Oh," I said. The doors slammed in emphasis.

A faint light glimmered through two small, barred windows in the double door. The truck was not merely a front: by the scant illumination, I made out several very genuine laundry bags. I sat down on one. The floor was cold; a chilly breeze settled in my pants leg just below the shin. I looked at my watch and, at just that moment, G'wain started the truck with a wrenching jerk. I was poorly prepared. The bag rolled toward the truck's rear, running up, over the backs of my calves. I fell heavily and slid about a yard on my chest. For a long moment I lay, painfully winded, my legs pinned by the laundry bag. G'wain stopped short. The bag rolled into the darkness.

G'wain began making erratic turns. I stood and I held to a window bar, swaying, breathing heavily. My coat front was filthy. A blob of grease lay in the middle of my gloved palm — I tried to keep the glove away from my coat. In the darkness laundry bags rolled against each other with solid, ominous thuds. A warning horn shrieked. G'wain came to a violent halt. The engine was cut off.

My heart began to pump brutally. I peered through the dirty window. The street was deserted; no crowds, no preparations were apparent. I stood back, but the truck doors did not open. Five minutes passed. I sat again, my feet alerted. I heard cars going by; then high, adolescent voices. Flattened hands slapped with resonance at the truck's side. My stomach whined; the mechanism of my colitis was unlimbering itself. Voices. Then footsteps. The doors opened. I stood up, hitching my pants on my hips.

"Got company for you. Ooops. Up we go," said G'wain as he handed a small, agile figure into the truck. The doors slammed shut.

"Hello," said the figure. The first syllable was stressed and its vowel slightly lengthened; an Eastern European, I thought. "Hello," I replied. Steel-rimmed glasses glinted faintly — round empty circles. The man was white and, I judged, about sixty years old; he wore a short, square beard. The cab door slammed. The starter whirred, then caught. The old man sat on a laundry bag next to mine. I braced my feet, but, even so, I had difficulty balancing when the truck lurched forward. My companion, however, took the jolt easily, as though he had long experience of dark trucks and laundry bags.

"Name is Pratt," I said. "Rector of St. Bartholomew's Church — here in Harlem." I stuck out my hand. Three soft fingers curled daintily around it.

"So. I am H. P. Krushinsky. Professor of sociology. City College."

"This — " The truck swerved; I was temporarily silenced by my own frantic gymnastics. H. P. Krushinsky removed his handkerchief, blew his nose daintily, and replaced his handkerchief, without once being inconvenienced by the truck's motion. "Wow," I said. "Some trip. Exciting, isn't it?"

"Exciting?"

"For me anyway. Have you — I mean this isn't your first time, is it?"

"Oh, no. Not my first time." He chuckled in a languorous, sad manner. "Is it yours?"

"Well . . ." I said, suddenly abashed. "Yes, it is." G'wain chose that moment to negotiate an unending turn — a U-turn, I think. I struggled as long as I could, then I toppled, grunting, into Professor Krushinsky's lap. "Sorry. Sorry." I said. An oppressive odor of tobacco and rich cologne distressed my nostrils.

"That's all right," said Professor Krushinsky. He helped me, rather firmly, to regain my seat. Then he began brushing at his coat front, as though contact with my body had left unsavory traces. I reiterated my apology; he demurred again. With quick, irritable movements, he extracted a small object from his trouser pocket. Nail clippers. Professor Krushinsky began arranging his cuticles.

"Excuse me," I said after a moment.

"Yes, my friend?" Krushinsky held his thumb at eye level, but the light was insufficient for his purposes.

"Ah . . . What — what will it be like?" He laughed.

"The rally?"

"Yes."

"Well. Our friends will be very angry. You must expect that. They will shake their fists and growl at us. They will throw things — soft, juicy things. You won't be frightened, will you?" His tone was condescending. "It's a game — a learning game. When they train a bull for the ring, you know — train him to kill — then they sometimes use dummies covered in red cloth. The bull sees red. He charges. He gores the dummy. That's what we are, my friend. Dummies in red cloth."

"Teaching them to kill?"

"Yes. I think so."

"But, in the ring — it's the bull that gets killed."

"True, my friend. In the ring. But the bulls are not organized. One at a time — yes, of course they get killed. Here we have not one bull, not two — thousands and thousands of bulls. A bull fight? No, a great stampede."

"I don't understand — at least I hope I don't understand."

"Yes. I hope so too. In fact, we are counting on it." I sensed that he was smiling, though, in the darkness, his nose and lower face were not visible. "The matador never understands. He is trained like the bull. It is a ritual, you know. But now there is time for new rituals. A seam splits here. A seam splits there. Rip. Rip. Rip. In time the whole rotten fabric falls to pieces."

"What fabric?"

He almost snarled. "What fabric do you think?" The truck came to a halt. "Ah," said Professor Krushinsky. "That will be Zeitzoff."

The doors opened and a huge, heavy-boned man climbed, without assistance, into the laundry truck. He wore a handle-bar mustache and one of those black wool hats. His hair was dark and very curly — the sort that is pervasive, that appears on insteps and wrist bones and inside ear holes. Despite the disparity in their heights, Zeitzoff and Krushinsky embraced with great enthusiasm. Zeitzoff planted a kiss beside each of the other man's ears. When Krushinsky sat, Zeitzoff, disdaining laundry bags, knelt eagerly at his feet.

"Did you speak to Purston? What did he say? Will he do it?"

"Easy, Max," said Krushinsky. "We have company." He nodded toward me.

"So," said Zeitzoff, "I didn't see."

"This is Mr. Pratt — or is it Father Pratt? Father Pratt, I think. This is his first rally."

"So," said Zeitzoff. We shook hands. "So. There must always be a first time."

"Uh — yes. I'm quite nervous actually. Don't know what to expect."

"So," said Zeitzoff. "So. Listen, my friend. Will you excuse my impoliteness? I must speak to Professor Krushinsky. Personal matters."

"Sure. Go ahead. Don't mind me."

But Zeitzoff did not wait for my permission. He commenced speaking at once in a thick, Slavic tongue. Occasional words, names like Smith and Purston and Mody, remained in English, but the rest was unintelligible. Zeitzoff did most of the speaking, and yet he appeared, in all matters, to defer to Krushinsky's judgment. The truck jounced forward. I looked at my watch, but I was too nervous, just then, to see or to comprehend the time. My intestines sputtered. My nose began to run in tiny spurts. What, I wondered, had Krushinsky meant by soft, juicy things? The truck came to a sudden stop. I heard the cab door open. Zeitzoff and Krushinsky stood.

"So. We are here," said Zeitzoff. "You will forgive our bad manners, Father Pratt."

"Don't mention it," I said. "Not at all."

The doors opened. Zeitzoff leaped down. Krushinsky stood at the edge of the platform, presenting his bent elbows like a surgeon who has just scrubbed. Zeitzoff reached up, cupped the older man's elbows in his immense hands, and then lifted him easily down to the street. I saw, in those presented elbows, many other such truck platforms, many other such rallies. Zeitzoff did not offer any further assistance; I, for my part, was determined to prove myself competent in these matters. I inhaled, swung my arms several times at my sides and then leaped. I hit squarely on my heels; my ankles seemed to telescope with the shock. I waddled, with an enforced bowleggedness, toward the sidewalk.

G'wain had parked near the stage entrance of what appeared to be a large theater. To the left, a naked, red bulb marked the stage door. In a widened alley that stretched back twenty feet to a high truck-loading dock, tabarded men were coming and going with chairs and ladders, platforms and bits of lighting equipment. Horn Greens wearing the black pointed-circle of the special police stood to the left and the right, barring the sidewalk to normal traffic; there were one or two as well on the dark network of fire escapes that lined the walls. The preparations were going forward, despite the considerable number of men, in an oddly determined silence. Zeitzoff and Krushinsky had already reached the stage entrance. G'wain held the door open as I approached it.

"*Nos morituri te salutamus,*" I said as I passed him. G'wain grinned and bowed, unperturbed by what must have seemed gibberish to him.

I followed my companions down a long corridor, illuminated by one or two red bulbs and perilously cluttered with a theater's functional equipment: fire hoses and axes, pails filled with sand, rostra, spotlights and coils of rope. The corridor opened suddenly on the spacious stage left wing of the auditorium. Zeitzoff and Krushinsky hung their outer garments on one of several skeletal costumers. A round table with a coffee urn and piles of paper cups stood near the wall. A female Horn Orange waited nearby. It was after eight, but the rally appeared to be still some minutes from its beginning. Between two curtain walls I could see a podium and a microphone and, behind these, about twenty chairs. The auditorium was nearly three-quarters filled and here, too, the silence seemed incongruous. Men and women sat quietly, coats in laps; there was little conversation. Horn Greens patrolled the aisles, hands clasped behind backs, faces impassive. I hung up my coat and sat a respectful few feet behind Krushinsky and Zeitzoff.

Krushinsky touched Zeitzoff lightly on the shoulder; the latter turned. A tall Negro had just entered through the corridor. Two men, Horn Greens, were taking his coat. He wore no tabard, just a very well-cut black suit with a large, blue pointed-circle pinned over the vest pocket. As soon as his presence became known, men approached from all parts of the auditorium. They gathered around, asking questions, gesturing, interrupting each other.

"Is that — ?" I made a gesture. The name had eluded me.

"Yes," said Zeitzoff. "That's Aylbrous Purston. A great man. The greatest man in Harlem."

"The greatest?"

"Yes, my friend. Time will tell — you mark my words. Aylbrous and his brother — G'wain there — someday they will be famous." I sat back. I put my hand to my forehead and stared, with clandestine interest, at this man, Aylbrous Purston.

He looked very much like G'wain — taller, heavier, perhaps broader in the shoulders. He would have been handsome but for his mouth: the lips were thick and his teeth, which protruded slightly, seemed to chew the air as he spoke. A scar ran from his hairline through the right eyebrow, to a point on the crest of his cheekbone. It seemed an old scar, but the instrument that caused it, I knew, had gone right to the bone. In his right earlobe there was an unadorned, gold earring. He seemed never to communicate directly — talking above people, through people, making little, oddly prim gestures with his fingers. G'wain stood behind his brother, arms folded across his chest. After a few moments Krushinsky rose and joined the small knot of Horn Blues. When he spoke, he was treated to no more apparent attention: Purston looked at his watch, wound it, said something to his brother and then, without ceremony, left Krushinsky where he was standing. Krushinsky dropped his hands to his sides. He shrugged.

Three other white men had arrived. They were standing against the far wall, each with his hands in his trouser pockets: a short, blond man with a severe crew cut; a short, wiry man with no upper teeth; a man with olive skin and Eurasian eyes. They stood shoulder to shoulder, within inches of each other; too close, I thought, to be total strangers. And yet, during the few minutes that I watched them, there was no conversational interchange, not one acknowledging glance. They stared ahead, their gazes fixed on exactly parallel lines. Two Horn Greens paused in front of the wall, a long extension ladder borne, at shoulder height, between them. And at that moment, each of those three staring heads appeared, decapitated, in its wooden frame, like so many ancestral portraits on a wall.

I rubbed the balls of my fingers together, then I pressed them until the fingernails whitened. I gasped. The hot needle of a cramp had begun stitching, drawing tight, within my abdomen. My intestinal piping bubbled like a chemist's boiling retort. I looked quickly for the men's room. G'wain Purston appeared at the coffee urn. I waited for the pain to achieve its cyclical ebb. Then I rose, pinched at the waist, and stepped hurriedly toward him.

"G'wain. Got a little trouble here. Where — where's the men's room?"

"C'mon," he said, grinning. "I'm goin' that way myself." G'wain picked up his coffee cup and led me to the right, down a narrow passage that ran along the auditorium's outer wall.

"I — uh. Damn cramps." I gasped. "Say," I said, "didn't know you were Aylbrous Purston's brother."

"Sure. Me'n Ayl been brothers for years. In here." He pushed open a door marked WOMEN. "Yo? Anybody in there?" No one answered. "Men's room just got flooded out."

"Oh," I said. Then I slumped, hands at my stomach, against the wall.

"Nothin' serious, huh?" G'wain stepped over to the sink; he poured half of his coffee down the drain.

"No. Don't think so. I've had it for weeks. Comes . . . and . . . goes . . . Oh, boy." I straightened up.

"Here," he said. "This'll do the trick." He reached in, under his tabard and removed a silver flask. He unscrewed the jigger top and filled it.

"Thanks," I said. I swallowed hastily. The strident liquid opened my sinuses and brought moisture to the corners of my eyes. "Counter-irritant. Wow!" I grimaced. G'wain filled his coffee cup to the brim. Then he sat, sidesaddle, on the sink's edge.

"Horn Smith don't want us Blues drinkin' — not in public, anyhow. Man, don't he ever have pussy cat ideas."

"Strange man. Won't even drink coffee." The pain subsided. I stood on tiptoe and lapped my fingers over the edge of a toilet cubicle. Then I hung there, extending my body.

"Y'met him?"

"Twice — only by chance. Quite an experience. Both times."

"Smith's got something." G'wain sipped at his cup. He seemed unenthusiastic. "I mean, people like him. He's a great boxer. Honest, too — I don't take nothin' away from him. And the horn — that's a real weird thing. Stands out. Helps with publicity an' all. But Smith ain't nobody without Ayl Purston. Ayl works mostly in the back, but it's him has the friends. An' Ayl's got experience — I mean, he makes Horn Smith look like an amateur."

"What kind of experience?" G'wain shrugged.

"Experience. Ayl's a few years older'n me — he's been around. Mmmmm." G'wain drained his cup. He refilled it at once. "I figured you knew Horn. Last man in St. Bart's give me a real hard time."

"How so?"

"Oh, man — Pierre was his name. He thinks he's God Almighty. He don't want t'get 'involved' in the movement. Won't come to no damn rallies. A real piss cutter."

"Why?"

"That cat — man, I try t'talk nice, but he tells me — " G'wain made a mimicking fist, " 'Get the hell outa my rectory and don't you never come near it again.' He thinks we got the wrong kinda people here, in the movement."

"Like Krushinsky and Zeitzoff?"

"Maybe."

"Are they Communists?"

"I don't know, man. I don't ask. They're Ayl's friends an' they seem pretty harmless t'me." He leaned forward, pointing. "But take some advice from a real nice guy. That's me. Don't get too particular. Mr. Pierre, he got no place fast — he opened his big yap just once too many times. Play a little ball an' you'll get along fine. Hell, it ain't no skin off your back." G'wain got down from the sink. "Okay. I leave you t'your privates. We start in ten minutes or so, probably more like fifteen." He took a last swig, threw the cup in the wastecan and left me.

When I returned from the men's room, eight white men and eight Negroes were standing in a line stage left, white and Negro spaced alternately. G'wain waved to me.

"Man, hurry. What took you so long?"

"I — it was more serious than I thought."

"Okay. Okay." He brought me to the front of the line. "When I say go — you lead these guys out. Go sit in that chair, the one way over on the end." G'wain looked back over his shoulder. A few seconds elapsed. I felt a pressure at the round dents on both sides of my temples. My vision unfocused: in the semi-darkness I saw, or thought I saw, great finger smudges on my eyeglass lenses. I took my glasses off. The house lights dimmed. I put my glasses on again. Something very like panic caused an itching tickle in my throat. I sucked my mouth in, rubbing the rough parts of my tongue against the roof of my mouth. G'wain tapped me on the shoulder. I hesitated. The man behind, a Negro, gave me a firm, painful push in the small of my back.

"Go," whispered G'wain. "Go." We walked out onto the stage.

I watched only my kneecaps as I stepped across that long platform. I suppose, with my chin nestled against my chest, I must have seemed the first figure in some tableau of contrition. A vise gripped my head, my neck, the axis of my vision. At first our entrance elicited little or no response. But, as I passed the center line, a low, sickening boo rose up — born of single, inciting boos, growing in geometric progression until the sound became so overwhelming that it appeared to produce echoes in all things — in the curtains, in my ears, in the air itself. "Good grief," I thought. "What, in God's name, am I doing in this place?" I reached the designated chair. I sat, the circumference of my vision still restricted. And then a resounding, harsh cheer arose, the inverse, it seemed, of the booing we had undergone. Aylbrous Purston was on stage.

I looked up. Purston had neared the podium. I realized then that I, alone, had presumed to sit. My fifteen companions were standing, now at almost military attention. I jumped to my feet. Purston looked from left to right. He bent at the knees and bellowed "Hoooorn!" pushing the word up, high into the old I-beam rafters of the auditorium. "Hooorn!" the crowd answered. Everyone brought their right hands high in front of their foreheads — in the dreadful "Heil Hitler" salute. But, at the final moment, the fingers of each hand angled sharply forward to form a symbolic Horn. I looked to my left, my right hand abridging the gesture as I did so. All my companions stood rigid. Their hands affirmed the Horn salute. And, in the very last, left seat, more rigid than the others, his right hand more palpably a miniature horn, there stood the Reverend John Meeker.

Purston turned, nodded. Everyone sat. Meeker looked behind him, an intent, joyous expression on his face. He recognized me just as his buttocks encountered the chair seat. I heard the short, hard explosion of his breath. Meeker stood quickly, half-crouching. I inclined my head. I smiled. And then, quite incredibly, Meeker began moving across the long platform toward me. His lips sketched words: words of one, brittle syllable. I waved him back. He continued to come, crabwise, his fists balled near his knees. A vigorous shout went up. Meeker hesitated, remembering then where we were. He paused. After a moment's deliberation, he backed reluctantly. He found the chair seat without once taking his eyes from my person.

"Do we hate white men?" screamed Purston.

"Yeeees!" roared the crowd.

"Do we want their segregation?"

"Noooo!" roared the crowd.

"Do we want their integration?"

"Noooo!" roared the crowd.

"Do we want our own?"

"Yeeees!" roared the crowd.

"Will we get it?"

"Yeeees!" roared the crowd. "Yes! Yes! Yes!"

Feet stamped rhythmically; hands were slapped against chair

backs. The platform quivered beneath us. Eight hundred-odd faces stared up in ecstatic hatred — stared up at dummies in red cloth. Directly in front of me, just beyond the stage apron, a young man of twenty stood, his eyes huge and tranced. He had singled me out. When Purston called, he would pound his fists, then shake a long forefinger at me. He did not answer yes or no with the others. He threatened me personally and, though the words were lost, I could read their import on his lips. "Get you. Get you. Get you." Saliva ran down his chin, spattered out against the lights. I thought, I hoped, he might be drunk. I wanted to ignore him, but there was a dreadful fascination in his bitterness. And I wondered — Can it be? Can any man hate me, C. B. Pratt of quiet Greensprings, with such unmitigated fury? Can I, so perfectly harmless, have caused a murderous rancor in this man? In a man I have never seen before? I didn't know. But the question itself, so reinforced, was bewildering.

"Are we through, brothers — through getting the dirty end of every dirty stick?"

"Yeeees!" answered the crowd.

"If the American people don't get wise — and don't get wise quick — will we teach them a lesson they'll never forget?"

"Yeeees!" answered the crowd.

"Will we fight their wars?"

"Noooo!" answered the crowd.

"Will we pay their taxes?"

"Nooo!" roared the crowd.

"Will we obey the white man's laws?"

"Nooooo! No! No!" roared the crowd.

Purston's fist came down on the lectern's edge; the thuds, amplified and distorted by the quivering microphone, lent a rhythmic accompaniment to the "No! No! No!" of the mob.

I stared down at my shoe tongues in despair. I knew. I knew the time had come. Had I been more a man I should, long before, have left the auditorium. But I could not rise. Horn Greens continued to patrol the aisles, ominous, goading in their silence. No one there, I knew, would dare rebuke Aylbrous Purston's demagogy. The young man in front of me had stretched his entire torso over the apron's rim. In a lull I could hear his threatening snarl. "Look at me, Whitey. Look at me, you stinkin' bastard. Honky. Honky. Honky." My fingers gripped the edges of the metal chair seat. I prayed. And Aylbrous Purston pursued his dreadful litany.

"If our people are beaten, will we strike back?"

"Yeeeees!"

"If our houses are burned, will we burn?"

"Yeeeees!"

"If our men are killed, will we kill?"

"Yeeeees!"

"Does the black man want power?"

"Yeeeees!"

"What kind of power?"

"Hoooooorn Power! Hoooooorn Power!" The gestapo salute was repeated. A seemingly spontaneous chant commenced, "Horn! Horn! Horn! Horn! Horn!" Bodies swayed in the aisles. Feet stamped. Hands clapped. A baseball was thrown up, onto the stage. The Eurasian-eyed man ducked, and the ball hit the far rear wall. It rolled harmlessly back between my legs.

The rally, meanwhile, had progressed to a further stage. Purston turned away. Max Zeitzoff rose and walked toward the podium. The crowd began to boo, but, at a signal from the Horn Greens, they became uniformly silent. Zeitzoff stood before the lectern, not speaking, his head bowed. A huge wrist

bone bulged beneath his cuff and I could see the black, matted
hair that covered his hand from knuckles to wrist. His suit was
creased: the jacket seemed too small; the pants too large even
for his long legs. One cuff had become lodged between shoe
and ankle. Zeitzoff sighed. He began to speak. His voice, at
first, was almost inaudible, as though constrained by emotion.
Then it rose, becoming shrill and very high, belying the
breadth of his massive chest.

"I am ashamed — ashamed to be a white man." His fingers
tightened on the lectern. Below, his knees bent and straightened, bent and straightened, as deliberately, carefully, he accelerated the rhythms of his speech. "To a man — to a man we
are despicable in our hypocrisy. Animals in our brutality. Corrupt in our selfishness. Obscene in our lusts. Inhuman — oh,
God above — we are inhuman in our tyranny. We — " His
right hand groped for a phrase of sufficient hyperbole. "We are
the scum of the earth. The lowest of all created things. If we
do not persecute you with our hands, we ignore your suffering
in our hearts. We are accomplices to murder, to oppression,
every day and night of our lives. But we will learn. The time
of dread reckoning is near. We will learn and that learning,
yes — yes, it will be a terrible thing. The white man will fall
— will fall — will fall — until his mouth is in the dirt, and his
pride is crushed by the black man's almighty greatness."

My fingers entered my right-hand trouser pocket. Once
there, they began pinching the skin of my thigh. I listened to
those pinches as though the pain were supremely audible, as
though it might outscream Zeitzoff's oratory. Faces glistened
with approval. Voices answered in surly threatening that was,
simultaneously, an affirmation. And Zeitzoff proceeded, without embarrassment, from one intemperate assertion to another.
He compared the Negro to the Jew in Hitler's Germany. In

obscene detail, he described the concentration camp atrocities. He named parts of the body that were burned, amputated, skewered, ripped open. Then he paused. He raised his fist. He brought it down with an impact that made the entire P.A. system sputter and shriek.

"And I am the worst," he shouted. "For I — I am myself a Jew."

An anonymous voice responded. "Dirty Jew! Jews are the worst!" And the crowd chorused its agreement. "Yeah! Yeah! Yeah! Kill the dirty Jew!" Two eggs sailed through the air. One struck Zeitzoff's lapel and exploded there like some grotesque boutonniere. Zeitzoff pushed his fingers into the goo. He spread it, in apparent ecstasy, over his jacket front.

"Thank you," he said. "Thank you. I know how you feel. We are the worst. We are — for we should know, more than any other people, we should know what it is to be choked and oppressed and ground under. Thank You!" He bowed his head again.

I averted my face in an impotent protest. Then I gasped. In turning, my eyes had met Aylbrous Purston's eyes. He was sitting to my left, legs crossed, and, all that while I knew, he had been observing me, appraising my discontent. My head began to twitch: uncertain whether to meet his gaze or to turn away. Purston licked his lips and his teeth appeared for one second. The single word "carnivorous" presented itself to my consciousness. Purston nodded, signaling, in that gesture, that my disapproval had not gone unnoticed. Zeitzoff returned to his chair. Purston stood. He walked to the lectern. "Oh God," I thought. "He's going to bring me up there." I exhaled and doubted, suddenly, the reflexive mechanism of my breathing. I choked as I struggled to control my lungs. But Purston did not do it. He knew what would happen. It was too soon, just then, to release the bulls.

The rally went on. It went on for nearly two hours. Voices became hoarse. Legs wavered. Men fainted and their limp forms were removed by paired, impassive Horn Greens. And yet the mob's vitality did not wane. If anything, exhaustion merely compounded the tranced, ecstatic stupor. The responses were more enthusiastic, not less. Single men seemed to be speaking from communal mouths. Three or four would throw arms over shoulders, their bodies and lungs would go into spasm, stiffen, erupt in shouts — like several cells coming together to form a single, more efficient organ. For myself, however, there was only a perdurable boredom, which, in time, blunted my fear, my anger, my humiliation. My ears no longer registered the shouting; the drums had become insensitive, skinned over with a dull, echoing roar. I stared at my hands and traveled slowly, as though in a tiny vehicle, over the lined roadways of my palms. It was all so barren, so predictable, so without taste or meaning. And yet not purposeless. For there was achieved, in this tumultuous, methodical uniformity, a stifling of reason and dissent; an unquestioned acceptance; another triumph in a series of triumphs for Aylbrous Purston.

Stage left someone yelled "Go!" at the apex of a sudden, explosive chant. The dummies were hurried out. I was last in line and, as I trotted down the long corridor, G'wain tossed me my coat and scarf, for I had abandoned them rather than delay my escape. G'wain ran behind, his opened palm urging at the small of my back.

"Get a move on, man. Pick 'em up. Some that crowd get 'round back — ain't nobody gonna help you."

Several trucks had backed into the loading alley. Horn Greens, armed, stood at either side, helping the white demonstrators in. A furniture truck began to pull out as I rushed down the short flights of steps. I saw Krushinsky and Zeitzoff, the one being boosted up, the other already seated on a fat laundry bag. Fumes erupted from each truck's exhaust. I had started to run, when a figure appeared to my right, in the blurred periphery of my vision. I sensed no menace in his approach, for his face was that of a white man. But as I attempted to rush past, the figure inserted itself quickly into my line of flight. I slowed; I stepped uncertainly aside. And then this white man hit me a terrific, numbing blow on the mouth. My glasses jumped off my face. My vision doubled, quadrupled, failed and then became unnaturally clear. It was Meeker.

"You fuckin' Jew bastard," he screamed. "I'm gonna kill you. I'm gonna break your neck."

He moved toward me, his fists held low, his legs wide apart. I dropped my coat and brought my palms up to my shattered mouth. Pain had overpowered numbness. I opened my mouth, moaning, and felt a front tooth pop free from a hole in my lower lip. Meeker was a breathing shadow above, around me. He swung left, right and his fists caught me at the belt buckle and in the solar plexus. I collapsed, my kneecaps painfully wounded in their impact against the rough pavement. Meeker grabbed me by the lapels. He lifted me to my feet. I tried to speak, to plead, and a huge wad of blood leaped out, spattering Meeker's forehead.

"You took them away. You took them away from me. Jew! Jew! Dirty, stinkin' Jew!" As he hissed these senseless, ethnic insults, his lips touching my lips, Meeker was forcing me back across the alley. His hands on my lapels became strangling hands. I scratched desperately at his locked fingers. Meeker pushed me away from his body. Then he kicked me squarely, ruthlessly in the testicles. And when my body folded, he brought his knee up, into my stomach. The breath heaved out of my body and then it would not return. The atmosphere became as thick, as unmanageable, as water. My hands clutched at the air, as though, by their means, I might feed my starving lungs. I fell on my hip. The pains from my groin settled high at my kidneys. I rolled from side to side. I bit crazily at the cement.

Meeker's legs straddled my body. And then he shrieked; it was a shout of joyous pain, placed high in the vocal register. I felt his body drop heavily onto mine. His fists began to hit, short, hard blows, at the back of my head. I tried to pin his arms. We rolled over and over, and, above us, a crowd of black, leering faces closed in. Bets were placed. Facetious encouragements shouted. I cried out for assistance. I pleaded, but no one offered me help. I will never know how I bore that excruciating pain. And Meeker, cursing, sobbing, mumbling; pummeling with his fists, striking at my groin with his knee, gnawing near my collarbone with his teeth. In desperation my hands closed on his throat. Momentarily Meeker's face rose up before my face. It was bloated and furious, the teeth snapping. Meeker was insane, with an insane man's determination, and I knew that I was lost. My body went limp. I prayed without coherence. I acknowledged the imminence of my end.

I did not die. They pulled us apart before Meeker could quite destroy me. I heard him sobbing, as they carried me, shoulder high, to the laundry truck. The crowd was ecstatic, inarticulate in their joy. They howled; they laughed; they gibbered. The mad matadors had gored themselves; it had been a glorious spectacle. Blood choked my nostrils. One eardrum, apparently, had burst. I swallowed and, in horror, felt a tooth loose on my tongue. Zeitzoff leaned down, helped to draw me into the truck. As the doors slammed, I could hear Meeker screaming in the fullness of his voice.

"I showed him! I showed the dirty Jew! I can handle myself! Don't nobody tangle with me!"

In the emergency room six stitches were sewn under my left eye; three where chin becomes lower lip. Large bits of gauze rushed to scarlet on merest contact with my face. Rivulets bubbled over my knuckles, became tacky, then crusted and almost purple among the hairs of my wrist. Pains arrived, departed; played contrapuntally. My eye sockets ached of harsh extrusion — I recalled pimentos forcibly squeezed from green olives. Every rib was as familiar to me as the individual bars in a xylophone, each with its distinctive tone of pain. Even my earlobe, unfeeling flesh excrescence, throbbed so insistently that I was constrained, again and again, to comfort it between bloody fingertips. I began to fear that the Reverend John Meeker had done me serious hurt. Internal, I thought, repeating that dreadful word. Internal injuries . . .

But my blood impressed no one else. G'wain, whose conduct was otherwise unexceptionable, suppressed sharp giggles throughout. The intern, a young, darkish Puerto Rican seemed on the verge either of boredom or of sleep. He yawned at least as often as I groaned, and applied his needle rather as a drunken seamstress might, encouraging his fingers in muttered Spanish. It was the first time my skin had been stitched and, frankly, I was terrified. I opened my mouth at the onset and droned "aaaaah" thenceforth in an unremitting monotone. My body rose into the air with the needle's upward thrust; cowered as it pressed downward through my skin. My eyes crossed while its sharp point lingered close to my left cornea. When he was finished, the intern said, "Get up, please. Get out of the chair," several times before I had comprehended. There were other faces yet to stitch; I had received my share of his busy compassion.

I rode home with G'wain, slumped against his shoulder in the laundry truck cab. When we reached the rectory, he half carried me down the alley and then, with surprising gentleness, helped me to remove my blood-sodden clothes. I was very grateful. I sipped at the whisky flask while G'wain spoke enthusiastically of other rallies — "real big" ones — that were to come. I hadn't the strength to protest. "Sorry, Father," he said finally. "Real sorry. But you'll be all right — you see." He turned off the bedroom light. "Sleep tight," he said and then he was gone.

I slept tightly enough. When I awoke, however, it appeared as though all Christ's miracles, applied in concert, would be insufficient to mend the parts of my body that were halt, lame, blind or totally paralyzed. My left eye was closed behind the pierced, swollen mound of my cheek. My right eye would not focus properly; the ceiling seemed on hydraulics, rising and falling like a gigantic but very undecided Spanish torture bed. I lay perfectly inert for several minutes. Then, gingerly, I plucked my blankets off and let them drop to the floor beside my bed. My knee joints would not answer the reiterated command of my nervous system. I began rolling from side to side, accumulating momentum, until finally I hurdled the mattress edge. I landed on my left hip. The shock, cushioned even as it was by the blankets, caused my vertebrae to jerk painfully, one against the other, like a long freight train starting.

My forehead, as I stood erect, seemed to pass through the ceiling. Nausea swirled in a small, tight eddy below my ribs. I began to teeter sideways and my fingers, as they reached for the bedpost, gave way like pipe cleaners. My shins were black with blood. My big toenail had purpled. "Wash," I thought as, in distress, I remembered my mother's face and her firm advice: "A wash, Calvin, is good for soul and body." I tottered to the bathroom, down, through the dark, long tunnel of the hall.

I bent over the sink and then, tricked by long custom, stared up, into the mirror. This for my morale's sake, was a tactical error. The mirror, itself cracked and dull, seemed a congenial frame for my face. Practically considered, I had no left eye at all — a blackened pucker, a white bandage and a bit of thread, no more than that. My right eye, though still serviceable, had been blackened as well. Blood had dried in my hair; clumps stood stiffly like week-old spaghetti. My mouth was swollen; the lower lip was orange with the stain of disinfectant, and it protruded further, I think, than the tip of my considerable nose. My neck and throat were covered with broad scabbed scratches, where Meeker, in his insane rage, had not scrupled to use his fingernails.

I cupped water in my palm. By half-lowering my head, half-raising my hand, I managed to pour a few drops down my forehead. I gasped and, in this sudden opening of my mouth, saw that my lower front tooth had been broken off at its base. My upper front tooth, too, was chipped at a severe angle. I slapped the heel of my hand against the sink edge. "God. God. God." I mumbled. The prospect of dental work quite appalled me. I dropped the plug into the sink drain and allowed the basin slowly to fill. Then I pushed my lacerated face deep into the icy water. When I resurfaced, the water was faintly discolored — orange-purple, the tints swirled gently in thin streaks. Tufts of hair floated on the surface. I dabbed at my face with a towel. As I did so, I first heard a heavy knocking at my front door. The towel slipped from my fingers. "Meeker," I thought, "come to finish me." I took my bathrobe from a hook and draped it over my shoulders. Then I wrapped my fingers around the neck of a large cologne bottle. With this concealed inside the skirts of my robe, I stumbled toward the knocking.

It wasn't John Meeker. It was the police, a single detective looking very much, I thought, as detectives are deemed to look.

A trench coat, a high-peaked waterproof hat, a face lined and tanned even then, just after winter. He flashed a badge and I, rather confused by his gesture, flashed my bottle of cologne as a countersign.

"Yes?" I mumbled, meaning, if I could, to contain his advance at my threshold.

"Police," he said unnecessarily. "Investigating an assault. Reported at Heights Hospital last night, one a.m. You the victim?"

"No," I said. "I always look like this in the morning." My lower lip stung where it had been stitched, exacting quick revenge for this small flippancy. My one eye watered.

"Look, buddy," he said, hand upraised. "I try t'do my job, that's all. Now — I got some questions to ask. You wanna cooperate?"

"I haven't been uncooperative," I muttered, but he had already strode past me, removing his hat, sliding his coat loose on his shoulders. He made an interrogatory gesture with head and eyebrows. I pointed to the left, toward my office. He nodded and, with a terse wave, indicated that I should follow him. I did so. His large feet seemed to bounce whenever they touched the floor, as though there were an excess of resiliency in his legs. He stood a few inches under six feet, but enormous breadth of shoulder and length of arm lent his torso a massive rectangularity. He sat in my armchair and drew a thick notebook from his inside jacket pocket.

"Sit — hold your horses. I'll get done here soon as I can." He thumbed at the pages, recollecting. Then he said, "Uh-huh" with an ominous finality. "Right. Your name is Pratt. G. B. Pratt."

"C. B." I said.

"It says G. B. here," he muttered, staring at me through wary and half-closed lids. He ran his thumb over a flat, much-broken nose bridge.

"Nonetheless," I said. "It's C. B., Calvin Beecher — ohh." I fingered my lower lip tentatively.

"You're the priest here?"

I nodded.

"Okay," he said. "Now we want t'get the guy or guys who did this. Can you give a description?"

"I can," I said. "But — I don't mean to be uncooperative — I don't intend to." He slapped his notebook closed.

"Why is that?"

"It . . . A misunderstanding. A moment's anger. That's all — forget it."

"Son-of-a-bitch." He began nodding his head vigorously and for the benefit of some unseen audience to his right. "Son-of-a-bitch. You guys make me sick. I mean it. Sick. I get this all the time. How — how the hell can we protect you? Huh? Are you crazy? Y'let these stupid niggers walk all over you. It's no wonder. Buddy, you're as guilty as they are."

"You're wrong," I said. A spasm of pain contorted my neck and throat. I tried to support my head by placing several fingers just under my damaged left ear.

"I'm wrong? I'm wrong, he says. Look brother — I hear this shit every day of my life. Anybody'd cut you up like that — believe me, some day he's gonna kill someone. And you'll be to blame. You, my friend."

"Excuse me," I said. "Just a moment, please. It's hard for me to talk." I paused. "The man who did this — he was white."

"Oh, come on— cut the crap," he made a vicious slash with the edge of his left hand. "Can it, Father."

"It's true. He's a friend of mine — "

"Can it. Can the crap."

"I don't want to make trouble for him."

"God-damn stupid bastard." He laughed bitterly. I stood up.

"I — I don't think there's anything more we have to say."

"Sit," he said. I sat.

"Okay. We'll play games your way. Where were you last night?" He grinned meanly.

"Out. It's none of your business."

"No? Isn't it true — you were at the Rabazz Ballroom? On the platform?"

"Perhaps. Still it's none of your business."

"I happen to know it's true. I got it right here. There was no white man, buddy. No white man."

"There was." He stood up. He began to pace with deliberate slowness, backward and forward, in front of me. As he stepped, his face held a slight colloquy with itself, a colloquy rich with dramatic grimaces, sneers, nods of agreement. Finally, as I had anticipated, he halted very near to my chair.

"Sorry," he said in a contrite voice. "Sorry I used those lousy words, Father." I met his eyes.

"You'll use them again," I said sadly. "When this soft sell doesn't work." He laughed, but I knew he was disconcerted.

"Probably. Okay — you're no fool. But me — I'm no fool either. See. I know how it is. We're both white. We both gotta work in this jungle. We don't want enemies. Right?"

"It was a white man." His right hand darted out at my reply, but he only scratched his arm, mitigating the violent reflex.

"That your story, or theirs?"

"Mine. And it's no story."

"You're afraid. I can see that. Me — I'm scared, too. We're all scared. They wanna kill us, don't they? They say it all the time. Then they're gonna rule this country." He paused. "You remember Watts and Newark? Detroit? Philly, last summer. What d'you think — you want that kinda stuff here?" I shook my head. "No. Well, man, I tell you — there's only one way t'stop it. Get tough. Crack down. Turn the other cheek and they'll cut it off your face."

"But these riots — I mean the conditions here, in those other ghettos. You — you can almost understand."

"Not me. What's the matter — you one of those lovesick liberal guys?"

"No. Yes — I don't know."

"You're not. I can tell. You're too smart t'swallow that crap." He stood in front of me, his huge pectorals defined even under the bulging, wrinkled surface of his shirtfront. He drew out a pack of cigarettes, extracted one, offered it, then, at my refusal, placed it between his own lips. The flash of his lighter, reflected on the prism of my blurred vision, seemed a shimmering, lovely thing. He exhaled, and, as my attention was distracted by the spiraling smoke, he said,

"Was it Purston?"

"Who?"

"Did he give the order — Aylbrous Purston?"

"You're a mile off base. It was a white man. A friend of mine."

"Okay, Pratt. Let me level. I need your help. I — we want Purston. We want him bad. He's a killer and he's a Commie."

"It was — "

"Right. Right. Have it your way. But Purston was there — I know that. Nobody moves an inch until he gives the word. All you have t'do — " I raised my hand. Then I worked my swivel chair away from him.

"I'm tired," I said. "Dizzy. And I'm not doing anything. Not anything like that."

"Pratt, listen. You don't like me — okay. But listen. Summer's coming. There's gonna be a riot here. A riot t'end all riots. A massacre. Purston's going t'let them loose. This is it — D-Day. And brother, when it happens, Harlem's going up like a bomb. It won't be pretty. A lot of people — black people, white people — they're gonna get killed."

"I don't understand all this," I shook my head. "Horn Smith changed things — that's what they told me. I read it in the magazines. In newspapers. The *Times*. The crime rate is down. The police — is it true or isn't it — the regular police don't even come to Harlem any more."

"Yeah. It's true. It's true. He's changed things all right? You know how?" He stubbed out his cigarette. "He let Purston loose, that's how. These poor niggers, they're so scared, they don't dare piss. And they talk about police brutality — oh, God!" He laughed. "They're savages. Cannibals. You know those Horn Greens — the ones with the black badges — they're the gestapo. There's nothing, man, nothing they won't do. And there's nothing we can do t'stop them." He paused. "Last year we found a kid in Central Park. He's about seventeen, eighteen. He stole some equipment. But he wasn't smart, the gestapo got him. They took his fingers and they broke every one of them. Broke them here, at the knuckles, then they taped the kid's broken fingers straight back, like this, so they were touching his watch band. Just a couple of palms, with the fingers bent back like inside-out umbrellas. He was crazy with the pain."

"Good God above."

"It's true. Stick around. Keep your eyes and ears open. Me, I don't care. Let the savages eat themselves up, I say. But you asked — you wanted t'know how Horn Smith did it. How he brought law and order to Harlem. Well, friend, he did it the way I would. The only way. Like this." He closed his fist on an imaginary, yielding object. "Now they want quiet. In a couple of months — then it'll be different. Then they'll want a riot. An organized riot. And you can bet, friend, there won't be a man in Harlem who tells them no. They'll move south. They'll cross the line at 96th Street and they'll keep going until we stop them. We have our informers. We know. Right down Park Avenue. This time they'll have firepower. Bazookas, maybe. Machine guns. And when it's all over, then there'll be editorials in the papers about how we're guilty. How we've frustrated the poor, black bastards. How we should feel sorry and forgive. It makes me sick."

He was silent. Outside a dog barked and then yelped. I looked up. The detective had picked up his hat. He stood with it in his hand — it seemed ridiculously small against his broad chest — watching me.

"My name is Slater," he said. "If you think of anything — give me a ring."

"Yes," I said.

"Get out of here, Pratt," he said, almost whispering. "You're a misfit. You're going to get killed." He turned then, fixed his hat on his head and walked quickly out of my office.

The swivel chair creaked, shifting on the edges of an equilibrium. I remembered our hammock at Greensprings, and the two great silver birches it had been slung between. I went to sleep then, but my sleep was troubled. Slater, Purston, Meeker, each presented me with a special threatening. And then the hard, concussive blows of my beating, now exaggerated, soundless, slow; the pain was visual — memory, not sensation. I awoke coughing, and the noise of my coughing was explosive in the silent rectory. A roach hurried to the desk edge. It peered over, its feelers semaphored. Then it rushed down the desk's face and crossed to my knee. I struck out with my hand, making too sufficient contact. I heard the clear cracking of its hard shell. I sat up. I took out a piece of notepaper. "Dear Bishop Hawkes," I wrote.

I put my pen down. The letters I had written were erratic in their size, disordered in their placement; my stiff fingers seemed incapable then of any constant pressure. I brought my face close to the desk top, reading with one, short-sighted eye. I added the colon: each dot placed with the overnice precision of a distracted mind. It was a petulant gesture, self-harassing. Now I could not resign. Now I was, in truth, a minister — with a congregation and immense responsibilities.

I turned the page over, and then I began to outline a sermon censuring Aylbrous Purston and the Horn movement. Meeker will thank me, I thought, Sunday they'll be heading back uptown, back to St. Catharine's. "Certainly," I wrote. "Certainly we are guilty. All — the ignorers as well as the persecutors. But there is no redress in murder. No prosperity in hatred. No hope, no future, in threatening and brutality. Stop this. Reject those who recommend violence. Unless you would compound your misery, and join us, as well, in our terrible guilt — unless you would sin against Christ in the same degree as now you are sinned against — stop this. Stop before it's too late." I panted as I wrote, fearful of retribution even in my solitude. And when Nicholas Breakspeare came in, I hugged the page to the secrecy of my bosom.

"Holy Jesus Cow," he gasped. He put his pail down and came cautiously forward, his brow pursed, his chin swiveling from left to right. I waved him back; the scrutiny embarrassed me. "Cap, who did it? Horn Greens — was it them?"

"No," I said.

"No? I thought — I mean, you were up on the platform last night. I didn't think it was right. I told my wife. You don't belong in a place like that."

"Nicholas. You, too? You were there? You go to those hor-

ror shows?" He shrugged. "How could you?" He shrugged
again. "I — I don't understand. Ooooh . . ." I put my hand to
my mouth, but the contours of lip and chin were so grotesque,
so unfamiliar that I withdrew it again in revulsion.

"Look, Cap. You can't understand. Me — I'm a Horn
Orange. That gives me privileges. I got a family. I got responsibilities. Next year I'm up for promotion. They tell me t'go
scream and stomp my feet — man, I go. An' I scream real
loud and I stomp real hard." He scratched at his scalp, still
fascinated by my face. "You said something, huh? I knew you's
not happy up there. You said somethin' an' they laid into you
good. Huh? That how it happened?"

"No. You know me: I'm no crazy hero. Believe it or not — a
white man did this."

"A white man? Jesus, Cap — I hate to say, but you're a mess."

"Well — I was never a beauty. But I lost a tooth, too. That
really upsets me. I've got more than enough skin — but, just
so many teeth." I tried to stand, but my knees betrayed me at
a critical moment. I fell backward, toward the chair seat, and
the chair, skittish on its wheels, gave ground under me. I began to fall. Nicholas Breakspeare rushed across the room and
caught my sliding body by its armpits. He kicked the chair into
place with his foot. Then he lowered me carefully until my
buttocks were settled.

"You belong in bed, man. No place else."

"I suppose. My head's very bad now." The veins at my temples seemed twice their natural size, fat, pulsing.

"You taking anything?"

"Aspirin. And the doctor gave me a shot. That's the trouble,
I think — it's wearing off."

"Look. I got just the thing — some half grain codeine. Hold
on they're in my bag." He jogged out and returned with a

medicine bottle, a glass of orange juice and a strange device.

"Sip 'n see straw. Father Pierre had it in his drawer — been there for years. Looks pretty clean." He shook a tiny cylindrical pill into his hand. "Pop this in your mouth. Hold it." He placed the long straw end into the orange juice. A clown in a red and green suit had been superimposed on the contorted upper tubing of the straw. Like my own, his jolly grin was toothless in two places.

"I feel silly."

"Go on." I pushed the pill past my swollen lip. Then I inserted the straw. The yellow-orange liquid rushed up the clown's leg, through his abdomen, around a hoop-like device in his hand — it turned his eyes and left ear yellow-orange and then it passed into my mouth. I swallowed and the pill went down.

"Good idea," I said. I began sucking playfully. The color lingered in the clown's stomach, shot up to his eyes, retreated to the hoop, dropped to his kneecap. It went up smoothly, went up in jerks, rose and fell swiftly, crawled slowly around the hoop's circumference. I made bubbling noises in the glass. "Fun," I said.

"Yeah — my kids liked them. But I don't see 'em in the stores any more. Drink up. Then you're goin' t'bed."

"No," I said. "I will, but first we've got to talk."

"About what?"

"About the rally. About . . . about things. I'm very upset." Nicholas Breakspeare examined his fingernails critically. He found a piece of dead flesh in the corner of his right thumb's cuticle, and he scraped at it with his upper front teeth.

"Later, Cap. Some other time — you're a sick man."

"Now. I must. Please."

"I don't like this. That's the truth. I've got a family and

talk can make trouble for a man." He shook his head, but sat
obediently, nonetheless, in my armchair.

"You know, Nicholas," I said, "when I came to Harlem, I was
terribly excited by Horn Smith and his movement. Really enthusiastic. I'd read the *Autobiography*. I'd read magazine
stories. It seemed, I thought, that something was really being
done. For your people. By your people. Something good.
Something that portended a great, a unique future for the Negro. Now . . ." I sipped and the tooth-gapped clown winked at
me. "Now I'm not sure. That rally last night. That was madness, pure and simple. An irresponsible madness; a sick madness. And now you tell me you were there. All right — I'll accept your reasons. I saw those Horn Greens in the aisles. But
just tell me — do you believe what Purston says? Tell me. I
give you my word — I'll never repeat what you say."

Nicholas Breakspeare was silent. I put a handkerchief to my
lip. A little blood stain, in the shape of a head, roughly decapitated, had formed on the fabric. Nicholas Breakspeare leaned
down and played desultorily with the nap of my carpet. He
looked up. His face was distorted, as though the muscles of his
jaw and cheek had tightened in an unnatural manner.

"Yes," he said. "I believe it."

"Then you hate me?"

"No need t'get personal — we gotta work together."

"No. Get personal. Please. If you really hate me, say so. But
tell me first — is it because of my skin or because I've done
something that merits your hatred? I want to know. I — I'm
curious."

"All white men are alike." He shrugged. "Enemies."

"But I've never shown myself to be an enemy. I don't hate
you. I came here — oh, clumsily, stupidly — but I came here
to help."

"I don't need your help."

"No," I said. "You don't. I — we all — may have presumed too much. But good intentions aren't an enemy's intentions." He looked at me, then away. He began whistling nervously.

"Plenty white men hate me — because of this, because of my skin. That's all — because of my skin. I never was no enemy, either. But, brother, they hate me all the same." His voice became slightly shrill, uncontrolled. He tried to smile in contravention of his anger. The smile was aborted.

"Yes. I know that. I don't pretend it isn't true. But not all white men — "

"No," he said, suddenly furious. "You whites are different from us. You all are, the good guys and the bad guys. You'll never know what's goin' on in here — inside me — even if you cared. You're different. We're different. I don't understand you and you don't understand me. Sure, you pee like me, you eat like me, you bleed just like me. So what? That don't mean nothin'. My wife pees and she bleeds, but nobody's gonna say she ain't different. Look, Mr. Pratt, you're a good guy — far as I can tell. Fine. I sit here with you an' it looks like we're real buddy-buddy, real friends. But it ain't so. I ain't never gonna feel free, feel comfortable talkin' to a white man. I like my own kind — they're different, too, but not so bad different. Where's the sin? Man don't go crazy 'cause lions and tigers don't get along. Everybody sees they're different. Well I got stripes, Mr. Pratt, and you don't. And I ain't never gonna feel right with you. And you," he leaned forward, "you don't feel right with me, neither."

"I — I don't feel wrong."

"You don't feel right. Don't lie." He spread his palms in a gesture intended to suggest reasonableness and honesty. Then he winked. "Tell truth now. Ain't you sayin' it in your **mind?**

Ain't you sayin', 'My. My. He's a Negro and he's still a nice
guy. My. My. Isn't it nice? We can talk like equals.' I mean
— aren't you surprised like?" I shook my head.

"No," I said, but in truth, I had been thinking in terms
very much like those.

"Well, I am — and I always will be." He slapped his hands
together. "I'm surprised when it's easy talkin' to a white guy.
I look at him and I say — see, he ain't so bad. He's talkin'. He
don't insult me. Not yet. He don't seem t'hate me. Here we
are, talkin' like brothers. Yeah — but all the time, every minute — I'm thinkin' he's white and I'm black and something
just ain't Kosher. No sir."

He seemed upset by his own vehemence and, in the silence
that followed, he could not meet my eyes. I sighed, too
troubled just then to answer him. Nicholas stood. He bent to
retrieve his pail, but it was only a token movement. He sat
again. The long harangue had enervated him. He felt, despite his frankness, that these things should perhaps have been
left unsaid. He was afraid, I knew, that he had damaged our
friendship. I, too, was afraid and for the same reason. I had
come to like Nicholas Breakspeare.

"So," I said finally. "Then it's war. Kill the white man because he's different. Kill me." Nicholas shrugged. "Do you believe in that, too?"

"No," he said.

"I'm glad." There was no intended irony in my voice.

"No. That's Purston. He's got his own ideas — he's got his
own plans. I don't know — " his voice trailed off.

"Know what?"

"I don't know why Horn let him get so big. Murder. Riots.
I don't want no riots. It's the black man gets killed in them
riots — not the white man. I don't want t'get killed — Purs-

ton, he'd kill me, soon's he'd kill a white man. Soon's he'd kill
his mother."

"Then why — why follow him?"

"We got to. He's Smith's man and Smith's our only hope.
Things weren't like this back a few years ago. When Smith
started things. Y'should've been there. That's all I can say,
Mr. Pratt. It was magic. Then, see, we were just tryin' t'improve ourselves. By ourselves. The white man wasn't helpin'.
Oh, he thought he was. He thought," Nicholas spat into his
pail. "Money. Money. Money. Mind I ain't got nothin' against
money — but I sure as hell wasn't seein' none of them billion
dollar things. We had this S.O.S. program — Save Our Slums —
right in my neighborhood. They got money, millions of dollars. Run by black men. You remember what happened —
Sam Somers run off with a big hunk of it. It's a game, y'know.
White man runs it — he knows about money but he don't
know nothin' about Harlem. Black man runs it — oh, he knows
all about Harlem, but he don't know nothin' about money. Both
men run it, man, they cut each other's throats. But Smith, right
from the start, he was different. He can't read or write. But
he's smart like a Jew. And honest. There never was a man more
honest."

"Where did he get the money to start?"

"That was it — he got it all himself. He didn't go beggin'
to the government." He thought a moment. "Where — I don't
know for sure. From boxing. From the book. Other places.
But it come, it come real good and every cent goes right back
into our movement. Now we got an org'nization. Now we
makin' money for ourselves. I tell you how I got started? How
I joined up?"

"No. Tell me."

"Happened like this." He rested his head on the chair's

back and lapped one knee over its right arm. "I was workin' at
the Shell station — two blocks up. Sixteen hours a day. See,
my wife's mother — she got cancer of the breasts. Got it real
bad. She's livin' with us, and my wife, she gotta give up her
job t'watch her. We got three rooms an' with two kids — I
mean, that's too much. The old lady lays in the livin' room —
she's groanin' all day long. Even when she sleeps. Little
squeaky groans t'drive you crazy. Doctor give her morphine,
but it don't seem t'help. She gotta be carried to the can. She
gotta be fed like a kid, though, God knows, she don't eat hardly
nothin'. But the worst of it . . . the worst," he shook his head,
as though to rid it of the memory, "Cap, she smell. Terrible. I
never smell nothin' like it. It burns your nose, makes you
wanna puke. The whole house stinks. I come home two, three
in the mornin', I don't wanna go in there. Sometimes I fall
asleep on the stoop like some bum. We sent the kids away to
friends — but they gotta be home sometimes. Months it was.
April, May, June. She gets a hump, just like a hunchback.
Then her legs swell up so, they break right open. I ain't never
wanted nobody t'die so much. An', yet, Cap, I spit at myself. We
live with old Ella early on, when we's first married. She's a real
good lady, a real straight arrow, a good Baptist. What am I
gonna do — there's no money t'send her away — not t'some
place decent? It's a mess. You know?"

"Yes. I think I do."

"Then one day — " he sat up, two hands together, fingertips
aligned. "I don't know even now — I don't know how they
come t'find out. A man comes on Saturday. A Horn Orange
dressed up just like me. He's got a girl with him, a nurse. He
asks us, do me an' my wife want t'come with him? He takes us
down near the park, to the Horn Rest — it's a nursin' home.
It's real nice there. Doctors, white and black. Clean. Spankin'

clean with plenty modern equipment." He thought a moment. "So I says, you know, 'How much?' 'Nothing,' he says,
'but we want you t'help us.' Cap, 'til that moment I ain't heard
of Horn Smith. In the sports section maybe, that's all. So he
takes us right up here t'Horn's Place, an' we join up. The old
lady did fine there — I mean, suffering as she was. Me and my
wife, we joined for life. There's never no backin' out once you
give yourself up t'the Horn. But I ain't yet regretted it, an'
that's the truth."

"It — it hardly seems possible," I said. "I still don't see:
nursing homes, doctors, medicine. These things cost so much
money. How can one man — how could Smith finance all that?
Even if he earned two, three million dollars from boxing. It
still wouldn't be enough. Not by half."

"But it's not one man," said Nicholas Breakspeare. "Not any
more." He stood, driven to his feet by enthusiasm. He threw
his arms behind his back; then began pacing busily up and
down in front of my bookcase. An insect, I thought. A jolly
beetle, wings folded behind, fat orange body propped on spindly
legs. His knees flexed with excitement; his fingers wriggled
behind his back like upended spiders. "Now we're workin'
together. Look, that's been our problem — we been divided.
Workin' only for our own selfs. Some Negroes, they don't think
they's black. Some, they don't like t'work at all. But now we
got discipline. We work an' we work together. Black or brown
or one shade from white."

"Then there are punishments?"

"Sure. Sure." He closed his eyes, impatient. "Sure, but we
need them. Look what we got now. A narcotics department
that gives free drugs and help. Believe me, there ain't a pusher
left in Harlem. An abortion department. A welfare department. Our own bookies, our own numbers game — man, even

our own whore corps. And the money, it all goes right back into the movement. Them white guys, the Mafia and the Cosa Whatsits, they're finished in Harlem. Finished. Horn's no crazy, sick reformer. We got problems, we got vices, but Horn makes them pay off — while he's curin' them."

"I see. I see."

"But that's not the best part. Best part's this — " He came close to my chair and then dropped to his haunches. As he talked, he poked his fingers at the rug, sketching irrelevant diagrams. "Horn started his own businesses. Now we got almost two hundred here — some in Brooklyn, too, Newark, places like that. Every kind of store. Shoe store. Drug store. T.V. repair. Supermarket. Ice cream parlor. You name it, we got it. And all the profits, they go back in. Take Rolly Thomas. He was a Horn Blue early on. Horn buys up a liquor store and he gives it to Rolly. Rolly runs it, makes a good salary, and then he gives back all the profits. But ten years from now, and all that liquor store is Rolly's own. Free and clear. He don't have t'share the profits no more. He will, maybe. But he don't have to. An' Rolly — he's on Welfare before he joined up. Now he's a respected man. That's why I gotta be a Blue. Don't you see, then maybe Horn give me a store. But Horn, he gotta be sure of you. Sure you're loyal. No black marks."

"That's — I didn't realize Smith did that."

"No. No, you don't. That's 'cause Horn don't want no white men interferin'. He don't want no publicity. Like some other Civil Rights men. He don't want no Nobel Prizes, Horn's too busy for that stuff." He paused. "But there's more. Like I said, Horn — he's smart like a Jew. Think a minute . . . Suppose there's five liquor stores where you live. Four of 'em, say — four is run by Cohen and Goldberg and those guys. Right?"

"Right."

"The last one, that's a Horn store. Say, Rolly's store — you known that 'cause it's be'n announced on Horn Radio, WGHS, or in the paper, *Horn's Voice*. Right?"

"Right."

"But Mr. Goldberg's store — it's right across the street and Rolly's store, it's five blocks down. Cold night, say. Snow on the ground. Right?"

"Right."

"Prices — well, Mr. Goldberg charges a bit more. Not so much more, 'cause the Horn liquor stores, they've forced him t'come down. Right?"

"Right."

"So. You and me — we probably go across the street. 'Stead of walkin' five blocks or ten. Right?"

"Right."

"Funny, ain't it? No, it's not funny. It's real sad. All the people here — they know which store is a black man's store. We know, we help the black man, we help ourselves. An' still — still we shop at Mr. Goldberg's. Why? Don't ask me. It's God's truth, we ain't never used our ec'nomic power. Not 'til now. You know what Horn did?"

"No." Nicholas grinned.

"You ever hear of Horn Stamps?"

"No. What are they?"

"Well. If y'don't go to Mr. Goldberg's store. If you're smart and walk them five blocks t'Rolly's place. Then, for what you buy, you get so many stamps. Like Plaid Stamps or Green Stamps. There's even a Horn Stamp book. But it's different — you don't get a toaster or a lamp or a Mixmaster. No sir, you get work done instead. See, that's what we got plenty of — labor. You want your apartment painted? Five books. Exterminator? Four books. House maid? A book for each day's work. Y'can even get the car fixed an' only pay for the parts. It's great. That's what, mostly, we Horn Oranges and the little Hornets do. Supervised by the Greens. An' the work is good. Real good. It's gotta be — the Greens see to that."

"That's brilliant," I said, genuinely astonished. "Brilliant."

"It works, too. We're pushin' the white man out. Earnin' money, buyin' our own places, livin' better. It's a dream, Mr. Pratt. A dream come true."

"Yes," I said. "Yes." I sat forward, for I was infected then with the vitality of his enthusiasm. But it endured only a moment, only as long, in fact, as it took my chair to tilt fully forward. My hopes were stunted, miscarried by the white man's curse — the knowledge of his own history and of the bitter experiences of men and their governments. "But," I said, as my chair sagged in response to my spirit's deflation. "But. There's only one thing — one thing wrong."

"No, Cap," said Nicholas, "no, there's nothin' wrong."

"There is, Nicholas," I said sadly. He stood up and a sneer that evolved slowly from a smile began to appear on his face.

"Yeah, what? What's wrong?"

"It all depends on Smith — that's what's wrong. It can live only as long as he lives. Or as long as he remains loyal to it. Don't you see — a good, wise king, that's what you've got. That's all you've got." Nicholas frowned. He walked over to the globe and peered closely at the continent of South America.

"How d'you mean?"

"It's simple enough. If Smith dies — then who takes over the movement?"

"Purston. Purston, I guess."

"And Purston, could he — would he — keep things going the way they are now?"

"Smith ain't gonna die."

"There was an assassination attempt. I read about it."
Nicholas Breakspeare stared into the light from my desk lamp,
and his pupils, oppressed by that stark illumination, narrowed.
But he was preoccupied and did not draw his gaze away, though
the light must surely have been irritating his eyes. He grunted.

"Well," he said. "You just better pray he stays all right."

"I'll pray," I said. "Nicholas. You know, I'm not going
again. Not to one of those terrible rallies. And this Sunday —
well, I'm going to tell them, my congregation, just what I think.
See. I've written the sermon already." He looked at me,
measuring the strength of my determination. His upper lip
receded slowly. He sighed.

"Why?"

"I have to. It looks like I support Purston. If I hadn't gone —
gotten up there on the platform — then I might have kept silent. But now — now I've got to speak out."

"Leave it alone, Cap."

"I can't."

"They'll leave you — they'll go back to that guy at St. Catharine's. You want that? You think it's better for them?"

"I have to. If they want John Meeker and his violence . . .
Then they can have him. But some may stay."

"No one," he said. "No one's gonna stay. And . . . you **may**
get hurt."

"Do you think so?" He shrugged and I stared down at my
bare foot with its blackened toes. The night's brutality was remembered then, and I could not, even for Nicholas Breakspeare's sake, dominate the fear that tightened my fingers and
cracked the timbre of my voice. He saw and was compassionate.

"If you got to," he said, "you got to. Only I wish you
wouldn't. I don't want t'see you hurt. Not you. You got **no**
part in this."

"We all have a part."

"Come," he said. "I'll lend you a hand t'bed."

Excerpt from the Autobiography of George Horn Smith

. . . They made it hard for me, the old white men with their cigars and thick eyebrows and their coughing throats. A whole year they let me wait. The lawyers talked, the newspapermen wrote, the boxing commissioners, they shook their heads no and Mr. Koch, he shook his head yes. One year is a long time to wait, to wait and not know what my future is. Should it be allowed, they ask, should a man with a horn put money in his pockets from boxing? No, too dangerous, they say. In seventy-four amateur fights, never once has my horn split a skull or popped out a man's eyeball. Seventy-four fights, seventy-four men beaten. Fifty men knocked out and all with my fists, not one with my horn. But now, when I would earn some money for Mr. Koch and for my poor, lovely mother, now I am too dangerous. And even a boy must wonder — a white man with a horn, would he be so dangerous? Would he be made to wait?

And then they came, the two of them. The famous black man, the tall basketball player, and the young white man from the commission, his nose bent like a green parrot's, his hair cut to the skin of his scalp. The white man smiles all the time, and the black man, he nods when the white man smiles. They are talking 'sense' to me. "Look," says the white man, "don't be stubborn, you're a great boxer. Give yourself a chance." "Look," says the black man, "Don't be stubborn. For the good of your race, get wise." Your race, he says, as if today he is being black for my sake. "What do you want?" I ask. "Good. Fine," says the white man. "I know a great doctor. He'll take it off — one, two, three. No pain. No bother." "For the good of your race," says the black man. "You'll look better, too," says the white man, "you'll have girls." And when I try to hit the white man's face the tall black man, he holds me tight by the arms. "Stupid nigger," he says in my ear. But I was not sorry, I am not sorry. For, if they cut it off, then today I could not be what I am. I could not be George Horn Smith.

These are hard times for us. Mr. Koch, he owns a big apartment house and for ten dollars a month and a room to sleep in, I must mop the floors, shovel snow, carry out the big ash barrels. My mother and me, we live in a little room near the boiler place, where people keep their baby carriages and their bicycles. My mother does not mind, but I mind for her. She is getting old and it is time, I think, she must have some easiness in her life. So, every night, I am at Mr. Koch's gymnasium, working out. Night after night. Sunday night and Christmas night. I know there is hope only in my fists, and soon my punches are so hard that big men will not spar with me. They moan when I hit them, even just on the arms. Amateur boxers, they start running even before the bell rings, but I hunt them down. A killer, they call me.

At last the big judges must decide. Mr. Koch, he has spent many thousand dollars. His lawyers are important men, with little eyes and squeaking voices — and their names, they all have the word 'gold' in them. Mr. Goldberg, he shows the judges a long film of my amateur fights. Mr. Goldstein, he says "See. This poor boy's horn, it points up, not out. Up. Harmlessly up. Touch it — see." And the judges must each touch. They watch when Mr. Goldfarb wraps my horn in soft foam rubber. They nod — then they decide, yes, that I can fight. Mr. Koch, he is happy, but very tired. He puts his hand on my shoulder, and his white, dead eye looks at me. "Kid," he says, "you cost me plenty. You better win." And I do. Mike Cortera, Pete Minelli, Armando Perez, Harry O'Shaughnessy, Joe de Santo, Benny Thomas, Ulysses Watts, Carmen Palucci — thirteen, fourteen, fifteen men. Fifteen men, eleven men knocked out. And already Horn Smith is famous.

Now, you see, my horn is good. What they call a human interest thing. The reporters, they go wherever I am. They ask stupid questions. "How do you put your shirt on? Is it heavy? Does it itch? Do you bump things?" I see myself in movie newsreels. I hear my name on the radio. The headlines, Thomas Jefferson, my trainer, reads them out loud. HORN WINS ANOTHER. HORN GORES PALUCCI. FIFTEEN FOR THE HORN. Now I am glad the doctor did not cut my horn away. People, you see, they are hungry for strange things. They pay to see me, even in my first, my little fights. The

promoters, men with big money, beg Mr. Koch to let me fight in
their places. They want me to win. The posters go up — posters
like Dr. Oddie's posters — all horn and no George Smith. I am now,
indeed, what they call me. The magnificent freak.

And when I come out from the dressing room, down the long aisle
to the ring, people stand — they go up on their toes, and their heads,
they seem to jump off their necks. "There! There! Look! See! See
his horn!" It gives me a thrill even now, a thrill of great power.
"Oooooh — Ohhhh," the crowd gasps, and the sound is like a big
train coming. Around the ring, where a seat costs much money,
there are only white men and white women. The women with furs
and jewels on their fingers, earrings in their little ears under high-
piled hair. The women cheer. "Go Horn," they shout, their hands
wave in the air. Then they laugh and their men, in fine suits, they
laugh with them. A rich man's game, you see — cheer the black
freak. And my own people, the people I love, far away, high up in
the poor man's seats. They cheer too — but for me. And for the
burden we bear together. For them, for me, this is no game. We
fight together. We fight for our lives and for our dignity . . .

. . . Fifteen wins and now my first main event in Madison Square
Garden. Already they call me champion. I am excited and proud. I
walk with my shoulders back, my horn pointing high in the air.
Hundreds of people come to watch me in my training, and Mr.
Koch, he teaches me to make the letters GHS inside a little horn —
for everyone wants my autograph, and I am ashamed that I cannot
write. Now, I think, there will be some money. I run to tell my
lovely mother. She is happy, yes, to see my happiness, but I know
she does not understand. When I tell her, she is sitting on our little
bed, in the baby carriage room, her head nodding like a man who
has taken many punches. I know then, even in my excitement, that
I am too late — my mother has suffered for too long. She waits only
to die now, afraid to hear, afraid to see. Like so many of my people,
the spirit of life is crushed by poverty and dirt and cruelness. "I
will win," I say. "I will win, little mother. We will be famous, you
and me." My mother, she says only these three words — "Georgie,
my son." And there is such sadness in those words; my great pride is
emptied of its joy. I think only of black mothers throughout this
ugly world, giving birth to children without gladness or hope. And

I know then that my success must be something more — that I must never, in pride, forget the blackness of my skin.

And so the big night comes — the most terrible night in all my young life. Adolph Vesey was already an old man when he fought me. A trial horse — an experienced boxer whose strength is gone, someone a young, fast boxer may beat and win a name in beating. But Adolph Vesey is ring-wise and tough. The bookmakers' odds are five-to-one against him, still Vesey does not worry. "I use the horn against the Horn," he says. Thomas Jefferson is troubled, but not me. Am I not the best? Am I not already champion? Vesey is old. He cannot punch. I will beat him good.

Adolph Vesey was tall and very thin, with gray hair coming already around his ears. He has a strange body — long arms, chest and stomach caved in, legs like sticks. He looks so weak I almost laugh when I see him standing there in his corner. His old bathrobe has holes — he looks like the scarecrow in Mr. Rebezi's field that shook when the wind blew through it. The crowd cheers as my name is announced, and I dance the fighter's proud dance, my gloves high in the air. Then we are standing, my strong chest to Vesey's bony, sunken chest, in the middle of the ring. Vesey doesn't look afraid. He chews his mouthpiece when the referee talks. He seems to be thinking, his mind far away. Vesey has fought eighty professional fights and, in that time, he has met everyone, the good boxers and the bad. Scar tissue is thick over his eyebrows and his coffee brown nose is crooked with big lumps in it. I am thinking already where my punches will land, seeing his long body stretched on the canvas. I am sorry only that Vesey is not white. Sorry that my victory must come at a brother's expense. The referee slaps us both on the back. Five rounds, I say to myself, five rounds Mr. Vesey and you are gone.

The bell rings. I leap up from the stool, dancing, full of my own great strength. Vesey will chase me, jabbing with his long arms, and then I will counterpunch to the body. That is our plan. But Vesey does not move. He stands where he is. Come, his face is saying, if you are so good, my man with the horn, then you must come and get me. I dance some more, teasing him, but he will not move. The crowd boos. "Go get him!" yells Thomas Jefferson. "Go get him!" I move forward, my head low, my knees bent, and I think, as I move, that old Adolph Vesey is smiling.

His arms, they begin to move, glove over glove, like a man reeling in rope. I circle to the left, my head still low, looking at that bony chest, far behind Vesey's long arms. And I think, this will not be so easy after all. I jab at his body and, as I jab, something very strange happens — my head jumps. I hook to Vesey's ribs and again it happens. My eyes dance, the punch misses. Now I see — see what is happening. Each time I set myself to swing, Vesey will lean out and tap at my horn, upsetting my balance, confusing me. I look up, and Vesey throws a right hand hard into my face. The crowd cheers. Vesey dances away. I chase him again, but Vesey's glove is out, tapping at my horn — using it like a handle to shake my head. The crowd begins to understand. And now I hear the name, "Vesey! Vesey!" The crowd roots for the punch, always for the man who is winning.

By the sixth round I am dizzy, wanting almost to vomit. Vesey is smart — he does not hit my horn hard, does not commit his body. Tap. Tap. Tap. Only that, playing with me. My eyes cross — sometimes I see three Veseys — and soon I am crazy with fear and anger. I am going to lose, I know that. In the eighth round I catch Vesey against the ropes with a left hook hard to the head. He goes down to one knee. The crowd cheers for me now. But Vesey is up, running, shaking his head clear. His thin legs wobble. The crowd roars for the kill, but the bell rings and my chance is gone. The judges vote 6-4, 6-4, 5-4-1. All for Vesey. Unanimous — the boy with the horn has been beaten. Beaten by an old man with gray already in his hair.

I am still a child, still with a child's fear. You must remember that. When we leave the ring, I break free from old Thomas Jefferson's arms, break free and run to my dressing room. But the reporters stand by the door, waiting to ask their stupid questions. "George! George! It's all right!" Mr. Koch waves at me. I see his little, short body, his bald head, and, to me, he is Dr. Oddie come to take me away again. I turn and run, pushing through the crowd, shouting, "Out, out of my way! Out, out of my way!" Then I am running up Eighth Avenue, not seeing in my panic. People stand still to watch this running man, with a horn, with a boxer's trunks, with his hands still taped and white. A man, they don't know, who hurries to find his death.

I run to 59th Street, then past the statue and into Central Park. The lake is there, waiting for me, flat and very peaceful, with the lights of the big buildings dancing on its water. I walk to the edge, then I stop, my hands on my kneecaps, gasping. Cool breezes touch the sweat on my chest. I shiver. The lake laps near my feet, and I can hear its sound — tap, tap, tap, like Vesey's glove. Tap. Tap. Tap. The quiet lake is saying, "Come, I am like your mother's lap. I will swallow your fear and all your hopeless dreams." My knees stiffen, for I know what I am going to do, and there is something yet in me that says no to the thought of death. I step forward. The cold water covers my right foot. Again. My other foot. Now I am walking very slowly into the lake, and its cold takes the life from my calves, from my thighs, from the warm parts of my groin. I sing to myself, sing a song I remember my mother singing, long before this night of my shame. The water licks at my fingers. It freezes them. All around my body the lake is quiet. I know, as in the world, that when a man dies, there are no great ripples, just the wide, flat surface. Soon unbroken. Not caring. Full of an empty peace. The water touches my stomach and the secret organs there under my skin come to a stop like little watches not ticking any more. "I have lost," I whisper. "I have lost."

And then another sound. My mind dreams, drowned already in the cold, soft water and, for a long time, I cannot hear it. A hollow sound. Clop. Clop. Clop. Like a tired man, applauding alone in some great building. I turn my head. There, far to the lake's other side, a horse pulls a carriage slowly along the road. A man sits alone, a tall hat on his head, his back bent in sleep. Nothing else moves in all the empty park — only that slow black shadow and the horse's clopping. And then I am a child again, watching as the old coffin comes slowly down Mulhaney's Way. "No," I say. I shake my head. "No." I raise my fist high in the air. Then I smash it down on the water's surface. "No! No, Mr. Smith!" I shout, in the night. "No! You promised me! Not like that!" And, across the lake, the horse and its driver, they hear my angry shouts. The horse begins to run, and the old black carriage, it rushes between the trees. I laugh. "No!" Not like that. Never . . .

I halted at my alley's neck: the Reverend John Meeker was

standing, his back toward me, near the rectory wall. As I watched, he commenced a sort of solitary game — rushing from window to rectory window, hopping, skipping in great agitation. He stood on tiptoe, shaded the glass with his hand and, sometimes, when the window's height demanded it, dragged the full length of his body up the wall in order to peer in. I retreated along the alley; as I did so, I lifted my small grocery bag up, against my face. I wanted to steal away, having no stomach, just then, for an unpleasant and possibly dangerous encounter. But at that moment Meeker abandoned his suspicious tactics and climbed the front stoop to tap, while alternately stopping to listen, at my front door. His elbows were out; in the case of the left, a hole in the jacket was superimposed over a hole in the shirt, baring the white skin of his elbow. His hair was disheveled, and one considerable clump jutted out at a sharp right angle to his part. His pants legs were abbreviated; they ended at mid-shin. Beneath the cuffs, there were two very different species of sock. I crossed the courtyard. Meeker's preoccupation was such that I reached the foot of the stoop undetected.

"Here," I said. "I'm here. What do you want?"

Ten seconds elapsed before Meeker had fully anatomized my ruined face. Then he said only, "God . . ." As he said it, he took a quick inventory of his own features with thumb and forefinger: eye, lip, earlobe, throat. Reassured, he stood back, dabbing at his recalcitrant hair. I took out my key. Meeker's face was quite as revealing as my own — crude, heavy lines and dark shadows, like a charcoal sketch of himself. I knew, even before he told me, that he hadn't slept since Sunday night.

"You're mad," he said. "I know it. You're mad at me."

"No," I said, as I unlocked the front door. "Not mad. Afraid. Confused. That's all."

"You're mad — go on, say it. You've got to be mad. God knows, I deserve it."

"All right — I'm mad."

"Shit . . ." he said, musing. "Look what I've done to you. Just look."

"I'd rather not. Shall we go in?"

"Are you all right? I mean, did you see a doctor?" I nodded. "Did you — you didn't tell the police, did you? You didn't do that?" I shook my head. "See. I knew you wouldn't. I told Helen you wouldn't. Are you sure you're all right?"

"I'll endure. Please come in." He moved across the threshold, unable, for the moment, to withdraw his glance from my face.

"Your eye." He reached out as though to touch at it, but, when my head dodged away, he repressed the action. "Can you see? It's all closed up. Stitches?"

"Six. And I've got three in my lip. And my lower front tooth is gone. Swallowed." He put his hand to his mouth. "My groin is black and blue. My ribs — "

"Stop. Please. I'm sorry, Pratt. I didn't know what I was doing. And I'm so strong."

"Yes. You are, indeed." I said. "Come into my office."

Hopefully, I indicated my armchair, but Meeker was too distressed, too full of a lively contrition, to sit just then. He strode up and down in the small room, striking out at chair, desk and wall with the soft underpart of his fist. I stood in the doorway while he acted out his repentance, aware that the performance was self-indulgent, that, in fact, he scarcely knew I was present.

"I'm apologizing, Pratt — sure," he said, beginning a monologue. "Sure. I didn't want you messed up, believe me I didn't. I could kick myself. I'm apologizing for that — for the stitches and for the teeth . . . But you made a mistake, not that I blame you. Here, baby, you don't play with lions and tigers, not unless you expect t'get scratched. I mean, Pratt, I can see in the dark, you know? Hear things, smell things. I'm not a man any more. There's a strength in me, in us . . . it's savage. And good. You, what can you know? I told you a long time ago — this is the jungle and you, you of all people, you don't belong here." He hit out at my bookshelf in emphasis and a row of heavy volumes toppled, one against the other, subsiding at a crazy angle. "So, you see, Pratt, I'm not really apologizing. I thought — I was dead wrong, sure — but I thought you'd pulled a dirty trick on me. But you didn't, did you? No. I found out yesterday. God, Pratt, if you knew what I've suffered. Now . . . Now I don't know what to do."

"Well," I said. "We'll talk about it." He stood near me, one hand out, cupped in petition. "Sit down. I'll make some coffee." I turned sharply away from him, purposely deferring my response to his appeal. I was still angry, I suppose, and I didn't care, just then, to sell my sympathy too cheaply. I took my time in the kitchen. I waited until the water was boiled, the coffee made and on a tray, before reentering. I wanted to allow him time, a few moments without an interested audience, so that he might calm himself. But when I returned Meeker was not calmed at all. He stood in the center of my office with a paper, my sermon, in his hand. His face was suffused with the red of an intolerable fury and, when he saw me setting down the tray, he charged, stammering. I backed away, moving evasively, forearms across my face.

"You bastard! You lying, sniveling bastard!" He held the paper in front of my face. I pushed his hand away. "You told Hawkes. You went and told Hawkes."

"Get away from me." I shoved him aside and retreated hastily toward my desk. Meeker followed gesticulating, pulling at his matted hair.

"Why?" he said. "Why? Why did you do it? Why?" He snarled. "Yes, I know why. You're jealous. You think I'm crazy. You want me ruined here."

"Stop it!" I shouted, harried quite beyond fear or patience. He hesitated. One hand, fingers askew, remained extended at his eyes' level. "Sit down," I said. "Sit in that chair. Now!" He backed away, uncertain, and, I think, exhausted by his own unrelenting obsessions. "John. You can sit or leave. I won't talk until you sit down."

"Pratt — "

"Sit! Damn it! Sit!" He sat down. "Now drink some coffee." He stared at me. His glance was vacuous, disoriented; I realized then that, without his anger, without his fear, without the sharp complicity of his hypertense body, Meeker was an insensate, fatuous thing. I pointed at the tray near my foot. He picked up the cup, his hand fluttering, and brought it to his lips. Coffee spattered on his shirtfront. I sat in my swivel chair. As much as I wanted my own coffee, I was yet too afraid to pass near him.

"John," I said, after several moments. "If you so much as raise a hand to me again, I swear, I'll set the police on you. Do you understand?" He nodded. The cup wobbled in its saucer. His eyes found mine after some uncoordinated groping.

"You told Hawkes," he said, his voice subdued, resentful.

"I didn't," I said.

"Dear Bishop Hawkes, that's what the paper says. Dear Bishop Hawkes." He repeated the phrase, turning the first, salutary word into an ironic adjective. "You wrote him a letter."

"I almost did — but I didn't. And it wasn't about you anyway. I was going to resign."

"Resign?" He looked up with a sort of sly hopefulness. "Resign? Yes, why don't you? That's a good idea. Then they'd come back."

"Who?"

"My congregation." His eyes opened wide and fixed themselves, I think, on my globe of the world. He muttered something, and then, with curiosity and a measured slowness, he dunked two fingers of his right hand into the coffee. He sucked at them. "You didn't tell Hawkes. Then maybe you're really my friend. What's your name — I mean, besides Pratt?"

"Calvin."

"Cal, will you help me?"

"If I can. But I don't think I'll be able to. The way you are now — John, you need psychiatric help."

"No, silly," he said. "Not that kind of help. Help me get my congregation back. Will you?"

"But . . ."

"Please, Cal. Don't play with me. I know I need help. Good God, no one knows better than I do. But I can't stop now, not now. Not when I've come so far." He spoke calmly, but with an eerie remoteness, as though he were remembering while he spoke.

"John. Be realistic. What can I do?"

"Give them back. That's all. You don't understand them anyway — you never will. You're a white man, Pratt — Cal — you'll never be anything else. At least I have a chance. I've gone all the way. Holy Jesus, I've worked so hard here. I've given my wife — " He shook his head. Then he laughed, embarrassed. "Freudian slip. You don't know about Helen — or did Hawkes tell you?"

"No. He didn't."

"That's unlike him. He hates me." Meeker paused. "Do you want to hear?" I shrugged, then nodded. "Well . . . One afternoon, in May it was, three men, boys really, Negroes, they broke into our home. We were living in a ground floor apartment, waiting while the rectory was being redone. They just wanted to rob us — God knows they have so little. But Helen was there." He sipped at his coffee. "They probably knew, sensed, how she felt about them. They have wonderful instincts and Helen, Pratt, she doesn't care for Negroes. That's the ugly truth. Anyway, they raped her. All three of them. And then they went once around again. Sloppy seconds they call it."

"Good God," I said. I remembered Helen Meeker's tears and the explanation she had given for them. That, I thought, that and Meeker too.

"Distressing business." He lifted his right leg and began carefully examining the sole of his shoe. There was a hole near the ball of his foot. He pushed his finger through, then extracted it and put it in his mouth. "I found her on the bed — it must have been hours after . . . tied to the four corners with my old neckties. She'd asked me, you know, just the night before, if I didn't want to throw them out. The ties, that is. She's a beautiful woman, was anyway. She seems a lot older now. And I couldn't help admiring her even then, while I was undoing the ties." He spoke without apparent emotion, so conversationally, that the hairs on my neck began to rise. "Yes . . ." he said. Then he yawned, while slowly rubbing the back of his hand up and down against his temple. "Sorry. I haven't had my proper rest. Where was I . . . Yes. They'd hurt her. And there was shock, too. She spent a week in the hospital." He slapped his hands together softly. "It wasn't easy for me, Pratt. At first Helen didn't understand — she's not a priest, after all — she wanted to press charges." He laughed nervously. "Good God, that would have finished me here. But she finally saw the light. I told her — it was cheap vengeance or me. Simple as that. She chose me. But you know, Pratt, she's never forgiven them. To this day. Can you imagine my position — a priest, loving these people as I do — and all the while, knowing my own wife hated them?

"Ah . . . what then? Oh — we found out Helen was pregnant. Pregnant. Yes, and, of course, we didn't know who the father was. It was very upsetting for Helen. After all, I was outnumbered three to one and I hadn't been too interested in — you know — in the family business." He chuckled. Then he raised and lowered his eyebrows four times in swift succession. "Do I embarrass you, Pratt?" I shook my head. "If Helen'd had a black child, I think it would have killed her. In fact she — and this is between you and me — she wanted to have an abortion. I had to, — uh, put my foot down. She's obstinate, perverse, the way women are. I told her, Pratt, black or white, they're all Christ's children. I told her. All equal, all deserving of her love. All — well . . . you understand, you're a Christian. But Helen didn't, she's so bigoted. Like I said, I had to put my foot down." He began whistling a lively tune, tapping the foot he had put down to its rhythms. A vacant smile opened up on his face, like a fist slowly unclenching.

"But God provides, you see. We had Kathy. Blonde, white and Aryan. No Negro blood there. I wonder what it would have been like — to raise a black child . . ." He sighed. "Helen had a rough time. The story got out somehow. Maybe one of them talked. Maybe it was someone at the hospital. She knows they know and I think — I don't know why — I think she's ashamed." He shook his head. "You wouldn't have a cigarette, huh? I need some smoke bad."

"We've been through this. I smoke a pipe."

"That's right," he said. "Maybe I'll try it. I never did before. That big curved pipe looks nice." I swiveled, hands outstretched, toward my pipe rack.

"No," I said. I pulled the rack possessively toward me.

"Why not?"

"It's not sanitary."

"Oh," he said. "I don't mind." He rose and started walking toward my desk. Sweat formed between my fingers. Quickly, while he was still distracted by the pipes, I dropped my pad of matches in the trash basket. He began fingering my pipes, weighing them in his palm. Then, one by one, he clenched them between his teeth and sucked noisily. My hands, my legs tensed; the skin of my face tensed as well, and my poor left eyelid was wrenched upward in my aborted fury. For one second I could see, and then pain, in colored specks of light, hammered at my skull. I stood hastily and walked across the room, away from him. My pipes . . .

"This one is nice."

"I — I have no matches."

"Matches I've got," he said. He began packing a small straight-grain Hardcastle. My favorite pipe. "Maybe I'll take this up. It's cheaper than cigarettes, no?"

"Yes," I said, my back turned to him. I heard the click of his match. Then the strong smoke reached my nostrils. My fingernails dug into the soft pads of my thumbs. I wanted to cry.

"Smells good. Guess I better not inhale." He returned to my armchair. I could hear the soft popping of his lips on the pipe's stem. "Where was I? Yes . . . Maybe you think I was wrong, Pratt. I know, you think I should have done something. Gotten revenge. Well, you know, I did." He chuckled. "I got my revenge. It was diabolical. Can you guess what I did? No . . . I don't think you can. What I did, Pratt, I made them love me. God's revenge, that's what it was. I went everywhere. To the whorehouses and the heroin dens. On the marches, at the sit-ins. The riots, too. I helped carry television sets and mattresses and cases of food. I showed up where no white man has ever been before. I worked with them; I played with them; I fought with them. It wasn't a picnic, believe me. But I wore them down. I took their snubs and their insults and their threats and I just kept on coming. It worked, Pratt. Never underestimate love's power. My congregation grew and grew. Negroes came from all over the world to hear me, to ask my advice, to pray with me. I was, I am a famous man. I had my revenge — oh, but good. I had — " he paused. The fingers of his two hands entwined, clenched. His knuckles cracked as they whitened. "Until last Sunday. Until — don't you see, Pratt? You've got to help me."

"Your wife," I said. "Your poor, innocent wife. What a savage, what an evil thing."

"Oh, no." Meeker puckered his lips. His voice became very soft, very tender. "You're wrong, Pratt. Not evil. They don't know any better."

"Are you mad?" I shouted it. Then I slapped my open hand against the wall. "Are you insane? We're not talking about dumb animals or trees or rocks. We're talking about men. They know better, John. They know a lot better."

"Well, perhaps . . ." His eyes began wandering around the room, then to my pipe in his hands. It had gone out. He laid it on the chair arm. Ashes fluttered down, onto the rug. "Perhaps. But after all, you can't blame them. You live here, you see their homes. Rats. Roaches. No jobs. No hope. We've martyred them, Pratt. Crucified them. Do you know how they came here?"

"In the slave ships? Yes. You told me all about it."

"Well . . . See. As a Christian, Pratt. Can you blame them?"

"Yes! Damn it all, yes! I do blame them. As a Christian I blame them. John, what's the matter with you? Are you so silly

and sentimental, so blinded by your own guilt — have you forgotten that we live in a real world?" He brushed at his eyebrow,
taken aback by my vehemence. "John, look . . . evil exists.
It's a real thing. It's hard and it's heavy — as hard and as heavy
as this ashtray. And it's dangerous. It exists, the devil exists, to
destroy us. Good grief, have you forgotten the history of your
own religion? Why do you think Christianity's lost its hold on
the world? Why?" Meeker shook his head. "Because, if God's
dying now, it's because the devil died and was buried and forgotten long before God even showed symptoms. Evil died, or so
men hoped. Now no one can sin. We have victims of environ-
ment and society and neuroses. But no sinners. That's why
Christianity's passing away, John. There's no one who needs
saving."

"Pratt — "

"Let me finish. Please . . . you and I, we're in this business
to teach men about Christ, about hope, about salvation. That's
our job. But we've missed the boat, me, as well as you. We
can't talk about doing good, about loving, unless we admit that
hate and evil exist, that men do wrong. On purpose. Deliberately. Maliciously. Heinously. You see, that's what doing good
is — not doing evil." I said the words slowly, separating them.
"Not doing evil. I'm sick of it. Sick of the nonsense I hear every day. Everybody's innocent. Innocent from the day they're
born to the day they die. Hitler and the boys that raped your
wife alike. No matter what they do society, Freud, anything —
anything else takes the rap. Jesus Christ, poor, unenlightened
Jesus, he died on the cross for nothing. We're all perfect." I
paused. "And the pity of it is — we're not helping them. They
can't believe in good; they've never been told what it is. They
can't even do penance for their sins. Our poor, pathetic, sin-
less generation."

"But, Pratt, Christ said, 'Forgive. Seventy times seven — ' "

"No! Don't be stupid. Christ forgave, yes. But after, after he had forgiven, he said, 'Go and sin no more.' Go and sin no more. That's the point. Without the admonition, forgiveness is a stupid, a dangerous farce. Christ knew what sin was. He didn't say, 'I forgive you because your home life stinks and you needed to let off steam.' No, my friend. And you, John — you didn't forgive those three men. You only think you did, my friend. What you did, you forgave the sin, not the sinners. You said, rape is fine, go ahead. Rape is no sin. Have a ball. Come jump my wife anytime. John, they don't even know you've forgiven them. If they're human — and I believe, more than you seem to, that they are — if they're human, then at least one of them feels guilty and miserable. He might even welcome punishment. But there is no punishment or expiation or repentance. You've denied it them. Know what that is, John? That's terror. A world where right and wrong, law and morality and justice no longer exist. That's terror."

"Pratt. Will you help me?" I stared at him. Meeker was leaning forward in his chair, thumb and forefinger inserted negligently in his left nostril.

"You haven't heard a word I said."

"Yes. Yes, I have. You speak very well. And . . . you may be right. I don't know. I'm not thinking clearly. Will you help me?"

"How can I? They came of their own free will. I can't just send them back."

"No! No, they didn't." Meeker jumped up; rushed over to where I was standing. "No. They were driven away. Ordered away. By Smith. By that nigger devil Smith. I found out last night. He hates me."

"I don't believe it," I said, stammering. Meeker clutched at my shoulder as I, in dismay, backed quickly away from him.

"It's true I tell you."

"It can't be."

"Yes. Yes it is. He threatened them." Meeker pressed his fist to his cheek. "God. What will I do? A *Life* magazine photographer's coming — next Sunday. And there'll be no one. My church, my poor church will be empty. What will I do?"

"Smith? But he hates me, too. He as much as said so."

"Said so? Do you know him?" Meeker's eyes narrowed. He took two menacing steps forward. His ears began to wiggle, and the skin of his scalp rose and fell weirdly.

"I — I've met him."

"How?" he shrieked. "How? I've been here for years. I've never met him."

"It was an accident."

"You did do it." Meeker's voice dropped into his throat, became a snarl. His fists closed. "It was your fault. You told Smith to do it."

"I did no such thing! If you insult or threaten me again — I promise you, John, you'll never see another Negro in St. Cat's. Ever." Meeker hesitated. His eyes became moist at the corners, his head wavered. The sight of him standing there, so pitiably cowed, was abhorrent to me. "I didn't ask him," I said. "As far as I know Horn Smith thought — thinks — I'm the most useless person born. But, we'll see. I've got his private number. If you're right — if they've come because of him — then I don't want them. They can go and good riddance. Now get out of here. I'm sick of looking at you."

"When will you call him?"

"As soon as you leave."

"I want to be there."

"No." I took him by the arm and led him out, down the corridor. He offered no resistance. The arm I held was limp,

and the vague odors of his body drifted feebly to my nose like
the tattered shreds of an old spider web. Meeker laughed several times as we walked. Then he spoke.

"How did you do it, Pratt? You of all people? His private
number? How?"

"That's my business," I said, as I unlocked the door. "As for
you — if you want my advice — go home to your wife. She's
the one that needs love and comfort. Not that you're capable."

He stepped out onto the stoop, seemed a moment confused
by the light, then turned and grasped the lapels of my jacket.

"Please, Pratt. You've got to bring them back. I'll commit
suicide if you don't. I will."

"You tempt me," I said.

I sat at the table in unabashed, audible conversation with
my own mind, until long after Meeker's departure. He didn't
leave at once. For nearly half an hour he lingered in the courtyard, shoulders pressed against the walls of my rectory. At five-
minute intervals, Meeker would pull himself up to the office window; I would see unkempt hair, furrowed brow and black
eyes staring toward my telephone. Only when I retreated, at
last, to the kitchen, could he prevail upon himself to leave. I
sat, sipping coffee, for hours then; with each sip a new and con-
flicting emotion perturbed me.

There was fear, certainly: fear of Smith and of Meeker, fear
of what, soon, I would have to do. Disappointment: I had looked
forward to my new, useful pastorate. Embarrassment at the
gullibility of my pride, for I had assumed, without doubt-
ing, that all these things were the result of some personal deserving. Suspicion of Horn Smith's odd and insistent involve-
ment with a man, myself, whom he apparently despised. Anger,
too, indignation, at his careless use, not only of myself, but of

the St. Catharine's congregation, and the sanctity of our shared faith. And, finally, abysmal confusion: I could not comprehend, nor even surmise, the motivations and the objectives. But, of all these, fear was the greatest. I would have to confront Smith; I should, already, have been confronting him. Then I thought of Greensprings and I wondered if, indeed, all this were necessary. I could leave the next day, and Meeker's transient congregation would return, warmer, more comfortable after all, not in the least mindful, instruments that they were, of their one cold Sunday with C. B. Pratt.

A roach scurried out from behind my napkin holder. It was a spherical, tiny thing; a dot on marvelously efficient legs. An infant form, perhaps, of the larger, antenna-waving varieties; or perhaps a quite different species. I was not certain. The roach hesitated where several grains of sugar had spilled from my bowl. I shooed it away with the shadow of my moving hand and then, as it scuttled toward the table's rim, I brought my cornflakes box down directly in its path. The insect reversed its direction without, seemingly, reversing its round body. I shifted the cornflakes box. The roach stopped again, made a northwest turn, then a south, southwest turn, east and again a northwest turn, rushing forward each time until the ubiquitous box appeared in its path. A very equal contest: had the box been less broad, my view of the battlefield less complete, the roach's swiftness and maneuverability would have won it freedom. The roach executed one complete circle, as though in joy, as though in thanks, and disappeared over the table's far edge. Myself, here in Harlem: stymied, toyed with by giants. And not even sufficient, in my world, as that brown, swift dot in its own. Despised, though; similar in that.

I looked at my watch. It was two o'clock, just after. I said a prayer for my flagging determination. Then I stood. Hands

on table, I rehearsed, tested the tones of my voice. "Mr. Smith.
Excuse my bothering you — I know how busy you are. I know.
I'm sure your intentions were good. Mr. Smith, I don't want
to insult you. You must believe that. But a man's faith, it
shouldn't be tampered with. I'm going to ask you — please,
please allow these people to return to St. Catharine's. I cannot
accept them. Not under these circumstances. I cannot. Here
I stand. Mr. Smith. Excuse me for — " The phone was
ringing. I rushed down the hall, my haste diminishing as I
neared the instrument. I touched it with a calming hand; it
continued to ring despite the gesture. I stepped back. The
phone shrilled, mocking my timidity. I picked up the receiver.

"Hello?" I said.

"Hello. It's me. Puppet."

"Puppet? Oh, yes — yes. Mrs. Prather."

"I just called t'confirm our meeting — Thursday night."

"Oh . . ." I said. I was annoyed, there is no milder word,
annoyed at this remnant of my discarded future. I had no
patience with her questions, her cheerful voice. I wanted only
to terminate the conversation, and, to that end, I became
stupidly devious.

"Father? You there?"

"Oh, yes. Look, Mrs. Prather — its lucky you called. In fact,
I was just going to ring you up. You see, I — well, I just
learned, ah . . . There's been a sickness in the family. I'm
afraid I'll have to leave. Right now actually. And I won't be
back until the weekend."

"Oh, my goodness. My. My, my, my. That's too bad. Is it
your mother or your father?"

"No. They — " I had already ceased listening and her questions confused me. And so, for lack of ingenuity and the sake
of time saved, I agreed with her. "Yes," I said.

"Which?"

"Both." I was recalling then my parents' joint deadness, not their imagined diseases and, too late, I realized the inanity of my remark.

"Both? Both sick? How terrible. But how did it happen?"

"Well. Ah . . . It was contagious. You know, catching. Look, Mrs. Prather, I'll give you a ring as soon as — "

"What — what sort of thing was it? Oh, dear — you must think I'm awful — I know you're very upset just now."

"Yes. Well . . . I am." I was.

"What did you say? A fever?"

"That's it — fever."

"Well now, Father — you take care of your family. That's your Number One concern. We'll pray for you — all of us."

"Yes, yes indeed. Thanks for calling, Mrs. Prather. I'll be seeing you."

"Right, Father. And see you don't get it."

"What's that?"

"The fever. Don't you come down with it too. Oh, I know — I know what you do. You go buy one of those little baby masks."

"I'll do just that. Thanks, Mrs. Prather."

"I guess that'd work. Or would it? Now I think, that keeps the baby from gettin' your germs. You think it works both ways?"

"I'm sure."

"Well, maybe. Are they guaranteed?"

"I don't know. I've never bought one."

"No, I mean your parents. Are they — what's the word when nobody can see you?"

"Invisible?"

"No — I mean because you're sick?"

"Oh. Quarantined."

"That's it. Look. I'll just take a peek in my medicine chest."

"No. No need t'do that. Wait — yes . . . Someone's at the door. My taxi. I've got to fly."

"Okay, Father. We'll be praying."

"Thanks. Thanks for the help. Good-bye."

I stood on tiptoes and did a graceless pirouette there by the cradled receiver, humming, groaning, chiding myself. Then, as an outward and visible sign of penitence, I slapped my sore knuckles sharply against the desk's edge. I was very angry: angry at myself, at the clumsy lies I had forced Puppet Prather to accept, but angry, too, at Horn Smith. He was the determining cause of this, of the bruises and lacerations on my face, of my present untenable position in Harlem. And from that moment's anger derived the strength and purposefulness I had lacked all afternoon. I drew out Smith's card. Then, without hesitation, I dialed his number.

"Smith here."

"Yes. Uh . . . hello."

"Hello. Who is this?"

"C. B. Pratt." There was silence. "Father Pratt, from St. Bartholomew's Church."

"I know where you come from. What is it you want, Mr. Pratt? My mother stands right here beside me."

"It's not about your mother. I have something important to tell you. It's about — "

"Can't talk now, Mr. Pratt. I am doing many things at once."

"Oh. But it's important." Silence. "Perhaps then — perhaps you could come over here this evening."

"No. I'm going away."

"But it's important."

"Well . . . All right. You can come over here. Come just

before six if you must — but not later than that — at six I must
catch a plane."

"Over there?"

"Yes, Mr. Pratt. Over here. Is it too far for you to walk?"

"No, but I mean . . . Yes. Yes, I'll come."

"Good-bye, Mr. Pratt."

The phone clicked. Sputtered. I held it to my ear in senseless, shocked expectation until the long hum of the dial tone
returned. When I put the receiver down, the clunk-clunk of
metal on metal suggested brutal blows and the hard paraphernalia
lia of mayhem. Blackjacks. Lead pipes. Gun butts. Horn
Smith was angry. He had planned my humiliation, perhaps
even my death, for a little before six. No white man had ever
before been allowed in Horn's Place. I began pacing up and
down in front of the bookshelves. It was two-thirty. More
than three hours yet. Three hours until . . . I looked up then,
at my bookshelf. I saw and my eyes momentarily comprehended,
doubted, rejected what they saw. Then my head swerved back
with such reflexive violence that my second-best glasses jumped
off my nose and bounced across the carpet.

I wanted to hurry forward, to retrieve my glasses and answer,
at once, the doubts that perturbed my mind. But I allowed
myself only the most deliberate movements, as an antidote to
what seemed incipient madness. "It can't be," I said. "It can't
be, because — because it just can't be." I picked up my
glasses, adjusted them on the bridge of my nose, over each ear.
Then, hands behind my back, as a precaution, I think, against
self-destructive acts, I walked slowly to the book case. It was
there. Thucydides was there. Where it had always been, between Tacitus and Trollope.

I ran my fingers lightly over the shelf edge. What else had
been removed? Augustine and Virgil. But there, in plain
sight, first book on the top shelf, was my copy of the *Confes-*

sions. Paranoia, I thought, these are the symptoms of paranoia. I searched the lower shelf: twice along its length from left to right. No Virgil. And now there was a gap, as well, just after Catullus. "What begins with C?" I asked. Cicero. My Cicero was gone. I lowered my head and allowed its weight to drag my torso down until my fingers hung suspended just over my insteps. I had begun to feel faint. I saw where the brown carpet padding showed through in an inch-square hole beside my right toe. "Frayed," I said. Then I stood upright and took my Thucydides down, caressing my cheek rhythmically with its cool binding. I walked to my chair.

Several of my assumptions now appeared invalid. Horn Smith was exculpated. He hadn't been to the rectory in a week, and during that time, two books had vanished and two had been returned. No. Only one had disappeared. Nicholas Breakspeare? But that assumption seemed hardly more just. Nicholas couldn't read Greek or Latin, and the books, certainly, had not been sold. I thumbed through my Thucydides. The pages offered no evidence. I smelled the book; that, too, was inconclusive. I lit my pipe and watched the tobacco strands wriggle like impaled snakes in the match flame. My pipe went out. I knocked the ashes into my trash basket and stood up.

Nicholas was seated in the choir loft. I heard him reading out loud in a low, uncertain monotone. When he saw me, he jumped quickly to his feet, and the book slapped shut with a sound that echoed far out into the nave.

"The Bible, Cap," he said, waving a thick book. "Reading the Bible. Gotta do the lesson next Sunday."

"Nicholas. Come into my office. I must speak to you." He frowned, suspicious of my tone. He took a step forward, smiled, then stopped.

"I do something wrong?"

"I don't know," I said. "Come in, please."

"Okay, Cap."

"Now look — " I said, pointing at my bookcase.

"A little dust is all. I just run a rag over it — "

"No. Listen, please. See — see that book?" He nodded patiently. "That's Thucydides. Remember? I told you he was gone. Well, now he's back. And that's not all — no sir. Two other books went as well, only . . . Only, one's come back and the other's still gone. It belongs here. And still a third book — sorry, a fourth book — a fourth book just this minute vanished. All I want t'know, Nicholas — I'm not accusing you of anything — all I . . . Just tell me what's happening, that's all." Nicholas thought a moment. Then he examined the empty spaces, rapped the bookshelves with his knuckles. He whistled softly for a few moments. And, as he performed these meaningless acts, I could feel sensation swiftly ebbing from my fingertips, replaced by a painful tingling. My breath came in short, hard gasps that lodged, like blows, just under my ribs. Round, red dots surfaced in my vision. I thought I was falling. I stumbled to the armchair and sat heavily. One of the arms cracked, seemed to give way, under my considerable weight. Nicholas stared at me. He frowned and gnawed thoughtfully at the insides of his cheeks.

"You're sure about this?"

"I knew it," I said. I began plucking nervously at the stem of a fat, bloated rose in the slipcover pattern. "I knew you'd say that. Your very words. I knew it." The weak fabric parted. I pushed my finger deep into the rose's throat.

"Simmer down, man. Take it easy. You're ruinin' that." He came over and sat on his haunches just in front of me. "I mean. You know — it's funny, ain't it? If I didn't take them books — and I didn't — who else is there?"

"I don't know," I said. Nicholas frowned. Then he whistled a single note, opened his mouth, closed it, opened it again.

"Of course," he said finally. "There's something else. It's possible, y'know. Possible."

"What?"

"Now don't get all het up."

"Yes? What? Go on?"

"You — ah . . . You ever walk in your sleep?"

"Fine," I said. I slapped my hands together. "Just fine. Just damn fine. Do I walk in my sleep? Oh, just damn fine."

"Wait now," he said, as he moved his hand slowly, more slowly, up and down in front of my eyes. "Relax. Relax. Let's think about this. Reason I ask — we had a lotta funny things happen back home when I's a kid. Couldn't figure it out. Crazy things — like one morning, there's a big, red heart painted on the living room ceiling. My father give me a good lickin' an' all the time it's Aunt Flora, my mother's sister. She'd get up — bake cakes, plant flowers in the yard, do the craziest things. And in the daytime — man, she don't know nothin' about it. Nice lady, about your age, too."

"Nicholas . . . I don't walk in my sleep. I never have. Look, I've lived with people all my life — ah . . . ."

"Remember something?"

"Well — but I was only a child." I dug my fingers deep into my thinning hair and scratched until my scalp burned. "Last couple of weeks — it's true — I've been having weird dreams. And I don't ordinarily dream at all."

"About books, huh?"

"No. But — I don't feel rested in the morning. Not at all. I'm not getting my proper sleep, that's partly why I'm like this." I held my hand out flat. Nicholas watched as it jittered between our eyes. He shook his head.

"See. I tell you what. I got some clothesline in my kit. You tie your leg to the bed. When you go t'sleep, I mean. Then, if you get up at night — bang, you'll know." He slapped his hands together.

"Bang. I'll know. Then I can use the rope to hang myself."

"Cap. This ain't you. This ain't the Cap I know — I thought you're cool, man." He stood and, to better represent his disappointment, turned his back on me.

"Is that so?" I said, not without a certain annoyance.

"Yeah. It's so. Like when they busted you up. I thought you took that real good. He don't look it, I say, but that cat's cool. Tough." He faced me. "Now — I don't know." He shook his head in long, very deliberate arcs. Then he sighed. It was meant as a friendly rebuke, I knew that, and I had a friendly answer to his rebuke.

"Are you cool, Nicholas?" I asked.

"Well. Sometimes, man." He flipped his palm open at shoulder height; a gesture of self-deprecation. Then, interested in his palm, he brought it close for examination.

"Maybe you'd do me a favor, then? It'd make me feel a lot better. A lot cooler." I smiled at him with as much harmless innocence as the stitching in my lower lip would allow.

"Sure, Cap. What is it?"

"Would you mind — ah . . . Would you take a little walk with me?"

"A little walk?" He leaned forward and cupped his ear.

"Yes. You see, it's not the books I'm scared of, Nicholas. Though they're part of it. I need your moral support."

"Where's this little walk to?"

"Not far. Just up to Lenox Avenue and — and over to Horn's Place." Nicholas smiled. He didn't believe me. For a short moment he returned to his haunches, then stood up suddenly, when my desperate, entreating grimace did not change. He laughed finally; the laugh became a sputter and several flecks of saliva appeared on his chin.

"You're kidding."

"No."

"Then you're nuts."

"No."

"No?" he snorted. "That's no little walk, that's a death march. The last mile — for you anyways."

"You aren't cool, are you?"

"Fuck cool, man. The morgue's cool."

"Look, Nicholas," I said. "It won't be so bad. Really. I'm not going t'storm the place. I've got an invitation from Smith. An appointment — for just before six. Just walk over there with me — will you? I'm a little nervous about it. I've had one bad experience already." Nicholas, meanwhile, had seated himself in my swivel chair. He was rocking, sending the chair backward with short, sharp toe movements. He pulled his lip back over his upper teeth and grinned uncertainly.

"Sorry, Cap. I can't do that. You'll be all right. I was exaggeratin'. If, like you say, Smith made an appointment — sure, you'll be all right. But you gotta see my position. If I go up there, arm 'n arm with you, it just ain't gonna do me no good. An' that's the truth. I mean, how can I explain — "

"But they must know you work here — "

"Yeah, but that's different. That's my assignment." His voice wavered as it crossed that last syllable.

"Your what?"

"Assignment." He shrugged a third time. "I ain't supposed t'say — well, Smith tells me t' work here." I opened my mouth; Nicholas, however, had changed the subject before I could question him. "But why's Smith want t'talk with you?"

"He doesn't. It's me. I'm talking with him."

"Why?"

"Because, Nicholas — " I hesitated. "Because I just learned the ugly truth. My lovely, new congregation — you know? They're not mine at all. They're Smith's. He ordered them over here."

"Yeah, I know."

"You know."

"Sure. What you think — I clean up this place for fun?" He giggled. "Smith told me 'bout it a good, long time ago. Told me t'get the place ready. But, man, you don't have t'thank him."

"I'm not going to. No, friend. I'm going to tell him to take his congregation and send them right back where they came from."

"Why, Cap? Why?"

"Why? You can ask that? I don't know how Baptists do things, but, sorry, to me, church isn't a game of musical pews. Besides, I'm suspicious of the whole lot. There's something fishy. There's got to be. Meeker told me, half of them, they aren't even confirmed. If you ask me, the whole thing's just a meeting place for the movement. Well. Let Meeker have them back. He's not particular."

"No, Cap." Nicholas shook his head. "You're wrong. Them people's as good Christians as any. I know. It's just different here and you don't understand. Here, man, the movement's everything. Nobody's gonna buck it. Nobody'd dare. Cap, look at it this way — who's better for them? You or that nut Meeker? He's a nut. We all know it. He think's he's a black man. Well, he ain't, brother, he ain't — takes more'n feelin' black t'be black. He ain't fish or fowl. If Horn's sick of him, that's good, real good. You don't do right t'send them back."

"Well. I don't know." I rubbed the back of my hand across my forehead. "Anyone who wants to stay can stay, but I won't have them being forced. I'll close the church first. Smith won't use me like this. I won't allow it."

"Cap," said Nicholas sadly. "We all bein' used. By the white man. By the movement. By our own wives and kids. It's the truth."

"Well. You may be right. But, thanks, they made a mistake — they let me know it." I stood up. "Are you coming with me?"

"Can't do it."

I nodded. "Right," I said. "I'll just have to go alone." Nicholas stood and walked slowly toward the chancel door. When he had reached it, he put his hand on the jamb, turned and smiled.

"One thing. Guess I don't have to do all this cleanin' and paintin' no more."

"No ill wind," I said, "but it blows someone some good."

"You are cool, Cap," Nicholas touched his eyebrow. "Different than I thought. But cool. Honky cool."

"Honky cool," I said. "That's me."

I rounded the corner and began walking irresolutely up Lenox Avenue to Horn's Place. I hesitated. They were there, just as I had feared; seven or eight Horn Greens loitered near that dreadful fence. Twenty minutes to six. I bent to straighten my sock, and, as I did so, maneuvered sideways, nearer to the building wall. Through a dingy plate glass front, I saw sinks and toilet seats, faucets, brass elbows, cans of Drano, and, on the walls, at least twenty faded cheesecake calendars. I pressed my nose to the glass. A. Krumnitz, licensed plumber. Black grime had invested A. Krumnitz' office. His desk, his

swivel chair, each was covered by a homogeneous blanket of
dark filth. A. Krumnitz, I knew, had been purged from Harlem. The wind poked reproachful fingertips at my back. My
nose dribbled. I took out a handkerchief, pressed it to my nose
and then turned my head to peer up the Avenue. The tabards
were still there; time had nearly run out.

My shoes weren't shined: I noted that fact and little else as I
walked toward Horn's Place. My hands fisted in their pockets.
I muttered a prayer. As I approached the fence, I sensed, rather
than saw, an alertness galvanize the lounging Horn's men.
Without raising my eyes, I proceeded toward the opening. A
hand grasped my jacket, pinching, as well, the skin of my biceps.
I jerked aside.

"Where you goin' Charlie?"

"I — " But I had forgotten my rehearsed explanation, my
purpose, forgotten, too, my fears. I had seen the balls.

Twelve balls on a fence. I reached out my fingertips and
touched the rough, mottled pate of the nearest. Measured vari-
ations on an extraordinary theme; yet more extraordinary in
their execution. From left to right, from the first ball to the
eighth, a ritual maiming heightened by degrees. The eighth
ball was its culmination: riddled, shrieking, agonized. And
then, from the ninth ball onward, a second sort of mutilation
was evolved. This, a wasting, a natural decay — rather like
the sad, slow melting of candles or the body's necessary putre-
faction. The twelfth was considerably smaller; it sagged, as
though on the edges of liquidity. I stepped back; I tried to as-
similate the entire sequence. Beyond roundness, there was no
patent anthropomorphism. And yet the progress of a specifically
human suffering was abstracted there. The modeling of each
ball was subtle and expert. It was a magnificent abomination;
I had not thought to find such sophistication, not certainly amid

the jungles of Harlem. A hand clutched at my lapel. It pressed
inward and rubbed its knuckles hard against my sensitive ribs.
I backed away.

"Who made those?" I asked.

"Max," said the man whose hand was on my chest, "let's take
this white prick and dump him someplace."

"No," I said. "I'm going in there. I have an appointment
with Mr. Smith."

"Mr. Smith?" he laughed. "That's a good one — man, Horn
don't need his ass wiped." There was concerted laughter.

"Lookit his face. Someone worked him over good."

"Hey, white man, what I'm gonna do — I'm gonna shit in
the corner and make you look for your supper."

"I'm — I have to go in. Right now. Mr. Smith is waiting
for me and I'm late."

I tried to push past him, but my bluff was not persuasive.
He grabbed at my collar with such force that the studs popped
loose. The collar came off in his hand.

"You scalped him, Percy."

"It just come off. It come off right in my hand."

"Maybe he's a fake."

"No. That's the way they go on." Percy slipped the collar
around his neck and fixed it in place with a lowered chin. He
rubbed his hands pompously over his stomach. "Jeesus Christ.
Jeeesus Christ, brothers. Believe in Jesus, the white man's cock
sucker. He'll take your pennies, then he'll fetch you a good,
swift kick in the chops. And you'd better like it, brother, 'cause
he's God." This bitter parody was applauded. I grabbed for
the collar, but Percy slapped my wrist aside.

"You had your fun, honky. Now I'm a priest."

"Hey, you cats — " A short man with a thin mustache and a
pencil behind each ear was standing at the door of Horn's Place.

He gestured impatiently, an inward movement of his left hand and forearm. "Send that man up. Horn's in a hurry. Come on, Percy — don't stand there — send him up." The short man disappeared. Percy stared at his comrades. Two shrugged. One said, "Son-of-a-bitch." Chastened, Percy began fumbling clumsily with my collar. I snatched it from his hand.

"Come on, big mouth," I said. "Game's over."

I hardly knew just what I expected to find there, beyond the double front doors. Something savage, grotesque, I suppose; certainly not the wide, deep room, in sound and aspect seeming no more malevolent than a busy newspaper office. There were about forty desks, mostly old, heavy, wooden things, separated by low railings. For sounds, there were shrill ringings, voices shouting names and numbers, the chatter of typewriters. Sets of three or four desks were grouped together and, above each set, a sign had been suspended on chains; "Security," "Transportation," "Housing," "Sanitation," "Medical," "Recreation," "Credit," "Legal," "H.W.C.," "Recruiting." People sat on benches along the four walls. Large colored cards were held in laps, between dangling fingers. I hesitated, distracted by my curiosity, but Percy pulled me roughly along. He led me to a metal staircase that stood by the far left wall.

"What — " I asked, "what are these people waiting for?"

"Mind your own business, Whitey."

"It doesn't look too bad," I said, chiefly to myself. "Looks like a government office, that's what."

The stairs were not lit. My eyes adjusted only with difficulty to the deep shadows on the upper steps. When we reached the top, two men appeared at either side of the landing. They wore guns. "Search him," said Percy. Sure hands examined me from ankles to armpits, rather too roughly for my sore body's comfort. I noticed, moreover, that Percy, himself, was not exempt, though he was treated more gently. The guards grunted simultaneously; then they let us continue. Percy guided me along the darkened corridor. We passed two doors that faced each other: "Mr. Mody" was on the left; "Mr. Purston" was on the right. Beyond these, at the far end of the hall, was a single, unmarked door. Percy knocked.

"Come in."

The door was opened. By the glare of a single, naked bulb, I saw Horn Smith. He was seated at a wide, low desk; the short, mustached man who had just rescued me stood to his right. I stepped forward, into the room. There was little in the way of furniture: one wooden armchair; the desk, its top bearing a telephone and a photograph of Cerela Smith; a costumer; a small table with boxing trophies, over which Smith had carelessly draped an overcoat. The walls were bare, but for the east, where the huge wedge of his horn rested in silhouette, projected, distorted, quiescent now. Watching. It swiveled and subsided as the single bulb swung on its wire.

"Sign here," said the short man. Smith made an X.

"Sit down, Mr. Pratt," said Smith. The short man whispered something, then slipped several sheets into his attaché case and left us. The door closed.

"I have five minutes, Mr. Pratt. What's your problem?"

"A favor. Not a problem." I looked down at my lap. My agitated, clenching fingers had crushed the collar: the two ends were bent at right angles to each other. Instinctively, I touched my throat.

"What favor? Quickly, please, Mr. Pratt."

"I want — " I swallowed. "I want you to send them back. My congregation. Let them go back."

"Back?" He tilted his head, frowned. The horn dipped and rose, making an invisible check sign in the air. "Back, Mr.

Pratt? I don't understand this. I thought you wanted people there," he indicated the window, "in that great, empty place. To worship your God."

"I do. Of course, I do. But they must have a choice. Don't force them to stay — or to go. They must be free, Mr. Smith."

"Free," he said, "Free . . . free . . ." He repeated the word slowly and with, it seemed, a private irony. Smith stood, hands behind back, horn pointed toward the floor, and walked slowly to the open window. He placed his palms on the sill and stared out. I realized then that his window opened onto my court-yard, that Smith was able to watch all my comings and goings. "I see," he said finally. "But if no one comes, Mr. Pratt. Then they knock the old church down."

"It doesn't matter," I said. "They'll knock it down anyway."

"Is that so?" He nodded, "and when?"

"Next April they'll start. Close it down first, I guess."

"More than a year." He stood upright and then he smiled. "Who knows, Mr. Pratt. I may be dead by then."

"Yes. We none of us know. But, Mr. Smith — about my congregation. If you did all this for my sake . . . Well, I deeply — deeply — appreciate your gesture. But it's not fair. You've hurt John Meeker terribly. Terribly. He's heart-broken. I can't allow that."

"So?" He returned to his desk. "So? What do you care? Mr. Meeker. He's no friend of yours. Look at your face, Mr. Pratt."

"Yes. You see, he thought I'd taken them away. He was angry. I don't really blame him. He's done great things here, Mr. Smith. Great things — "

"No. You are wrong, Mr. Pratt. He did nothing. I did it. Without me, Mr. Meeker is dead in Harlem. I gave and now I will take away. Meeker is a fool."

"That may be. But it's his congregation, no matter what you

say. I won't be a servant of your whims, Mr. Smith. I'll close
my church first."

"But Mr. Pratt — " Smith smiled. "I chose Mr. Meeker. Now
I choose you. Mr. Meeker, he is too violent. He's not good for
my people. You are a gentle man."

"Too violent! You've got a nerve. Excuse my frankness,
Mr. Smith, but you're no one to talk about violence. You — of
all people. You retail violence. You buy and sell it. I was at
the rally last Sunday. Don't tell me about violence." I almost
stood in the excess of my indignation. "You've got a bloody
nerve."

"Is that so?" Smith leaned across the desk. His eyes opened
very wide beneath the sharp, now malignant-seeming pro-
tuberance. I gagged. My kneecaps danced, slapping together
in my lap.

"That — yes, it is so." Horn Smith nodded. He closed his
eyes. Then his hands began moving slowly up and down over
the surface of his desk. As a blind man's might, searching.

"All right, Mr. Pratt. We don't see eye to eye. I hoped we
could work together. But it's not possible. I will do what you
ask."

"You will?"

"I will."

"Thank you, Mr. Smith. I didn't mean to get angry. Really,
it's none of my business — " He raised his right hand.

"You don't let me finish."

"Oh. I didn't know. I'm sorry."

"I will do what you ask, yes — but on two conditions."

"Conditions?"

"Yes. Do I use the wrong word?"

"No."

"Conditions, then." Smith took a cravat from his desk

drawer and began to play with it. A smile appeared on his face.

"What conditions?"

"One," said Smith. He draped the cravat over his horn, and held the two ends in either hand. "One," he repeated, he pulled his right hand down; his left hand rose, almost to the horn. "They all go. All your people. Nobody comes to your church. Ever again."

"Why?"

"I have my reasons, Mr. Pratt." He pulled his left hand down.

"Okay. All right. I agree."

"Two. Condition number two." He began pulling his hands up and down in rapid alternation. Thick ropes of muscle formed at either side of his neck. "Two — that you, Mr. Pratt, you come to the party I give. One week from this Saturday night."

"A party?"

"Yes. A nice, little party. A celebration — for some of my friends. You are a friend, no — you will come?" I frowned so severely that my eyes and forehead began to ache.

"No, Mr. Smith. Please. I don't think I could."

"You will, Mr. Pratt." He slipped the cravat off his horn and wrapped it around a huge right fist. "If you don't come — I promise you — that congregation of yours, they won't go back to St. Catharine's. No. I will make them all Baptists. One. Two. Three. Like that." He snapped his fingers. "Don't think I can't do it. Baptists are nice. They're easier to handle."

"But — will there be other white men?"

"No," he shook his head sadly. Then he knotted the cravat around his neck. "No. I don't have so many white friends. A shame. But you came here to meet Negroes. Is that not so? Not white men."

"What is it, Mr. Smith? Will you have me killed?"

"Mr. Pratt," he said in a neutral, merely declaratory tone. "When you are killed — there will be no party. I ask once more. Are you coming?"

"I'll come."

"Fine. That's what I like about white men — they make such good servants." He grinned. "I'll send Nicholas with your invitation."

"Don't be so sure of yourself," I said. "I know you're using all of us. I saw Zeitzoff and Krushinsky. But some day, Mr. Smith, your time will come."

"But not you, Mr. Pratt." He pointed a sudden forefinger at my chest. "How could I use you? You're not an angry Jewish Communist like Mr. Zeitzoff. Not a stupid, guilty liberal Christian like Mr. Meeker. I eat those men for breakfast. I suck their juices out. I live on them. But you, Mr. Pratt. You're not angry. You're not guilty. I cannot use you."

"I'll go now," I said. I stood up. "Thank you for your time." I turned my back on him and walked to the door.

"See you Saturday, Mr. Pratt."

"As you please," I said.

"What is it, Mr. Pratt? You think I'm a tyrant? A black Hitler?"

"Perhaps I do." I opened the door.

"Be happy then," he said. "What do they say? *Sic semper tyrannis?*"

"What?" I whirled around. "What was that?" Smith's eyes opened wide.

"Percy," he said. "Show Father Pratt out."

Excerpt from the Autobiography of George Horn Smith

. . . I was seventeen when this thing happened and still only an amateur. There is a famous boxing tournament in the big city of Washington, and Mr. Koch, he sends me there. It is my first time on a train. I remember now, I jump up and down in my seat, push my hands against the glass window, ask questions all the time. I am so excited. "Look at this!" I say. "Look at that! Look! Look!" Thomas Jefferson, my trainer, he shakes his head. Then he pulls his hat down over his eyes and he goes to sleep. I don't mind. I talk to the people and my horn taps at the window when I speak. "See that building! See that river! Do you know what place this is? Do you know how fast we are going?" And the people, they say nothing. White people. People who look at each other, they shake their heads. People who hide themselves behind big newspapers. People who close their eyes but do not sleep. White people. I am going south where hatred lives.

Mr. Koch has a room for us at the YMCA, but it is hot in Washington and me, I cannot sit still in that little room. "Go to the gym then," Thomas Jefferson says, "One block down the street. Go. You make me nervous." And so I take my little bag and I walk in the street until I see the gym place. It is almost night, dinner time and no one is in the gym. I change my clothes, then I run for twenty minutes. I feel very good, full of my young life. Proud. Strong. I slap the light bag. I jump rope. Then, when I am tired, I think — yes, I will use some of the little money Mr. Koch gives me. I will see a movie show. I walk into the shower room. Whistling. Very happy.

I am still whistling, when I come out of the shower, naked, with only a towel to cover my body. I rub my back, stretch my body — and then my ears hear something. A man is clearing his throat. I look around. Two white men sit on a bench near my locker. They do nothing, they say nothing, but their eyes are always watching me. Now I can see another man and this man is behind me, his hand is on the windowsill. I know that something is wrong. My heart begins to beat. I cover my groin with the towel. I don't want to go near them, but I am naked and I must get my pants. I walk down the aisle, down to where my little bag is. The men watch me as I walk. I pick up my bag. The bag is empty.

"Get the door, Em." It is one of the sitting men. He says this in a quiet voice, as if there is business to do but he is very tired. The two men stand up. I am very afraid. I know already that they will hurt me. The man who speaks is small, like me. His face is dark with not having shaved and there are no teeth in one side of his mouth. He walks near to me. The other man is very, very big. He walks around behind me. I look from one man to the other. The aisle is very narrow and I have no room to move. The little man laughs. He knows I am helpless. I hold out my bag to him.

"All my things are gone," I say.

"If it ain't the big, black hornhead. Come all the way from New York City."

"Mister. Did you take them?" I say.

"A real snotty nigger, thinks he's big stuff."

"Did you take them?"

"Sure, hornhead, we took them."

"Give them back to me." The little man looks at the big man. He shakes his head.

"Must be they're right, Clem. Must be. He sounds real snotty t'me. Guess, up in New York City, they treat their niggers too soft."

"Mister," I say. "I don't want no trouble. Just give me my things."

"Hornhead. Who told you t'come in here?"

"I —"

"In here, hornhead. Don't you read signs?"

"Mister. I don't learn to read."

"Is that so? Must be pretty stupid — even for a nigger. Clem, I think we better give hornhead here a little reading lesson." He looks at the man called Clem. I turn my head, but, before I can move, Clem jumps at me from behind. He holds my arms back in a half nelson. The little man laughs. Then he punches me, with all his strength, hard where a man's ribs end.

"Stupid nigger," says the little man. He hits me again. I shriek like a pig when its insides are cut out. The pain makes my eyes go crossed. "Stupid nigger. This locker room, see, it's for white men only. That shower, that's for white men only. That there john, that's for white men only. You don't respect a white man's property — but, brother, you're gonna respect this." He steps back like a football player who measures for a long field goal. Then he kicks me in the soft, naked parts of my groin. My legs, they lose their feeling. I want to fall to the ground, to clutch my body. But the big man, Clem, he holds me up, he shakes me like a little doll. The pain is so bad, a knife twisting in my back, that, even hanging there, I must bring my knees to my chest. And the white man kicks me again. Under, where I hang exposed.

"Em. Come on over here." The third man comes. "Put his watch and his wallet in the bag. This here other stuff — well, just throw it away. He ain't gonna fight, not tomorrow he ain't."

"That's a funny thing. That there horn," says the man called Em. "I ain't never seen a thing like that."

"Don't touch it, stupid, you'll get the clap."

"Yeah?" says Em. He pulls his hand away.

"Clem. Drag him over to the door. No. Over there."

Clem drags my body to a door at the far back of the locker room. The door, there is a red light over it. It opens out onto a metal fire escape. Em kicks my bag out. "No!" I say. "No!" I think they will throw me down to the street. But they do not. Clem, he just drops me there, on the fire escape. The door slams shut. Locked. I hear the noises of a busy street down below, down where the metal stairs go. And I am naked.

In that night, I, George Horn Smith, I suffered many things that do hurt to a man's pride. I will not tell you those things, for, even this day, so much later, I feel anger when I think of what happened that night. The man who kicked me, his name was Zeke Foss. Maybe you will remember him. I fought with Zeke Foss in a boxing ring five years later in the city of Cincinnati. In the fourth round I knocked him unconscious with a strong right hand. No one was holding him from behind. A fair fight. Zeke Foss was dead that night.

If I tell you this now, I tell it as a warning. I was not sorry that I killed Zeke Foss. No. I am not sorry now. I wanted to destroy him then, just as now I want to destroy anyone that hates the color of my skin, that shames the dignity of my people. Any man. Any man. I mean to destroy them. And I will . . .

PART THREE

Getting Out Again

Sic semper tyrannis . . . That phrase, spoken — as it had been — as an explicit challenge, tantalized my imagination during those ten days before Smith's party, tempted me to certain assumptions that, just a week before, I would have considered preposterous. *Sic semper tyrannis* . . . It represented no greater sophistication in the classics, certainly, than *Veni, vidi, vici* or *E pluribus unum:* common enough mottoes, phrases that any man might encounter in his lifetime, although far less likely in an illiterate. And Smith had pronounced it impeccably. He had not anglicized the vowels, especially not the long "e" in *semper.* Taken by itself, of course, the event had little significance; juxtaposed, however, against the disappearance of my books, it became a patent, a purposeful insinuation. At times there seemed to be no other option: Smith could read and speak Latin and most probably Greek as well. And yet this supposition was so incongruous — when presumed in conjunction with his horn, with the autobiography and with the native Caribbean sing-song — that I began to question the processes and powers of my reasoning. "A wish fulfillment," I thought. "Next he'll be a Christian — and chasing butterflies."

By Thursday of the second week I was in execrable shape. I seldom could sleep through two successive hours. My stomach

squeaked and sputtered, then sagged in a disabling nausea. On
Monday my stitches were taken out; the next morning a dentist,
against the strong objections of my cowardice, removed the
root of my broken tooth — an experience which worried me
beforehand, terrified me in its actuality, and haunted me for
days afterward. I was in a state of unremitting hypertension.
My fingers and knee joints quivered. My eyeballs ached whenever I shifted focus. My shoulders shrugged of their own accord, sometimes quite to my ears. Unexpected noises became
my chief foe, and the old rectory, in apparent spite, growled
and crackled, throwing up odd words, notes of music and dozens of sharp, unexplained pops. Nicholas Breakspeare deserted
me for five days, pleading Horn business, and, on Sunday, as
threatened, St. Bartholomew's was empty. I might have borne
all these things, but for my dread of the coming Saturday night.
I expected the very worst. Wednesday I spent an hour packing; and two hours, thereafter, undoing what I had packed.

By three o'clock Thursday afternoon I no longer doubted the
literacy of George Horn Smith. In the morning I had begun
desultory work on a monograph — one I had long intended
writing — on aspects of Catholicism in medieval England. My
research lasted no more than a few hours: I discovered at the
outset and to my astonishment, that the real name of Adrian
IV, the only English pope, was Nicholas Breakspeare. I realized
then why the name had seemed so familiar. I called Nicholas
into my office, but he knew nothing of his Horn name's origin.
Like all the others, it had been given him by Smith. On a
hunch I asked Nicholas for a list of Horn names and, by the
evening, I had placed nearly all of them. They fell into two
major categories: the Percivals and Gawains derived from
Malory's *Morte d'Arthur* and selected French romances; the
Nicholas Breakspeares from esoteric portions of medieval his-

tory. Some — like Aylbrous Purston and Cubert Mody — were apparently the pure products of Smith's imagination. But there could be no question of coincidence. Nicholas had supplied forty-two names: I had traced thirty-six in no more than two hours work.

And then, on reflection, I realized just how thoroughly Smith's medievalism had influenced the Horn movement. The tabards and hosen; Smith's own burgher's robes; the musicians and their triumphant processionals. Even the unicorn emblem, I found, had been reproduced from a portion of the Bayeux tapestry. The movement's tenor, the relationships between the men and their leaders was explicitly feudal. Not only could Smith read Latin and Greek: he was, most probably, a scholar-historian as well. I reread the Autobiography, but there was no intimation, in the uncompromising and monosyllabic style, of secret abilities suppressed. Smith was determined to appear a freak, an animal — essentially a liberal white man's Negro: the eighteenth century's noble savage.

There occurred, that week, still another extraordinary event: it happened on Friday morning. The weather had turned mild, a breezy, near-cloudless day, and these preliminaries of spring had lured me to my front stoop. The cat, I saw, had returned from her winter's retirement. She sat in my courtyard's center, her back, as before, presented to the recory's façade. I stepped inside and returned with some tuna fish remnants from the previous day's lunch. I placed these near the basement: to my surprise, the cat left its haunches, approached the plate and proceeded to eat while crouching no more than two yards from my feet. I was both pleased and honored. I stepped discreetly backward and looked up into the morning sky, the same sky that was, give or take a few clouds perhaps, spreading itself over Greensprings as well. And, at that moment, I saw it.

A butterfly: an emblem. I saw a butterfly — blue and gaily dotted white. It floated, fluttered, then floated high above me, and, when I saw it, I thought, "This must be a sign." It seemed, you see, such an explicitly personal thing. And its appearance there was so anomalous that, standing, even as I was, in the midst of the twentieth century, I might have considered it a supernatural — God or demon given — symbol. Butterflies do not often mature in early March, less often at a great city's heart. And large, white-dotted blue butterflies are not, I think, indigenous to New York City. But these reflections were after the event. My immediate reaction was conditioned: I rushed in to get my net.

When I returned, the butterfly was still circling my court-yard, then at a twenty-five foot altitude. I shook my head. But-terfly hunting, contrary to common prejudice, is a superbly ex-acting pastime. Butterflies are very swift and wonderfully maneuverable; they are quite incapable of level, sustained pat-terns of flight. I realized, at first appraisal, that there was scant likelihood of a catch — though, certainly, I had never before so wanted to catch a butterfly.

It was flying counter-clockwise. I began my stalk in the op-posite direction. The butterfly appeared upset; as much aston-ished by its presence there as I was. My heart thumped. The butterfly, I saw, was spiraling gently downward, losing several feet of altitude at each circuit. I stopped walking, cleared the net's mouth and raised it slightly above my head. There was yet little hope — nine of ten successful catches are made of stationary butterflies. But here there were no succulent flowers; almost no chance of my butterfly's settling. I would have to risk a moving shot. The butterfly continued to swoop lower, now only five feet above me, and my opportunity came on the very next round. The net's mouth shot forward. The butter-fly hit the upper rim and bounced off, stunned. Terribly disappointed, I began hopping, skipping, making random, futile lunges. I rushed across the courtyard, stabbing skyward, but the butterfly rose up and fluttered easily over the nave of St. Bart's.

There was applause. I swerved, panting, my net still held at full cock. Almost every window in the rear of Horn's Place was occupied — some by several torsos each. I felt a flush of shame rise along my throat. "Everybody together now!" shouted a voice second story left. "Hip, hip hooray for honky!" And the chorus followed *con moto*. "Hip, hip hooray for honky!" But it was not unanimous: there were those whose hatred was too strong to be assuaged by mere irony — I heard boos, and raspberries as well. I acknowledged their sarcasm with a curt bow, took time to furl the net and then, reddened by embarrassment, ran up the rectory steps. And behind me . . . "Pick on someone your own size, you fat, white fart!" I might have cried.

And that afternoon it arrived:

George Horn Smith
requests the appearance
of
C. B. Pratt
at an informal party
to be held at
720 E. 126th Street
beginning at nine o'clock
Saturday, March 11th

Nicholas Breakspeare frowned when I opened the envelope; frowned as I read; frowned more severely as I, too, frowned. The invitation was printed on an excellent grade of paper. The lettering was embossed, Gothic, gold. My own name had been elegantly hand-printed. I placed the invitation under my nose and sniffed at it — as some fearful animal might.

"Well," I said, when I handed the card to Nicholas. "Some-

thing for the scrapbook." He read it — several times over, I
suppose — for he didn't comment immediately. Then he
whistled once, an off-key, unformed note.

"You going?"

"Are you?"

"Me?" He thumbed his left nipple. "Me? I don't get invited to these blasts. Not me. I'm nobody. But you — you going?"

"I have to, Nicholas. He threatened me. I'll be in big trouble if I don't. God knows, I wish there was some way out. I
wish. I wish. What — what're they like?"

"I said, Cap. I ain't never been."

"But you must've heard something."

"Yeah. I heard."

"Well . . . ?" He drew his upper lip back, and, when it
was fully withdrawn, his two rows of teeth joined to abuse the
lower one; gnawing, plucking at it.

"It ain't the place for you, Cap."

"I know that. Don't you think I know that?" I sighed. "Just
tell me what it's like."

"There's goings on."

"What goings on?"

"Drinking — "

"Drinking? You can do better than that. There's drinking
at the Bishop's annual lawn party."

"Sex," he shrugged again. "Heavy sex. Women and men.
Men and men. Women and women. Um — men and . . .
Men and women."

"You mentioned that. It's the same as women and men."

"Yeah. I guess."

"What else?"

"Dope. And acid. And initiation things — "

"Initiations?" A circular, cold spot appeared then in the center of both my palms. "What kind?"

"I don't know — honest. I only hear from other guys and they don't get no invitations neither. It's for Blues mostly 'n their women. They do — like . . . like they want t'do."

"White men there?"

"Uh-uh. Never. That's what's so funny. I mean. It's like Horn Smith bein' invited to George Wallace's place. It's real funny."

"Funny . . ." I slapped myself sharply on either cheek. "Do you think I'll get hurt?"

"Anything could happen. Me, I'd be scared t'go."

"Oh, boy," I said.

"Well," he shrugged and then put a fingertip delicately into his earhole. "Maybe it won't be so bad. Maybe they're 'xaggeratin'. You know how guys talk. What you could do — you could go and leave early."

"Yes." I thought a moment. "Yes. That's the answer. I'll show my face and leave. He said come, but he didn't say for how long."

"Sure, Cap. That's the trick."

"Will Purston be there, you think?"

"Yeah. He's a big ladies' man — they say his thing's a foot long. And he drinks big, too. Gets real nasty when he's bagged."

"Oh, boy," I said.

"Tell you what, Cap. Sunday, I'll look in here early. If you ain't back, I'll ring the cops."

"Oh, boy," I said. I rubbed the back of my wrist against my forehead. "Yes. You better do that."

Night fell on Saturday with the abruptness of some sorcerer's illusion. Afternoon was indistinguishable from morning; neither seemed more lucent than the earliest shades of dusk. The sky remained overcast throughout, and, from noon until just after three, an unenthusiastic drizzle misted down. The first hours of the evening, however, were dry and perceptibly cooler. When I stepped out onto the stoop, my cheeks, warm from agitation and the electric fire, seemed radiant embers in the chill air. My front door slammed; the sound reverberated behind me in the courtyard's confines, a blunt intimation of menace. I looked at my watch: only eight-fifteen. I had planned to arrive very early, depart very early — well before the festivities, whatever they might be, had properly begun.

Horn Smith's party was thirteen blocks downtown and three to the east. I had determined to walk, the better, I hoped, to ensure my anonymity. But I had never before been afoot during a Harlem Saturday night, and, after just the first few blocks, I regretted my decision. Despite the cool, whole apartments, it appeared, had been transplanted to the pavement. Kitchen tables, chairs, crockery, utensils, a bird cage and a bird, two cribs, pillows, phonographs, children's games, an army cot and blankets. And people moved among these items, easily, comfortably, as though in some communal living place. Music was ubiquitous: strident, jumbled; thrown from open windows, portables, parked cars, upthrust throats. Salutations were defamatory shouts; handshakes became turbulent wrestling holds. I could scarcely make progress along the sidewalks, and, fearing a challenge, I stepped finally out, into the avenue itself. Large crowds milled at every corner: aimless and expectant, resembling crowds before some climactic and brutal sporting event. And, indeed, I sensed in these people an appreciation of death, death considered as fearful and superb entertainment.

As I walked, I jerked my hat brim down and raised my scarf up, over my white neck and ears. There was a fire to the east, just off Seventh. Short-lived sparks rose up and faltered above the building roofs; I smelled an acrid smoke. Fire apparatus and the gray arteries of its acting spilled out, into the avenue. A bull horn was chiding the crowds that pressed forward against an insubstantial line of policemen. I looked to my right: a side street there, a black crevasse between the brighter avenues. I could see but three inefficient circles of light along its entire length. I shook my head. I turned in. My own footsteps coaxed echoes from the high, silent stoops, encouraging my legs to yet more resolute efforts. I started to run, and then, abruptly, two figures loomed in my path. They halted me, not by force but by the suddenness of their appearance, by the close contiguity of their bodies — situated, as they were, between a stoop's outcropping and a thick cluster of garbage cans. I peered uneasily at them. The bodies seemed one, joined at the shoulders. The man at the right, I saw, held a whisky bottle by the throat, a weapon at ease. I glanced hastily to my rear.

"Brother . . ." said the man to my left; his tongue unfurled clumsily as he pronounced each word. "You . . . got . . . dollar . . . dollar?" The man to my right let out gas with a terrific, popping rush. He laughed and his head bobbed like a flower's on a broken, wind-agitated stalk. "Seee . . . he needs help . . . bad . . ." Another laugh. "Fart again . . . Thumbs. Go on . . . show the man . . ." Thumbs complied.

I fumbled for tribute and drew a single quarter from my overcoat pocket. Fingers reconnoitred my palm. "Fuckin' quarter . . . Thumbs blow his brains out . . . for a fuckin' quarter . . . Gimme more, man . . ." The fingers clenched, then they reached uncertainly forward, toward my pocket, an elephant's trunk nuzzling for peanuts. "No," I said; I pushed it away. The hand came back. "Stop it!" I struck sharply at his extended forearm. He staggered. Thumbs, whose entire weight had been propped against his shoulder, fell heavily across his friend's body. They both collapsed in a thrashing confusion at my feet. I backed, then leaped; my left heel descended on something soft, perhaps a finger. I ran. Behind me, the bottle smashed and a siren commenced its hoarse, low climb to shrillness.

I had three blocks yet to go: one south, two to the east. I hesitated under the last street lamp to reexamine my invitation once again. Sweat, in the hollows of my spine, conducted chills from hips to the vertebrae in my neck. For several moments I clung to the humming metal post. A quarter to nine. Above, a window opened in an upper story. A figure came to the sill, leaned out, peered left, peered right. Then it lifted a tall, vaguely cylindrical object to its chest and shoved outward. The window was closing as the object fell. It struck the pavement with a muffled thud. An animal, startled, scuttled from the courtyard, out between two parked cars. A large animal, piebald and with a vestigial tail. A pig, I thought insanely. I stepped back into the shadows and began walking sideways along the building wall. The moon appeared and disappeared; it glowed through clouds of an inconsistent depth. It peered down to witness my passage along the jungle-dark streets. White, it was; pocked with shadows. And I thought, as I saw it, of an aging man's naked buttocks. Pale. Veined. Bruised black by time. The moon went in.

It was a modern apartment building, six stories tall. I backed into a doorway opposite and stared covertly upward. Lights showed without exception at each window. Bright lights; ominous, tinted lights; at a few windows quick-alternating reds and

blues and yellows. Cars were double- and triple-parked in the
streets and on the sidewalks; several Horn Oranges walked
among them. Six men entered the apartment building. I heard
their boisterous, expectant calls to each other. My fingernails
picked at the doorway's wooden frame. "Lord God, protect
me from harm this night. Teach me not to fear, for all things
are ordered by Thy governance for the good of Thy creatures.
Should this be the last night of my existence, I pray thee, re-
deem Thy promise given unto us in Jesus Christ, lead my soul,
repentant, unto an everlasting life." A table lamp smashed
down onto the pavement, thrown from some upper story window. An amen to my prayer.

I crossed the street, threading my way between the close
bumpers. Two Horn Greens flanked the building's entrance;
I expected, indeed hoped, to be checked there, but I was not.
Smith, it seemed, had forewarned his men. A Horn Green took
my hat and coat with unexceptionable courtesy. Then he
pointed into the lobby. There were two elevators and a service stairway.

"What floor is it on?" I asked.

"All floors, man. Take your pick." He laughed pleasantly.
"It's pretty crowded up there."

"Crowded? But it's just past nine o'clock."

"Man, but the blast started at eight. They's even on the roof
by now."

"At eight . . . Then he must have tricked me."

"Who that?"

"Uh — just a friend. What floor would you recommend?"

"Hey, Tris — which would I recommend?" Tris opened his
eyes wide. Then he parted his lips in a lavish, superbly-toothed
grin. His companion laughed, understanding the man, Tris's,
insinuation. He turned back to me.

"I got diff'rent tastes, friend. Y'better find out for yourself."

I pushed all six buttons; none seemed to represent sanctuary. At each floor dense crowds shouldered the elevator, threatened to obstruct its doors. On the second and fifth floors loud jazz music was playing. On the third I could hear an eerie, harsh chant — very like something from *Carmina Burana*. The fourth floor was weirdly lighted, the colored tints changing in some mechanically prearranged pattern. The doors opened onto the top floor to let in a burst of laughter, a burst of applause. Then the elevator started down again. I extracted my lower lip from between clenched teeth. Now I would have to decide. I chose the second floor: a fall from these windows, I thought, might only be crippling.

I raised an open hand to my forelock — a blinder against reality — and tried to wedge myself into the mob. I was not successful at first. The elevator doors closed several times on my rear parts before I made any headway. The lighting here was chiefly red; gels had been taped over the hall bulbs and the faces around me were shiny, scarlet-purple things, like bloody calves' livers. "Excuse me," I said, but no one heard: the noise level was prohibitive. I expected recognition at any moment. At the hall's far end some transaction of bodies occurred, creating a wave that pushed me and those around me back fully a yard. I was making no progress. I saw an apartment door ahead and to the right; simultaneously, a tiny aisle opened between swarming bodies. I turned sideways, my right hand held low and ahead of me as a prow, and pushed toward the doorway.

I gasped, stopped. The edge of my right hand had become wedged in something. I stared down incredulously. There, at the end of its arm, my dreadfully white hand was jammed in the buttocks' crease of a young and very naked Negro girl. I withdrew it so abruptly that my hand cuffed the side of my head. The girl giggled. Deviously, I glanced in her direction: naked, no doubt about that. Naked, smoking a cigarette and — and talking to another girl. Also naked. This second girl's body was presented full front to my view and there were parts of her that — I will confess it — I had previously seen only in female infants. These parts seemed very different now. In vicarious modesty, I placed both hands over my eyes. But then I could see nothing. I turned around entirely, executing tiny steps in my restricted space. But then I was headed in the wrong direction. I backed to where I thought the apartment's doorway would be, using my weight ruthlessly, and, at last, came to ground against the wall. Eyes closed, I sidled along until I felt the opening with my fingertips. "Hey, man, don't walk so hard," said a voice, but I had already escaped from the hall.

It was less crowded inside. I maneuvered through a narrow foyer, past a fully equipped kitchen, to what must once have been a capacious living room. There was no furniture, and the room now easily contained its more than thirty people. I stood, hesitant, at the doorway, giving like some hinged device when people pushed past me, as yet too dreadfully impressed by what I had just seen for relevant action. Another. There was another. I sent my glance to the ceiling; then, gradually, retrieved it. A short girl, rather plump, whose naked hips and buttocks quivered when her heels struck the floor in walking. A blue medallion, with the letters HWC in silver, was somehow attached to her skin, just above her left nipple. "Can't be a pin," I said to myself. Then I giggled.

I saw cups, a few soiled paper plates and then, to the left, a refreshment table. On the table, opalescent green punch, a quenching color, lapped at the sides of its bowl. I shouldered a way to the table and pointed at the bowl, not willing as yet to

commit my voice. An attendant Horn Green quickly grasped
his ladle, and, when he did so, my head dodged involuntarily
in expectation of a blow. But the attendant said merely, "Here
you are," and, without further comment or apparent interest,
passed me the paper cup. Encouraged, I backed into a corner,
near a lavishly spread hors d'oeuvres table, determined to watch
for fifteen minutes, to fulfill the merest letter of my obligation,
and then to leave.

The punch was sweet, licorice flavored; altogether quite
pleasing. I sipped and, alternately, reached down to the table
for tidbits of pâté and caviar and a savory jellied substance. I
ate and drank without pausing, compelled by my agitation. A
trio came in: a drummer, a bass and a clarinetist. They set up
their instruments at the far side of the room and began playing.
Dancers paired off. I tapped my foot. Then I looked down, saw
my foot and giggled. My foot stopped, abashed by this scrutiny,
but it would not be disciplined for long. I giggled again. Then
I started stuffing myself, scarcely swallowing before I had refilled my mouth. I was feeling very well — very well, indeed.
I peered at the greenish liquid in my cup and winked at it.
The punch and my nervousness found each other congenial; a
strong intoxication was compounded between them. Apparently I was safe here. The Horn people, out of uniform for the
most part, seemed not to notice or to care that I was white.
"Pratt," I mumbled, "you're going to make it. You're going to
make it, baby." I giggled. Then I treated myself to another
cup of punch.

A half hour passed; an amiable half hour. Now both my feet
were tapping; occasionally, too, a knee or a hip would flex in
sudden self-expression. In that time, moreover, forty years'
training in propriety, it seemed, had rapidly become superan-
nuated. I now observed nude women with neither bashfulness

nor indignation. With interest, in fact. After all, I instructed
myself, they're wearing pigment, they're a shade from nakedness. Properly speaking, the naked are always white. It's like
some African documentary. "Dr. Livingstone, I presume?" I
said, handshaking the air. I laughed out loud at that. Then,
mortified by my growing intemperance, shoved a soft candy
into my mouth. But the candy would not be chewed. I worked
at it diligently: between my molars, between my incisors; I
shaped it like bubble gum. At last, however, I had to spit it
out. I peered into my palm, tilted my glasses for more intense
magnification, but my gnawing had left it unrecognizable. I
turned to the hors d'oeuvres table. Then I slapped my right
ear: not a candy at all. A contraceptive. A rubber condom.
The very same sort of thing I had been shown in hygiene class
— a whole Lazy Susan full of them. I belched and almost vom-
ited; then I downed my entire cup of punch. "My God," I
said. "They'll never believe this in Greensprings. They'll
never believe it." I dropped the contraceptive, now distended
like a windsock on a placid day, into a trash basket behind the
table.

"Yummy," said a voice. "Yummy num num. A white man."
A tall, very thin Negro approached my corner. He had thick
lips and long, greasy hair that lay in frizzled waves; his hands
and forearms reposed at chest level like those of some delicate
praying mantis. "Oh," he said. Though already thin, his voice
heightened in pitch as he pronounced the vowel sound. "Oh —
hhh — oooh. A priest. A lovely, big white priest."

"H-hi," I said, as I backed into my corner.

"H-hi to you, too, big man." He placed his middle finger at
the corner of his eye, and then leaned his head against it. He
wore a tiny nose ring: a gold band with a single, small depend-
ing pearl, like an escaped drop of mucus. His dinner jacket was

gold and of some reflective material; his shoes were white san-
dals; at his throat was a cravat, latticed with red, retiform
streaks. He leaned very close to me; his head bobbed when he
did so, as though he had difficulty focusing his vision. "Just
what I need," he said with an elaborate and stylized sigh.
"Some ex-treme unction." He placed the flat of his hand on
my lapel.

"Oh?" I said, "Uh — are you dying?"

"I am. I am — every time I look into your big, blue eyes.
I die. Give me some unction, quick. Unct me man,
uhunct . . ." He began rubbing his hand vigorously up and
down my lapel. I could feel the warm friction on the skin of
my chest.

"Oh," I said, as I tried to avoid his hand, "Are you — I mean,
are you a homosexual?" He ceased rubbing. Then he frowned,
narrowed his eyes.

"Why do you ask?" he said after a moment. "Do I look like
one?"

"Well . . . I've never met a homosexual before, but I've
read some things — nothing very scientific — just an article in
Time magazine. It's the way you talk, I guess."

"Do I talk funny?"

"Well — it's a bit Baroque. Sounds like Tallulah Bankhead
sometimes."

"Baroque . . ." He pouted. "Tell me, are you prejudiced?"

"I have nothing — you must believe me — I have nothing at
all against Negroes."

"Who cares about that? I mean queers — are you prejudiced
against queers?"

"As I said," I cleared my throat. "I've never met one. But
no, I don't think I'd find much common ground."

"Well, you're meeting one now, blue eyes. And he's making a pass at you."

"My eyes are brown. Very brown. And, really, I wish you wouldn't bother."

"I've only had a white man once," he said.

"Oh . . . ?"

"And he was just twelve years old." He giggled. "What is it Jesus said — 'Suffer little children to come under me.' "

"Unto," I corrected, "unto me. Oh — it's a joke."

"He didn't think it was. He wriggled and squealed. It was soooo tight. You should've been there." A spasm of remembered excitement quivered upward from his groin. "My name is William C. Garrett. What's yours?"

"C. B. Pratt." We shook hands and, as we did, he tickled the center of my palm with his forefinger.

"Ready when you are, C. B."

"William C. Garrett? You're not the novelist?"

"You've recognized me. What a thrill."

"I read *Devil's Hill* and *The Hunger Man* just before I came here, to Harlem. I was impressed. Shocked. You have an exciting style." He giggled.

"Don't I? Don't I just? Come up to the fifth floor, Ceeby, and I'll show it to you. *Au naturel.*"

The drummer began his cadenza. Dancers slowed to listen, and the noise precluded conversation. William C. Garrett lit a flat, unevenly packed cigarette, and I observed him with curiosity as he did so. His hands were unresponsive; coordination of the most elementary sort seemed absent. The match refused to light and then, when lit, cigarette tip and flame could not easily be made to conjoin. The drummer threw one stick in the air and caught it behind his back, while maintaining a vivid, savage rhythm with the other. The smoke from William

C. Garrett's cigarette encountered the sensing portions of my nose. I grimaced: a rich, unpleasant smell, as though of spices undiluted. William C. Garrett, I knew, was not smoking tobacco.

I shook my head: a gesture meant to reprove my naïveté. I had seen him once before — on a television seminar. He had appeared so masculine then and his subject, I remembered, had been that very masculinity. He talked of the Negro male without ever smiling, each sentence an explicit threat. Of the Negro male's terrible awakening, of his strength, of his inevitable triumph — secured, necessarily, at the white man's expense. I had judged him then: an articulate speaker; a brutal, uncompromising writer; a male redolent of sexual prowess, dominant. And William C. Garrett — now otherwise redolent — made a smoke ring and, daintily adorned his little finger with it.

"Have a little drink with me. Huh, Ceeby?"

"Well, yes . . . I think I will. The punch is very good."

"Here you are, pretty boy." He handed me the cup, and raised his own in an unannounced toast.

"What is this?"

"Absinthe mostly. Are you a Catholic priest?"

"No. Episcopal."

"Oh — then you can screw around?"

"Ah — we can marry, yes . . ." William C. Garrett drew me back into the corner.

"Are you married?" he asked.

"No."

"Why not?"

"I — " I shrugged. His questions had become disagreeably personal. Moreover the absinthe and Garrett's exhalations had begun to affect me. The picture before my eyes would drop

suddenly, to be replaced by another, an identical picture — a
television screen, rolling. William C. Garrett pinched his cigarette tightly and inhaled, his fingers pressed against his nose,
as though, almost, he were preparing to eat the lit ember.

"You know why?"

"Why?"

"Because you really like men, that's why."

"No. Please, Mr. Garrett, that's not true. I'm normal, a bit
overshy, perhaps. Don't get your hopes up."

"It's not my hope that's up now." He pressed his groin
against mine. Horrified, I turned sideways to his thrust.

"Good grief," I said. "Can't we talk about something else?"

A brown hand appeared at William C. Garrett's right shoulder. It pulled at him. William C. Garrett turned sideways,
slapped at the hand, rebounded back into place. The hand appeared again. Individual fingers asserted themselves; they
made little gutters in the glinting fabric. William C. Garrett
cursed. He jammed his elbow backward, forgetting the absinthe which leaped from his cup onto my cuff and shoe. He
had misjudged the blow. William C. Garrett tripped, stepped
on his own foot and toppled forward. The hand, seconded by
another, appeared at his hip, steadying him.

"Damn you, go away."

"Please, Billeeee. Don't be mad." A short, pudgy Negro
appeared. He glanced once indignantly at me and then set his
face in a stereotype of pleading. His forehead wrinkled; his
eyebrows reached out at each other; his lips puckered austerely.
And yet, in the midst of this careful agony, his cheeks remained
unchanged — apparently his most characteristic feature. They
bulged as though they were loaded with breath and, when he
opened his mouth to speak, I was surprised not to see them
subside, hissing.

"Go away, Fred." William C. Garrett plucked Fred's fingers from his sleeve one by one; each finger resumed its grasp as he passed on to the next. I stared at Fred's cheeks: they shone in their tautness, highlighted like soap bubbles — each with its small, square window of reflected light. Wonderful things, I thought.

"Billee. Come on back. Herb says he's sorry. He is, Billee. He is. He won't do it again. Never. You're the only one. He's just weak, Billee. He's just weak."

"What d'you think? Huh, Ceeby? Huh? Should I forgive them, Ceeby?"

"Uh — "

"Come on, Billee — "

"Shut up, you little toad." He slapped Fred on the perfect hemisphere of his right cheek. The cheek did not collapse, nor even give way; it merely shimmered and then settled in its pristine, round resilience. "What d'you say, Ceeby?"

"F — forgive," I said, stuttering. "Forgive seventy times seven."

"Well . . . If you say so. But look, Ceeby, come up to the fifth floor later on. Apartment 5H." Fred took William C. Garrett's arm in both hands and began hauling him away. "Promise now. Promise." He waved. I waved back. "Don't dis — a — point meee!" he shrieked as Fred pulled him backward across the room. People began to stare, and I ceased waving at once. Fred had difficulty negotiating a passage through the crowd, especially as William C. Garrett, in his wake, insisted on goosing every other man he encountered. The band extemporized, "I must go where the wild goose goes." There was laughter. William C. Garrett hit the cymbals with his fist as he passed. Then he was gone.

I glanced discreetly toward the room. The dancers persisted.

A noisy huddle still screened the refreshment table. I scanned the faces sedulously from left to right, analyzing expressions for hostile intent. I sensed no threat. Despite William C. Garrett, they were ignoring me. Encouraged, I made my way through the crowd, past the band's blare, to where, I judged, the apartment's bathroom should be. I walked without confidence; the floor seemed to give with and, alternately, repel my feet. I stepped on the outer edges of my soles, my arms swinging high for balance. Every few paces I would giggle uncontrollably and without motive. To the bathroom mirror I said, "Pratt, you're just a little bit drunk." And, on my way out, I made a short, unnecessary detour through the empty tub.

Once outside, I leaned against the bathroom door's jamb. I belched. Beyond the band, past the foyer, I could just see the outer hall: it was still packed, impervious to my disordered movements. At that moment, moreover, I was struggling with a difficult exercise in casuistry — should I be allowed more absinthe? I knew it was wrong; I knew I risked utter disorientation. But my safety, my continued acceptance, seemed somehow related to this state of intoxication. Sober, I feared, I would be white again; inhibited and vulnerable. I peered around me. There were four doors near the bathroom. The fourth and nearest door was ajar about a foot and a half. Six of those HWC medallions adhered to it. A red light, neither dim nor bright, lit up the crevice. I tottered over, pushed the door fully open, and peered in.

I won't forget what I saw there. I see it now with an undiminished clarity. They lay like dark, fallen logs — a dozen of them on two huge beds. The red light was reflected from pair upon pair of moving buttocks, and I knew from the glint's keenness that they were sweating. There was such teeming nakedness: so many flanks, so many breasts, so much soundless, sinuous movement. And the dozen bodies, the half-dozen busy conjunctions, seemed to derive enthusiasm from the act's communality, as though the pleasure were compounded by it. Pairs on the beds were not distinguishable, they melded into one another. Into one dark, heaving mass — a many-celled organism expressing a single appetite. Perhaps not even that, not even an organism: a huge, labor-saving machine, its drive shafts shunting up and down, cranking out ream after ream of sensual pleasure. I observed this for precisely as long as it took my arm's reflexes to answer. Then I threw my body outward, into the hall. Two hands caught me at the shoulders as I fell.

"God," I said. "That was a mistake."

She was tall and remarkably handsome; a young lady of about twenty-four or twenty-five. Her hair was piled high and was surmounted by an expensive-seeming jeweled tiara. Her features were Caucasian, delicate and very regular. The color of her skin was more red than dark. But her eyes, certainly, were her most extraordinary part. They were vast and almond-shaped, with a huge sufficiency of soft, brown pupil. For several seconds my own eyes met hers and were subsumed in their cushioning depths. Then, uncertain of the distance between our two faces, I reached out with my fingers to touch her cheek. She suffered my touch. And smiled.

"You're Father Pratt," she said.

"I am, yes," I shook my head. "Yes, but poor Father Pratt shouldn't be here — in there . . ." I pointed. "In that room. I mean . . . so many of them. Someone should put up a sign."

"They did, sort of. Those blue badges with the HWC, the girls take them off when they go t'work. Stick them on the door. It means 'Do not disturb.' "

"Oh," I said. "I should have guessed. One, two . . . four . . . six of them. What does the HWC stand for?"

"That's Horn's Whore Corps."

"Whore Corps . . . it rhymes."

"Yes." She laughed at my perturbation. "It does."

"But — how did you know my name? And what's yours, if — that is, if you don't mind telling me."

"Mine's Godhild. Horn told me yours. He said t'watch out for you."

"Godhild — did he give you that name?"

"Yes. Really it's my second Horn name. The first one was even worse — Folkenhild."

"Folkenhild? Where'd he get a name like that?"

"Search me." She shrugged. I frowned and then, as though innocently, I said —

"He must read a lot, I guess?"

"Read?" She snorted. "Where you been? Horn can't read. Not a word. He drives me crazy. I got t'read him everything — even where it say, 'Men's Room,' things like that."

"No kidding? Do you know him well?" She laughed.

"You really don't know nothin', huh? I'm a Godhild. God-hild number six. All Horn's own, personal girls get called that. I been around a year now. More'n the others. A year an' eight days."

The band accomplished a prolonged, strident coda. There was applause. A single man stepped out of the HWC room, pulling the door closed behind him. He looked around, a drawn, somnolent expression on his face. Then he tightened his tie and tucked the ends under his waist band. I stared at my cuffs in embarrassment.

"Mr. Pratt — you mind if I ask you something? You mind?"

"No. Not at all. Go right ahead."

"How d'you know Horn?"

"Uh — just a chance acquaintance, that's all." Godhild narrowed her eyes. Her tongue swirled in her right cheek near her lips. Then she smiled, and, by that smile, indicated that my response was hardly credible.

"Mr. Pratt — I know you're a priest an' all, but I just can't believe that. I mean, how'd you get an invitation here — if it's like you say, and Horn don't hardly know you?"

"That's a good question, Miss Godhild. Something I'd like t'know myself. He didn't just give me an invitation, either — he made me come. Made me. Otherwise I wouldn't be here, you can bet on that. Not that I haven't had a good time. I have, all things considered." I peered at the HWC door.

"Then you don't know about it?"

"About what?"

"About where he goes?"

"How'd you mean?"

"Where he goes at night sometimes. He disappears, Mr. Pratt. Nobody knows where, not even Cubert Mody and Cubert's his best friend. I thought since he cares so much about you — "

"Cares?" I frowned. "But does he? I don't think so. After all, Miss Godhild, I am white."

"So?" she smiled. Then she brought her mouth so close it touched my earlobe. "I'm half white myself. My father was. I figure that's why I last so long with Horn. My skin's different and my face, too. Can you see?" I nodded. "So, y'see, Mr. Pratt, you an' me, we ain't so different. If you wanna tell me anything, I'll keep it quiet. Horn ain't gonna find out."

"But — I'm sorry — I don't know anything. You say he goes someplace?" But Godhild had ceased being interested. Having judged me ignorant, she no longer cared to discuss these private matters. She stood straight and brushed several times at her dress, as though to dismiss our brief intimacy.

"Then you're having a good time? Is that right, Mr. Pratt?"

"Yes. Yes. Everyone's been wonderful, just wonderful. I

can't tell you. I hardly expected . . . I mean, I didn't know what to expect. It's been, ah — very, very interesting."

The HWC door opened. A face, a body appeared. At first they were only just familiar — something remembered of the lips, of the scar at the temple. Then they were dreadfully familiar. Aylbrous Purston saw Godhild and smiled. He took a step forward, toward her, and, abruptly, saw me in the periphery of his vision. He stopped. I heard the sharp crack as a blue mechanical pencil snapped in his tightening fist.

"Godhild," he snarled. Then, with great deliberateness, he paused. I knew he was restraining himself; I observed the unpleasantness of that restraint. Purston approached Godhild, nodded once toward me, and said, "This your idea of a joke?"

"Not my idea. Horn's. He invited Mr. Pratt." Purston laid the back of his fist flat against his temple, to the place where his flesh had been torn apart. A vein appeared there, tumescent, pulsing. He inhaled: it was a sigh reversed.

"Horn," he said. I pulled out my invitation and held it toward him between quivering fingers.

"Horn," said Godhild. She enjoyed the emphasis that her repetition gave.

"He didn't tell me."

"No — guess not. You're only God, Ayl. Sometime, maybe, you'll be Horn Smith." He laughed; an arid sound.

"Maybe."

"Still have to buy it — that so, Ayl?" She pointed toward the HWC door.

"Man, bitch — what is it with you?" He rested his hand easily on her shoulder. The shoulder dipped an inch or so, as though to indicate displeasure, and yet it did not renounce his touch entirely. I backed along the wall, away from them, but Purston's body barred my retreat.

"You're touching me, Ayl."

"Yeah. Was a time you got all wet just thinkin' my hand's on you. Was a time."

"Things change."

"You always a kinda prissy bitch. Get that from your daddy."

"No, Ayl. It's you. You don't light no fires — no more, man." He kissed her then, hard and on the mouth. She returned his kiss, with an equal but passionless thrust, as though this were some new test of strength.

"Horn here?"

"No. Not yet."

"Come on — up the sixth floor. Schozz Allingham's playin' there."

"How much, Ayl? How much you pay me?"

"Uh — " I said. "Excuse me. Think I'll be moving on. If you'll just . . . ah — just let me squeeze by. I'll go then." But they did not hear me. I tried to edge past Purston, but I could make no progress, not without reentering the HWC room.

"Pam, baby. You might be payin' me. Like you used to."

"Godhild. Not Pam. No more."

"Okay — okay, bitch. I play it your way. Just you play."

"Uh," I said. "Uh . . . If you don't mind. I think I'll go." Purston turned toward me. His eyes widened, as they had done on the platform those many days before. Then he closed them abruptly. I inhaled, cherished the air, as though soon I might be deprived entirely of it. But when Purston reopened his eyes they were empty, not focusing, lined with red blood vessels. He moved aside.

"Have a good time, Mr. Pratt," said Godhild. Purston laughed.

"You better pray, Whitey. Pray Pam here's nice t'me. Otherwise — I'll be lookin' for trouble soon. Lookin' — I might find you."

"Uh," I said. "Yes — well you enjoy yourself. Have fun now." I waved. But he ignored me.

I should have left then. God knows, I was mad not to. Purston had fairly warned me, and I deserved everything that was yet to happen. But I was in a rare mood: busy compensating for that long six months of loneliness and enforced silence. "Hey, excuse me, man," I said. I bullied a passage to the refreshment table and had one, then another, then another cup of absinthe — my talisman. My mind was oddly clear, though this clarity was never successfully transmitted to my limbs. I tottered out of the room and into the teeming corridor. For several moments I merely stood, tossed backward and forward like some buoyant thing on a great swell. "Man! Man!" I shouted. "Man! Man!" I suppose then that a lifetime's conditioning was momentarily abnegated. There was no longer cause or consequent effect. Just a senseless, happy noise in which I joined senselessly, happily. A billowing roll, as when, a child, I would throw myself into the comforter-piled, huge bed of my parents and, for just a moment, my body relaxed, would allow the resilient springs to toss me gently about.

In time I drifted near to the service stairway. The current carried me upward. Nothing is very clear now, certainly not the exact sequence of events during that extraordinary ascent, but the third floor, I think, was devoted to lascivious games. I remember watching men ride on women's backs, women on men's backs; equestrian trappings, bridles, saddles, sharp spurs and crops. One room, a slave auction; another in which the reverberating sound of wood on flesh could be heard and the bleating of a sheep. Yet another, where, I believe — I am not sure, I left it so quickly — prizes were given for the length and diameter of certain organs. There was a game called, "Pin the donkey on the tail"; another called, "Spin the Bottom" — where a naked woman, pointing finger and arm extended, was rotated on a huge turn table. Lurid, yes; scandalous. But also, I thought, superbly imaginative. *Panem et circenses.* A Bartholomew's Fair for satyrs. Even to my inexperienced sight, the promiscuous sex act became, in that melee, almost unremarkable. I observed everything. I asked naïve questions and was patiently answered. This profusion of the bizarre was, I supposed, my security. For among such things my unique whiteness and clerical collar seemed a suitable prop — serving the same function as the Christ effigy in a black mass.

The fourth floor seemed deserted by comparison: the dry center of a swirling eddy. Most of the early throng, it appeared, had left. This was the level of the flashing, tinted lights. Even in the corridor a many-faceted ball of mirrors rotated, orbiting, as it did so, tiny dots of reflected light. An unseen projector placed rich landscapes of color on the walls and ceiling with the unrepeated variety of a kaleidoscope. Somewhere nearby electronic music droned: toneless gongs whose echo preceded their striking; sudden, rushed noises like the vast insuck of soup from spoons. I walked forward a few paces. There, close to the elevator, were twin, arrowed signs ←pot rot→. "Oh. Ha!" I exclaimed. "Narcotics. Dope." And I remembered then what I had been smelling — William C. Garrett's pungent cigarettes. I shook my head and followed the right hand arrow. Toward the rot.

The door to apartment 4C was open. The foyer and kitchen were dark, but, beyond, in the living room, I could see again the irrational flashing of colors. I stepped forward cautiously. A small table with cookies and coffee stood near to where the foyer became the living room. I picked up a cookie and nibbled

while I watched. There were men and women on the floor —
a dozen at most. The majority were inert, sitting rather like
shrubs on a twilit lawn. I could hear conversation, but the
sounds, though facile and clearly enunciated, seemed only to
approximate speech. A few figures lay prostrate; others
moved in regular patterns, as though executing a restrained
calisthenic. One man, near the window — which was strongly
barred — seemed intent on turning himself inside out. Another was climbing the wall: placing finger and shoe tips
against the plaster, securing an imagined purchase, moving
upward without leaving the floor. And vastly satisfied with his
progress. Incense burned in holders near the ceiling; jungle
gym-like mobiles drooped downward. I started to retreat, backing toward the foyer, when a man appeared next to me. He
had a thick, handle-bar mustache and, on his lapel, a button
that said GUIDE.

"Hello," he said. "You new t'this stuff?"

"Yes," I said. "It's LSD, isn't it?"

"No, man," he laughed. "You're really new — new as a
baby. Last time I saw LSD was in 1969." The teeth under the
bushy mustache appeared in a pleasant, familiar grin. And,
suddenly, I remembered my Uncle Tim, with just such a mustache and such a grin. My father's younger brother.

"Tim," I said.

"No. Tom. Tom Aquinas. Glad t'meet you." He shook
my hand. "This here is ROT, Father. Specially imported
from Switzerland by Horn. Gives y'all the kicks of LSD, but it
don't mess up your balls. Smoother ride, too. No bumps."

"Is — is that so?" Couldn't be Tim, I realized that. Tim had
died three years before my father. I had only seen his picture
— once. In the third left drawer of my mother's vanity. The
drawer with the lion's head knob, the lion's ears worn round

by the pulling. And it smelled, the drawer, of orange sachet
and Camel cigarettes.

"That's so," said Tom. "It's cool goo. I'm the guide in this
room — I see to it y'have a safe trip. Nothin' t'worry about.
You'll like it."

"Me?" I said, thumb at sternum. "Oh, no. Not me. I'm just
a visitor." Tom Aquinas frowned.

"Yeah. But you done ate 'most all that cookie — that's a
pretty fair trip right there."

"What!"

"Take it easy."

"What! What! What!" I glanced at the cookie fragment and
then hurled it away from me. I commenced a dry, futile retching, doubled at the waist.

"Calm down, man." I began to run, but Tom caught the hem
of my jacket and pulled me roughly toward him. I struggled
against his hold. He cursed. Then he inserted thumb and forefinger where my collarbone crossed near to my throat. I knelt
against my will.

"Easy. Easy," he hissed. "Calm down."

"All . . . right," I gasped. "But do something. Isn't there
an antidote?"

"Listen t'me. It ain't so bad — you'll like it. I promise.
Don't fight it — you go in easy, you come out easy. It ain't
gonna screw up your crome-zomes."

"Uncle Tim," I said. "That's why you were . . . ah."

"Come. Sit inside. You didn't take too much. Maybe only
an hour or so. Stand up."

I stood and that, of reality, is all I can now remember . . .

Among many excursions, few recalled, few pertinent, I met
myself coming slowly along the road that leads yet from Greensprings to Sturgis Forge. I was at least fourteen; I know be-

cause the terrible blue-purple pimples were there. I gestured
to me, and we sat to talk by the side of the road. I had many
things to explain and he, too, seemed burdened. The sky was
blue and the grass was green: where they met there was no compromise, no bluish-green. The road was empty, silent, not
implicit even of other travelers. There was no breeze, and yet
all things, though dreadfully static, seemed breeze blown. I offered grass to myself and he took it. In the eating, it was as
bread. We touched fingers in this transaction and we felt (I felt,
saw him feeling) each other's clammy palms. We were
repulsed. "Cold hands," I said. "Cold hearts," he said. We
nodded.

I told him then what he yet would learn, and he, in his turn,
reminded me of things I had willingly forgotten. We talked
for compact hours. Though it was neither hot nor cold, young
Calvin showed a pesky sweat in his ruined skin. His thick glasses
slid forward and left red commas, I saw, that must have pained
beside his eyes. These little disappointments were but a learn-
er's prelude — I told him that gently. And he nodded, for we
both, in our times, have been fatalists. I mentioned the young
ladies and the awkwardnesses and the fear. And he, in recom-
pense, showed me my mother and some things perhaps that we
did not owe her, however great our debt of gratitude might
be. I couldn't help remarking how insipid, how stolid, he looked
sitting there on his heels. And his eyes, appraising me, were
quite as unforgiving.

Then it was time for us to part. His bicycle was there, by the
side of the road. Pipe, book and butterfly net in the wicker
basket — I touched each of them and perceived how little, in
fact, I had progressed. He climbed clumsily astride the saddle.
I stood near. He was more shy even than I was, and so I placed
my hand on his shoulder finally, to acknowledge our only known

comradeship. He thanked me; and I him. The bicycle wavered as it started forward, silent here, not creaking, false in that alone. I sensed big tears on my cheeks. He was far before me now pedaling toward the place where blue met green without once surrendering a shade of either's integrity. And I cried fully. Cried for all the things he would have to suffer yet, and for his great, bovine patience, and for the mass of his buttocks dwarfing my bicycle's seat . . .

"How'd it go?" My chin was cupped in Tom's hands. I felt the tips of his fingers then at either eye. The skin of my scalp was, as a foot or hand, asleep; it tingled painfully in its awakening — grasping my skull again and again like a closing hand.

"I've been crying," I said. "Really, I mean." My cheeks were wet; the pouches beneath my eyes seemed swollen.

"Yeah. 'Bout half an hour ago you started. Been at it pretty good. Sobbing like. Kinda sad, huh?"

"Exquisitely." I smiled as I remembered. "I — I never expected it to be like that."

"Look, you're gonna get flashbacks now and then, for a couple hours. Nothin' t'worry about. Try standin' up."

"I want to puke," I said.

"Yeah. But you probably won't. Try not t'look down."

"How long — ?"

"Ninety-five minutes by my watch. Just a run 'round the block. Come out into the hall." We stood for several moments at the doorway to apartment 4C. Tom, I knew, was examining me for signs. I inhaled.

"I think maybe you better go on home now. Get some sleep. You're more tired than you figure."

"Yes . . . I am."

"I gotta go back in. Somebody might need me."

"Yes," I said. He left me there.

The corridor was nearly deserted now. I followed a satellite of the mirrored ball as it rushed obliquely from wall to ceiling to wall again, spreading itself like a drop of liquid as it passed from one plane to another. And then, standing there, I was abruptly feeding the fish in my eldest sister's tank. I returned to perceive my right hand still outstretched in pantomime; ball of thumb and ball of forefinger rolling one against the other to scatter tobacco-like food thinly over the water's surface. In my embarrassment, I stood very straight against the doorjamb.

She was watching me. A pigmy of a woman, scarcely five feet tall. Quite naked, with an incongruously ornate beaded bag hung from her left shoulder. Her hair was very short, very fuzzy. Her breasts were small and precisely conical; her belly seemed somewhat distended; her buttocks, in compensation, seemed rather flat. But my interest in her was incited by her very apparent interest in me. She stood about fifteen feet to my right and across the corridor, ostensibly waiting for an elevator. Yet, when the doors opened, she made no attempt to enter. Again she peered at me, and I was disturbed by the covert, purposeful unfolding of her glance. I had a quick intimation then of menace. But, unfortunately, I supposed it a last illusion of the ROT.

"Hello, there, Mr. Big."

"Uh . . . hello," I said. She hitched the bag high onto her shoulder and came rapidly across the corridor to where I had slumped against the wall.

"Need some help?"

"No," I said. "I'll be all right." But her tiny arm had already encircled my body at the waist. It squeezed me, and its fingers explored my shirt. I felt her naked hip as it insinuated itself into the pit of my well-clothed thigh.

"Just lean on me."

"I'll be all right. Just have t'get home is all. Get a night's rest."

"You're good looking," she said.

"No," I said, correcting her, "I'm not good looking at all."

"Well . . . I like the way you look." She smiled a deliberately sexy smile: the kind television models cultivate — opening and closing their lips very slightly, but in quick alternation.

"Let's go over to the elevator, huh?" I tapped her on the shoulder and pointed. "And push the button."

"You just take a trip?"

"Yes. Let's go push that button."

"Okay. Okay." We crossed the corridor. I kept my hands chest-high, lest our contact become accidentally intimate. I pressed the button.

"Uh," I said. "Sorry I'll have to leave. But you were waiting for someone, weren't you?" I struck the DOWN button several terse blows with the flat of my palm.

"No. What's your name?"

"Pratt?"

"That's your last name. What's your first?"

"Calvin." She nipped at the skin of my belly. I made a fist and pounded the button.

"You'll break it, Calvin. Don't be so rough. My name's Gun — Gunniver."

"Gunniver?"

"Something like that. I just got it today."

"Oh — Guenevere." I tried squeezing the button gently.

"How d'you say it?"

"Guenevere."

"Gun-i-ver."

"Gwen."

"Gun. Gwen."

"Gwen."

"Gwen."

"Gwenevere."

"Gunniver." I laughed in spite of myself. "That Horn Smith man's crazy. I never heard such a stupid name. Gunniver. My name used t'be nice — Sharon. Then I join the Whore Corps and he gives me a name sounds like the clap. Gunniver."

"Today? Uh — don't do that, Guenevere. Please." I jerked my zipper back up. Then I placed my hand, fig-leaf fashion, over the mechanism. "You were saying — did you get that name today?"

"Yup. This is our 'nishiation day — seventy of us girls. That's why the party." She took off her HWC medallion. On the back it said Guenevere IV. She stuck it on my chest. "We had a big ceremony at Mr. Horn's Place. I passed all the tests real good."

"Tests? Putting round pegs in square holes?"

"Don't you make fun of me." She punched at my solar plexus.

"Where is that damn elevator?"

"I like big white men."

"Don't do that, Guenevere." I slapped her wrist.

"You've got long johns on. I saw."

"That's my business."

"Ooooh. Your face is all red. I think you're shy."

"I am. Very. So Please. Ah — " The elevator doors opened. I rushed in, away from her, but my escape was illusory, permitted. Guenevere followed me in. She hesitated for a moment near the control panel. Then she tackled me at the waist and propelled my uncoordinated body to the elevator's rear.

"Calvin. You see — me an' you's gonna have a real nice time tonight."

"No, dear," I said, as the doors closed. "I'm going home."

"You an' me, we'll — "

"Hey! You pushed the wrong button. We're going down too far." I tried to reach the M button, but Guenevere leaped up then, wrapping her legs around my waist, her arms around my neck. She kissed me on the mouth. It was difficult for me — I had to remove her body without touching it — and the elevator reached B before I was allowed to succeed.

"Come on, Calvin — this is where I live."

"No," I said. I stamped my foot. "You're making me mad, Guenevere . . . taking advantage. I'm going back up." I pushed her aside. But, when I pressed the M button, there was no response. Guenevere stood, arms folded on chest, nipples, like dark eyes, supported on her forearms — and with one foot wedged against the door.

"Come in — just a minute. Just for a drink. Huh? Be a sport."

"Guenevere — please. Get away from the door."

"No."

"Please."

"I won't."

"I'll have to use force."

"Calvin, baby, you can't even stand up straight." I punched the DOOR CLOSE button. There was a frustrated clicking in the mechanism. Only that.

"Guenevere."

"I'm not movin'."

"Please."

"No."

"Oh — nuts." I tottered out of the elevator. Guenevere, suspicious, pressed the outside button at once. The doors closed behind me.

She uprooted the HWC medallion from my chest, kissed it, and then stuck it just under the B4. I shook my head and became, for the moment, Dean Trumbull's cheerful German Shepherd, shaking dry after a dip in the Dean's gigantic birdbath.

"Damn ROT," I said. "Now I'm a big dog." Guenevere pulled me into her apartment skipping, snapping her heels together a full foot above the floor.

"Beee-beep," she chortled. "Watch out — chug-a-chug — we're a train." She was, I thought, a most unlikely whore. "Well. How d' you like it?"

"Woof," I said. The apartment had been decorated in contemporary motel style. There was mostly living room and, in the far corner, a tiled area that contained kitchen appliances and a table. Chairs like wood buckets, lamps that puttered across the ceiling on little tracks. Cubed hassocks marked like dice. Pillows everywhere. It seemed very clean. To the right I could see the bedroom's gaping maw. I made up my mind: no further than this. I would roll over and play dead on the floor rather than be drawn into Guenevere's bedroom.

"Huh?"

"Very nice."

"I'm gonna like the Whore Corps stuff. Even though I's makin' a good livin' before. Sit down."

"No. I'd never get up again. What did you do? Before, I mean."

"I was a bondage model." I inclined my head.

"A bandage model? How — how d'you model bandages?" She made tocking sounds between tongue and roof of mouth. Then, as coda to this improvisation, a very wet Bronx cheer.

"Don't be silly. A bondage model. Bond-age. Like, you know, James Bond. Not bandage. Gosh, you sure are silly."

"So? What's a bondage model?"

"Y'mean — y'don't know for real?" I shook my head and, bang, was back again in the Dean's birdbath. "Man, you priest people. A bondage model's somebody that gets herself all roped up. In real crazy positions. Then they take pictures of her — for the magazines."

"But why?"

"Why? Why, he says." She slapped herself smartly on either flat buttock. Then she began hopping up and down — like a child being the Easter bunny. "So the old men can see and jerk off."

"Ask a silly question . . ."

"Hey, look." I started. A dreadful grimace, a grimace of such persuasive dread crossed her face that I searched quickly behind me for an intruder. Then Guenevere began to improvise. Eyes wide. Lower lip quivering, distended in a noiseless sob. Nostrils flared. Face now pleading, now anguished, now anticipating a blow, now suffering after a long day's torment. I applauded. She shrugged in self-deprecation. "See. That's the trick. You gotta look afraid. That's what the old gawks pay for. Some girls, they laugh and giggle — nobody believes they're all tied up. It's not real." She leaned close, as though to make some aesthetic distinction. "And they don't get paid that much neither."

"I see, but — do they really tie you up?" No question: I had insulted her.

"Man. You're God-damn right they do. Me, anyway. Some girls throw a fit if y'do. But not me, I'm tough." She threw herself roughly to the floor. I stumbled backward. "See," she said, grunting as she demonstrated. "Watch close now. Sometimes . . . they tie, uh — a rope around my throat and I gotta bring my hands up between my legs, like this. Ugh. Then they tie the rope t'my hands. After a few minutes your face goes red.

Then blue." She performed an agile somersault. "Or like this. One arm — aaah — tied to one leg and the other leg tied t'the neck. That's a crotch buster, friend." She jumped up. "Best of all, though, is when they tie you t'the ceiling by your wrists and then they bring up your legs — and tie them t'your throat. Three minutes an' you're dead. No foolin', dead. I'm one of the few in New York City can do it."

"Good God," I said.

"Come on in my bedroom. I got pictures."

"Uh-uh," I said.

"What you mean — uh-uh? You scared t'go in my bedroom?"

"Uh-huh," I said and nodded.

"Y'think I's gonna rape you? That it? Huh — big man?"

"Let's change the subject, what say? Why'd you give up the bondage job?" She frowned then and looked guardedly at her wrist, but there was no watch.

"What time is it?"

"Uh — quarter to two. Time I was in bed."

"Yeah. Ain't that the truth?" She leaped forward, grabbed me about the waist and planted her bare feet on my insteps. "You asked why I quit. It's the benny-fits. I got a kid, Calvin. A girl — already two years old. The HWC give me free medical and free baby-sittin'. I don't gotta worry."

"I see." She hung there, silent, her head on my chest. I could feel her heart beating and her toes through the leather of my shoes when she wriggled them. She spoke sadly and in a hoarse whisper.

"It's nothin' personal, Father Pratt. I got nothin' 'gainst you, not 'gainst the white race. Whatever happens, you know." She stepped off my feet. She took a deep breath. "I got a kid t'think of."

"Yes?" I said. And then a fragment of concern, concern for me, mussed the fragile features of her face. It was quickly gone, overwhelmed by a smile, but that had been my warning. And I ignored it.

"Mr. Pratt — you good in bed?"

"Oh, yes," I said. "I go right to sleep." She giggled.

"You're sure a kookie cat. Guess it's because you're a priest." She cocked her head. "You don't want t'go in there? In my bedroom?"

"No, Guenevere," I said gently. "No, I don't. Nothing personal."

"Okay," she said. She clapped her hands together. "I save you a trip. I got me a swell Castro Convertible."

She seized my right elbow between both hands, and then wrenched my body entirely around. I tottered backward. Desperate, I sought balance in a large chair that stood just behind me, but the chair itself was designed to spin. It gave way. I pursued the direction of its turning as long as I could, my fingernails seeking purchase in the smooth vinyl upholstery, and then centrifugal force separated us. I toppled backward and sideways, chiefly on the insecure platform of my left heel, halting finally against the room's far wall. When I looked up, Guenevere's sofa had become a sheeted, blanketed double bed. She was standing at the foot. I belched and got to my feet.

"You're doomed to failure," I said.

"Ain't you even tempted, Mr. Pratt?"

"I'm tempted to put you over my knee, little girl."

"I like it any way you like it, big man." She slouched across the room in her best sensual manner. Her buttocks rose and lowered themselves. Tightened and untightened. Guenevere took her small breasts in either hand and squeezed the nipples.

"Uh — don't do that, please, Guenevere." She began run-

ning her fingers up and down my shirtfront. My stomach
growled. On the sixth downstroke she pulled several lengths
of shirt from under my belt. I placed my hand on hers and
gently removed it. She stamped her foot.

"You don't think I'm sexy."

"Well . . . Uh — you might be. If you had some clothes
on."

"Yeah? You think so?" The concept intrigued her. She pondered it, the dynamics of her pondering patent in the working of her mouth and forehead. Then she ran to the bed and,
with one agile movement, pulled off the spread. This she
draped about her body, as though it were a giant's toga. Guenevere began promenading up and down in front of me, pur-
posefully revealing, now and again, a select segment of her
anatomy.

"Now you're talking," I said. "That's better. The old
devil's at me now."

"Yeah? How much more I got to do?"

"Oh. Keep coming. Keep coming."

"Man, this spread's heavy." She danced near. "Here. Hold
this." She handed me one corner of the bedspread and unraveled herself. Then she ran once around me and refurled her
body until we were cocooned chest to chest. We stood for a
while like a pair of mummified Siamese twins. Guenevere
poked at my body desultorily, but the spread thwarted her ex-
pertise. After a while she became bored.

"You got too many clothes on."

"An occupational hazard. What say I go home?"

"No sir, Mr. Pratt. You can't do that. No sir. It's getting near
two o'clock."

"So what's two o'clock?"

Guenevere unraveled herself once again. She walked back-

ward and, in a stentorian voice, counted each step as she took
it: a broad jumper, I thought, aligning some crucial approach.
Bemused, the bedspread at my feet, I observed her with the
stolid intentness of some public monument on its unveiling
day. Guenevere glanced once at me, once at the bed, estimated
our relative positions and then charged forward. She tackled me
at the waist, fuzzy head buried at my crotch and drove my body
before her until the backs of my knees encountered the mattress
edge. I sprawled on the bed. Guenevere, her breasts thrusting
like vengeful darts, straddled my rib cage backward before I
could roll over. I heard my jacket sleeve rip. Then there
was a pleasant giving at my abdomen as my belt buckle was
brusquely unloosened. I strove to sit up, but Guenevere's mus-
cular buttocks were planted squarely on my sternum, calves
clamped at either of my ears so that my shouting and the sound
of her labors were subsumed by a loud, inner rushing.

"No! No! No!" I screamed. "That's not the way!"

"It'll have to do," she answered, panting. "Have — to —
do." I grasped her busy left hand in my own, but her little fingers undid my grip at once and bent my thumb back until I
cried uncle. There was a distinct coolness now about my hips; I
could feel the working of her warm fingers. Guenevere leaped
off my chest and, simultaneously, doubled my left arm back
on itself.

"Turn over."

"No — uuummmph." Despite my protests, I was easily
turned; at once the coolness progressed down and over my
buttocks. This last assault on my posterior dignity was more
than I could bear. I took a deep breath, wrenched my body to
its knees, and brought my right hand, fisted, flailing backward.

Aylbrous Purston was there.

Three men stood behind him and in a semi-circle. They were
black men, but their blackness was special — so uniform, so

terrific that it seemed an artificial, not a human pigment. And the white of their eyes and teeth was so exaggerated by the contrast that they appeared luminous. One of these men, a Horn Green whose left ear was but a nibbled crust, held a large pail in one hand, a heavy paint brush in the other. I saw steam rise from the pail's rim in ominous, curled fringes. Their mouths spread one after the other, beginning at the earless man's mouth and proceeding right with the precision of some carefully rehearsed performance. Purston did not smile. He raised his hands to his chest, as though in an Eastern obeisance and then, deliberately, he cracked each finger knuckle.

I heard the snaps. I numbered them: the first through the eighth. The room was very silent then — six anticipations, five lustful, one horrified — and the sound of his cracking possessed an inordinate resonance. Six, seven, eight: the teeth in my upper jaw pierced the insides of my lips. There were intense aches at the heart of either palm. My eyes closed, for Purston's face had become radically more grim. "This is the end," I said. I would have screamed, but I had no voice at all. And my ROT and absinthe befuddled mind repeated the formula, "This is the end. This is the end. This is the end." In my apprehension, I clutched at Guenevere's torso; pressed my face against her sharp, comfortless nipples.

"Thank God you come," said Guenevere. She shoved my head away and hopped swiftly off the bed. "He was raping me."

"Guenevere!"

"He was raping me. It was terrible. Can I go now, Mr. Purston?" Her back was toward me. I watched as, with languid fingers, she scratched between the cheeks of her behind.

"Raping a Negro woman," said Purston. "A girl — a girl no more than sixteen. That's very bad."

"Can I go now, Mr. Purston?" He nodded impatiently. The

earless man put his pail down. It touched the floor heavily. Then, slowly, he began pushing up his sleeves.

"I — I want to see Godhild."

"See?" said Purston. He snarled and a thick patina of phlegm was scraped from the depths of his throat. It dribbled down, as he spoke, from the corners of his mouth. "See? See? White man, you may never see again."

"No," I said. "Please. Not that." And my eyes, terrified, rolled to the very tops of their orbits.

"You're finished in Harlem, Mr. Pratt. Finished meddling. Finished, period." He drew an object from his pocket and touched at it lightly. There was a click. A long blade leaped out. The point was so sharp, so thin, that it was almost invisible. I crawled backward, toward the head board.

"Mr. Purston — "

"Your balls or your eyes, Mr. Priest?"

"Mr. Purston, please. I never did anything. I didn't mean any harm — "

"Answer me, Whitey," he came forward, the blade longer yet at the end of his extended arm.

"Please. Please. Please. I'll go away, I'll go. I promise. I'll never come back. I promise. As God is my witness. I promise. Don't hurt me. Don't — "

"Answer me!"

"What — what? Please, what do you want?"

"Your balls or your eyes, Mr. Pratt. You get a choice."

"I — " The blade darted suddenly toward my face. "My balls! My balls!" I shrieked, my forearm pressed across my precious eyes. "My balls!" And the three men laughed.

"He ain't got none is why," said the man with the nibbled ear. "He ain't got no balls." He spat on the carpet: a thick wad of sputum. I watched as it subsided, seeping into the thick nap.

"Yeah," said the man behind Purston.

"He ain't got no balls is why," repeated the man with the nibbled ear. He said it with emphasis, as though the reiteration were a new thought. His two companions nodded.

"Get on your feet, Pratt."

"What — what will you do?"

"Get up!" I stood, my hands held high and near my eyes. My pants slumped down. When I bent to pull them up, Purston kicked at my wrist with a brutal swiftness. The toes of his shoes were encased in metal, and, at first, I thought my wrist had been broken. I stood there sucking the bone, my pants at my knees. I knew that my nearly nude thighs were shuddering. I knew because all three of Purston's henchmen were leering at them. There was enjoyment in their watching: enjoyment that was heightened by my helplessness. Enjoyment as pure as carnal lust.

"What's — what's going to happen?" I sobbed just once. Then bit my tongue instead.

"Pratt," said Purston. "You better take them glasses off." He leaned over to remove them. I thought it an oddly considerate gesture. Purston snapped my glasses in half at the bridge, and I was glad. There was a sort of withdrawal in this blurring of my vision. Faces' threatening became vague — black skin, white embedded eyes and teeth — it approximated a dream, and I wanted very much to be dreaming.

"We feel sorry for you, Pratt," said Purston. "We know you hate bein' white. We know y'like layin' little black girls. So we're gonna do you a favor — we're gonna make you nigger for a night." He stepped back. "Humphrey. Luke. Take his clothes off."

I helped. I unhooked the special studs for them; I bent low when they drew off my undershirt. They, in their turn, manhandled my body ruthlessly, ripped, came close to my ear to curse and to threaten. The man called Humphrey used a long scissors on my hair; lopped clumps dropped to my shoulders like tattered epaulets. My legs never once ceased shaking, and often it was impossible for me to stand upright. A very painful blush, almost a fever, suffused my cheeks. I was silent: too apprehensive for prayer, watching Purston with feeble eyes. He knelt near the pail throughout my preparation. With patent satisfaction he worked the brush backward and forward. It was black and very thick. Still emitting strands of steam. Pitch, I knew. Black as pitch.

"Shit, man," said Humphrey. "This cat's white — I mean real white. White all over, white like a dead frog's belly. It makes me sick."

"Shut up," said Purston. He carried the pail over and set it down near my bared right foot. "Hold him." Purston dipped his brush. He held it flat side up and thrust under the pitch's surface, scooping as though with a spoon. Thick, dark strands plopped on to the carpet. For several moments Purston's big, fish's mouth opened and closed, the teeth perfect but too large. He appeared to devour the air — straining some special, subtle nourishment from it. I turned away, for he seemed not human then. But Purston grasped my earlobe and drew our faces together until I could smell the meaty odor of his breath. "This is a warning, Pratt. I don't give warnings twice. Get out of Harlem. Get out fast."

The brush rose, the bristles top heavy with their burden. When it came, the blow turned my head a full ninety degrees, and the pitch was driven into my mouth, high up into my nostrils. I began to choke. I strove to double up, but Humphrey's grip held me erect. The odor of the pitch seemed now to be behind my eyes, an exudation of my own brain. Purston set to work in earnest. Industriously, he dug the brush into the slight-

est corners of my face. He dabbed at my ears: my hearing
faded and was beset by echoes. Once I fainted, and then was
roused suddenly as my life reflexes fought asphyxiation. Eyes
tight shut, I heard, as though in the distance, the happy sounds
of their playing.

"Hey, Ayl — you splashin' me."

"Hold him up."

"Get him down there, too."

"No, man, leave that white. That ain't no black man's thing."

"Hold him up."

"Hey — even his teeth're black. His fuckin' teeth're black."

"Paint a white collar on him."

"Turn him sunny-side."

"Y'missed a spot."

"Come on, Ayl — let me have a go. Come on."

The pitch was very warm, not hot. I remembered then a wide
mud puddle near our house in Greensprings, and a child my age
whose shoes had been muddied there. He was disgusted; fearful of a mother's anger. He sat and, with torn up grass clumps,
tried to wipe his shoe tops clean. But, when he rose from his
labors, another boy pushed him mischievously between the
shoulder blades. He fell lengthwise and forward into the puddle. We expectantly awaited then his anger and dismay. But
when he rose to his knees, he was laughing. He began to roll
there in the puddle until body and clothes were an even ooz-
ing red-brown. And we, still unbesmirched at the puddle's
edge, were filled with wonder. But this was understandable
after all: he had committed himself, been committed, to mud-
diness; there remained only to enjoy. Now I, too, stood patiently, no longer resisting my captivity. My eyes were shut
tight; my hearing distanced; my smelling and my tasting were
only of the pitch. The brush and my body met some other place

but the meeting was not unpleasant. Choiceless, I capitulated and was almost willing though still afraid.

"Open the door, Luke." Something sharp, perhaps the knife's point, prodded at my spine. "Walk, Pratt. Keep walking and no tricks."

It seemed we went a long way, I with my arms outstretched before me. I heard voices, sounds of persistent festivity, yet no one offered aid. Now and then one of my captors would kick me sharply, but their brutality was discouraged by the pitch. A door opened. It became oppressively hot, and I knew that we had entered a boiler room.

"Stop," said Purston. I stopped. Another door was opened and, with the opening, there came a chilling draft. "You been lucky, Pratt. Next time you're a dead man. We cut you apart and there'll be pieces all over Harlem."

I felt the flat of his shoe sole at my hips. It rested there a moment. Then, when he had achieved sufficient leverage, Purston shoved me powerfully forward and into the cold. I tried to balance, but the ground dropped rapidly away beneath my feet. I fell, tumbling head over feet. The door slammed shut behind me.

Cold air touched my new skin and began to congeal it. The supple areas of my body — my joints, the loose fat of my stomach and buttocks — sensed the restriction and protested. Cracks developed at points of stress; a thousand body hairs were painfully uprooted. I rose to my knees. Then, in terror, I tried to see. The left lid, already weakened, would not part: the right lid opened only with difficulty and my vision through the eye was badly obstructed, striated by thick strands of pitch. I knew better than to touch it with my blackened hands. I stood. Pieces of trash — newspaper, cigarette butts, cellophane — adhered to my back and rustled in the breeze as I walked. It

seemed very cold. My skin sought to form goose pimples but
was thwarted. And, above me, as though on some poorly tuned
frequency, the noise of Horn's party chaffed my plight.

I was alone and in a dark rear alley. On either side were two
high wooden fences topped with wire. The alley appeared to
extend from the HWC building's rear door, across the block
and then under another, taller, apartment building, some thirty
paces ahead of me. I stepped forward cautiously, crab-wise,
leading with my right leg and eye. Something deep and slimy
oozed up from between my naked toes. I gagged — in frantic
revulsion I tottered sideways against a loaded garbage can.
The handle caught me painfully at the place where kneecap
touches shinbone. I grasped the rim for comfort, and, in so
doing, encountered a bit of bedsheet that was tolerably clean.
I pinched a segment between my fingers, then attempted, very
gingerly, to free my vision. I succeeded, but not gingerly — at
the cost of nearly all my eyelashes. My right eye watered, then
cleared. And I could see.

I saw first my nakedness. Though alone, I imitated Adam's
dread enlightenment and his shame. Instinctively the flats of
each palm reached down to hide my private parts. Then, fur-
tively, I peered up at the lighted windows, but they were in-
different, not seeing. I looked beyond them to the sky and,
through one watering, myopic eye, I perceived the moon again
— itself still an image of nudity, innocent still. My hands parted
as fists. They sought sheltering pockets in the black flesh of
my hips. And then I stood quite motionless. I was awaiting, I
think, annihilation.

For all the things around me were clothed. I saw that. I
knew they must abhor my nakedness. The very earth under
my feet, the hard granite of Manhattan, had not seen sunlight
in a hundred years, and its rough armor broke the skin of my

feet. I was terrified by my uniqueness and, in this terror, abruptly wise. I began to pray. My nudity was an intolerable reproach to all the countless shells — the soft, the impervious, the insensitive, the distorting —that were about me. Tough, square buildings. Enveloping cloth. Words and gestures. Standing there I understood my mortality and was appalled. The bones of my skeleton were there almost to touch. My heart pulsed a scant few inches from the bitter wind. And death — inside. Inside. At fortress center. Coexisting with my precious life, cancerous, thriving on its substance. I prayed and was rewarded, as never I have been before or since, with an awesome, unmitigated humility. And then I knelt to let the pavement bruise my knees as well.

It could not last. These things are not so ordained. Existence is selection: a thorough, careful exclusion of all doubt. Until the last, agitated moment of life, until then, we are all immortals. And that night in the alley, my immortality returned in a sound — a loud hailing. "Pratt! Pratt! Over here. It's friends!" I stood. The cry seemed to emanate from the place, where, in darkness, my alley plunged beneath the taller apartment building. I walked forward hopefully, quite disregarding the fact that I knew no friends in Harlem. The blackness was intact below the building. There were obstacles — carriages, bicycles, all on recalcitrant wheels. I made slow progress. The voice became perturbed: urgent, perhaps impatient, I could not judge, nor could I answer it. I encountered, at last, a tall flight of stairs, and this I climbed on hands and knees. When I reached the street's level I stood upright, oblivious, once again, to the state of my nudity.

It was Smith. He sat under a streetlamp, astride a huge, golden motorcycle. As I emerged from the alley's mouth, he began to laugh; his laughter was strident and oddly female. It echoed in the quiet side street; in the baffled passages of my hearing. It echoed and reechoed for he could not seem to stop. His horn pointed at the heavens and shook like some reproachful forefinger.

"Help me," I whimpered. I stretched out my right hand, imploring. "Help me, please."

But, for a long moment, Horn Smith could scarcely help himself. God only knows what I must have looked like tottering there: it was enough, certainly, to abrogate even his sublime demeanor. Smith had placed both fists on the handlebars, his face on the backs of his fists, and now his horn pointed downward — the beak of some shortsighted bird. "Oh no. Oh. Oh. Oh." He shrieked. "Too much. Too much." His shoulders bunched, relaxed, shuddered; bunched again. I looked left and right, for this loud hilarity, I feared, would draw attention to my state — and, indeed, windows had already begun to rumble open on the street's far side.

"Please," I hissed. "Please. Help me get home." While begging, I retreated further into the alley's shadowed mouth. Smith's eyes watered with the excess of his merriment; he dabbed at them with his shirtfront. Then, without forewarning, he leaped high and brought his full weight down on the motorcycle's starter mechanism. The machine roared.

"Hop on," he shouted. I backed down the steps, waving a refusal with my still extended hand.

"No. Please. Call a taxi."

"Hop on, man. It's a kick. Besides — you got no choice." I gripped my bare chest with the nails of all ten fingers and Smith laughed once again.

"I can't. I can't. I'm afraid."

"Hurry up," he said. "I ain't got all night."

There was no option. I realized that. "God. God. God," I moaned as I stumbled toward him. Smith observed my progress, too bemused by comedy to offer aid. "Hey!" a voice shouted from above, a woman's voice. "He ain't got no clothes on!" The motorcyle bucked and jiggled as I tried to straddle it. Cold metal gave my groin a numbing shock that I assumed was the pain of injury. Smith gunned the engine.

"Hold onto me," he shouted, and, before I was securely astride, the motorcycle lurched ahead.

The force of that first acceleration was merciless. The palm of an iron hand drove itself into my windpipe, forced my chin irresistibly backward. My fingers were tangled in Smith's jacket belt, but, even so, my bare feet soared up until they had over-topped his shoulders. For an interminable moment I was quite upside down. The asphalt, the snarling rear wheel hung above me. I pulled on the thin material; the belt gave, then be-came taut. I pulled and the tension made my arms solid, joint-less bars. The motorcycle dipped to the right. My stomach spiraled up and then obtruded against my diaphragm, preclud-ing breath. As Smith turned onto Seventh Avenue the mo-torcycle rolled further and further onto the inner portions of its tires, until it seemed to ride on the glinting spokes them-selves. I yanked my right arm in as the street snatched at it. My head was suspended but eighteen inches from a hard de-struction, saved only by the perverse laws of centrifugal force. I was screaming: I had screamed all the while. The sounds I was making now were low and guttural, as though the cords of my voice had frayed. And Smith, joyous, shouted his laughter at the building tops. We roared down the avenue at fifty miles an hour, still accelerating. The wind blew the fat of my ab-domen into pocked ripples. I was so bitterly cold that I could no longer feel coldness. The sensing part of my flesh seemed sheared away. For the first time, I stared forward — for two blocks ahead of us, the lights were red.

"Stop! Stop!" I screamed. "Are you mad? Are you drunk? Stop! For God's sake stop!"

"Noooooo!" he howled. Beneath me, a raucous siren began to wail. On the pavement late walkers went rigid in extreme postures of motion. One aged woman snatched a tremendous German Shepherd up, into her protecting arms. Cars from the side streets came to screeching stops at odd angles to the avenue. A policeman hurried from the curb, hand upraised, his whistle blaring in his mouth. Without hesitation, Smith drove the motorcycle at him, and the policeman, whistle still in mouth, dove headfirst over a parked car's hood. What an infernal apparition we must have seemed — the man with the horn and the naked black white man, near panic, bouncing on bared buttocks. And screaming at the height of a shattered voice.

"Hold — on — tight!" Aghast I watched as Smith deliberately headed the machine left, into the oncoming traffic. I shrieked and tried to pull at his right arm, but Smith shrugged me off. The lights of the first cars were bearing down on us. Already their drivers had begun to slow in alarm; they turned left, right erratically. Smith roared between the two cars, through a gap no more than five feet wide. The driver to our left lost control and rammed a parked car's rear. I tried to close my eyes, but my dread fascination was compulsive. Then, just a block ahead, I saw a huge, empty bus pull out. Smith seemed not to notice. He swerved outside a black Cadillac, then suddenly back, across the traffic flow, scarcely avoiding a Volkswagen's low, snub nose. I thought I felt cold metal on my shin. Smith howled and gibbered, then accelerated again. He began leaping up and down on the seat like some naughty, irrepressible child.

"Watch out! Watch out!" I shrieked. The empty bus loomed up, now no more than half a block away. Smith howled defiance at it, but did not slow. Then, to my horror, another bus appeared on the right, overtaking the first. Their brightly lit

fronts drew even and presented an impenetrable wall — a wall
that rushed forward at one hundred miles an hour. And Smith
accelerated. I braced my poor, bare frame for impact. Suddenly as the nearest driver threw his hands over his face, Smith
swerved left. The motorcycle leaped the curb, grazed a hydrant
and scattered six men who had been pitching quarters against
the building wall. We raced down the sidewalk a full block
and then, I think, Smith headed out into the oncoming traffic
once again.

I fainted then. My head was moving left-right, left-right
against the force of Smith's firm slapping when I awakened.
The motorcycle reposed in silence beneath me. St. Bart's was
there, monstrous and unperturbed; I heard the creaking of its
sign. I slipped off the seat and Smith, ignoring the pitch, held
me up as I toppled. The tension had damaged every sinew and
muscle in my legs. One knee seemed irreparably bent. Smith
carried me to the alley's mouth. Then he settled my shoulders
against the wall of St. Bart's.

"Oh, my God," I said. "Oh, my God."

"You made it, Pratt." In unaccountable glee he began pounding me on the shoulders. "You made it, man. You made it."

"I — " Then I puked. In short, silent bursts the yellow
detritus poured down over my feet. Smith danced away from
the splashing and laughed. I shivered, inhaled against the bitter flow and choked. I took a few steps away, halted, drew
my arm across my lips and slumped against the wall again.

"You made it," said Smith, quietly now. He came close.

"Why?" I whimpered. "Why?" Smith took my face in both
hands and lifted it up. Then he peered intently into my eyes
— my eye. He smiled.

"I know, man. I know. But you're all right. You're all right,
my good friend, Pratt. And you made it."

"I made it," I said. Smith stepped back. With a graceful

gesture he bowed slightly and touched his horn. Saluted me.
"Ave atque vale, magister," he said. "I'll be seeing you."
And then he was gone.

. . . And, of course, my dearest sister, they had taken my key
away. What a dreadful moment! You can't imagine. You can't
imagine. I threw myself at the rectory door, I throttled the handle,
I banged my fists until they bled. And then, when exhaustion overwhelmed me, it was so, so cold. I cried, Eleanor. I knew there was
nothing for it but to wait — four long hours in that courtyard,
naked and the temperature no more than thirty-five degrees at best.
Nicholas came early, thank God, I might not be here now if he
hadn't. As it was, I had a high fever. Poor, dear Nicholas. I shall
bring back to Greensprings only one pleasant memory — of his
kindness. He put me to bed. Saw to it the pitch was removed from
my more sensitive parts. He spent the whole of three days and
nights here, and, on Monday, when my fever had become quite
frightening, he risked compromising his career and perhaps more
than that to bring a doctor. A white doctor. Very nervous he was
— the doctor. And with good reason.

I'm better now. Still very weak of course. My eardrums are swollen — they almost burst — but I hope the terramycin I'm taking
will relieve that. Nicholas has scraped most of the pitch off, still . . .
I must prepare you, dearest. I haven't a hair on my body. Bald
as a bulb. My scraggly topping never was much, but now I haven't
even got eyebrows. Eyebrows. Eleanor, you can't imagine how
essential eyebrows are. Well, you'll know soon enough. My face
is still pretty badly scarred from my first beating. I haven't told
you about that one! I will. I will. I've so much to tell you.

You've guessed, haven't you? I'm coming home. Coming home
and soon. Greensprings is all I can think of now. I've had some
fine, if rather delirious, dreams of you and Harold and the old house
in the last four days. I called Bishop Hawkes this morning. I tried
to speak calmly, but the tone of my voice must have warned him.
He refused to see me until Saturday. He's a crafty old fox and probably suspects — wants to give me time to think it over. Not much
chance: I'm too scared. Let him deal with Purston, it's time I went
home.

As for Horn Smith — God only knows his mind. Unbalanced, at the very least. Did I tell you? He can read Greek and Latin, let alone English. Eleanor, I'm absolutely sure of it. You've read the Autobiography, you know what it sounds like. And everyone here, even his mistress, thinks he's an immaculate illiterate. But I'm sure of it. Not only that, it seems he imagines some weird bond between the two of us (could it be the classics? Ha!). C. B. Pratt and George Horn Smith . . . All for one and one for all! I don't know, half the time, whether he's trying to seduce me or get me killed. Nicholas is loyal, he refuses to believe Smith had anything to do with my humiliation last Sunday morning. I'm not so certain. Well, whatever Smith's guilt may be, Nicholas agrees with me on one subject. He thinks I should get out of Harlem and quick. He doesn't say it, but I know he's afraid. Purston's displeasure, when and if he decides to manifest it, is likely to be quite indiscriminate. Catholic, I might say. Nicholas may suffer for the kindness he's shown me.

I could endure still more, I suppose. I could be more determined, more the insensitive John Meeker. But is there any point? The indignities I've suffered are paltry compared to what the martyrs underwent. But their suffering was vital, it forwarded Christ's work in the world. Here it's a game. If, instead of being stoned, St. Stephen had had his pants pulled down — well, I imagine the church would have had second thoughts about canonizing him. Besides, no one needs my help. Not here. And, when it comes to that, what help have I to give?

And so, my dearest sister, I shall soon be back in your attic thumping and pottering and dropping things. I dread the sensation my face will cause in Market Square. I dread the explanations and the looks of "I told you so." But, at least I'll be home — home among people who aren't so fearfully alien. Prepare my way, if you can. And don't worry — it was a close thing, but I'm all right now. And wiser. So much wiser.

> Your brother,
> CAL

I was in my kitchen when it happened — at five minutes past eight o'clock precisely, Thursday evening. I was standing near

the sink, scraping my plate into the mouth of a garbage bag. A
roach, I recall, disturbed by my rustling, circumambulated the
can's rim once and vanished down the far side. My glasses
had slid very near the tip of my nose. I interrupted the action
and brought my right hand up to readjust them on the bridge.
I was very careful, for the scraping knife was still in my hand.
My eyes watched my fingertip as it approached. I held my
breath. And this trivial gesture remains now fixed in my memory, because it was then that I felt the shock.

My glasses disappeared. I blinked and they were gone. A
knuckled right fist inserted digits under my right mastoid.
Both my ear drums sputtered and then, with excruciating pain,
seemed to contract. My head swerved, and I saw, at the right
side of my vision, four panes of the kitchen window, intact and
in symmetry and suspended two feet above the sink. They fell,
but the sound of their shattering was subsumed in the clap of
a tremendous explosion. It knocked me nearly senseless to the
floor. There was a loud hissing and an even louder whooshing
noise, as of a great burner in ignition. Two terror-stricken
mice scurried across the kitchen floor, collided with each other,
struggled, tiny feet treading the air, and then rushed to sanctuary beneath my refrigerator. The lights went out. Blunt
forceps were inserted at either of my earholes and jerked upward. Through the roar of my tormented hearing, I listened to
screams, to crackling as of great sticks being snapped, and, from
above me, to the cheerful thrumming of Landowska's harpsi-
chord.

My spectacles had not been broken. I found them just under
the stove. Above, the gas jets were hissing, for the shock had
snuffed them out. I stood and turned each off; I turned off my
portable radio. Though the lighting had failed, the entire eastern wing of my rectory was flooded by a midday brightness. The

catastrophe, I knew, had occurred close to home, was still occurring. With the windows gone, the house was abruptly pervious to sound. As I approached the front door I heard sirens, shouts and then a dreadful crashing noise, succeeded by hundreds of smaller, more brisk retorts. I pulled open the door.

I had to shade my eyes. The upper story of Horn's Place — along its entire length — was on fire. Flames rushed upward in a furious arc, a titanic cresting wave that seemed about to break above my head. A terrific gust of hot wind blew my jacket open. The conflagration was so intense that I clapped both hands over my newly shaved skull, for it seemed, even at that distance, that my flesh was being seared. Before me, in the courtyard, were strewn odd bits of debris, poignant in their heterogeneity. A telephone receiver. A dead, headless rat. Half a coat rack. A huge, still-flaming, wooden beam. A filing cabinet drawer. Dozens of books, hundreds of loose pages. An umbrella, furled. The insides of a typewriter. A mattress lay against my stoop, smelling vilely of charred hair. And, as I looked, smoking, black missiles dropped onto the pavement. I backed into my doorway. It appeared certain that my rectory would be consumed as well.

Suddenly a window, a shattered frame, in the lower story of Horn's Place was worked up. A leg appeared. Then another. The figure of a man burst through the smoke and jumped, fell to the courtyard pavement. His jacket tails had been wrenched up, over his head; yellow flames and smoke leaped out of his shoulders as he reached the open air. He rolled backward and forward on the ground. I ran toward him — I took four steps and was pummeled to my knees by cyclonic winds. The air scorched my nostrils and seemed to expand balefully against the membrane of my lungs. I crawled forward on all fours. A heavy block of wood fell just a few feet to my right; it bounced crazily on its corners. The man was still rolling, arching his back, seeking to crush the flames that danced near his neck. He coughed: his inhalations were the hunting cry of some savage dog. I tore off my jacket and threw it over him. When I did so, he started violently and struck out with his arm. His jacket slipped down, and I saw the horn.

"Pratt . . . Quick! Get me inside."

"The flames!" I gasped. "The flames out." I fell on top of him, smothering the red embers with the weight of my body. He groaned, and I knew I had caused him pain.

"Inside — get me inside." I fell back onto my knees, then shrieked. A piece of tissue in my shirt pocket burst into flame. I smashed it out with my forearms. Smith was struggling to his feet. A great section of the upper story thundered inward. I tried to stand, but couldn't. My lungs, expanded to bursting, could not give up their air. A searing shock covered the small of my back, and spread outward. "Oh, God. No! No!" I gasped. The thin material of my shirt had begun to smoulder. And then, miraculously, a stream of water, thrown by miscalculation over the building, spattered down onto my back. Steam seemed to spew upward from my own body; it blinded me. But the fires on my back were doused.

"Hurry. Hurry." Smith began lifting me by the armpits. I tried to shrug him off — I knew how weak he was — but the pinching, frantic grip of his fingers would not be denied. He hauled my unresponsive weight across the courtyard in short, wrenching spasms of a yard or so: bending and driving backward on his heels, as an inchworm moves. My knees were scraped bloody by the pavement, and yet Smith would not wait for me to stand. I cried out; my nails scratched at his mutilated shoulders. And he repeated that single word, "Hurry! Hurry!" with scarce conscious resolution. At the foot

of the stoop he tottered and collapsed on top of me. I thought
he had passed out, but he was up again at once. With one hand
inside my collar, he drew me up the steps and half hurled my
body through the doorway. Smith kicked the door shut behind
him.

We lay prostrate, chest to chest, in the tiny foyer. Smith began to cough with an alarming ferocity. I felt the tip of his horn
against my shoulder: it pecked at me like the beak of some
insistent bird. His cough lost its distinguishing form. He
choked, sputtered, sobbed; he took his own throat between infuriated hands, but he could not stem the reflexes of his hungry
lungs. I reached out and touched him tentatively at the hips,
a useless commiseration. I thought of my mother and how she
would pound her children between the shoulders when they
choked. But I could do nothing. Smith grabbed my forearms
and squeezed fiercely as he struggled to contain the paroxysm.
The sound of human voices penetrated from the courtyard.
Smith leaped up; he pressed the flat of both hands over his
mouth and the coughing became an ominous, internal growl.

"Fireman," he hissed. "They'll want in. Quick." He
wrenched me to my feet. "The church. Hurry. They'll be
here — now."

"Why?"

"Come."

"You need help."

"Come!"

He knew the way. That, in itself, should have seemed suspicious. Still coughing, striding while doubled at the waist,
Smith led me hurriedly down the corridor, through my office
and into the chancel. And there we both stopped, astonished.
It was the light. To our left, the glass and most of the board-
ing in the northeast wall of the nave had been blown out. We

could see the huge fire, and the fire, in turn, projected its shimmering oranges and yellows onto the walls of the nave. St. Bart's itself appeared in sympathetic conflagration. The flickering light peopled the aisles with dodging shadows; it set the fan tracery undulating like sea anemones. The statues of the saints beneath the shafted imposts nodded and gesticulated. The fire's light illuminated the pathetic wedges of glass that remained in the flamboyant windows on the far wall. Here and there a pentagon of blue, a trapezoid of pale green, glinted dully through the wavering yellows, like jewels seen at a shallow stream's bottom. The entire nave seemed to oscillate. For quite the first time my church approximated a living thing — a busy device of many glowing and interrelated parts. Only the chill, the moistness that condensed on the sore, hot bits of my back, betrayed its sorry dereliction.

"Weird," said Smith. He looked once through the broken windows, at the flaming ruin of his work. He started to shake his head, but completed only one half-arc. Then he spat on my chancel carpet: it was half in defiance, half a necessary act. "Come," he said; he drew me down the steps and into the nave.

We proceeded to the left-hand aisle, and along it, shattered glass crunching beneath our feet, until we reached the door that led down to the disused basement. Smith halted before it. He began fumbling in his pants pocket.

"It's locked," I said. "The keys are in my bedroom." But, to my amazement, Smith produced a long, old-fashioned key from his pocket. He inserted it and turned: the door opened inward.

"Quickly," he said.

I found myself on a narrow, stone spiral staircase. Smith closed the door firmly and shot a bolt home. The darkness became absolute. I backed against the cold masonry as he edged past me on the stairs. He descended only a short way, perhaps a dozen steps. A dim light was turned on. I stepped down. One twenty-five watt bulb had been installed at the foot of the staircase; even its dull illumination was partly obscured by a dirty piece of rag. Smith smiled.

The basement of St. Bart's was spacious. To the right, through an unhinged double door, I could see a large, long meeting room. It appeared to occupy a good part of the rectory's length toward Lenox Avenue. Ahead, a corridor extended some distance into shadows. To the left, along this corridor, was a series of low arches. Beyond these arches, stretching under the nave itself, was a considerable area — used, apparently, for storage. I saw chairs and kitchen appliances. Piles of magazines and damp newspapers. A filing cabinet. A folded Ping-Pong table. It was all very much as Nicholas had described it. We passed three of these arches as we proceeded along the corridor, but the fourth was different. A rough, rounded door had been fitted across the arch's mouth and padlocked. Smith drew out another key.

"I've been squatting here for some years, Mr. Pratt. Like a little mouse. You will forgive me, I hope." He tore a piece of charred material from his jacket sleeve. Then he began to shiver. He unlocked the door, leaned in and snapped on a switch. His teeth chattered as he spoke. "Please," he said, "come in."

Once, when I was a grammar school boy, I, with several other children and their parents, was invited to tea at the headmaster's house. Mr. Herridge was very old, nearly eighty then. He reminded me, reminds me now, of Mr. Casaubon in *Middlemarch* — gray-fleshed, with wens and hairy warts like purses of surplus skin thriftily set aside. He was tall and stooped, yet affected a very loud voice which contrasted violently with his apparent feebleness. Tea was served in the rose garden, but, after a while, there being more guests than expected, another boy and I were sent to fetch chairs from the kitchen. Along the way, we happened to pass Mr. Herridge's study. I peered in, too awed by his august, lingering presence to place even a foot beyond the threshold. There was an odor of stagnant tobacco smoke. A broad desk dominated the room, and it was untidily strewn with books and sheaves of paper, pipes and three, I recall, three quite different pairs of glasses. There was an electric desk light, green-shaded and constructed to resemble a kerosene lamp. Books lined three of the four walls. Busts of the classic poets and emperors stood high atop the bookshelves. Wood cuts hung in several places, so poorly illuminated that they seemed, from where I stood, but magnified thumb prints. A globe, a dictionary on a stand, and two stuffed chairs, arms bloated and splayed outwards by the burden of their own weight. And now, as I peered in from the basement corridor, I saw all these things again. Differently arranged; an item added; an item missing. But essentially the same — the paraphernalia of a nineteenth-century scholar.

"What do you think of it?" he asked.

"Uh — " I stammered. "But . . . where did all this come from?"

"It was all here, you know. In bits and pieces. From some priest man's old office. From upstairs, I think. The chairs were in the big room. The silly heads — Nicholas found them in a box. Some of the books were already down here." He looked significantly at me. "And some of them are mine."

"Yes." I nodded. "I guessed as much."

"Come in. Come in, please." He closed the door behind us. "Just give me a moment."

Smith removed his jacket and shirt carefully. An emblem,

I saw, hung around his neck on a leather thong — some
animal's eyetooth. I knew from the uncertain, quick flinching
of his eyes, that the shirt fabric had taken skin with it. Here
and there on his back, flecks of white were imbedded, melded
into the dark surface. Smith walked over to a small, screened
enclosure where a sink and toilet were partially hidden from
my view.

I examined his library. The books were old, some had Dewey
decimal numbers printed on them in white ink — as though
they'd been removed from some public institution. The shelves
nearest the door held, chiefly, volumes of history: ancient, classical and medieval. The books themselves belonged to history: few had been published later than the First World War.
I took down a volume of Breasted. On the flyleaf was written,
"Dr. Francis Oddie, 1918." The toilet flushed abruptly. I
slapped the book shut.

"That's it!" I shouted. "My toilet. That's why it flushed
in the middle of the night. I'll be damned." Smith came toward me. He was massaging Vaseline into his forearms.

"Please, would you rub this on my back?" He withheld the
jar, however; insisting first on some explicit gesture of my
willingness.

"Sure." I took the jar. He presented his back to me.

"Gently, I think," he said. I dug my fingertips into the goo.

"Are you sure this is all right? Vaseline is fine for minor
burns, but . . ."

"Please." I touched his skin. It quivered, shied away from
the shocking chillness of the Vaseline. I hesitated.

"Does it hurt?"

"Go on, Mr. Pratt."

"I think you should see a doctor." He inhaled sharply.

"At the moment, I'm afraid, that is not possible. Go on." I
did. Smith made a humming noise: a groan disguised. "Mr.

Pratt — when we came in — you seemed to know about this. About my reading books. May I ask, what made you know it?"

"Lift your arm a bit. Well . . . Several things really. The names of your people, of course. And their uniforms. But it was the books — the ones you borrowed — that first made me suspicious. Your neck, too?" He nodded. "I see now how you got them from my shelves. You came up through the church while I was asleep or out. But what I can't see — I mean, how did you get down here in the first place? Do you have a key to the church?"

"Oh, yes." He laughed. "That's all I need, Mr. Pratt — to be seen letting myself in and out of a white man's church. My people, they wouldn't understand. And Aylbrous . . ." He laughed again. "Thank you. Give me the jar now." He took it; then turned me by the shoulders. I sensed a ripping as he pared away the ruined parts of my shirt: then the tips of his fingers and the cold, soft Vaseline in the small of my back.

"How — how did you manage it then?"

"Well, Mr. Pratt. There was a girl's school — called St. Agnes, I think. It was burned down in 1921, and the stores — the ones that are . . . were . . ." He paused, disconcerted by the recollection. "Ah. Horn's Place was built on the old school's foundation. It seems there was a tunnel. It ran, you know, from the school's basement to the church — it comes out at the end of the hall there. For rainy days, I think. So the girls could go to chapel in the mornings. You can still see — have I missed any places that hurt you?"

"No. That's fine. I'm in pretty good shape, thanks to that lucky downpour. Go on."

"It's nothing really. You can see, here and there, where the little girls wrote on the walls. Names of boys. Dates — 1890, 1900. Some silly rhymes. A few bad words." He returned the jar to his medicine cabinet. "When I bought the old stores, you see — I started all by myself to put new panels in the cellar walls, and I found the entrance. No one else knows. Just me and Nicholas. And you, Mr. Pratt."

"And this is where you learned to read? You taught your-self — down here?"

"No, my friend." Smith shook his head. The horn passed through the air, left-right-left, just inches from my forehead. "I have known how to read for some time now. Since I was eight years old, I think."

"What? But how can that be, I — " He raised his hand, then touched his horn lightly, as though to restrain it.

"I know. My book says something else. I'm sorry. The book is a big fake, Mr. Pratt. I made it that way. A little truth. A lot of lies. I'm sorry."

"A fake? Your own life story? I don't understand."

"You see — the truth, it was not so interesting." He smiled wistfully. "For a man with a horn, I have lived a very simple life."

"But pretending to be illiterate all this time. Why that?"

"Why not? Everyone expects it. They think I am an animal. And my own people, they don't like an educated man. He's an Uncle Tom to them. They will never trust an Uncle Tom. The whites, the ones that call themselves liberals, they like a man who has made himself from nothing. I needed the money from a big selling book. And besides . . ." He walked over to his desk. With an exaggerated carefulness, he slipped on a pair of dark horn-rimmed glasses. I smiled instinctively. "See," he said, "now I am Ferdinand the Bull smelling flowers. Babar the Elephant when he reads the Sunday papers. Some silly storybook animal, not a strong, angry prize fighter. My eyes are a bit farsighted. It helps when I must pretend not to read."

"I'm amazed," I said. "In fact — I feel like a bloody fool. All those things you said to me, up there, when we first met . . .

And I felt sorry for you. Can you read Latin, too?" He sighed. Then he took off his glasses.

"Yes. I'm trying. I started once many years ago — with Dr. Oddie. He was a good friend, not like the things I wrote about him. Most of these books are his. Just a while ago, I think to myself, I will take it up again. To learn more about your people." He picked up a book: it was a second year Latin school text. "I borrowed your books for that, to see if I was learning. I get tired of *puella pulchra est*. I wanted to read some poetry. But the Latin poets are very hard, and I have so little time now."

"And no one guessed? Of all the thousands and thousands who read your Autobiography. Not one of them guessed?"

"Of course not." He pointed to his horn and grinned. "This makes all things true. If a space ship would land in Central Park, Mr. Pratt — a space ship with men who had six eyes in their heads — would anyone doubt what they said, even if it was the greatest lie? No, my friend, we would see only the six eyes in their heads — only that. And we would believe."

A siren shrilled. The sound was distant: it seemed the ultimate cry of some living thing. Smith glanced at the ceiling. For one long moment his eyes appeared to stare intently, then the intentness became fixed, inert, and a sort of film misted across the lenses. His hands were held slightly outward, the wrists drooping down, like an animal surprised while feeding. I wanted to speak, but I was afraid. I imagined that I could see his ears moving, animate in the delicate act of hearing. Then, suddenly, the trance dissolved. Smith looked about the room hastily, as though numbering the things that were his.

"And Greek?" I said stupidly, not aware that the time for such questioning had passed. "Did you start learning Greek, too?"

"Enough — please, Mr. Pratt. Enough. I would like to talk,

but not now." Smith raised both hands deliberately, made them into fists, and seemed to examine each set of knuckles. "Now I must be doing things. Doing. Doing." He whispered the last two words, as though to some recalcitrant portion of his will. "You understand, Mr. Pratt — up there my eyes are being cut out and my arms are broken off. My . . ." He hesitated: his teeth appeared within a grim smile.

"I understand."

"Yes . . . You understand." He said it as though he thought I really couldn't. He turned and looked once again toward the room. "I need your help, my friend. Right now. Will you help me?"

"If I can." He turned back and began to speak very swiftly. "Tomorrow, when the fire is dead, they will find my tunnel. The firemen will follow it — and others will follow them. And they will find my room."

"Perhaps I can keep them out," I said. "After all, this is private property."

"Not in Harlem. In Harlem there is nothing private." He came close. His horn moved slowly, left-right; I thought he was using it as a hypnotist might use a swinging pendulum. "For the next few days, Mr. Pratt, I must be dead. It's the only hope I have. No one must think I came down here. No one must think I hid in this room. Before it is morning, you and I must make this room like it never was. And then I will leave."

"That's easy," I said. Smith shook his head. My eyes followed the horn's tip, blunt, the size of a quarter, faintly shining.

"Not so easy. There are two filing cabinets here — and my desk. They are filled with papers — names of people, addresses — they are very important, Mr. Pratt. With these papers someone, even you, could embarrass me very badly. Not only me — believe what I say — senators, even the President of the United States would be embarrassed with me. I want you to take these papers upstairs to your office and hide them there. Will you do it?"

"Yes."

"I must be honest — if someone should find out. Aylbrous, for instance. Then, Mr. Pratt, you might be treated very badly." I touched my bald head.

"I think I'm getting used to that. I think . . . A bit, anyway." I swallowed. "No. I guess you never really get used to it."

"You will do it then?" I nodded. He wanted to shake my hand, I know that. His own right hand began an involuntary movement. But he didn't. I think he was simply too shy. "Good. No more said. There are cardboard cartons outside — in the long meeting room. Bring them in here."

There were twelve cartons, all piled at crazy angles. The damp had rotted the bottoms from those nearest the floor, but there seemed about eight that were useable. I balanced four, one atop the next, and carried them to the door of Smith's room. Then I returned. I collected four more in the semi-dark of the meeting hall and started again to cross the corridor. I stopped. There was a noise: a scratching, the sound of small, clawed feet. Cold areas formed on my neck, just behind my earlobes. I peered cautiously around my armful of boxes. A little shadow had appeared near an empty drum, some ten paces from where I stood. The shadow moved. I yelped and threw the boxes from me.

It was an animal. When the boxes fell, it jumped from behind the drum, seemed to bounce several paces away from me. Then it hesitated, jumped once again and turned to peer. I opened my mouth; a long, low interrogative sound issued out.

A mouse, of course, but a very odd mouse. It seemed tall for its size, with long hind legs and an outsized, rather thick tail, on which it appeared to be reclining. The mouse watched me, waiting for a move that might indicate my intentions. It cocked its head, and, with it, a pair of bulging eyes, and a pair of large, spade-shaped ears. It looked rather like a five-inch kangaroo. I stepped forward. The animal bounced away, jumping as far vertically as it progressed horizontally — using its tail as a lively spring. It disappeared into the darkness.

I bent to retrieve the boxes, then stood upright and empty-handed. My fingers, preoccupied with the last event, had difficulty closing on the smooth cardboard sides. The animal was gone. The silence that now pervaded the long, cold corridor seemed to belie the realness of what I had just seen. I bent again. As I stood, balancing my awkward burden, I seemed to watch myself tottering there with an odd sort of objectivity. And I felt pity: my fingers were trembling, my heart pulsed, and my mind, withdrawing from reality, began to repeat nonsense lines with a maddened rhythm. "Spinx and ousels sing divinely. Spinx and ousels. Spinx and ousels. Ousels . . . Ousels . . . Ousels . . ." Very soon, I thought. Very soon, Pratt. You're coming to the end of your strength. I hurried to the door of Smith's room.

Somehow, in my wild anxiety, I had forgotten about his horn. For some time then, I suppose, I had seen it without appreciating the thing's uniqueness and now it shocked me. I stood in the doorway for several moments, staring with the special intensity of ominous night dreams. Smith was on his knees, reading, the heavy spectacles near the tip of his nose. The light gleamed from his naked, greased shoulders, and his horn, appearing to exceed his eyes, perused the page like a single dull orb on a stalk. I shook my head. There were notebooks, littered file folders, and three large piles of paper in front of him. Abruptly, I lost all faith in my own sanity. It seemed that, walking forward to that circle of light, I would pass from the real to the wholly infernal. "No," I whispered, and I turned to go.

"Mr. Pratt?" Smith looked up.

"Y-yes?"

"You can bring those boxes here." I walked toward him. "What's wrong? Did you hear anything?"

"No."

"They can't come through that fire." He said it to himself. "Not yet. We have time." He pulled open the lower desk drawer. "Take those three piles — put them each in a box. Put some books on top or some rags."

I nodded and took up the first pile. The top page was covered with a tiny, fastidious handwriting. Instinctively, I looked at Smith's arms and their terrific biceps. He pushed the glasses back on his nose, then stroked his horn in absent concentration. A siren howled. Smith crushed several pages in the fierce closing of his right fist. He looked at me.

"Who did it?" I asked.

"Who . . . ?" He smiled: an unpleasant grimace, as though he were repressing a spasm of nausea. "Who else? Aylbrous did it."

"Are you sure?" He nodded, then pulled a sheaf of papers from the desk drawer. "But why?" He shrugged. "Don't you want to talk about it?" He shrugged again.

"Nothing personal, Mr. Pratt. He likes me. He's told me that many, many times. Oh yes . . . But now, I'm no longer useful. That's all. He must be about his business." Smith looked up. "That box is too full. Start another one."

"Yes. Business? What business?"

"Aylbrous is a professional. From Curaçao. Trained in Cuba. I didn't know at first." He laughed. "Now I know."

"You mean — a communist?"

"Well, no . . . Not Aylbrous. He'll forget them too — when they can no longer help him. Aylbrous believes in himself, that's all. He's made a deal, you see, to deliver my people to a certain organization at a certain price. He doesn't care. No — there were a dozen people on the floor tonight. Just people. Secretaries. Errand boys . . ." He paused. "But his time will come. And soon. I promise you, Mr. Pratt."

His voice was low, obstructed by phlegm and the excess of his indignation. It intimidated me. I stood and carried three boxes to the door, one by one. When I returned, Smith was standing near the larger of two filing cabinets. He turned and handed me several folders.

"I suppose you think me a fool, Mr. Pratt. But you don't know Aylbrous, you've only seen him at his worst. He can be very charming when he wants to be. What you call a fair-haired boy. Full of ideas and enthusiasm. A flatterer. A wonderful, wonderful organizer. I think — you know, it's strange — I think I like him even now."

Smith took half a dozen sheets from the top drawer, examined them, then brought them over to his desk. He lit a match. He held it under the lower edges of the paper and burned them carefully above a large ashtray. He watched the flame with a strange fascination, so intently that his fingertips were singed and the black, spark-laced ashes were scattered suddenly across the desk top.

"I needed him — a scapegoat, that's what you call it. Someone to do my hating for me. Someone to keep the stupid liberal whites away with their speech-making and their useless handouts. Castrating my people, making them beggars. Give me the Ku Klux Klan any day, Mr. Pratt. An enemy, it unites a people, but these friends, they want to buy our souls. We will stand on our own. It's high time for that." He passed me six or eight hand-written pages, stapled together at the upper left-hand corner. "Take a look at this," he said.

It was a list of America's great corporations. To the right was a cash figure. Next to one chemical company the amount was over a million dollars. The heading read: "1966: Cash Amounts — shares held in Unicorn Enterprises." Smith smiled. He took the papers back.

"What is it?"

"The Horn movement, Mr. Pratt, is a corporation. A secret corporation, and we have capital to ten million dollars. All — except for sixty thousand of my own dollars — all that money has come from big business. White big business. Not beggars' charity. No. An investment. We pay eight percent this year. My stores are making good money. We earn just as much now as A & P, and we have certain advantages."

"But how?" I said. "How did you do it? Why wasn't it done before?"

"It's power. The water runs down the hill — but if no one builds a dam or a mill wheel, then the power, it runs away to the sea." He turned back to the filing cabinet and began passing me heavy folders, talking as he did. "You don't know it, my friend, but I have great power. No — my people have the power. I am the mill wheel, the dam. I can swing the Negro vote here in Harlem. And in Newark. Philadelphia. I proved that two years ago and four years ago. The President was very grateful. He'll be more grateful before the next election. I will see to that." He laughed. "Are we running short of boxes?"

"Yes. Only two left."

"There are some suitcases there, in the toilet place." I went over and carried them back.

"You were saying?"

"I met the President himself six years ago. A big secret. He was coming here to the U.N. and they brought me up the backstairs in his hotel. They were very careful, very smart — no one has yet found out." He paused to help me carry several filled cartons out into the hall, lifting two to my one. "The income tax man. Mr. Pratt, he is a very, very important person. When you are a good friend of the President, then no one looks at your taxes. It's not against the law. Unfair, but not against the law. The list I showed you — all those companies can deduct from their taxes the money they gave to me. And, if they give enough, then the tax man is too busy to look at their reports. Oh my. Everyone was so quick to hand me money. I had to say, 'No. Please. That's enough.'" He laughed. "Now everyone is happy. The white man and the black man. Now, all at once, there are jobs for Negroes in those companies. Good jobs. We have made it worth their while. And Mr. President, he is the happiest. He gets the Negro vote and nobody knows why. That's the part he likes best." Smith winked. "There is, you know, a white backlash in the country just now."

"That — I mean, it sounds so corrupt." Smith shook his head vigorously.

"No. No. No. It's democracy, my friend. Democracy — I mean that. And it's good. We are outnumbered, remember that. Nine to one. At the voting place, Mr. Pratt, we must lose. But in me, in me, the Negro can use his power. As — as a lobby. That isn't corrupt. If the majority always ruled, if that was democracy, then . . . then we would have been killed a long time ago. We are learning, Cubert and I — " he slammed the drawer shut.

"What is it?"

"The time, Mr. Pratt. The time. Quickly."

"Nine — nine-thirty."

"When it went off. What time was it then?"

"Eight. Just after."

"No," he said.

Smith walked away from me. There was still a folder in his hand, but it slithered down as his fingers forgot their function. The papers scattered before his feet, and he stepped on them, crumpled them. I staggered back, repulsed by the turbulence of his emotions. Smith sat at the desk. He pulled the chair out and seated himself carefully, upright. He stared ahead with his hands folded precisely before him.

"What is it? Please tell me."

"Cubert is dead," he said.

"How do you know?" He answered, but not my question; questions of his own asking.

"I didn't think it was so late. The light — it's still so bright now. Spring is coming. But Cubert was in his office. I know that."

"You can't be sure."

"I am sure." He turned and looked at me. Angrily. "Now the question is — if I die . . . who will there be? These papers, I was saving them for Cubert. He knows. He's the only one. Purston may guess, but he can do nothing without this. Nothing. And he won't get it, he — " he bowed his head. "But who is there?"

"I'll go upstairs. Right now. I'll find out."

"No!" He stood up suddenly. He brushed at his face, as though some unseen material had obstructed it. "I need you now. I might break down. You see, I have known the man for fifteen years, and he was good. I might break down but I won't . . ." He smiled. "Not in front of a white man. Shall we go back to work, Mr. Pratt?"

"Uh . . . Yes, yes."

There was another explosion: less clearly defined than the first, more a prolonged and thunderous rumbling. It lasted a

full five seconds. One after another, the prints fell from the wall
and shattered near the wainscoting. Above and in front of me,
the busts of Socrates and Caesar vibrated, turning inward on
their pedestals, until they nearly faced each other. The lights
went out. Then they flickered and came on. I saw that Smith's
body had gone rigid. His eyes were tightly closed, and his fingers grasped his thigh, so that it seemed the material of his
clothing must part. He opened his mouth; his tongue appeared
and licked once at his dry lips — as, I remembered, I had
seen frightened dogs do. Then slowly, and with exact coordination, he brought both hands up to his cheeks and pressed them
there. "Leave me something," he whispered. "Leave me something. Please." The lights went out again.

The blackness was absolute. I stood, my head dodging
quickly from left to right, as though, at some place, the dark
might be penetrable to my vision. I heard Smith moving, and
the noises were made sinister by my blindness; I imagined that,
in his excruciating anguish, he would attack me. Something
fell to the floor, bounced, threw up metallic vibrations. I turned
sideways and projected my right hand, palm flattened, to fend
off the instruments of his assault. Smith cursed. Then a match
sizzled into flame, illuminating the room with its first fiery explosion. He held it aloft.

"This is unfortunate," he said. "Have you got a flashlight,
Mr. Pratt?"

"No."

"Candles?"

"Yes. Of course."

"Where are they?"

"Uh — in a closet. Just beyond the kitchen. The first door
on the left." The match went out. "Oh — and there are two
on the altar."

"Yes. Could I get them? The light may not come on again."

"Certainly. I'll go up now."

"No. I'll go. I want to look anyway."

"Are you sure?"

"Yes," he said. I sensed then that he had begun to move past me, toward the door.

"Can't I come with you? I — it's dark down here." His fingers touched my shoulder, then they followed along the full length of my arm. He found my hand and took it.

"Come along. There is a chair over here." I stumbled after him. "Sit. I'll come right back. There are no such things as ghosts, my friend. Only big rats."

He left me there. As I felt my way into the soft, upholstered chair, I could hear the door closing behind him. I sat back. The chill seat material touched my skin through my torn shirt. I put my knees together, my hands on my kneecaps. A siren hummed sadly in its lowest registers and the sound recalled my vocation. I knelt to pray for him, for the ones who had been hurt and for my own people . . . those who needed a different prayer.

There was a sputtering noise. I stood quickly upright. The noise faded, to be superseded by the sound of an invisible hand thumbing pages. I jumped into the chair and pulled my legs in behind me, just as, on cold winter mornings, I would snuggle into the soft armchair in my mother's bedroom. There was a creaking of successive floorboards. I stared at the door, but I could see nothing. Above, on the bookshelves, there was a vague whiteness: the busts, I knew, peering before them with pupil-less eyes. My fingernails dug painfully at my cuticles. I looked at my watch and the luminous eye startled me. I began to hum, but the sound of my own voice was intimidating. "Oh my," I said. "Oh my. I'm very frightened." Again the sound of tiny, clawed feet. I rose higher on the chair, until I was uncertainly balanced on the arms and back. The door latch lifted abruptly with a loud tocking noise, and my leaping heart echoed it a hundred fold.

"Who's there?"

"Me."

"Light the candles," I said. "Please. Quickly."

"I have no candles." He came toward me. I could barely distinguish his deeper blackness against a dozen other blacknesses.

"Don't touch me," I shrilled. Smith stood still.

"Why did you say that? Why would I touch you?"

"I —"

"What's the matter, Mr. Pratt?"

"I'm sorry," I said. I leaned my forehead on the chair's back. "I'm scared. This — the dark. The explosion . . ." Smith moved closer. He sat in a chair just opposite mine, not more than a yard away.

"Such stupid fear, my friend. Be careful. Hatred begins that way."

"I don't know what came over me. I scared myself, I guess — the way a child will. I didn't mean, when I said don't touch me —" I cursed. "Why — why can't we have some light?" Smith struck another match. His horn leaped out at me, lengthened by grotesque shadows. It seemed to waver, as though it were hinged where it met his scalp. I turned fully around and sat, hoping to compose myself.

"There are people upstairs," he said. "In your church. I saw their flashlights."

"Firemen?"

"No," he said. "I don't think so. I had to come back." The match flame turned blue, then vanished.

"What can we do?"

"In the dark, nothing. Wait. Talk, perhaps. That's all, Mr. Pratt. I'm not going to hurt you."

"I know. I know."

"But you don't. You're not sure. How could you be?" I said nothing. "No. How can anyone be? A drink, maybe that would help."

"Yes. Do you have something?"

He rose and made his way slowly toward the far right wall. A piece of furniture, I was not sure what, toppled and fell with a muffled banging. He carried a bottle back. I heard his thumb as it worked at the seal. Then the bottle was placed in my hand. I hesitated.

"There are no glasses," he said. I put the neck to my mouth and swallowed. The ardent liquid and the fullness of its outpouring surprised me. I sputtered and a few drops went up my nose. I choked in earnest for several seconds. My eyes ran, and rum dribbled from my nostrils. Smith took the bottle.

"What will you do now?" I asked. "Tomorrow?"

"Tomorrow . . ." he said. "Tomorrow or the next day, then I will appear at my own funeral. Surprise, that is my only chance. I must be quick. Quick." Smith was silent. His fingernails tapped on the glass side of the bottle. He exhaled; it seemed a sigh. "But, you know . . . tonight . . . I am very tired, Mr. Pratt. I'm not sure just what I should do. I have no clever plans. Maybe, in the morning, when my head is clear, maybe then it will come to me. Do you think?"

"Yes. Yes, I'm sure." He laughed.

"I'm glad you are. But sometimes when I sit alone here, Mr. Pratt, I have a feeling. For all these muscles, I think, when I get up — you know — my legs will break like children's candy canes. I'm forty-two years old. No one knows that. And Aylbrous, he is only twenty-nine, with just himself to think of. Another drink?"

"Yes." He handed me the bottle.

"Just now, Mr. Pratt — just a minute ago — I was thinking

this thought. Why not be dead? Why not? Disappear. Go to some other country. Let them take care of themselves. I've given them a start, a very good start." He paused. Then I discovered his hand searching mine for the bottle. "And I decided no. I would stay. But for the wrong reasons. For this, my horn. For the first time I did not think of them. Just of this: how can a man hide who has a horn in his head? Wear dark glasses? Grow a long beard? I'm in this to the end. I must try to take him with me, that's all."

"Why?" I said. "You're no fool? How could you let him get such power?"

"How? How else? I made a mistake. I wanted to use him, Mr. Pratt. I was so clever. But he used me . . ." Smith was silent for several moments. "Perhaps you've heard this. We have our own police force here. It was needed. Believe me that. Believe me, too, when I say, Mr. Pratt, that I didn't like to do it. But sometimes my people, they don't know their own good. We have bad habits, like spoiled children. We don't like to work." He drank again; licked noisily at his lips. "If a man doesn't do his job, then we have to . . . to punish him. But this punishing. It was nothing — we never hurt anyone."

"Excuse me," I said. "Don't be angry, but — I have heard differently."

"That was Purston. I swear it to God. I couldn't watch everything, could I?" I shook my head, quite forgetting that the gesture was invisible to him. "Could I?"

"No."

"No. This is a big thing, the Horn movement. I travel all the time. And my boxing, remember that."

"I do."

"Yes. But you would have done it better. I know. You all would have done it better." There was an unpleasant silence.

I stared into the dark, waiting for some distinct movement that might betray the outline of his body.

"I'm not criticizing," I said finally. "I just — just want to know."

"All right. Yes, I had heard some things, too. And I asked Aylbrous — but he always had answers. Maybe, who knows, maybe I thought he was right. Maybe I am the guilty man. I don't know. No. But Aylbrous knew. Yes — he broke a man's teeth with his fist and he said, 'Horn Smith did that to you.' He snapped a man's fingers back one by one and he said, 'Smith. Smith. Smith.' This man with no teeth and this man with no fingers, they didn't love me any more. Then Aylbrous would give him money. A hundred dollars. A thousand dollars. Aylbrous gets money from the party, from a man in New Jersey called Hammer. To buy my own men from me. And what can I do? Can I join the John Birch society?"

"It's the same story," I said. "It's always been the same. Power corrupts."

"I have not been corrupted."

"No. Not you. But you couldn't watch, you said that yourself. And anyway — was there a judge and jury? When a man had to be punished, who would decide?"

"I made the decisions. I'm a just man, Mr. Pratt."

"Only God is so just," I said. "Only God — and even His justice is hated."

"But there is no other way. You must believe it. I know. There is always some bad in the good. But the good is bigger. A hundred times. A thousand times."

"Up there," I said. "Your good may be dead."

There was no reply. I could sometimes see him: an uneven obscurity superimposed against the quadrilateral obscurity of the bookshelves behind him. He was breathing with difficulty

it seemed — from his mouth and as one caught up in a
troubling dream. Nothing was said for nearly fifteen minutes.
His sudden reticence was disturbing. In the unrelieved dark,
conversation had been the one rational business left to me. I
began once again to experience an intense apprehension. I
wanted to speak, but I had nothing to say and I was afraid to
provoke him. Smith, moreover, seemed oddly restless. An arm
or leg would move in an abrupt reflex. He would grunt as
though avoiding blows. The chair creaked under his weight.
He was, I realized, quite elsewhere, being buffeted by the vi-
olences of his imagination. And then, as if there had been no
pause in our talking, he spoke.

"Tell me about Greensprings, Mr. Pratt." I sat forward,
peered into the darkness, incredulous of what I had just heard.

"Greensprings? How did you — I mean . . ."

"I hope you will forgive me." I felt his hand on my kneecap.
"A few weeks ago, when I was in your office, I found some letters
on your desk. It was a wrong thing, but I am glad — they were
very beautiful letters. From your mother, I think."

"My mother is dead. It was Eleanor. She's my sister."

"Your sister?" He withdrew his hand. "Yes? I thought —
well, you must be very close."

"Yes."

"You live in the same house, I think,"

"Yes. Well, Eleanor and her husband live downstairs. She's
married. I rent from them — it's a very modest rent. Really
it's our family house. I've lived there all my life."

"Go on."

"Do you really want me to? I can't understand why. And —
well, I'm embarrassed to talk like this."

"Have another drink." He handed me the bottle. I drank,
more to postpone what I had to do, than to find solace. Smith

moved: I think he lapped one leg over his chair arm. He was content to wait patiently.

"Uh . . . Let's see. Greensprings is very small. Quiet. Full of big trees. Dogs. Old people, many old people. Scotch-Irish. A few Germans. The seminary where I teach is three miles down the road. Students come to town, but they get bored pretty quick. One movie theater. One shoe store. One book store. One of everything, I guess. That's all."

"And you were happy in Greensprings?"

"I was. I — I wish I were back there now." Smith made a reflective noise, a long hmmmm, his fingers evidently near his lips.

"Mr. Potts, who is he?"

"Our mailman, for thirty years at least."

"Mr. Curtis?"

"A neighbor — a retired bookbinder."

"Are there Negroes in Greensprings?"

"One or two. Farm help. There's George at the filling station. It's different."

"Yes. Different. I'm trying to see it in my mind." He paused. "What is the Isle of Capri?"

"Capri?" It surprised me again: to hear private things; things from my sequestered past life, in that starkly blackened room. "It's an island. Not really. A child's imaginary island. Where the stream makes a loop and almost meets itself. I used to go there — to read. To think. To dream. It was my secret place for many, many years. Nothing special, not even very nice — there were mosquitoes most of the time. But I would puff on my pipe. Puff and read. Feel sorry for myself."

"Alone?"

"Eleanor came sometimes."

"But alone."

"Yes. It was spoiled if someone else came. I would leave then."

"Why?" I squirmed in the seat; clutched at my knees. "Why?" he repeated.

"Well — I guess you want me to say it. I was a misfit. I was fat, fatter than I am now. I had pimples. I couldn't see very well. I stammered. Boys made fun of me — I didn't mind it really. I thought I deserved it. But it tired me out. It was nice just reading. One makes compromises, you know. You look in the mirror and say: well, I'm this or I'm that — no use trying to be something else. The Hindus think the body is a symbol of the soul's condition — I don't know. It might be the other way around. But they're very close. Siamese twins."

"I know what you mean, Mr. Pratt, about looking in the mirror."

"Yes. I suppose you must."

"Have you ever been in love?"

"Of course. Yes."

"Did she live in Greensprings?"

"Yes. No. I mean — I don't want to talk about it. I really couldn't. It's too much to ask."

"All right," he said agreeably. "But for all this — the pimples and the fat — for all this you were still happy?"

"I'm a simple man. I guess you couldn't understand my sort of happiness. To read. To teach. Catch butterflies. In a place where I can comprehend what's happening. Where there is a winter and a spring, and the spring is different from the winter and very wonderful. But still the same as the spring before and the spring before that."

"Yes," said Smith suddenly. "Yes, I would like to be white."

"You would? Why? Whatever for?"

"Don't get me wrong, Mr. Pratt. Not for the little things —

not for the jobs and for the restaurants. Not for the color. I like my color."

"Why then?"

"Once, Mr. Pratt, you said to me, 'I'm a timid man, Mr. Smith.' I remembered that. Of all the things you said."

"I don't see . . ."

"Because we are all of us timid, Mr. Pratt, every mother's son. All of us. But only you can say it. And this is because you're white." I stammered. "Please. I know you are special — that very few men of any race could be like you. The liberal white man — the Jews and the Hippies and the Mr. Meekers — God knows, they are more like us. Frightened. Not trusting. But you, you have that thing, what you call Western Culture. That's why I read these books and I try to learn Latin. And your religion, that too, that perhaps most of all. You know who you are, Mr. Pratt and we — none of us can ever know that. I admire your timidity. It makes me jealous. Only a white man can say — 'I am afraid.' "

"Please," I said. "I'm never certain — are you making fun of me?"

"You can't tell? Yes, I think you can — you are timid, but not a fool. The rest of us, the rootless ones — black and white — we have one reality. We do things. We do. That, for us, is God, is everything. To do and to do and to do." He pounded his fist, in time, on the chair arm. "Always making things. And when we stop doing, then we don't live any more. We're like — you know, the cartoon show cat that runs over the edge of the cliff and keeps running and running on the air. And while we run it's all right, we think we have something there, beneath us. But stop once. Look down. And we fall."

"Oh no," I cried. "No. You've got it all wrong. All wrong. My life has been nothing. Narrow, sterile, frustrated, lonely. Self-centered. If I can be happy, then it's just a measure of my

pettiness. The books, the little learning. They're the best part.
The rest is hollowness."

"What, Mr. Pratt? You don't believe in God?" I lowered my
jaw and bleated once like a sheep, he had so taken me unaware. But I could not answer. "It seems," he said, "it seems,
for a priest, you say very little about the things of your religion.
Why is that?"

"I repeat. I'm a timid man, Mr. Smith. I've spent most of
our time together — these three or four meetings — trying
not to offend you through some indiscretion. I know your opin-
ion of . . . our religion. I thought it wise — no. That's not
true. I was afraid. And now I'm ashamed."

"But. It is important to you. God and Jesus Christ and the
great, big, clumsy church."

"It's my life. What little I have been or have done that becomes manhood, that was God's. What remains has been — is
— pathetic."

"You see." His hands reached out from the darkness and
again gently cupped my knees. "That is the difference between
you and me. That's why I'm jealous. Life — that's all we have.
We talk about it all the time. Living conditions. Living stand-
ards. The sacredness of human life. And life is always this
doing. Doing. But, to you, life is not so important."

"Don't be silly. Of course it is. It's very important.
Threaten it in me, and you'll see just how important it is."

"I'm not talking about an animal's fear, my friend. We all
have that. But human life, it isn't everything to you."

"No. Not everything."

"And you can rest. Nicholas tells me you sit sometimes an
hour up there in your office. With your feet on the desk and
your hands folded across your belly. Resting. Not doing things.
Peaceful." I laughed.

"Good grief — being lazy, that's what you mean."

"Laziness. That's death to us." He was silent. "You know, I've grown very old very fast. After tonight, I must expect my death at any minute. I begin to think, Mr. Pratt, for human life to have meaning, there must be more than just this. Otherwise, you see, I am only like a blade of grass pushing up through the sidewalk."

"There — " I cleared my throat. "Uh — excuse my presumption — but there is another life."

"Aha!" shouted Smith. He clapped his hands together sharply. "At last. At last. For a time, Mr. Pratt, I didn't think you would say it. I didn't think my soul was worth saving."

"I didn't know," I said. "How could I? But I'll be glad to show you — "

"Stop! Please. Don't spoil it. I don't want to go to your party, my friend. I just wanted an invitation."

"Oh . . ." I said. "I see. It was all a trick. You were just making fun of me."

"No. No. I haven't the equipment to be a Christian. That's all. My knees don't bend that way. It may be a very good thing — as the nun said to the whore — but not for me."

The lights went on. Our bodies became inflexible, fixed. Smith and I saw each other clearly once more: my whiteness was remembered and his blackness. We were both shy again. I squinted, for the sudden, bleak illumination had bruised my eyes. Smith cocked his head; then his glance engaged mine as though to ask, "Has anything been changed by this?" I shook my head, and the action was reprieved. Smith stood up.

"We must get back to work," he said.

We did. It took half an hour to find all his papers (Smith had hidden some behind a false panel in the wall), pack them and carry them to the foot of the spiral staircase. Then he tore all the references to Dr. Oddie from his books, burned them, and gave me the books to disperse in various places about the basement. We put sheets on the furniture, turned the chairs on their faces and unhooked the sink so it dangled from the wall. Smith filled the toilet bowl with newspapers, packing them so that the water was concealed. Then he poured the contents of the trashcan over the newspapers. While I rolled up the rug, he methodically smashed the two classic busts, leaving the plaster fragments scattered where they fell. Together we removed the door from its hinges and left it leaning uncertainly against the corridor wall. Smith put the padlock in his pocket. Then, without apparent emotion, he stared at his gutted den.

"Is there anything else? Do you see anything, Mr. Pratt?"

"I don't think so."

"There's no dust — but that can't be helped."

"No. I guess we're done." He shook his head.

"Not yet — I have one more thing to do. One more thing to show you. Come."

We crossed the room, crushing bits of plaster underfoot. There was a door in the back wall. An old door; a borrowed door. The apartment designation, 7F, remained and, above it, a peep hole with a web of cracks in the glass. Smith put his hand on the knob. Then he looked at me.

"Ready?" he asked.

"For what?"

"I'm showing off, Mr. Pratt. Excuse me. I want you — a man of learning — to know this: had I been born white — I would have been, I think, as great a man as the best of you."

He opened the door. A light was turned on. I looked quickly from left to right, curious, a bit frightened. It was a small room, obviously a workshop. A wooden carpenter's table occupied the center and, on it, were the implements of a sculptor who works in several media. Mallets. Chisels for marble. Tools for shaping clay. A welding torch. A large square of red wax. An armature of a man and one of a dog. Near my foot, on the floor, were two cubic feet of marble, surrounded by odd bits of scrap metal. Smith pointed, and my eyes followed the line that extended from his fingertip.

A polygonal object in dark metal stood on the table. It was almost a cube, but slightly longer in one of its dimensions. I stepped closer. The edges and corners had been rounded off. It shone dully under the single bulb. The size and the texture were familiar. I dabbed at the corner of my mouth with tentative fingertips. And then I remembered.

"It's the thirteenth ball," I said. Smith cleared his throat and nodded. "You did them. Those extraordinary sculptures. I should have guessed."

"Ah . . . Mr. Pratt. You are now — this moment — my dearest friend. You noticed. You even counted them. I will hug you." And he did. I felt my bare scalp reddening as his naked chest pressed close to my shoulder.

"I was struck dumb the first time I saw them. And brutalized. But this, it's not a ball."

"No," said Smith, distracted. "It's not. I think that is the point of it — but I'm not sure why. I made this in the fall. The others: they come from six to eight years ago. From the time of my greatest anger. I haven't had a chance to bring it upstairs and," he shrugged, "and anyway there is no room on the fence."

"The fence isn't the whole world. Or maybe it is. But this belongs apart."

"Well. As I think now, the fence must be gone."

I touched the smooth sides with my hand. And laughed. "I've got good news for you, my friend. What we were talking about before — I think someday you may come to the party." Smith snapped off the light.

"Don't please make sermons on my weakness. Turn your

head." He took a hammer from the table, reached up and smashed the bulb. Jagged teeth of glass protruded from the socket. "We can't move all these things. But without the light, maybe no one will bother to look. And you will say, will you not, that Mr. Pierre did sculpture?"

"Yes. All right."

"Come. It's getting late."

He took me by the arm. Behind us we left the door of the workshop slightly ajar. Smith then retrieved the three-quarters empty rum bottle from the desk, drank deeply, and handed me the bottle to finish. I did. He opened the drawer of a small side table and removed a can of brown shoe polish and a long buffing cloth. "It's really not so nice. So warm and brown. In places it is almost white. So I must improve on nature."

I looked: what had seemed areas of whitish powder — ashes from the fire, I had thought — were, in fact, the thing's true color. There were dark brown parts and parts the color of dirty ivory and parts indiscriminately mixed. Smith dug his two first fingers into the waxy polish. Then he dabbed it on his horn. When he had sufficient polish, he raised both hands and massaged it in with his fingertips: he seemed to be playing some odd, silent wind instrument through his forehead; enjoying it, as though his horn were a specially sentient thing. After a moment he looped the buffing cloth over it and began pulling vigorously.

"What now?" I asked.

"I must leave you, Mr. Pratt — and that may not be so easy." He rolled up the buffing cloth; then he slipped both it and the shoe polish tin into his pants pocket. "I can't go through your house. There will be firemen in the courtyard."

"We could go out through the church — right into the street."

"Yes. I thought of that — if the way is clear, and if there are no more flashlights upstairs." He took his charred jacket and slipped it on over his naked shoulders. The rough material hurt him; I could see that. But Smith ignored the pain and removed what seemed to be a piece of burlap from the jacket pocket. "My old hat," he said.

"How will you get away from here?"

"I have a little Volkswagen. It's parked just around the corner on Seventh Avenue — not mine. Nicholas' car, but I have a set of keys. If I can reach it, then I should be safe. And after I go — you will take those boxes upstairs. Yes?"

"Yes."

He adjusted the cap so that the flabby brim lapped over his horn's tip. The material sagged down on either side. His appearance was very odd, but, in the dark, a casual onlooker might not realize what the hat concealed. Smith reached up and gingerly unscrewed the hot bulb from the ceiling fixture. The room went dark, only casually lit by the dim bulb outside in the corridor.

"Good-bye my little room," he said. He slipped on his glasses and walked out into the hall. When we reached the foot of the spiral staircase, Smith unscrewed the last light. We ascended the narrow passage in total darkness. At the top, he pressed his ear to the door; then, satisfied, he slowly inched back the bolt.

"What time is it, Mr. Pratt?" I squinted at my luminous dial.

"Ten after one."

"You go first. If anyone is in the church and they see you, say you were hiding down here. But don't go into the other place — the lights are on there I think. Someone will spot you from the courtyard."

"All right."

I moved past him on the stairs. My fingers touched the bolt and slipped downward; at once they had become coated with a sheet of cold, treacherous perspiration. The door gave outward; its hinges popped every few degrees. I paused. Then I stepped up, into the nave. There was light, but it was hardly sufficient for precise vision; it entered uncertainly through the broken windows and from the direction of Horn's Place. It was white and inert — the flames had apparently died out. I could smell an unpleasant, acrid odor of burned things. Voices shouted to each other, but they were outside, in the courtyard. Occasionally an errant beam, a small spotlight perhaps, would glance high against the far wall of the nave. I crouched and began moving along one of the pew rows, toward the center aisle. The chancel was darkened, yet I imagined I could see a sliver of light entering from my office doorway. I waited, searching for movement, listening. There was no one inside the church. I turned back toward the basement door: Smith had already emerged and was moving between the pews.

"All clear, I think."

"Yes," he said. "Now we must see what's outside." Smith stared toward the broken windows. "I don't like this. It sounds like many people."

We walked up the center aisle and into the small vestibule. The coat rack had, for some reason, been moved across the entrance way, and I, leading, struck it full on. The coat rack fell noisily. Smith helped me up.

"Sorry," I said. "I'm so damned clumsy." But he was looking back toward the chancel.

"All right. That proves one thing — no one is in here. Open the front door. Just a little now. Just to see. Which door opens first?"

"Uh — the one on the right."

"Good. Look up to Lenox. See if there are any people. Just an inch now. Carefully." I unlocked the door, pushed it outward, then yanked it quickly closed again.

"No good," I said.

"What is it?"

"An ambulance and a police car — just outside by the alley. They were . . . uh. They were putting something in the back. On a stretcher."

"A body. How many were there?"

"I'm not sure. At least four. Two policemen. Two attendants."

"Could you see up the block?"

"There are people on Lenox and it's all lit up. There's a fire engine at the end of this block, but that's pretty far away. You're going in the other direction."

"Yes. We must wait. Not too long I hope." He stepped over the fallen coat rack and began moving into the nave. "This way — where we can see that no one comes in."

We sat in the furthest rear pew like two glum but expectant parishioners. Smith, nearest the aisle, sat in an alert, upright position, necessitated by the tenderness of his back. I sat leaning forward, my elbows on my thighs, my chin cupped in my hands. Voices outside shouted back and forth, yet the interplay seemed, after a while, to become less frequent. Equipment was dragged down the alley. There was laughter and excited cursing, as though those who remained had little to do but watch. A siren moaned behind us. Smith walked back to the vestibule and peered out. The ambulance had left, he said, but the police car was still stationed by the alley's mouth. It was one-thirty.

"Two o'clock. I must get out by two."

Getting Out Again

"Can you sleep?" I asked. "I'll keep an eye out — you probably won't get another chance tonight."

"I don't — " a shout interrupted him.

"Hey, Jimmy! Jimmy! What's the word? How many they found?" And Jimmy's voice, evidently from the alley's mouth, remote and yet distinct.

"Nine dead so far. Five missing."

"What about Smith?"

"Nothing yet. But he's in that mess someplace."

"You playing poker at Chief Black's Saturday?"

"Yeah. If I'm off. You?"

"If I can sneak out."

"Okay. See you there. Give my regards to Judy."

"I better not. She says you're a bad influence."

I heard Jimmy's satisfied laughter. Then Smith's fist struck the hard wood of the pew bench. He kicked out and the kneeler came loose. One end struck me on the ankle. "Nine," he said. "Nine. And it's my fault. I killed them."

"It's not you," I said. "It's this damned hatred and bigotry. I pray every day that it will end. I pray for love, so many of us pray for love. I — "

"Please, Mr. Pratt. Please." He stood up. "You know nothing about it. Love . . ." He laughed bitterly. Then he walked out into the aisle. I was going to speak, when I saw him fall suddenly forward onto his hands.

"What — what happened?" I rushed to the pew's end and looked, terrified, into the aisle. Smith was doing push-ups. His hat had fallen off, and I could hear him counting under his breath. "Thirty, thirty-one, thirty-two . . ." It was a grotesque sight. I turned away. He went on like that, tormenting his body, taking an athlete's refuge in this mindless, physical toil. The counting slowed as he neared one hundred, but he continued for fifty more. Then he stopped and rolled over onto his side, panting, shaking his head. His anger and guilt had not been exorcised.

"Love, you said," he pointed at me. "Love. Are you really so stupid? What is your God, Mr. Pratt — *The New York Times?*" He stood there wavering; his breathing was still agitated by the push-ups. He came close to where I was sitting, and I could feel the heat that radiated from his moist, heaving chest. "Use your brains, Mr. White Priest. There is no such thing as racism. There is no such thing as bigotry. There is no such thing as prejudice." He slapped the sides of the pew. "These are all stories that you tell little children. Sometimes . . . sometimes, I even think, there is no such thing as love."

"I don't understand you." As I spoke, I moved farther away from him, for his vehemence was terrible.

"No," he exhaled. Then he bent down and picked up his hat. "No one understands me. That's why we have come to this — whole cities burning in the summer. You — all of you — you are too proud or too stupid to admit the truth."

"What is it then? Tell me. What is the truth?"

"That there is no hatred. No hatred. Only fear. That there is no prejudice. Only fear. That there is no bigotry. Only fear." He cursed. "You, Mr. Pratt, what do you care for truth? You get up in that pulpit there and you say, 'We must love the black man. We must love him.' And you are surprised when there is no love. How can there be? How? There is still fear. You haven't taken away the fear. It's your fault — not the white man's, not the black man's. It's the fault of men like you — educated men, men who must do our thinking for us. You — you have failed. Not them."

Smith dropped his hat on a pew, then sat heavily just across the aisle from me. But for his panting, there was silence. I stared at my kneecaps. His anger, directed personally as it had been, had both hurt and dismayed me. I cleared my throat several times, but I was determined not to speak first.

"I am sorry," he said at last. "This is not the time. Nine . . . Whoever they were, I knew them all."

"Even so," I said sullenly. "I can't just let this go. You've said something, and it has upset me. You must understand, I don't often hear Negroes say that there's no prejudice. If you meant that, then I want you to explain it. Seems to me, for years we've treated you like an inferior race. We've — "

"No!" he said. "You see. You see. That's wrong." He came quickly back across the aisle. "Listen to me. If I think you are inferior, Mr. Pratt — I don't hate you. No. I feel sorry for you. Maybe I just don't think about you at all. But I don't hate you, because I don't fear you. Cats and dogs are inferior and yet we love them. Children are inferior and we love them best of all. But snakes. Oh, yes. Snakes. They are inferior, but they bite too. I hate snakes."

"All right. I'll accept that for the moment. Go on."

"If we — what's the use . . . ?" He exhaled. "Even if I teach you, who are you? Just another priest. The newspapers and the radio and the television, they are still saying it, 'Love, love, love.' Even the President's Commission — men who should know better — what do they blame all these riots on? White racism." He laughed without enjoyment. "What a stupid thing to say. Does it help? Does it teach us anything? Does it explain why you hate the black man? No."

"So explain. Why do I — we — why do we hate the black man?"

"For a very good reason, Mr. Pratt. You are afraid of us." He folded his hands at his waist. In the semi-dark his horn was invisible, merely a strange shadow cast by his forehead. "Think a minute. You are a smart man. Think of the people in history who have been hated most. Think of the Jews — we all fear the Jews. I fear them. And yes, I hate them. They are clever. They stick together. They are so good with money. And they have been persecuted for this. Shot. Gassed. Made into soap. For the fear they have caused." Smith bent down and put his head close to mine. "But the Red Indian. When last did someone say to you, 'I hate Indians.'" He sneered. "Not lately, I think. Not here in the east. Not since Mr. Custer made his last stand. We don't fear them. We don't hate them." He paused. "Tonight, when I came to you in the dark. When you said, 'Don't touch me — ' Even you, Mr. Pratt, even you were filled with fear. And you were ready to hate me."

"No. You're wrong there. I didn't mean it that way."

"Yes. I know," he said. "You're a special thing. You're different from the rest of us. I forgot."

Smith left me there. He walked up the aisle to the vestibule. I heard the lock tumbler click. A distinct draft of cool air touched my naked back; I turned quickly around, as though it had been a cold, questioning finger. A piece of glass fell out of the leading and crashed to the floor. I leaped up, too agitated then to sit. Had he been right about my reaction? Despite his vehemence, I didn't think so. Smith came back.

"The police are still there. What time is it?"

"Almost two. Listen, I — "

"Soon I must make a break for it — no matter what. I have too much now to do."

"Listen. Please. I was just afraid back there. Just afraid." He put his hand on my shoulder.

"Yes. I know." He sighed. "I have been picking on you, my friend. You *are* different. I have watched you. When you fear something, you blame yourself, not the thing you fear. That is

very strange. I have never met a man like you. In the town of
Greensprings, where there is only one of everything, where
every man has his strong castle — even if the castle is only in
his mind — in that wonderful place, I think, the fear is very
small. You have been lucky. If I were you, I would run back
there. Run as quick as I can. If you stay here, Mr. Pratt, then
you will catch the disease. And I would not like to see that."

"But tell me then? What is your answer? How do we end
these irrational fears?" Smith grunted.

"You make a mistake, Mr. Pratt. A big mistake. They are
not irrational. That is the terrible thing. Oh, some fears are
stupid, but the most of them have roots. Deep roots. Look.
If a Negro moves into your street, then the value of your house
will go down. It will. It shouldn't, but it will. This is no fairy
tale. If a Negro joins your union, then there will be one less
job for you. That's arithmetic, my friend. If a Negro marries
your daughter, then not all your friends will say hello when you
walk down the street. If your neighborhood becomes a
ghetto, then a Negro may rob you or rape your wife."

"But not all Negroes — "

"Yes. Yes. And very few snakes, they tell me, have poison.
But I take no chances. Do you? Please. Come away from your
books. Think like the little man. People — your people, my
people — they are very simple and life is too big for them.
They have jobs to keep and children to teach and wives to make
happy in bed. They have no time to decide who is a good black
man and who is a bad black man. And it is the same with us.
You are all honky. Abraham Lincoln and George Wallace. All
honky."

"Okay, but — "

"Let us sit down. My feet hurt." We sat again in the last
pew.

"Okay. What would you have us do?"

"First, my friend, get rid of the dirty words. The words that mean nothing. Racial prejudice. Brotherhood. Bigotry. And those stupid four letter words, love and hate. They must go. We can't think clearly until they go.

"Then we must be very careful and very wise. We, the leaders. We must take each problem as it comes, and find the fears. They are all so different. There is no one answer." He paused. "I'm a Negro. I want to move into a white neighborhood. The white men, they don't like it. Remember: this is a money problem, not a race problem. Fear. The white man's house is very important. He has saved money to buy it. When he dies, it will be his children's property. I'm not defending him. He's my enemy. But charity, you know, it begins at home. Only a madman will risk his child's home for a black stranger. If you want war, call the white man a bigot and move me in by force. Yes. And the white man will throw rocks at me and burn crosses in my yard. Or he will just move away. No one is happy. And now I am afraid. Then we *will* have a race problem. And it is you who made it.

"But if you want peace . . . Then the government must make promises. Tell the white man we will buy his house back at its full price, no matter what the real estate man says. If he stays five years. Money problems. Money answers. It might just work, you know. No one likes to throw rocks. No one wants to move away from their home. But fear makes them do it. We must be wise and kind to both peoples. Both. But we have never been. We punish the Negro for fifty years, and then we punish the white man for fifty years. It's our fault. Not theirs. They are children, stupid and frightened. We must find their fears. Find them and take them away."

"It — it seems too simple."

"No. No. It's not simple. That's my point, Mr. Pratt. That's my point." He slapped his hands together in irritation. "Fear will always be with us — as long as men are different. And they will always be different. It won't be cured by saying, 'Let us love our fellow man.' Never by that. And some fears, the dark ones, the ones that live deep in a man's mind, not just in his pocket — those fears will never go away. The white man who dreams in the night that I come to cut his penis off; that man will always hate me. But not because he is a bigot, Mr. Pratt, not because of that. Because, like a little child in his bed, he fears the dark." He paused and looked up toward the high, vaulted ceiling. "I can feel it — my people are dogs, straining on the leash to catch a wounded animal. They smell fear. After years and years of being afraid, they smell fear. They can cause it now. There are more cities to be burned. And those who stand by and say, 'Love, love, love.' Their voices will be choked by the flames."

"They can smell it in me," I said. "God knows, I reek of it."

"We are all frightened for our lives. For the soft parts of our bodies — the eyes, the throat, the balls. That is the greatest fear. The fear that most makes wars." He looked down at his hands. "I have learned and it was a bitter lesson. I thought my own policemen would make peace in Harlem. And they did. But in the wrong way. Without law. And now my own policemen have destroyed me.

"You see, Mr. Pratt, all the policemen in New York City, all those thousands of men — they exist for one reason. To keep just you from doing wrong. Just you. One man. You can take the subway: burn a house in Flushing, kill a man in Harlem, rob a store in Red Hook. Give me fifty men and I will bring this city to its knees. And that is what Aylbrous will do. He will say, 'I am fighting for my civil rights,' and he will tear New

York apart. He will bring such dreadful fear that there must be war." He paused. Then he chuckled sadly.

"You learn, Mr. Pratt. You learn. All my life I have hated the blue coats. Hated the honky policeman with his blackjack and his billy club and his gun. I hate him still. But he is the law. We must protect all the people; protect them from their fears; protect them from themselves. We must have police, my friend. And hard laws. If we don't, I promise you, then the fear in our streets will bring a civil war."

"Dear Jesus. Dear sweet Jesus," I said. "When will it end? How will it end?"

"Well . . . Don't take it so bad." He smiled. "It's only life. Step out to the stars and look back on us. It will pass. There will be other wars. There are other wars. The poor man fights the rich man. Every day. The male fights the female. Every day. The father fights the son. Every day. They are all as different as — as black and white are different. And they fear the differentness. When someone says to you, 'We are all equal. We eat and we sleep. We bleed. We die. We are all the same.' Spit in his eye, Mr. Pratt. He is an idiot. And a very frightened man, whistling in the dark." He stood up in the pew aisle and looked down at me. "Just one more thing, Mr. Pratt. And then I must go."

"Yes?"

"It's about your religion. The religion of Jesus Christ. Do you mind — I am an atheist and a mocker — do you mind if I say what's wrong with your church?"

"Dear me . . . No. No, go ahead. I might as well hear the worst."

"All right then. You once had a great power. You once ruled the world. Now you are dying away," he made a gesture that encompassed the whole of my derelict church. "I have wondered about that, and now — now I think I see why." He paused. "In this time I have listened to your priests. It seems to me they talk only about the man Jesus Christ and what he said about love. But he was not a great man, was he, because he told us to love our brothers? No. Many men have said that, and they are not Jesus Christ. Your Jesus was great because he taught his people how — taught them how to love. That is the difference. You have forgotten that."

"Well . . . Taught them? How do you mean?"

"How else?" He grinned. I could see the whiteness of his teeth in the dim light. "He took away their fear, Mr. Pratt. That's how. He said, give up your money and your houses in the suburbs. Come with me — even if there is pain, even if you starve, even if you die — it doesn't matter any more. I will give you another life in another world. A beautiful life. A life that will last a thousand times longer than this." He paused. "I don't believe his words, my friend, but the men who did — they could turn the other cheek, they could let nails be driven into their bodies. They could love. Because they had no fear. And that, excuse my nerve in telling you, that is why now your church is falling apart, why the roof leaks and the pews are broken. You preach only the words. And they are hollow words because you have forgotten his promises. Maybe these promises are all lies. I think they are. But they are powerful lies. If I knew there was a heaven, if you had taught me that, then I would not hate Mr. George Wallace or the man who killed Martin Luther King. But all I have is this life. This body. This task to do. These things. I am afraid to lose them. And my fear fills me full of hate." He leaned forward and touched my forehead lightly: a mockery of a blessing. "You have failed me again, Mr. Calvin Beecher Pratt."

An engine coughed in its ignition. Smith slapped his hands

together, then rushed past me into the center aisle, stepping heavily on my left small toes as he did so. I followed with a limp. He was already at the door, and, when I approached, he hissed at me and I froze. Smith opened the door and peered cautiously out. He closed it. Once again, he began adjusting his cap.

"All clear?"

"All clear to the left. Now you must poke your head out and look the other way. When it is clear to the right, then I will go."

He made a sign with his hand. I moved obediently to the door and tried the handle. Smith stepped behind me. I knew he was ready to leave, whenever the way was clear. I knew and I didn't want him to go: not before I had had a chance to speak. He touched my shoulder, impatient with my hesitation. But I turned to him instead.

"When it's clear," I said. "You'll go right out?"

"Yes."

"Then I must say something. Now. While the moment gives me a courage I'll never have again. Pardon the stupidness of these words, Mr. Smith, and their profanity." I looked at my feet. "But I want you to know I — I admire . . . No. That's not the word I meant to use. I love you."

"So," he said. He touched his cap. He fumbled in his jacket pockets. "So," he said. He turned his head away from me, then back to me. He cleared his throat.

"Don't say anything." I shook my head. "No. I just had to tell you." I turned, pushed the door open and stuck my head out.

It was clear all the way to Lenox. At the corner there were several dozen people, but their backs were turned to us. I edged my head out further, around the door, and looked to the right.

Two people — a man and a woman — exited from a door
across the street. They walked away from St. Bart's, toward
Seventh. A car approached the end of the block. The driver
hesitated, having seen the crowd on Lenox. Then he backed
and turned down Seventh Avenue. I ducked in.

"Get ready. Two people on the other side, going to Seventh.
That's all. No one else. When they get there I'll give you the
go sign." I slipped my head out again.

They were just a few yards from the corner now. I looked
back, checked the Lenox side, the windows across the street,
the alley's mouth. A fire engine proceeded slowly down Lenox.
Policemen held back the crowd. I turned my head right again.
The couple had disappeared and the street, momentarily, was
cleared.

"Go," I said.

He brushed past me. I thought, as he did so, that he had
grasped my upper arm gently — as a farewell, perhaps as more
than that — but I cannot now be certain. I saw him run down
the steps and across the street. The hat dwarfed the rest of his
body, it flapped as he ran. In the shadows of the far sidewalk he
slowed his pace. Then he was beyond my line of sight. I closed
the door and locked it.

Behind me the great church suddenly yawned with an eerie
menace. I walked out of the vestibule bravely enough, but I
could not pass beyond the first pews. I remembered what Smith
had said about the flashlights, and my breathing became short,
hard. A shout from the courtyard caused me to leap clumsily
aside. Something seemed to be moving below the pulpit; then
it was moving near the altar rail. I slipped quickly between
the pews and sat, huddled out of sight.

After a moment I bent down and straightened the long,
broken kneeler. I prayed. I prayed first for him and then for

what he meant to Harlem. I prayed for the children, all of us, who were afraid of the dark. At the last, I prayed for my church, that we might not forget Christ's great, freeing promise. I sat then. Alternately I dozed and shivered, trying not to imagine things in the shifting gloom. It was nearly three o'clock. Fatigue slid up my body, deadening my feet, my knees, the hands clasped in my lap. My head. I slept to await the dawn.

The morning light was less flattering to St. Bart's than had been the flames of the night before. The sky was overcast. Fragments of colored glass littered the pew seats. A chill wind blew transversely across the nave, subsuming all the annoying, petty drafts in one endless gust. I rose and walked stiffly up to the chancel. When I knelt to pray, I saw that my cross had been stolen. The chancel, indeed, had been stripped by some Puritan thief of all adornment. They had entered through the shattered bedroom window; my bedspread was soiled and resoiled with their footprints. Whatever appeared of slightest value had been expropriated. My extra pair of shoes. Two jackets. All my ties and nearly all my underwear. Candlesticks and the snuffer from my storage closet. My alarm clock. A barometer. My pipe lighter. For convenience' sake, even my battered suitcase. I found a place in the hall where my things had been carefully sorted. Old pens, pipes, bits of clothing — rejects — lay strewn about. I went into the kitchen: my radio had somehow been overlooked. I turned it on.

A report was aired almost at once. Eleven people had been killed in the explosion, including Cubert Mody. At least four — Smith himself, of course, among them — were listed as missing. Harlem had been troubled by riots throughout the night. And then Purston himself was there, shouting beside my stove. "The right wing whites got him — they hated him and they

got him. But their turn is coming. This is war, brother. This is
war." And then there was a singing commercial.

I pulled the window shade aside; it left dark smudges on my
fingertips. From an unused sitting room in the left wing I could
see nearly half the length of Horn's Place. There was nothing
left: merely a shell of the lower story. Police and firemen patrolled desultorily in my courtyard. A photographer used up
two or three flashbulbs. I could hear them talking and their
talk was already of other things: of home and of the new baseball season. They were bored by the event. A sort of haze, not
smoke, rose up over the ruin, as though to veil it. My eyes
smarted. The heavy air was filled with odors: odors of a thousand different charrings. A slight drizzle began to fall. I withdrew my head and crossed the sitting room; my shoes pow-
dered the tiny gray and black ash flakes that covered the floor.
Swiftly I returned to the kitchen: it was there that I heard the
bulletin.

Horn Smith was dead. His body had been found, the chest
broken by a dozen bullets, lying naked in Morningside Park.
And his magnificent horn — it had been sawed off at the base.
Before the bullets. Before. "I repeat," said the announcer,
"George Horn Smith, Negro leader and athlete, has been found
murdered in Morningside Park." Not alone. Some few yards
to the right lay Nicholas Breakspeare. Dead, and without fingernails. I understood how Purston had found Horn Smith.
And how, in time, he would find me.

I was still a child. I knew it then. For forty years self-shel-
tered from what is most precisely human: suffering and love
and loss. In all my living, the greatest tragedy I had ever known
was the death of our Lord upon the cross. As I stood there in
the kitchen, I saw, more than any other thing, my own inepti-
tude and selfishness. My friends — so hard won, so precious

— were dead. I couldn't cry. I knew no sufficient curses. My hands moved in the air. They moved as fists, they moved as clawing fingers. But they were expressionless. A coffee cup stood on the table. A spoon beside it. Sugar. Some cookies. On the stove, my water slowly came to boil. It hissed and bubbled. I lifted my left hand, made it into a fist, and placed it carefully in the roaring pot. And then I could cry, for I had found their pain.

It didn't last long. I put butter on my hand and bandaged it. And in these few self-regarding acts, my distinctive person, my Pratt-ness began again to assert itself. The pain in my hand became merely my pain. I yawned and it was my own weariness. I feared and, in fear, I schemed to preserve my own body. Preserve it for what? I had motives enough, but yet the objectivity to suspect them. I breathed out; saw my own breath crystallized in the chill, vented rectory. My own breath. And, for some reason, I cherished it.

For ten minutes I stood, unmoving, amid the ruins of my bedroom. "Less to pack," I thought. It was not even eleven o'clock. I could make myself ready by three. There was nothing left for a priest to do at St. Bart's. But one formality remained: to call the police, to show them the room; tell them what Smith had told me and hope they wouldn't believe. Make myself Purston's greatest enemy. "God help me," I said aloud. There was sweat on my body. Beneath me, my knees began to quiver. They rocked my hapless torso backward and forward. My fearfulness was abject; unmitigated. It has been so since.

I returned to the basement and brought the cartons and the suitcases back to Smith's room. I put some books back on the shelves; a few of his personal things on the desk top. The thirteenth ball was too heavy for me to lift. I had wanted to take it with me to Greensprings, but I settled instead for Smith's last

bottle of liquor. Upstairs, a lone sparrow was chirping on the
pulpit rail. Lost. Rain blew in on me as I passed under the
broken window. With the bottle beside my knees, I prayed in
the naked chancel. It seemed to me that I was praying differently. To the same God. There is only one. But as someone
enlightened by his sorrow. Ravished. No longer cumbered
with illusion. As a man, I think.

"Pratt — where the hell have you been?" I yelped. In fearful anguish, I hurled the chancel door from me. Bishop Hawkes
leaped from my swivel chair and came angrily toward me, hugging at his chest with spindly forearms. I gasped. I tried, in
instinctive, foolish embarrassment, to hide the bottle behind
me. But he saw it. "A drink. That's what I need, Pratt. My
teeth're chattering. What is it, scotch? Rum — well . . . it'll
do. It'll do. I'm frozen to the marrow — been sitting in this
God-forsaken wind tunnel for fifteen minutes. Where have you
been anyway? Hey . . . You haven't got any hair. You used
to . . . didn't you? No? Oh, I see. I see what's wrong. No
eyebrows. You haven't got any eyebrows, Pratt." I swallowed
and then suppressed a cough. I must have seemed very odd:
half degenerate, half furtive. Bishop Hawkes frowned. I
thought he looked none too well himself. There were red lines
in the whites of his eyes and bluish-purple half-circles beneath them. "Pratt? Are you all right? Your hand — your
shirt's just hanging on your back. Well? Say something, man."

"I'm glad — glad to see you."

"Wouldn't guess it. Can't say the same myself — nothing
personal you understand. Hey. That bottle's not open." He
took it from me. "Where d'you keep the glasses? Never mind,
I'll find them. Just sit down." He hurried out into the kitchen.

I sat in the armchair. My head ached and the skin of my
cheeks was flushed. I tried resting it between my hands, but

one was too sore and the other too clammy. My heart was still pounding from the start he had given me. I inhaled, then touched my aching eyes with the cold pads of thumb and forefinger. I would have to speak now and with some coherence: the effort, in prospect, appeared monumental. Bishop Hawkes returned with two large glasses. He put them on the desk and, in unseemly haste, began fumbling with the bottle's seal. He poured a glass and brought it to me. I drank half at once.

"God. What a time I've had, Pratt. What a time."

"The church is finished," I said suddenly. "The cross — everything is gone. It's finished."

"That's nothing," he said. He poured a second glass. "They broke off my antenna. Again. The third time. Smashed the no-draught. Started to rock the car sideways. I prayed, Pratt. I haven't prayed so much in ten years. Bouncing I was — so my poor head hit the ceiling a dozen times. I wonder it isn't cut right open." He bent to show me his pate. But the white, curly hair was unblemished. "The cops came. In their own sweet time. I tell you, this Smith thing's stirred up a hornet's nest. But what happened to you? Outside a fireman said no one was in here. Where have you been? In the church?"

"It's a long story," I said. "I'll tell you. But you shouldn't have come out in this. It was very brave of you."

"Well . . ." He sat in my swivel chair. "That's nice of you, to say that. But I didn't come because of you — I've been here all night. Over at St. Catharine's." He exhaled wearily and, for a moment, paused to admire his breath. "Have you heard? John Meeker's in Bellevue."

"No — " I sat up. "What happened? What did they do to him?" Bishop Hawkes shook his head.

"Nothing. He cracked up, Pratt. And I can't help thinking it's my fault. Bad judgment. Very, very bad. He wasn't sta-

ble, I knew it, he knew it. Everyone did. But it's hard to give
up on a man." He drained his glass. "This civil rights business.
You know, I got the diocese to pay his way down to Okaloosa.
He was crazy to go — wouldn't give me a moment's peace. Hell,
I thought we should be represented and . . . well, I don't have
to tell you. He was bad enough before, but after that — he was
possessed." He sighed. Then touched each of his knuckles, as
though it were an old ritual. "I'm over seventy now. I can't
fight with these young men. Not any more. Meeker got damn
good publicity, and, of course, St. Cat's became the garden spot
of Harlem. He had me over a barrel. I couldn't remove him,
not then. So I just waited and hoped. Prayed, too." He smiled.
"But it didn't work out."

"Is he — is he very bad?"

"You can't get much worse. He's in a straitjacket. Was,
anyway, when they took him out. I just spent the night with his
wife. Do you know her?"

"No. I met her once. Meeker told me one or two things — "
I stared at my feet.

"About her being — "

"Raped. Yes."

"I think he was proud of it. I think he was. Does this heater
work?" He leaned down and switched it on. "Poor Helen. She
had to put up with it . . . all of it. He gave his money away.
Came home without his shoes one night. Smelled like a bear.
Wouldn't speak to her or the children for weeks at a time. And
she put up with it. A wonderful woman. I love her. I've had
to support them out of my own pocket since last June. He
would have let them starve."

"He — I thought he seemed a bit strange, but — "

"Never mind that nonsense. I owe you a debt — and I'll
make it up to you. I promise." He smiled. "Helen told me

what Meeker did at the rally. And, forgive me, that's why I haven't been around here much. I — I didn't want to face you. Believe me, I — we all appreciate what you've put up with. If half our priests were as solid as you — " Bishop Hawkes trailed off. He saw me shaking my head. "I know what you're going to say. I know. I'm not blind. I can see you've been packing."

"It's not — "

"Relax. Let me finish first. This heater isn't much damn good." He got up and refilled my glass. "We should all feel sorry for Meeker. It wasn't his fault. He was crazy — pure and simple. Last couple of weeks, Pratt, Helen sent me letters that made my hair stand on end. Seems he began calling her Desdemona. Started walking with big strides. Bought himself a turban and a long robe. A scimitar, too, from God knows where. I saw them with my own eyes." He drank, belched. Drank again. "Night before last he tried to strangle her . . . but got interrupted. Confused. He couldn't follow through. It was like he forgot the lines, she said. Helen was afraid for the children, so she finally gave in and asked me to come down. It was lucky, too. All this hullabaloo drove him wild. It was pathetic." The chair squeaked reflectively beneath him. "Lawrence Peters has taken over at St. Cat's — for the time being. But I don't think he'll have much to do. Helen's sending the kids up to her sister in Rochester. They're staying at my place now. So," he slapped his thighs. "Tell me. I'm ready. What's your story?"

I told him. With uncompromising deliberateness I began at the beginning and followed through. It has become a ritual: the retelling of my story. It was then; it is now. A sort of debt, owed to myself and to those I loved. Bishop Hawkes smiled a great deal — affirmed my statements with a thoroughness that

betrayed his incredulity. He thought, I know, that he had two
mad priests in his diocese. But then I showed him Smith's
room, and, after that, he looked at me only with awe. I told
him, before he had fair time to regain composure, that I was
going back to Greensprings and nothing he could say would
change my mind.

"But. But from what you've told me, Pratt . . . Calvin —
that is your name, isn't it? Cal, you're the most valuable man
we could have here. No one knows more about the conditions,
the problems than you seem to."

"I'm not valuable dead. After I call the police, if I stay here
— believe me — my life won't be worth two cents."

"Bosh," he said. "You're exaggerating. I know the blacks.
They don't kill white men. They kill each other. They talk
about it, sure, but they're still afraid of us. Don't forget it."

"Fear is hate," I said. "I won't be any good here, not scared
as I am. And I'm very, very scared." I began taking books
from my shelves. I placed them neatly in the bottom of my
trunk. "Besides — you've seen the church. There's nothing
left. No one ever came — not even when there were windows
and a cross."

"I'm not talking about St. Bart's." He grinned, I realized
then that he was playing his ace. "I want you to take over at St.
Cat's. You're the only man fit for it. Even Meeker said so. Last
night, when he knew he was finished in Harlem."

"No," I said. "I'm honored. But no thanks."

"Cal. You're upset now. Any man would be. But there are
important things at stake. The future of our church here. Not
to mention these people and their spiritual health. Take a holi-
day. Take a month. Think it over. Things will be quieter
down here. People will forget. Think of all the good you can
do."

"Good?" I looked at him. Then I took more books from the shelf. "What good have I done? Get a Negro priest — these people want their own kind. They trust their own kind. They deserve that, at the very least. Why must we keep imposing our own strange ways on them? I'm a white man — not the best of wills, on both sides, can change that. And anyway — I'm afraid."

"Think it over."

"I've done nothing but think. These last six months. And learn."

"That's it," he said. "That's what we need. Your learning. It's precious."

"Not what I've learned. You don't want that."

"How d'you mean?"

"I've learned one thing here — in all this time. That I do not, cannot, understand the Negro people. That's what I've learned. And by learning it, I've learned some few things about myself. That's all I've learned."

"Balderdash. Poppycock. Understand? What's there to understand? They eat, they sleep. They've got two legs. What's so mysterious about that?" I straightened up; I looked at him with curiosity. Then I shook my head. And smiled.

"Hand me those books," I said.